NOT AT NIGHT!

edited, and with an introduction,

by

HERBERT ASBURY

MACY-MASIUS : THE VANGUARD PRESS
NEW YORK

1928

PUBLISHED NOVEMBER 1928

THESE STORIES WERE ORIGINALLY PRINTED IN ENGLAND IN "WEIRD TALES," AND WERE SELECTED AND ARRANGED FOR THE ENGLISH EDITION BY CHRISTINE CAMPBELL THOMSON.

MANUFACTURED IN THE UNITED STATES OF AMERICA

CONTENTS

INTRODUCTION

HERE ARE SHIVERS APLENTY! TWENTY-FIVE CREEPY TALES that are calculated to tingle the spine and roach the back hair of the most confirmed and blasé addict of mystery and horror yarns! I am perhaps not too optimistic in predicting that the reader who prefers his horror stark and unadorned will here find his every want satisfied; and that when he has concluded the final story in this collection he is quite likely to go to bed with the "willies," and with his night-light burning to protect him from the grisly phantoms which will most assuredly visit him under cover of the brooding darkness, assuming grotesque and horrible shapes and weaving mistily but threateningly before his horror-choked eyes.

Blood and the supernatural are essential elements in the composition of the modern popular horror story, and throughout this volume ghosts and evil spirits fresh from hell run rampant, and the life fluid flows freely. Indeed, the flow is practically continuous. And with these vital factors are compounded such favorite and time-tried ingredients as snakes, blood-sucking bats, werewolves, vampires, voodoo, witchcraft, the abhorrent rites of the Satanist; the man-eating plant, exquisitely perfumed but extraordinarily treacherous, which lures its victims into its gaping maw; the hairy, uncouth "thing" that slides sobbing out of nowhere and commits horrible murders; the parasitic hand which clutches and rends the vitals of its unlucky possessor; the hellish chemical mixture which causes heads and limbs to disengage themselves and fall to the ground while the body to which they had been attached writhes in agony; and the human brain and soul which are transplanted by surgery and black magic into the gross and obscene body of a sea monster. One of the most fearsome tales of the lot describes the wicked machinations of a mad and tricky scientist who gradually transforms an unfortunate victim into a gigantic lobster, with claws and feelers complete. Another recounts the terrible activities of a surgical wizard, apparently insane, who revenged himself upon the world for fancied wrongs by kidnaping innocent and handsome young women and removing the bones from their bodies, and otherwise marring their beauty. The others contain material equally shocking, and in most of them it is handled with considerable skill.

Perhaps largely because of the quickened interest in things psychic and supernatural that followed the World War, the reading and writing of mystery and horror stories has increased tremendously within recent years. Authors who produce straight detective fiction are more and more including an element of horror in their concoctions, and the most popular mystery novels of the past few seasons have been those which provided shock and terror as well as complexity of plot and mystery. And a whole new school of writers has arisen to contribute to the scores of magazines in this country and England which specialize in tales of horror and the occult. All of these periodicals appear to be enormously successful, and their number is rapidly increasing.

A writer in the *American Mercury* several months ago, discussing the popularity of the Western story, expressed the opinion that the formula for a successful tale of this type was simply "bang! bang! bang! ride! ride! ride!" Similarly, the formula for the popular horror story, of the sort that is being so widely read to-day, may be set down as "shock! shock! shock!" with a dash of "My God!" One who examines the successful magazines which specialize in horror cannot but be convinced that this is the correct method, and that what the reader wants is a series of successive shocks similar to the explosions of a gasoline engine, and culminating in one great, nerve-racking blast of shuddering terror. The average man devours his fiction in great gulps solely for the thrill that comes from even a vicarious contact with the mysterious and the unknown, and he is little concerned with literary finish and fine workmanship, or with the niceties of style and syntax. He is, indeed, inclined to resent what he calls "fine writing," and considers that an author who so indulges his muse not only obscures his story and retards the action, but makes an offensive effort to air his learning. Moreover, the average reader, especially the lover of horror stories, will not condemn an author for even the grossest implausibility of plot and situation. If a story makes him gasp, and feel creepy and afraid, and perhaps causes bad dreams, he is apt to vote it a grand yarn and a veritable masterpiece. And, after all, it may be, if it accomplishes the purpose for which it was obviously intended.

Most of the authors represented in this collection appear to be comparatively unknown in this country (Seabury Quinn is the only one whose work I have ever seen before), and scholars and critics will look in vain for evidences of the skill and erudition displayed by such masters of the horror story as Edgar Allan Poe, Ambrose Bierce and Algernon Blackwood. But any such comparison would be manifestly unfair, for the only criteria applied in selecting these tales from the many which were available were shock and gruesomeness.

HERBERT ASBURY.

New York City,
September 1, 1928.

THE PURPLE CINCTURE

By H. THOMPSON RICH

IT WAS A DAY IN MIDSUMMER, I REMEMBER. I HAD BEEN tramping over the densely wooded and desolate hillside the greater part of the morning, getting with each mile farther and farther from the tawdry haunts of man and nearer and nearer the rugged heart of nature.

Finally (it must have been after noontime) I paused and made a light lunch of the sandwiches and cold coffee I had brought with me from town, sitting on the edge of a great slab of granite rock, swept clean and smooth by ages of winds and rains and snows.

All about me was a veritable garden of great projecting rocks, jagged and broken, flat and polished, needlelike, giant flowers of earth in a thousand different forms.

Here and there a short, dwarfed pine or spruce tree struggled for a footing amid its rocky friends, and the resistless undergrowth surged up through every crack and crevice, while energetic mosses and lichens clutched at the granite walls and crept bravely up. One had a feeling of awe, as if in the presence of elemental, eternal forces. Here, I thought, if anywhere, one might commune with the voiceless void.

Suddenly my eyes chanced to fall upon a fissure in the rock to the left, and I sprang up with a low exclamation. What I had beheld was to all appearances a human skeleton!

Advancing reluctantly, yet with that insistent inquisitiveness which surrounds the dead, I bent, and peered into the fissure. As I looked, a cry escaped me. The object I beheld was indeed a skeleton—but what a skeleton! The head, the left hand, and the foot were entirely missing, nor was there any sign of them at first sight.

Thoroughly fascinated by the morbid spectacle, I began to search for the missing members, and was finally rewarded by unearthing the head some twenty feet away, where it lay half buried in the soft loam and decayed vegetation and sifted shale. But a painstaking and minute hunt failed to reveal the missing hand and foot.

I was successful, however, in finding something immeasurably more important—a manuscript. This I found by the side of the mangled skeleton.

It consisted of several pages of closely written material, in a small pocket notebook, which fact, in connection with the partial shelter afforded by the crevice where the body lay, doubtless accounts for its preservation through the years that have passed since its owner met his hideous fate.

Picking up the notebook with nervous fingers, I opened it and turned the damp and musty pages through, reading it at first hastily, then slower and more carefully, then with a feverish concentration—as the awful significance of the words was riveted into my brain.

The writing was in a man's cramped, agitated hand, and I give it to you just as I read it, with the exception of the names and places, and a few paragraphs of vital scientific data—all but a few words at the very beginning and end, where the manuscript had been moulded into illegibility by the gradual action of the weather. Here follows:

"——as strange. I had a sense of apprehension from the start, a vague, indescribable feeling of doubt, of dread, as if some one, something, were urging me out, away, into these sullen hills.

"I might have known. The law of retribution is as positive as the law of gravity. I know that now. Oh, irony!

"But I was so sure. No one knew. No one could know. She, my wife, least of all, until the end. And the neighbors, her friends, never. She had merely pined away. No one dreamed I had poisoned her. Even when she died, there was no thought of autopsy. She had long been failing. And had I not been most concerned? None in the little town of —— but who sympathized with me. And I mourned. Oh, I mourned! So it was that she paid the price of her infamy. Ah, but revenge never was sweeter!

"And he? Oh, but I despised him—even as I had formerly admired him, even as I had once loved my wife—so I despised him. And despising him, I killed him—killed him, but with a poison far more subtle than I had used to destroy my wife—killed him with a poison in effect so hideous, so harrowing, that I can scarcely think of it without sickening even as I write.

"The poison I inculcated into his veins was a germ poison —a disease I, a physician of no small repute, had discovered and bred—a disease I had found existed only in a particular and very rare species of virulent purple and orange-banded spider—the genus ——. [Here follow in the original manuscript seven paragraphs of elaborate scientific data, of no particular interest to the average reader, but of incalculable import to the scientific world. These paragraphs I have omitted from this account for very significant reasons, but I hold them open to scientific examination at any time, and will welcome investigation by reputable parties]—a disease which was responsible for the extreme rarity of this particular species.

"By careful investigation I was able to learn the exact manifestations and working of the disease—which by their frightful ravages upon the system of the unfortunate victim fairly appalled me.

"By segregating and breeding diseased members of this particular species of spider, I was able to produce the disease in the young in its most virulent form. You can well imagine the care I used in handling these spiders, to prevent infection. Briefly, the symptoms are as follows: The spider about to be stricken apparently first experiences a peculiar numbness of the first left foreleg, to judge from its inability to use or move the affected member. A day or so later the leg, which in a healthy condition is a dull brown, turns a pale, sickening shade of yellow, which deepens rapidly until it has taken on a flaming orange hue. Then, in a few hours, a deep, vicious-looking blue cincture, or band, appears just at the first joint of the affected member. This cincture rapidly deepens to purple, which seems somehow to sear its way into the flesh and through the bone, so that in a surprisingly short time the whole leg is severed at the joint where the cincture has been.

"The spider then appears to regain its normal condition of health, which it maintains for about a week; then once again the hideous disease manifests itself, this time in the left feeler, or antenna, which in turn becomes yellow, then orange, whereupon the same blue cincture appears and deepens to purple; then, in about the same period of time as in the case of the leg, the antenna drops off, seared as if by some hellish flame.

"Once again the spider appears to regain its health—then in about a week the whole *head* of the stricken insect turns slowly yellow, then orange—then the cincture appears—and as a last manifestation, the head is seared off in flaming agony—and the spider dies in horrible convulsions.

"That briefly, is the process—as I was able to note after weeks and months of tireless research and observation.

"So what more perfect punishment for the man who stole from me my wife, while pretending to be my friend?

"Loving her as I did, I had not the heart to kill her in this hideous way: so I put her to death with a painless and insidious poison.

"But for —— I had no mercy. In fact, I gloated as I worked over my vile and diseased spiders, breeding them together until I was convinced that I had the germs of the disease in its most virulent form. Even then I was not sure what their effect would be on a numan being—but that much, at least, I must hazard.

"So having finally made all my preparations, I invited him to my house and placed one of the diseased spiders upon his forehead one night as he slept.

"It must have bitten him, for he awoke with a cry, and I had barely time to close his door and get back to my room before I heard him rise and turn on the light.

"Then he called me, and I came to him, burning with a fiendish satisfaction. 'Something has bitten me, horribly,' he said. 'I feel as if I were going to be ill.'

"I managed to reassure him by telling him that it was very likely nothing but one of our uncommonly large mosquitoes, and he returned to bed.

"But he did not sleep. All night I heard him moaning and tossing. And in the morning he was very pale.

" 'I do not know what is the matter with me,' he said, and I thought he looked at me queerly, 'but I feel as if a little rest would do me good. I feel choked. I think I will pack up my knapsack and go off to the hills for the week-end. Want to come?'

"I longed to go with him, to see the dread disease work, but I feared its deadly contagion, and was anxious to get him away before I myself became contaminated. So I said no—and he left.

"That was the last I ever saw of him—but once.

"He went away, as he had promised, and he seemed apparently well—all except the curious little inflamed spot on his forehead, whose significance I knew so well.

"He went away—and he failed to come back.

"Days passed, and there came no word from him. People began inquiring. It was odd that he should have left no address. His business suffered.

"Weeks went by—and no word. Search parties were sent out. The river was dragged. The morgues of near-by cities were searched. And all the while I laughed. For who would think of turning to those far-off hills?

"And yet as the days went by, I found myself turning to them again—wondering, wondering, wondering. I grew nervous, agitated. I got so I couldn't sleep.

"Finally, on a day in late summer (it was the 8th of August—date I shall never forget!) I packed a few things and set off. In search of him? God knows. I tried to tell myself not—but at any rate I found myself strangely, magnetically drawn to those distant somber hills—and thither I went.

"It was one of those gorgeous mornings that only August can produce, and the exhilarating air would have lifted my spirits, but instead I walked along depressed, and the knapsack strapped to my shoulder served only to intensify the feeling.

"In spite of all I could do, I found my mind reverting to the hideous revenge I had wreaked on my wife and her lover, and for the first time repentance stole in upon me.

"I walked along slowly, and it was well toward noon before I left the beaten road and started off at random over the hills, following a narrow and little used path.

"Progress now became doubly slow and painful, leading often up steep inclines and hard descents, with the aspect momentarily becoming more and more rugged, as I left the lower hills and climbed toward the mountain.

"By this time, however, I had got a kind of exhilaration sought in vain during the earlier hours of the morning, and climbed on and on, glad to free body and mind thus of the poison of brooding and lassitude. I would return to the town at night and take supper at one of the small inns that abounded thereabouts. This would give me some hours yet before I turned back. For the time being, the thought of searching for —— was forgotten. I had freed my mind of him entirely.

"Presently the path I had been following branched and

the right half narrowed into an all but obliterated trail, leading up a laborious slope. Forcing my way over dry, snapping underbrush and under low hanging spruce boughs, occasionally starting an indignant partridge from its hidden nest, often put to a wide detour to avoid some hazardous gully cut deep by centuries of spring and autumn freshets, I at last emerged upon a small, circular clearing, evidently the work of some lone wood-chopper.

"Here I sat down, tired by the climb, and refreshed myself with a sandwich from my knapsack. Then I pushed on to the summit, pausing frequently to examine some uncommon species of insect life with which the hills abounded.

"So much was I enjoying myself and such scant notice of the time did I take, that sunset came upon me unawares and I found myself, with darkness settling in on all sides with a startling rapidity, still on the summit of the mountain, with a good three mile descent before me. Indeed, the prospect was not altogether a cheering one and I reproached myself for my heedlessness. But I had found a species of spider for which I had searched in vain for months, so, somewhat reassured by its precious body in a pill-box in my pocket, I started down.

"In spite of my best speed, however, night shut in on me before I had made one quarter of the return, leaving me to grope the rest of the way in utter darkness, with not even the light of a dim star to go by. Vague fear awoke within me, but I shielded my eyes and stumbled to the bottom, sliding, falling, clutching here and there at some projecting tree-limb to check my headlong descent. Finally, torn and disheveled and shaking, I emerged upon the clearing. Pausing only for breath, I plunged on into the dark. Fear was growing—growing—that peculiar fear of the dark which is the heritage of those who have taken human life.

"What was that? Something lay gleaming queerly ahead, with a dull phosphorescent glow. I stooped and picked it up—and flung it from me shuddering. It was the skeleton of a human foot!

"I groped on, my every heartbeat choking at my throat. Of a sudden I came forcefully against a barrier of rock. I tried to feel my way around it, to get beyond it, but could not. It seemed continuous, a solid wall that would not let me by. Had I fallen into a trap in the darkness? Terrified, I turned—and there lay something else gleaming with that same weird, phosphorescent glow! Sick with terror and dread, half fearing what it might be, I sprang on it and picked it up—*picked it up*—the rotting hand of a human being! With a stifled gasp, I flung it from me, reeled, tripped through some vines, and fell swooning.

"When I came to myself, I struck a match and looked about me. Its feeble flame revealed a pair of damp, rocky walls, low and vaulted. I was in some sort of cavern.

"Later on I crept out, collected an armful of sticks, brought them back, and soon had a fire started. By its light I observed that the rear of the cave was still in darkness, and judging that it must extend back indefinitely, I gave my attention to my immediate surroundings—when, with a shock I saw, directly in front of me, a granite slab. On it lay several loose sheets of manuscript, scrawled wildly on odd scraps of paper.

"With a prophetic dread I bent forward and gathered the loose sheets together. Holding them near the fire, I peered closer. Then I think a cry must have escaped me. The writing was in ——'s hand, curiously scrawled and scraggly, but still recognizable.

"So fate had brought me to my victim!

"For the rest, there is little more to say. I am doomed as I deserve, even as he was doomed. His words speak all that can be spoken. They follow:

APRIL 4TH—*I had meant to spend only the week-end in these hills, yet here I am, after two weeks—still here, and suffering the pains of hell. What has come over me I cannot imagine. And yet—can I not? I am not so sure! Perhaps —perhaps —— has in some devilish way managed to poison me. He is insanely jealous. He thinks there was something between his wife and me. Verily I believe he harassed her to death on the subject. And having thus brought her to her grave, he wishes to send me there.*

Perhaps he will succeed—if it is true that in some fiendish way he has got some of his germs into my blood. That bite at his house that evening. I am not so sure. It was a most unusual bite. It seemed upon the instant to sour all my blood.

And yet if he accomplishes my death, how vain it will be —for as God is my witness I swear I never harmed his wife. We were the best of friends, nothing more. And she loved him with a wholeness, a passion that any but a man maddened by groundless jealousy must at once have seen.

How he has wrecked his life! A mind so brilliant—and yet, with her dead, a closed room.

However, I may be wrong. I will wait. By the symptoms I will know. I write this down for I must do something.

APRIL 5TH—*It is he now, his hellish work. I am sure of it. To-day my left leg, which for two weeks has felt positively numb, turned a sickening yellow, from the ankle down, which began at once to deepen, until it now flames orange. And oh! the pain is hellish! Yes, I am sure it is ——'s work. But I will still withhold judgment.*

APRIL 6TH—*To-day a deep, virulent blue cincture has appeared just at the ankle of the affected leg. What a hellish contrast to the orange!*

It is ——. I am sure, now. Oh, what a fiend!

APRIL 7TH—*The cincture has deepened to purple, and seems to cut into the very flesh. It seems sometimes as if the pain would drive me mad.*

APRIL 8TH—*My flaming foot* dropped off *to-night, seared at the ankle by the purple cincture, and I flung it outside the cave. I wonder. Perhaps I may yet live to return to the world. Ah, I will be avenged for this!*

MAY 23RD—*I am cursed,* cursed! *To-day, just as I was beginning to believe the hellish thing had left me, it returned, this time in my left hand. Oh, I can see it all: to-morrow and the next day and the next,* for just two weeks, *my hand will be numb; then will come that frightful yellow; then the orange; then—then the purple cincture!*

Curse the man who discovered this hellish disease—and turned it into me! I could tear him limb from limb. Oh, I pray to return! I would go now, yet I fear my malady is of a vilely contagious nature. I have not the heart to menace a whole community, perhaps a whole nation, perhaps humanity itself—merely to avenge myself on one man.

JUNE 6TH—*I was right! This morning I awoke with my hand that death-yellow. Oh, it is too regular, too certain—too cruelly certain!*

JUNE 9TH—*Thank God! My hand is gone—out there where my foot went. It happened to-night. Perhaps I may yet return! Perhaps I may yet be avenged. I wonder.*

JULY 21ST—Doomed! *That fearful numbness again—this time in my head. I cannot think—I cannot write—I can scarcely breathe. Oh, the pain, the pain——.*

"Here it ended in a sputter of ink. Trembling in every limb, filled with a horror and anguish and remorse no man can know, spellbound by the awful tale those few sheets told, I sat there motionless.

"So I had been wrong. Oh, my jealousy, my insane jealousy! As I sat there, all desire of life suddenly left me, and I thrilled with joy at the remembrance of the hand and foot I had come upon, outside the cave. They were his. I had touched them. I was contaminated with the dread disease.

"What was that? I listened, straining every nerve. From the back of the cavern had come a sound.

"Five minutes passed—ten—fifteen (I was oblivious of time)—but it was not repeated. Slightly I relaxed my aching nerves and tried to think. Already I fancied I could feel the fearful poison of the diseased spider working in my veins.

"Suddenly the significance of that last entry in ——'s diary burst upon me, and I sat shivering as under a sudden deluge of icy water. *'July 21st.'* Two weeks more would make it *August 5th,* and three days more would bring it to —*August 8th!*

" 'Great God!' I cried aloud, 'to-night is the night!'

" *'Yes, to-night is the night!'* echoed a sepulchral voice from the cavern's inner darkness.

"In an agony of dread I looked, and the blood within me paled to water at the sight that met my gaze. Something—*something with but a single hand and foot*—emerged from the shadows of the back of the cavern and began to come forward, leaning heavily upon a rough staff for support.

" 'Stay back—*stay back!* For the love of God!' I shrieked. But the terrible thing came on and on, and the awful eyes fastened themselves upon my person and suddenly recognized me—and it smiled a hideous smile.

"When it drew nearer, I could see that all above the shoulders flamed orange, while around the neck a livid purple cincture seemed actually to be searing its way into the flesh.

" 'This is your revenge,' it spoke. 'And this is mine,' raising the hellish stump of its mutilated left arm and panting heavily at me. 'My suffering is over—but yours is all to come. And to the bodily pains of hell will be added the mental tortures of hopeless remorse—knowing your wife was innocent. With that I curse you.'

"Even as it spoke, the eyes rolled out of sight behind horrible lids, the tongue protruded itself in flaming agony, and the whole head, suddenly severed at the neck, thudded the cavern floor.

"I came to my feet with a mad cry, that, shattering the silence beyond the deepest shadows, swelled up in a thousand echoes, from the wail of a soul in torment to the screech of a crucified demon. Then I rushed headlong out.

"For the rest——."

The last page was illegible, as the first had been, worn and corroded by the slow action of years of decay.

I put the notebook slowly in my pocket and sat there thinking, sickened and awed by the astounding manuscript.

Again I went over to the skeleton there in the fissure. Now I understood why the hand and foot were missing, and why I had found the head many feet from the body.

There it lay, mute evidence that the retribution was complete.

THE HORROR AT RED HOOK

By H. P. LOVECRAFT

There are sacraments of evil as well as of good about us, and we live and move to my belief in an unknown world, a place where there are caves and shadows and dwellers in twilight. It is possible that man may sometimes return on the track of evolution, and it is my belief that an awful lore is not yet dead.

Arthur Machen.

NOT MANY WEEKS AGO, ON A STREET CORNER IN THE village of Pascoag, Rhode Island, a tall, heavily built, and wholesome-looking pedestrian furnished much speculation by a singular lapse of behavior. He had, it appeared, been descending the hill by the road from Chepachet; and encountering the compact section, had turned to his left into the main thoroughfare where several modest business blocks convey a touch of the urban. At this point, without visible provocation, he committed his astonishing lapse; staring queerly for a second at the tallest of the buildings before him, and then, with a series of terrified, hysterical shrieks, breaking into a frantic run which ended in a stumble and fall at the next crossing. Picked up and dusted off by ready hands, he was found to be conscious, organically unhurt, and evidently cured of his sudden nervous attack. He muttered some shamefaced explanations involving a strain he had undergone, and with downcast glance turned back up the Chepachet road, trudging out of sight without once looking behind him. It was a strange incident to befall so large, robust, normal-featured, and capable-looking a man, and the strangeness was not lessened by the remarks of a bystander who had recognized him as the boarder of a well-known dairyman on the outskirts of Chepachet.

He was, it developed, a New York police detective named Thomas F. Malone, now on a long leave of absence under medical treatment after some disproportionately arduous work on a gruesome local case which accident had made dramatic. There had been a collapse of several old brick buildings during a raid in which he had shared, and something about the wholesale loss of life, both of prisoners and of his companions, had peculiarly appalled him. As a result, he had acquired an acute and anomalous horror of any buildings even remotely suggesting the ones which had fallen in, so that in the end mental specialists forbade him the sight of such things for an indefinite period. A police surgeon with relatives in Chepachet had put forward that quaint hamlet of wooden Colonial houses as an ideal spot for psychological convalescence; and thither the sufferer had gone, promising never to venture among the brick-lined streets of larger villages till duly advised by the Woonsocket specialist with whom he was put in touch. This walk to Pascoag for magazines had been a mistake, and the patient had paid in fright, bruises, and humiliation for his disobedience.

So much the gossips of Chepachet and Pascoag knew; and so much, also, the learned specialists believed. But Malone had at first told the specialists much more, ceasing only when he saw that utter incredulity was his portion. Thereafter he held his peace, protesting not at all when it was generally agreed that the collapse of certain squalid brick houses in the Red Hook section of Brooklyn, and the consequent death of many brave officers, had unseated his nervous equilibrium. He had worked too hard, all said, in trying to clean up those nests of disorder and violence; certain features were shocking enough, in all conscience, and the unexpected tragedy was the last straw. This was a simple explanation which every one could understand, and because Malone was not a simple person he perceived that he had better let it suffice. To hint to unimaginative people of a horror beyond all human conception—a horror of houses and blocks and cities leprous and cancerous with evils dragged from elder worlds—would be merely to invite a padded cell instead of a restful rustication, and Malone was a man of sense despite his mysticism. He had the Celt's far vision of weird and hidden things, but the logician's quick eye for the outwardly unconvincing; an amalgam which had led him far afield in the forty-two years of his life, and set him in strange places for a Dublin University man born in a Georgian villa near Phœnix Park.

And now, as he reviewed the things he had seen and felt and apprehended, Malone was content to keep unshared the secret of what could reduce a dauntless fighter to a quivering neurotic; what could make old brick slums and seas of dark, subtle faces a thing of nightmare and eldritch portent. It would not be the first time his sensations had been forced to bide uninterpreted—for was not his very act of plunging into the polyglot abyss of New York's underworld a freak beyond sensible explanation? What could he tell the prosaic of the antique witcheries and grotesque marvels discernible to sensitive eyes amidst the poison caldron where all the varied dregs of unwholesome ages mix their venom and perpetuate their obscene terrors? He had seen the hellish green flame of secret wonder in this blatant, evasive welter of outward greed and inward blasphemy, and had smiled gently when all the New Yorkers he knew scoffed at his experiment in police work. They had been very witty and cynical, deriding his fantastic pursuit of unknowable mysteries and assuring him that in these days New York held nothing but cheapness and vulgarity. One of them had wagered him a heavy sum that he could not—despite many poignant things to his credit in the *Dublin Review*—even write a truly interesting story of New York low life; and now, looking back, he perceived that cosmic irony had justified the prophet's words while secretly confuting their flippant meaning. The horror, as glimpsed at last, could not make a story—for like the book cited by Poe's German authority, *"er lasst sich nicht lesen"*—it does not permit itself to be read.

II

To Malone the sense of latent mystery in existence was always present. In youth he had felt the hidden beauty and ecstasy of things, and had been a poet; but poverty and sorrow and exile had turned his gaze in darker directions, and he had thrilled at the imputations of evil in the world around. Daily life had for him come to be a phantasmagoria of macabre shadow-studies; now glittering and leering with concealed rottenness as in Aubrey Beardsley's best manner, now hinting terrors behind the commonest shapes and objects as in the subtler and less obvious work of Gustave Doré. He would often regard it as merciful that most persons of high intelligence jeer at the inmost mysteries; for, he argued, if superior minds were ever placed in fullest contact with the secrets preserved by ancient and lowly cults, the resultant abnormalities would soon not only wreck the world, but threaten the very integrity of the universe. All this reflection was no doubt morbid, but keen logic and a deep sense of humor ably offset it. Malone was satisfied to let his notions remain as half-spied and forbidden visions to be lightly played with; and hysteria came only when duty flung him into a hell of revelation too sudden and insidious to escape.

He had for some time been detailed to the Butler Street Station in Brooklyn when the Red Hook matter came to his notice. Red Hook is a maze of hybrid squalor near the ancient waterfront opposite Governor's Island, with dirty highways climbing the hill from the wharves to that higher ground where the decayed lengths of Clinton and Court Streets lead off toward the Borough Hall. Its houses are mostly of brick, dating from the first quarter to the middle of the Nineteenth Century, and some of the obscurer alleys and byways have that alluring antique flavor which conventional reading leads us to call "Dickensian." The population is a hopeless tangle and enigma; Syrian, Spanish, Italian, and negro elements impinging upon one another, and fragments of Scandinavian and American belts lying not far distant. It is a babel of sound and filth, and sends out strange cries to answer the lapping of oily waves at its grimy piers and the monstrous organ litanies of the harbor whistles. Here long ago a brighter picture dwelt, with clear-eyed mariners on the lower streets and homes of taste and substance where the larger houses line the hill. One can trace the relics of this former happiness in the trim shapes of the buildings, the occasional graceful churches, and the evidences of original art and background in bits of detail here and there—a worn flight of steps, a battered doorway, a wormy pair of decorative columns or pilasters, or a fragment of once green space with bent and rusted iron railing. The houses are generally in solid blocks, and now and then a many-windowed cupola arises to tell of days when the households of captains and ship-owners watched the sea.

From this tangle of material and spiritual putrescence the blasphemies of an hundred dialects assail the sky. Hordes of prowlers reel shouting and singing along the lanes and thoroughfares, occasional furtive hands suddenly extinguish lights and pull down curtains, and swarthy, sin-pitted faces disappear from windows when visitors pick their way through. Policemen despair of order or reform, and seek rather to erect barriers protecting the outside world from the contagion. The clang of the patrol is answered by a kind of spectral silence, and such prisoners as are taken are never communicative. Visible offenses are as varied as the local dialects, and run the gamut from the smuggling of rum and prohibited aliens through diverse stages of lawlessness and obscure vice to murder and mutilation in their most abhorrent guises. That these visible affairs are not more frequent is not to the neighborhood's credit, unless the power of concealment be an art demanding credit. More people enter Red Hook than leave it—or at least, than leave it by the landward side—and those who are loquacious are the likeliest to leave.

Malone found in this state of things a faint stench of secrets more terrible than any of the sins denounced by citizens and bemoaned by priests and philanthropists. He was conscious, as one who united imagination with scientific knowledge, that modern people under lawless conditions tend uncannily to repeat the darkest instinctive patterns of primitive half-ape savagery in their daily life and ritual observances; and he had often viewed with an anthropologist's shudder the chanting cursing processions of blear-eyed and pock-marked young men which wound their way along in the dark small hours of morning. One saw groups of these youths incessantly; sometimes in leering vigils on street corners, sometimes in doorways playing eerily on cheap instruments of music, sometimes in stupefied dozes or indecent dialogues around cafeteria tables near Borough Hall, and sometimes in whispering converse around dingy taxicabs drawn up at the high stoops of crumbling and closely shuttered old houses. They chilled and fascinated him more than he dared confess to his associates on the force, for he seemed to see in them some monstrous thread of secret continuity; some fiendish, cryptical and ancient pattern utterly beyond and below the sordid mass of facts and habits and haunts listed with such conscientious technical care by the police. They must be, he felt inwardly, the heirs of some shocking and primordial tradition; the sharers of debased and broken scraps from cults and ceremonies older than mankind. Their coherence and definiteness suggested it, and it showed in the singular suspicion of order which lurked beneath their squalid disorder. He had not read in vain such treatises as Miss Murray's *Witch Cult in Western Europe;* and knew that up to recent years there had certainly survived among peasants and furtive folk a frightful and clandestine system of assemblies and orgies descended from dark religions antedating the Aryan world, and appearing in popular legends as Black Masses and Witches' Sabbaths. That these hellish vestiges of old Turanian-Asiatic magic and fertility-cults were even now wholly dead he could not for a moment suppose, and he frequently wondered how much older and how much blacker than the very worst of the muttered tales some of them might really be.

III

It was the case of Robert Suydam which took Malone to the heart of things in Red Hook. Suydam was a lettered recluse of ancient Dutch family, possessed originally of barely independent means, and inhabiting the spacious but ill-preserved mansion which his grandfather had built in Flatbush when that village was little more than a pleasant group of Colonial cottages surrounding the steepled and ivy-clad Reformed Church with its iron-railed yard of Netherlandish gravestones. In this lonely house, set back from Martense Street amidst a yard of venerable trees, Suydam had read and brooded for some six decades except for a period a generation before, when he had sailed for the Old World and remained there out of sight for eight years. He could afford no servants, and would admit but few visitors to his absolute solitude; eschewing close friendships and receiving his rare acquaintances in one of the three ground-floor rooms which he kept in order—a vast, high-ceiled library whose walls were solidly packed with tattered books of ponderous, archaic, and vaguely repellent aspect. The growth of the town and its final absorption in the Brooklyn district had meant nothing to Suydam, and he had come to mean less and less to the town. Elderly people still pointed him out on the streets, but to most of the recent population he was merely a queer, corpulent old fellow whose unkempt white hair, stubbly beard, shiny black clothes and gold-headed cane earned him an amused glance and nothing more. Malone did not know him by sight till duty called him to the case, but had heard of him indirectly as a really profound authority on mediæval superstition, and had once idly meant to look up an out-of-print pamphlet of his on the Kabbalah and the Faustus legend, which a friend had quoted from memory.

Suydam became a "case" when his distant and only relatives sought court pronouncements on his sanity. Their action seemed sudden to the outside world, but was really undertaken only after prolonged observation and sorrowful debate. It was based on certain odd changes in his speech and habits; wild references to impending wonders, and unaccountable hauntings of disreputable Brooklyn neighborhoods. He had been growing shabbier and shabbier with the years, and now prowled about like a veritable mendicant; seen occasionally by humiliated friends in subway stations, or loitering on the benches around Borough Hall in conversation with groups of swarthy, evil-looking strangers. When he spoke it was to babble of unlimited powers almost within his grasp, and to repeat with knowing leers such mystical words or names as "Sephiroth," "Ashmodai" and "Samael." The court action revealed that he was using up his income and wasting his principal in the purchase of curious tomes imported from London and Paris, and in the maintenance of a squalid basement flat in the Red Hook district where he spent nearly every night, receiving odd delegations of mixed rowdies and foreigners, and apparently conducting some kind of ceremonial service behind the green blinds of secretive windows. Detectives assigned to follow him reported strange cries and chants and prancing of feet filtering out from these nocturnal rites, and shuddered at their peculiar ecstasy and abandon despite the commonness of weird orgies in that sodden section. When, however, the matter came to a hearing, Suydam managed to preserve his liberty. Before the judge his manner grew urbane and reasonable, and he freely admitted the queerness of demeanor and extravagant cast of language into which he had fallen through excessive devotion to study and research. He was, he said, engaged in the investigation of certain details of European tradition which required the closest contact with foreign groups and their songs and folk dances. The notion that any low secret society was preying upon him, as hinted by his relatives, was obviously absurd; and showed how sadly limited was their understanding of him and his work. Triumphing with his calm explanations, he was suffered to depart unhindered; and the paid detectives of the Suydams, Corlears, and Van Brunts were withdrawn in resigned disgust.

It was here that an alliance of Federal inspectors and police, Malone with them, entered the case. The law had watched the Suydam action with interest, and had in many instances been called upon to aid the private detectives. In this work it developed that Suydam's new associates were among the blackest and most vicious criminals of Red Hook's devious lanes, and that at least a third of them were known and repeated offenders in the matter of thievery, disorder, and the importation of illegal immigrants. Indeed, it would not have been too much to say that the old scholar's particular circle coincided almost perfectly with the worst of the organized cliques which smuggled ashore certain nameless and unclassified Asian dregs wisely turned back by Ellis Island. In the teeming rookeries of Parker Place—since renamed—where Suydam had his basement flat, there had grown up a very unusual colony of unclassified slant-eyed folk who used the Arabic alphabet but were eloquently repudiated by the great mass of Syrians in and around Atlantic Avenue. They could all have been deported for lack of credentials, but legalism is slow-moving, and one does not disturb Red Hook unless publicity forces one to.

These creatures attended a tumbledown stone church, used Wednesday as a dance hall, which reared its Gothic buttresses near the vilest part of the waterfront. It was nominally Catholic; but priests throughout Brooklyn denied the place all standing and authenticity, and policemen agreed with them when they listened to the noises it emitted at night. Malone used to fancy he heard terrible cracked bass notes from a hidden organ far underground when the church stood empty and unlighted, whilst all observers dreaded the shrieking and drumming which accompanied the visible services. Suydam, when questioned, said he thought the ritual was some remnant of Nestorian Christianity tinctured with the Shamanism of Tibet. Most of the people, he conjectured, were of Mongoloid stock, originating somewhere in or near Kurdistan—and Malone could not help recalling that Kurdistan is the land of the Yezidees, last survivors of the Persian devil-worshipers. However this may have been, the stir of the Suydam investigation made it certain that these unauthorized newcomers were flooding Red Hook in increasing numbers; entering through some marine conspiracy unreached by revenue officers and harbor police, overrunning Parker Place and rapidly spreading up the hill, and welcomed with curious fraternalism by the other assorted denizens of the region. Their squat figures and characteristic squinting physiognomies, grotesquely combined with flashy American clothing, appeared more and more numerously among the loafers and nomad gangsters of the Borough Hall section; till at length it was deemed necessary to compute their number, ascertain their sources and occupations, and find if possible a way to round them up and deliver them to the proper immigration authorities. To this task Malone was assigned by agreement of Federal and city forces, and as he commenced his canvass of Red Hook he felt poised upon the brink of nameless terrors, with the shabby, unkempt figure of Robert Suydam as archfiend and adversary.

IV

Police methods are varied and ingenious. Malone, through unostentatious rambles, carefully casual conversations, well-timed offers of hip-pocket liquor, and judicious dialogues with frightened prisoners, learned many isolated facts about the movement whose aspect had become so menacing. The newcomers were indeed Kurds, but of a dialect obscure and puzzling to exact philology. Such of them as worked lived mostly as dock-hands and unlicensed peddlers, though frequently serving in Greek restaurants and tending corner news-stands. Most of them, however, had no visible means of support; and were obviously connected with underworld pursuits, of which smuggling and bootlegging were the least indescribable. They had come in steamships, apparently tramp freighters, and had been unloaded by stealth on moonless nights in rowboats which stole under a certain wharf and followed a hidden canal to a secret subterranean pool beneath a house. This wharf, canal and house Malone could not locate, for the memories of his informants were exceedingly confused, while their speech was to a great extent beyond even the ablest interpreters; nor could he gain any real data on the reasons for their systematic importation. They were reticent about the exact spot from which they had come, and were never sufficiently off guard to reveal the agencies which had sought them out and directed their course. Indeed, they developed something like acute fright when asked the reason for their presence. Gangsters of other breeds were equally taciturn, and the most that could be gathered was that some god or great priesthood had promised them unheard-of powers and supernatural glories and rulerships in a strange land.

The attendance of both newcomers and old gangsters at Suydam's closely guarded nocturnal meetings was very regular, and the police soon learned that the erstwhile recluse had leased additional flats to accommodate such guests as knew his password; at last occupying three entire houses and permanently harboring many of his queer companions. He spent but little time now at his Flatbush home, apparently going and coming only to obtain and return books; and his face and manner had attained an appalling pitch of wildness. Malone twice interviewed him, but was each time brusquely repulsed. He knew nothing, he said, of any mysterious plots or movements; and had no idea how the Kurds could have entered or what they wanted. His business was to study undisturbed the folk-lore of all the immigrants of the district; a business with which policemen had no legitimate concern. Malone mentioned his admiraiton for Suydam's old brochure on the Kabbalah and other myths, but the old man's softening was only momentary. He sensed an intrusion, and rebuffed his visitor in no uncertain way; till Malone withdrew disgusted, and turned to other channels of information.

What Malone would have unearthed could he have worked continuously on the case, we shall never know. As it was, a stupid conflict between city and Federal authority suspended the investigation for several months, during which the detective was busy with other assignments. But at no time did he lose interest, or fail to stand amazed at what began to happen to Robert Suydam. Just at the time when a wave of kidnapings and disappearances spread its excitement over New York, the unkempt scholar embarked upon a metamorphosis as startling as it was absurd. One day he was seen near Borough Hall with clean-shaved face, well-trimmed hair, and tastefully immaculate attire, and on every day thereafter some obscure improvement was noticed in him. He maintained his new fastidiousness without interruption, added to it an unwonted sparkle of eye and crispness of speech, and began little by little to shed the corpulence which had so long deformed him. Now frequently taken for less than his age, he acquired an elasticity of step and buoyancy of demeanor to match the new tradition, and showed a curious darkening of the hair which somehow did not suggest dye. As the months passed, he commenced to dress less and less conservatively, and finally astonished his few friends by renovating and redecorating his Flatbush mansion, which he threw open in a series of receptions, summoning all the acquaintances he could remember, and extending a special welcome to the fully forgiven relatives who had so lately sought his restraint. Some attended through curiosity, others through duty; but all were suddenly charmed by the dawning grace and urbanity of the former hermit. He had, he asserted, accomplished most of his allotted work; and having just inherited some property from a half-forgotten European friend, was about to spend his remaining years in a brighter second youth which ease, care and diet had made possible to him. Less and less was he seen at Red Hook, and more and more did he move in the society to which he was born. Policemen noted a tendency of the gangsters to congregate at the old stone church and dance hall instead of at the basement flat in Parker Place, though the latter and its recent annexes still overflowed with noxious life.

Then two incidents occurred—wide enough apart, but both of intense interest in the case as Malone envisaged it. One was a quiet announcement in the *Eagle* of Robert Suydam's engagement to Miss Cornelia Gerritsen, of Bayside, a young woman of excellent position, and distantly related to the elderly bridegroom-elect; whilst the other was a raid on the dance-hall church by city police, after a report that the face of a kidnaped child had been seen for a second at one of the basement windows. Malone had participated in this raid, and studied the place with much care when inside. Nothing was found—in fact, the building was entirely deserted when visited—but the sensitive Celt was vaguely disturbed by many things about the interior. There were crudely painted panels he did not like—panels which depicted sacred faces with peculiarly worldly and sardonic expressions, and which occasionally took liberties that even a layman's sense of decorum could scarcely countenance. Then, too, he did not relish the Greek inscription on the wall above the pulpit; an ancient incantation which he had once stumbled upon in Dublin college days, and which read, literally translated:

> "O friend and companion of night, thou who rejoicest in the baying of dogs and spilt blood, who wanderest in the midst of shades among the tombs, who longest for blood and bringest terror to mortals, Gorgo, Mormo, thousand-faced moon, look favorably on our sacrifices!"

When he read this he shuddered, and thought vaguely of the cracked bass organ-notes he fancied he had heard beneath the church on certain nights. He shuddered again at the rust around the rim of a metal basin which stood on the altar, and paused nervously when his nostrils seemed to detect a curious and ghastly stench from somewhere in the neighborhood. That organ memory haunted him, and he explored the basement with particular assiduity before he left. The place was very hateful to him; yet after all, were the blasphemous panels and inscriptions more than mere crudities perpetrated by the ignorant?

By the time of Suydam's wedding the kidnaping epidemic had become a popular newspaper scandal. Most of the victims were young children of the lowest classes, but the increasing number of disappearances had worked up a sentiment of the strongest fury. Journals clamored for action from the police, and once more the Butler Street station sent its men over Red Hook for clues, discoveries, and criminals. Malone was glad to be on the trail again, and took pride in a raid on one of Suydam's Parker Place houses. There, indeed, no stolen child was found, despite the tales of screams and the red sash picked up in the areaway; but the paintings and rough inscriptions on the peeling walls of most of the rooms, and the primitive chemical laboratory in the attic, all helped to convince the detective that he was on the track of something tremendous. The paintings were appalling—

hideous monsters of every shape and size, and parodies on human outlines which cannot be described. The writing was in red, and varied from Arabic to Greek, Roman and Hebrew letters. Malone could not read much of it, but what he did decipher was portentous and cabalistic enough. One frequently repeated motto was in a sort of Hebraized Hellenistic Greek, and suggested the most terrible demon-evocations of the Alexandrian decadence:

> HEL. HELOYM. SOTHER. EMMANVEL. SABAOTH. AGLA. TETRAGRAMMATON. AGYROS. OTHEOS. ISCHYROS. ATHANATOS. IEHOVA. VA. ADONAL. SADY. HOMOVSION. MESSIAS. ESCHEREHEYE.

Circles and pentagrams loomed on every hand, and told indubitably of the strange beliefs and aspirations of those who dwelt so squalidly here. In the cellar, however, the strangest thing was found—a pile of genuine gold ingots covered carelessly with a piece of burlap, and bearing upon their shining surfaces the same weird hieroglyphics which also adorned the walls. During this raid the police encountered only a passive resistance from the squinting Orientals that swarmed from every door. Finding nothing relevant, they had to leave all as it was; but the precinct captain wrote Suydam a note advising him to look closely to the character of his tenants and protégés in view of the growing public clamor.

V

Then came the June wedding and the great sensation. Flatbush was gay for the hour about high noon, and pennanted motors thronged the streets near the old Dutch church where an awning stretched from door to highway. No local event ever surpassed the Suydam-Gerritsen nuptials in tone and scale, and the party which escorted bride and groom to the Cunard pier was, if not exactly the smartest, at least a solid page from the Social Register. At 5 o'clock adieux were waved, and the ponderous liner edged away from the long pier, slowly turned its nose seaward, discarded its tug, and headed for the widening water spaces that led to Old World wonders. By night the outer harbor was cleared, and late passengers watched the stars twinkling above an unpolluted ocean.

Whether the tramp steamer or the scream was first to gain attention, no one can say. Probably they were simultaneous, but it is of no use to calculate. The scream came from the Suydam stateroom, and the sailor who broke down the door could perhaps have told frightful things if he had not forthwith gone completely mad—as it is, he shrieked more loudly than the first victims, and thereafter ran simpering about the vessel till caught and put in irons. The ship's doctor who entered the stateroom and turned on the lights a moment later did not go mad, but told nobody what he saw till afterwards, when he corresponded with Malone in Chepachet. It was murder—strangulation—but one need not say that the claw-mark on Mrs. Suydam's throat could have come from her husband's or any other human hand, or that upon the white wall there flickered for an instant in hateful red a legend which, later copied from memory, seems to have been nothing less than the fearsome Chaldean letters of the word "LILITH." One need not mention these things because they vanished so quickly—as for Suydam, one could at least bar others from the room until one knew what to think oneself. The doctor has distinctly assured Malone that he did not see *IT*. The open porthole, just before he turned on the lights, was clouded for a second with a certain phosphorescence, and for a moment there seemed to echo in the night outside the suggestion of a faint and hellish tittering; but no real outline met the eyes. As proof, the doctor points to his continued sanity.

Then the tramp steamer claimed all attention. A boat put off, and a horde of swart, insolent ruffians in officers' dress swarmed aboard the temporarily halted Cunarder. They wanted Suydam or his body—they had known of his trip, and for certain reasons were sure he would die. The captain's deck was almost a pandemonium; for at the instant, between the doctor's report from the stateroom and the demands of the men from the trap, not even the wisest and gravest seaman could think what to do. Suddenly the leader of the visiting mariners, an Arab with a hatefully negroid mouth, pulled forth a dirty, crumpled paper and handed it to the captain. It was signed by Robert Suydam, and bore the following cold message:

> In case of sudden or unexplained accident or death on my part, please deliver me or my body unquestioningly into the hands of the bearer and his associates. Everything, for me, and perhaps for you, depends on absolute compliance. Explanations can come later—do not fail me now.
>
> ROBERT SUYDAM.

Captain and doctor looked at each other, and the latter whispered something to the former. Finally they nodded rather helplessly and led the way to the Suydam stateroom. The doctor directed the captain's glance away as he unlocked the door and admitted the strange seamen, nor did he breathe easily till they filed out with their burden after an unaccountably long period of preparation. It was wrapped in bedding from the berths, and the doctor was glad that the outlines were not very revealing. Somehow the men got the thing over the side and away to their tramp steamer without uncovering it.

The Cunarder started again, and the doctor and a ship's undertaker sought out the Suydam stateroom to perform what last services they could. Once more the physician was forced to reticence and even to mendacity, for a hellish thing had happened. When the undertaker asked him why he had drained off all of Mrs. Suydam's blood, he neglected to affirm that he had not done so; nor did he point to the vacant bottle-spaces on the rack, or to the odor in the sink which showed the hasty disposition of the bottles' original contents. The pockets of those men—if men they were—had bulged damnably when they left the ship. Two hours later, and the world knew by radio all that it ought to know of the horrible affair.

VI

That same June evening, without having heard a word from the sea, Malone was desperately busy among the alleys of Red Hook. A sudden stir seemed to permeate the place, and as if apprised by "grape-vine telegraph" of something singular, the denizens clustered expectantly around the dance-hall church and the houses in Parker Place. Three children had just disappeared—blue-eyed Norwegians from the streets toward Gowanus—and there were rumors of a mob forming among the sturdy vikings of that section. Malone had for weeks been urging his colleagues to attempt a general clean-up; and at last, moved by conditions more obvious to their common sense than the conjectures of a Dublin dreamer, they had agreed upon a final stroke. The unrest and menace of this evening had been the deciding factor, and just about midnight a raiding party recruited from three stations descended upon Parker Place and its environs. Doors were battered in, stragglers arrested, and candle-lighted rooms forced to disgorge unbelievable throngs of mixed foreigners in figured robes, miters, and other inexplicable devices. Much was lost in the mêlée, for objects were thrown hastily down unexpected shafts, and betraying odors deadened by the sudden kindling of pungent incense. But spattered blood was everywhere, and Malone shuddered whenever he saw a brazier or altar from which smoke was still rising.

He wanted to be in several places at once, and decided on Suydam's basement flat only after a messenger had reported the complete emptiness of the dilapidated dance-hall church. The flat, he thought, must hold some clue to a cult of which the occult scholar had so obviously become the center and leader; and it was with real expectancy that he ransacked the musty rooms, noted their vaguely charnel odor, and examined the curious books, instruments, gold ingots, and glass-stoppered bottles scattered carelessly here and there. Once a lean, black-and-white cat edged between his feet and tripped him, overturning at the same time a beaker half full of red liquid. The shock was severe, and to this day Malone is not certain of what he saw; but in dreams he still pictures that cat as it scuttled away with certain monstrous alterations and peculiarities. Then came the locked cellar door, and the search for something to break it down. A heavy stool stood near, and its tough seat was more than enough for the antique panels. A crack formed and enlarged, and the whole door gave way—but from the *other* side; whence poured a howling tumult of ice-cold wind with all the stenches of the bottomless pit, and whence reached a sucking force not of earth or heaven, which, coiling sentiently about the paralyzed detective, dragged him through the aperture and down unmeasured spaces filled with whispers and wails, and gusts of mocking laughter.

Of course it was a dream. All the specialists have told him so, and he has nothing tangible to prove the contrary. Indeed, he would rather have it thus; for then the sight of old brick slums and dark foreign faces would not eat so deeply into his soul. But at the time it was all horribly real, and nothing can ever efface the memory of those nighted crypts, those titan arcades, and those half-formed shapes of hell that strode gigantically in silence holding half-eaten things whose still surviving portions screamed for mercy or laughed with madness. Odors of incense and corruption joined in sickening concert, and the black air was alive with the cloudy, semi-visible bulk of shapeless elemental things with eyes. Somewhere dark sticky water was lapping at onyx piers, and once the shivery tinkle of raucous little bells pealed out to greet the insane titter of a naked phosphorescent thing which swam into sight, scrambled ashore, and climbed up to squat leeringly on a carved golden pedestal in the background.

Avenues of limitless night seemed to radiate in every direction, till one might fancy that here lay the root of a contagion destined to sicken and swallow cities, and engulf nations in the fetor of hybrid pestilence. Here cosmic sin had entered, and festered by unhallowed rites had commenced the grinning march of death that was to rot us all to fungous abnormalities too hideous for the grave's holding. Satan here held his Babylonish court, and in the blood of stainless childhood the leprous limbs of phosphorescent Lilith were laved. Incubi and succubæ howled praise to Hecate, and headless mooncalves bleated to the Magna Mater. Goats leaped to the sound of thin accursed flutes, and Ægipans chased endlessly after misshapen fauns over rocks twisted like swollen toads. Moloch and Ashtaroth were not absent; for in this quintessence of all damnation the bounds of consciousness were let down, and man's fancy lay open to vistas of every realm of horror and every forbidden dimension that evil had power to mold. The world and nature were helpless against such assaults from unsealed wells of night, nor could any sign or prayer check the Walpurgis riot of horror which had come when a sage with the hateful key had stumbled on a horde with the locked and brimming coffer of transmitted demonlore.

Suddenly a ray of physical light shone through these phantasms, and Malone heard the sound of oars amidst the blasphemies of things that should be dead. A boat with a lantern in its prow darted into sight, made fast to an iron ring in the slimy stone pier, and vomited forth several dark men bearing a long burden swathed in bedding. They took it to the naked phosphorescent thing on the carved gold pedestal, and the thing tittered and pawed at the bedding. Then they unswathed it, and dropped upright before the pedestal the gangrenous corpse of a corpulent old man with stubbly beard and unkempt white hair. The phosphorescent thing tittered again, and the men produced bottles from their pockets and anointed its feet with red, whilst they afterward gave the bottles to the thing to drink from.

All at once, from an arcaded avenue leading endlessly away, there came the demoniac rattle and wheeze of a blasphemous organ, choking and rumbling out the mockeries of hell in a cracked, sardonic bass. In an instant every moving entity was electrified; and forming at once into a ceremonial procession, the nightmare horde slithered away in quest of the sound—goat, satyr, and ægipan, incubus, succuba, and lemur, twisted toad and shapeless elemental, dog-faced howler and silent strutter in darkness—all led by the abominable naked phosphorescent thing that had squatted on the carved golden throne, and that now strode insolently bearing in its arms the glassy-eyed corpse of the corpulent old man. The strange dark men danced in the rear, and the whole column skipped and leaped with Dionysiac fury. Malone staggered after them a few steps, delirious and hazy, and doubtful of his place in this or any world. Then he turned, faltered, and sank down on the cold damp stone, gasping and shivering as the demon organ croaked on, and the howling and drumming and tinkling of the mad procession grew fainter and fainter.

Vaguely he was conscious of chanted horrors and shocking croakings afar off. Now and then a wail or whine of ceremonial devotion would float to him through the black arcade, whilst eventually there rose the dreadful Greek incantation whose text he had read above the pulpit of that dance-hall church.

"O friend and companion of night, thou who rejoicest in the baying of dogs [*here a hideous howl burst forth*] and spilt blood, [*here nameless sounds vied with morbid shriekings*] who wanderest in the midst of shades among the tombs, [*here a whistling sigh occurred*] who longest for blood and bringest terror to mortals, [*short, sharp cries from myriad throats*] Gorgo, [*repeated as response*] Mormo, [*repeated with ecstasy*] thousand-faced moon, [*sighs and flute notes*] look favorably on our sacrifices!"

As the chant closed a general shout went up, and hissing sounds nearly drowned the croaking of the cracked bass organ. Then a gasp as from many throats, and a babel of barked and bleated words—"Lilith, Great Lilith, behold the Bridegroom!" More cries, a clamor of rioting, and the sharp, clicking footfalls of a running figure. The footfalls approached, and Malone raised himself to his elbow to look.

The luminosity of the crypt, lately diminished, had now slightly increased; and in that devil-light there appeared the fleeing form of that which should not flee or feel or breathe—the glassy-eyed, gangrenous corpse of the corpulent old man, now needing no support, but animated by some infernal sorcery of the rite just closed. After it raced the naked, tittering, phosphorescent thing that belonged on the carven pedestal, and still farther behind panted the dark men, and all the dread crew of sentient loathsomeness. The corpse was gaining on its pursuers, and seemed bent on a definite object, straining with every rotting muscle toward the carved pedestal, whose necromantic importance was evidently so great. Another moment and it had reached its goal, whilst the trailing throng labored on with more frantic speed. But they were too late, for in one final spurt of strength which ripped tendon from tendon and sent its noisome bulk floundering to the floor in a state of jellyfish dissolution, the staring corpse which had been Robert Suydam achieved its object and its triumph. The push had been tremendous, but the force had held out; and as the pusher collapsed to a muddy blotch of corruption the pedestal he had pushed tottered, tipped, and finally careened from its onyx base into the thick waters below, sending up a parting gleam of carven gold as it sank heavily to undreamable gulfs of lower Tartarus. In that instant, too, the whole scene of horror faded to nothingness before Malone's eyes; and he fainted amidst a thunderous crash which seemed to blot out all the evil universe.

VII

Malone's dream, experienced in full before he knew of Suydam's death and transfer at sea, was curiously supplemented by some odd realities of the case; though that is no reason why any one should believe it. The three old houses in Parker Place, doubtless long rotten with decay in its most insidious form, collapsed without visible cause while half the raiders and most of the prisoners were inside; and of both the greater number were instantly killed. Only in the basements and cellars was there much saving of life, and Malone was lucky to have been deep below the house of Robert Suydam. For he really was there, as no one is disposed to deny. They found him unconscious by the edge of the night-black pool, with a grotesquely horrible jumble of decay and bone, identifiable through dental work as the body of Suydam, a few feet away. The case was plain, for it was hither that the smugglers' underground canal led; and the men who took Suydam from the ship had brought him home. They themselves were never found, or at least never identified; and the ship's doctor is not yet satisfied with the simple certitudes of the police.

Suydam was evidently a leader in extensive man-smuggling operations, for the canal to his house was but one of several subterranean channels and tunnels in the neighborhood. There was a tunnel from this house to a crypt beneath the dance-hall church; a crypt accessible from the church only through a narrow secret passage in the north wall, and in whose chambers some singular and terrible things were discovered. The croaking organ was there, as well as a vast arched chapel with wooden benches and a strangely figured altar. The walls were lined with small cells, in seventeen of which—hideous to relate—solitary prisoners in a state of complete idiocy were found chained, including four mothers with infants of disturbingly strange appearance. These infants died soon after exposure to the light; a circumstance which the doctors thought rather merciful. Nobody but Malone, among those who inspected them, remembered the somber question of old Delrio: *"An sint unquam daemones incubi et succubae, et an ex tali, congressu proles nasci queat?"*

Before the canals were filled up they were thoroughly dredged, and yielded forth a sensational array of sawed and split bones of all sizes. The kidnaping epidemic, very clearly, had been traced home; though only two of the surviving prisoners could by any legal thread be connected with it. These men are now in prison, since they failed of conviction as accessories in the actual murders. The carved golden pedestal or throne so often mentioned by Malone as of primary occult importance was never brought to light, though at one place under the Suydam house the canal was observed to sink into a well too deep for dredging. It was choked up at the mouth and cemented over when the cellars of the new houses were made, but Malone often speculates on what lies beneath. The police, satisfied that they had shattered a dangerous gang of maniacs and man-smugglers, turned over to the Federal authorities the unconvicted Kurds, who before their deportation were conclusively found to belong to the Yezidee clan of devil-worshipers. The tramp ship and its crew remain an elusive mystery, though cynical detectives are once more ready to combat its smuggling and rum-running ventures. Malone thinks these detectives show a sadly limited perspective in their lack of wonder at the myriad unexplainable details, and the suggestive obscurity of the whole case; though he is just as critical of the newspapers, which saw only a morbid sensation and gloated over a minor sadist cult when they might have proclaimed a horror from the universe's very heart. But he is content to rest silent in Chepachet, calming his nervous system and praying that time may gradually transfer his terrible experience from the realm of present reality to that of picturesque and semi-mythical remoteness.

Robert Suydam sleeps beside his bride in Greenwood Cemetery. No funeral was held over the strangely released bones, and relatives are grateful for the swift oblivion which overtook the case as a whole. The scholar's connection with the Red Hook horrors, indeed, was never emblazoned by legal proof; since his death forestalled the inquiry he would otherwise have faced. His own end is not much mentioned, and the Suydams hope that posterity may recall him only as a gentle recluse who dabbled in harmless magic and folk-lore.

As for Red Hook—it is always the same. Suydam came and went; a terror gathered and faded; but the evil spirit of darkness and squalor broods on amongst the mongrels in the old brick houses, and prowling bands still parade on unknown errands past windows where lights and twisted faces unaccountably appear and disappear. Age-old horror is a hydra with a thousand heads, and the cults of darkness are rooted in blasphemies deeper than the well of Democritus. The soul of the beast is omnipresent and triumphant, and Red Hook's legions of blear-eyed, pock-marked youths still chant and curse and howl as they file from abyss to abyss, none knows whence or whither, pushed on by blind laws of biology which they may never understand. As of old more people enter Red Hook than leave it on the landward side, and there are already rumors of new canals running underground to certain centers of traffic in liquor and less mentionable things.

The dance-hall church is now mostly a dance-hall and queer faces have appeared at night at the windows. Lately a policeman expressed the belief that the filled-up crypt has been dug out again, and for no simple, explainable purpose. Who are we to combat poisons older than history and mankind? Apes danced in Asia to those horrors, and the cancer lurks secure and spreading where furtiveness hides in rows of decaying brick.

Malone does not shudder without cause—for only the other day an officer overheard a swarthy squinting hag teaching a small child some whispering patois in the shadow of an areaway. He listened, and thought it very strange when he heard her repeat over and over again:

"O friend and companion of night, thou who rejoicest in the baying of dogs and spilt blood, who wanderest in the midst of shades among the tombs, who longest for blood and bringest terror to mortals, Gorgo, Mormo, thousand-faced moon, look favorably on our sacrifices!"

A HAND FROM THE DEEP

By ROMEO POOLE

SOMEWHERE NEAR MIDNIGHT MY ROOM TELEPHONE RANG, and according to well-formed habit I rolled out of bed and answered almost before I was fully awake.

"Ambulance trip for you, Marsh—Whitby Home."

That brought me wide awake, and hustling into trousers, shoes, shirt and white uniform coat I descended to the main office. Dr. Lang, the superintendent, met me at the foot of the stairs with a heavy overcoat.

"Here," he said, "put this on—it's a pretty chilly night. Here's your bandage kit; you may need it. Ambulance in the back drive. Explosion and fire out at the Whitby Home. Send back for help if necessary. Now use some speed."

I used some speed, and when I got into the ambulance the driver used some more. We tore up the street at a hazardous rate, the chauffeur giving himself over to the task of driving, while I turned the crank that ran the shrieking signal horn.

The so-called Whitby Home was an obscure little institution occupying a shabby ten-room brick building in a low-class residential district in the outskirts of the city. The place bore a rather evil reputation, and it was hinted that its owner and operator, Dr. Whitby, was guilty of various illegal practices in connection with his hospital work. However, no complaint of any importance had ever been lodged against him, and consequently no investigation of his activities had ever taken place and the general opinion of his character remained unconfirmed.

For aught I knew, the rumors about Whitby might have

been born of the natural resentment of all medical men toward a practitioner who declines to be governed by their standards and becomes, therefore, a "quack." For Whitby had belonged to no medical society; he was careless about collecting anything for his work; and he practiced any kind of medical theory, old or new, that happened to appeal to him, totally disregarding the ethics of the profession. He had no general practice, and the inmates of his would-be sanitarium were usually people of little learning and nearly always the victims of disabling accidents. I must mention, however, that my gratification at the thought of investigating the Whitby Home and some of its curious inmates entirely overcame my resentment at losing most of a night's sleep.

In a matter of seconds we drew up as near the place as we could get, the Fire Department having the narrow street blocked. The building was almost completely gutted by the fire when we arrived, and, grabbing my first-aid kit, I ran up to the captain who was directing the fire-fighting to inquire about the victims.

"Only one alive," he panted. "Rest all killed in the explosion. Come over here."

The survivor, whose room had been on the ground floor, had not been injured by the accident, although he had been stunned temporarily by the shock of the explosion. The firemen had wrapped him in a blanket salvaged from the burning house and laid him in a sheltered place to await the ambulance. Passing the mangled bodies of the dead, we found him sitting up, looking a little dazed at the excitement, but feeling cheerful and apparently comfortable. He was a common-looking little man of probably thirty years, a laborer of not very extensive intellect, but alert and sensible in answering our questions. He had been staying at the place on account of the amputation of his left arm a little above the elbow. I sat by his side on the return to the hospital, and questioned him regarding the cause of the fire.

"Gas, or gasoline explosion, I guess," he responded readily. "Fox, the fellow that did the odd work around the house, was in my room along about 10 o'clock, and sat there and talked to me awhile. Finally he said he smelt something like gasoline or escaping gas, that seemed to come down the stairs, and he went up to see to it. After a while I heard him open the door at the top of the stairway, and that's about all I knew till I come to, out there in the yard. Something must've blown the whole top of the house to pieces. I was lucky, for I was the only one that slept downstairs. Are any of the rest of 'em—alive?"

No, not a soul, I told him. The patient's face betrayed genuine regret at this.

"Too bad. Doc Whitby was a good fellow. I got this arm cut off in a smash-up over at the barrelstave mill, and Doc Whitby just happened along before I even got it wrapped up, and he took me in and took care of it ever since, and never asked for a dollar. I had a coupla weeks' wages with me, and I turned that over to him, but he didn't seem very anxious to get it. Wanted me to wait and see what a nice job he'd do on that arm—some new scheme he had."

Arriving at the hospital I installed my patient in a ward bed, made out his record card in the name he gave me, Simon Glaze, and then proceeded to look after the dressing of his arm, which I found soaking wet. I removed this and applied iodoform gauze, dry, covering it with a linen bandage.

"Aren't you going to soak it up?" he asked.

"Soak it? No. That's no way to take care of a stump."

"Doc Whitby kept it wet all the time."

"It's a new one to me," I told him. "We always keep wounds like that clean and dry. You'll be all right with this dressing."

"Well, maybe," he said doubtfully as I left him.

The next morning I went in for a look at my patient, who appeared to have spent a rather bad night.

"Doc," he began eagerly, "couldn't you stretch a point and

wet this bandage for me? I haven't slept a wink all night with that dry rag on it."

I wondered what kind of faith cure Whitby had been practicing on Glaze, and I maintained my position that the wet bandage was not the proper treatment. Glaze stared at me with red, sleepless eyes, misery showing in every line of his face.

"Doc," he finally said, "I want to talk to the regular top boss of this concern, and I want him pretty soon."

We had considerable argument over this, but ultimately I went and brought up Dr. Lang in compliance with Glaze's request. Glaze had been lying face down on his bed during my absence, and when Dr. Lang and I returned we opened the felted door with its silent latch, without a particle of noise and had stepped into the room before Glaze was aware of our approach. Dr. Lang started to speak and his heavy voice broke on the stillness of the room with quite a jar. The effect on the patient was most startling. He gathered his legs and his good arm under him like a flash and sprang backward, clear on to the next bed, which, fortunately for its occupant, was empty at the time, the patient being in the dressing room.

Lang gasped.

"Aha, a mental case, as I might have suspected."

He crossed quickly to where the patient lay, still crouched in the same posture, speechless, doubled up. The doctor laid a hand on him, spoke to him, turned him over on his back, all without evoking a word from Glaze, who lay with eyes half-closed like a man playing dead.

"Well, let's have a look at the arm, anyhow," said Lang, and he proceeded to uncover the unresisting man's stump.

"Bad-looking job," he commented. "No infection, but just doesn't look right. I suppose Whitby was trying some wildcat scheme on him, and so long as he has no infection maybe we'd better continue it for a while just to keep him calmed down. Then we'll gradually break in on some reliable modern treatment. Didn't you say he was perfectly rational last night?"

"He certainly was."

"Next time he has a lucid interval, just call me, will you, Marsh? No matter what I'm doing. This is an interesting case, and I'd like to know what the late Whitby has been doing to him."

Some time later in the day Glaze recovered his poise, and Dr. Lang talked to him at length, questioning him about the treatment administered by Dr. Whitby but the answers only increased our curiosity. Glaze admitted that he had been under chloroform a number of times since Whitby had first cared for his arm stump, which seemed rather unusual to us. Questioned as to the purpose of this, he said he didn't believe the arm had ever been touched when he was under the anæsthetic as it was never sore afterwards. There was an injury in the roof of his mouth that bled a good deal, he said, and there were little sore spots on his back that were quite painful for a day or two.

"And then," he finished, "there was a good deal of time I can't remember at all. Guess I been kinda feverish or something, for there's long stretches of time go by that I can't remember anything. This morning was one of them.

"And say, Doctor, I wonder if you could fix it so I can have a bath pretty often—say every day, or twice a day. I don't want much hot water—just plain cold is good enough for me. Doc Whitby always let me bathe two or three times a day, and I just can't seem to get enough of it."

Dr. Lang was interested enough to assent to this, although he hardly expected to collect a cent from the patient. He was retaining Glaze for the satisfaction of his private curiosity.

"That's the weirdest case I ever saw or heard of," said Dr. Lang to me later. "Call it intermittent insanity if you want to, but he hasn't a trace of fever, nor a sign of locomotor ataxia, both of which lunatics practically always have. In fact, when he is in those silent fits his temperature is actually *below normal.* And how he takes to water! Whatever is wrong with him, it isn't hydrophobia."

I prepared Glaze's bath for him several times, and he demanded water that was practically unheated, although the time was early winter and the temperature outside well below freezing.

Glaze was removed to a room by himself, with a bath attached, where his eccentricities would bother no one else, and during the next two weeks he showed very little change in symptoms. I was careful not to startle him unduly, but even under the most careful treatment he still showed that curious inclination to double up into a ball and go backward —always backward—away from any one who approached him. His talkative intervals grew shorter, and if allowed he would spend hours in his tub of cold water, hardly moving a muscle.

Making an examination of the arm-stump one morning I noted for the first time three or four little warty growths in the suture where the skin had been drawn together over the stump. As the patient was feeling apparently normal at the time, I held a hand mirror up to the stump so that he could see the warts, too, and told him they would probably have to be cut off. He looked intently at the reflection of the end of the stump for a few seconds and then turned to to me with a startled expression in his face and voice.

"Don't cut them off," he pleaded, and on the instant he doubled up again into a ball, rolling on the floor of the dressing room like a wooden thing.

When I told Dr. Lang of the incident his curiosity at Glaze's behavior put a severe strain on the good doctor's self-control.

"If that man Whitby were alive to-day," he remarked with studied restraint, "I'd be inclined to put him on the operating table and persuade the truth out of him with a red-hot iron. It's some devilish work of his that makes a man act like a dried armadillo every time any one looks at him.

And that subnormal temperature! Where does he get it?"

Two days later we took the somewhat unwilling Glaze into the operating room to care for his unhealthy stump. Dr. Lang, of course, superintended the work, and the actual cutting had been turned over to my fellow-interne, a young Irishman named Lancey with a flaming red head and a likable manner, whom every one considered to be destined for a brilliant future. As I gradually whiffed the ether into the patient's nostrils Lancey was busy unwrapping the stump. When the cut-off member was exposed, Lancey's eyes rested for only a second on the bits of flesh he was expected to remove; then his whole face changed as if he had been struck with a club.

"Holy cats!" he gasped, his lips turning gray-white. "Cut out the ether, Marsh. I don't want to operate on *that.*"

I stopped and turned toward Dr. Lang, who was a little nonplused at Lancey's sudden refusal to carry out his commission.

"Pardon my abruptness, Doctor," apologized Lancey to his superior, "but I'd like to have six or seven days' time before going ahead with this cutting."

"*You'd* like it?"

"Yes, Doctor. If you'll give me a week before you disturb this man's arm I think I can tell you something about the honorable Dr. Whitby's work that'll make your eyes open. But I've just got to have that much time."

"One week," ruminated the superintendent, slowly, "won't kill nor cure him, in his present condition. I presume we can wait that long. But aren't you forgetting that I am in charge here, and that this man is being kept here solely on my responsibility? Do you have to be so extremely reticent with your theories? I feel that I'm entitled to know something about what you think you've discovered."

"I know what Whitby has done," said Lancey simply. "And in a week I can tell you what he did it with. Can I have that much time?"

"Yes, take your week," exploded the doctor, with some irritation. "But I'm holding you strictly responsible for the condition of this patient."

"That's all right—that's what I want."

"And I still think you might give me an idea of what you're talking about."

"Take a look at that, then," pointing to the bared stump.

Dr. Lang scrutinized the growths. As he had not recently been reading on the subject that had given Lancey his sudden inspiration, it is possible that he did not see anything definite on Glaze's arm; also it is possible that in his dignified conservatism he doubted even his own eyesight. But as he retreated, dissatisfied and silent, I bent close and looked. What I saw took my breath away and made me wonder if I were really awake. Lancey hurried away, and I trundled the unconscious Glaze back to his bed.

During the next two days Glaze lost nearly all that was left of his normal human instincts and speech. He moved and obeyed mechanically when spoken to, but seemed to understand motion better than speech, so that it was often necessary for me to point to a thing in order to make him comprehend what I wanted. His mania for the cold bath increased, and if I went into his room quietly in the early morning I frequently found him doubled into the familiar ball, sleeping with his eyes half open.

Observing Glaze's eyes so much brought out another revelation. Upon first seeing the man I had noticed his bright, intelligent-looking eyes, which were rather prominent; but now since his recent prolonged lapses into semi-consciousness, I noticed that his eyes were sunk deeper into his head and seemed to be losing their luster. Now, this condition might be induced by anæmia or something of the sort, but Glaze was in the pink of physical condition and not in the least emaciated, and I was at a loss to explain the change in his eyes. He had certainly grown less talkative at the same time, and vaguely I wondered if something were influencing a part of his brain, causing it to shrink, and thus by natural consequence causing his eyes to sink farther back in the bony structure. As I sat observing him it suddenly struck me that the crown of his head seemed to be less prominent than when I first saw him, and after a careful survey I was positive that the man's head was losing its prominent crown and sinking into a more brutish line.

Of course, any physician knows that man's skull can change shape in the course of time, if something happens to develop a new portion of his brain, just as the bones in a coal-heaver's shoulders bend under his heavy loads; but a change like that in one's skull would hardly be perceptible in less than two or three years, and the apparent alteration in the shape of Glaze's skull in the three weeks we had known him seemed like a preposterous dream of some kind. Not wishing further to upset my good superior, Dr. Lang, I kept still about this weird discovery until Lancey returned to the hospital that evening, he having been out by special permission all day. Late that night I brought Lancey up and told him about the patient's eyes and asked him what he could see in the shape of his head. While Glaze lay in his habitual stupor, Lancey felt his head and turned it right and left. Then he placed his hands behind him and said:

"It all fits together—perfectly. But, my God, where will it end?"

I could only stare at my friend.

"I've got it, Marsh, I've got the whole story—up to date. And I don't know but that it would be a kind deed to chloroform this poor wretch and let him out of it. I never dreamed it would work so fast. To-morrow, Marsh, I'll tell all of you what I have found out."

And Lancey went back to the laboratory.

I now studied Glaze's habits more closely than ever, for I did want to get some idea about the mysterious case, before Lancey had to tell me every detail as if I were a child. Glaze was not inactive all the time. He varied between his rolled-up playing-dead attitude and sudden snappy, erratic movements. He was beginning to snap at his food and devour it hastily, almost without chewing, and this habit caused him some little stomachic disturbance, as of course it would with anybody. In his frequent visits to the bath-tub he would dive for long periods beneath the surface of the water and come up half strangled, yet seeming to enjoy it all. And if anything surprised or startled him it was always backward that he retreated from it—backward and suddenly.

Finding time to visit Glaze along in the afternoon, I dropped into his room and found him sitting up in his chair, apparently his old, cheerful self. I spoke to him gently and without startling him, and he smiled and looked as if he would like to reply, but simply could not. Hoping to draw him out into one more conversation, I sat down beside him and continued talking to him about little things around the house with which he was familiar. Finally, unsuccessful in getting Glaze to talk, I playfully shook hands with him, preparing to leave. The hand that gripped mine nearly broke three of my fingers, and the smile left Glaze's face as he shut down on me with a grip of inhuman strength. Tugging at his hand with my own left, in an effort to free my sadly pinched right member, I saw that his thumb reached clear across my own very large palm and had almost an inch to spare. How could I have escaped noticing that huge thumb before? Then I saw the nail. It bore a sharp ridge, like the gable roof of a house, down its center, and it occupied the entire end joint of that monstrous thumb. This certainly had not been the case when I had held Glaze's right hand a few days previously while administering chloroform to him. When I finally extricated my right hand Glaze kept opening and shutting that huge pincer with a motion that reminded me of the jaws of a hungry alligator.

What was this superhuman influence that caused a man's firmest tissues to alter their shape completely within a few hours? And what was it that that ghastly, gripping claw resembled?

I left the room with cold chills running up my spine.

The next morning Lancey arranged to explain to Dr. Lang, two or three other doctors who had become interested, and myself, regarding his findings about the mysterious patient, for which purpose they gathered in Dr. Lang's back office at 10.30 o'clock.

You may be assured that it was a highly interested little group that gathered in that room considerably before 10.30, Dr. Lang himself being almost rabidly impatient.

"Well, shoot, Lancey," he said, before the door had closed behind the last man. And Lancey shot.

"There's just one man in the room, I think, who saw and understood what was growing on the end of our patient's arm a week ago to-day. At that time it was four perfectly good little fingers and a model thumb!"

This statement was greeted with voiceless gasps.

"It's something different now—in fact, I hardly know what to call it in its present form, but we'll go up and look at it presently. Anyhow it is now perfectly plain that what Whitby tried to do, and partially succeeded in doing, was to modify the regenerative process in his patient so that a new forearm would grow in place of the lost one.

"The theory is nothing very new. As early as 1906 it was observed that when a limb is amputated at the middle of a bone, the bone starts to grow out again, but increases only about one-fiftieth of an inch in length before it is halted by some other influence. You know also, of course, about the little warts of so-called 'proud flesh' that apparently try to replace the original muscular tissue in case of injuries, but which are misshapen or misplaced. What Whitby was trying to get at, as I see it, was to so control these misdirected efforts of nature as to produce a new and perfect limb.

"The human body is already able to repair damaged bones by rebuilding small particles of the bony tissue; it is also able to replace muscle, nerve and even finger-nail tissue, although in somewhat imperfect forms. Whitby was trying to induce it to build a lost member in perfect form.

"Seeking this result, his studies naturally took him to observing the water animals that have this power of regeneration. A crab, for instance, when it gets a limb broken, promptly bites off the rest of the limb, and a new one grows in its place. The same is true of the lobster family, down to the tiny crawdad, no larger than a cricket. Specimens of these little creatures are frequently found with one limb far smaller than the others as a result of such occurrences.

"It seems that Whitby has been experimenting for years with the ductless and other glands of shellfish in pursuance of this theory of regeneration, and we have upstairs the living proof that he was able to prepare a glandular extract that changes the bodily cell-structure as well as influencing the building-up processes of nature; but it appears that he never succeeded in isolating the one influence from the other, both being present in his preparation.

"I have found that Whitby bought the little crawdads, which are really dwarf lobsters, from children around the neighborhood, and that his purchases ran into tens of thousands of these little creatures, and I also find that he bought live lobsters in a quantity that his dining table would never have warranted.

"In short, this patient, Simon Glaze, has had his body so saturated with the glandular extracts from lobsters that he has actually developed regenerative powers, and the bits of proud flesh on his arm stump which you saw only a week ago became quite well-developed fingers. At that time, of course, they were getting natural human material for their reconstruction. All that has changed now, and as a result of the other influence of his medication he is now coming more and more every day to resemble a gigantic shellfish, in both body and mind—if a shellfish can be credited with a mind.

"You remember what he told about a wound in the top of his mouth? That was the easiest access to the region of his pituitary gland, a seat of powerful influence over any structural change in a man's body. Other injections were administered along his spinal column, and I firmly believe that Whitby was successful in providing the man with something that he has used since Whitby's death in promoting the change, not understanding the real results."

I objected a moment to state that Glaze had positively had possession of nothing he had brought from the Whitby home.

"I've got it!" he ejaculated, his steel-blue eyes snapping. "This infernal lunatic Whitby was afraid somebody would take his patient away from him before he got through his nice little experiments. So he just lodged bodies of oil soluble extracts along his spinal column where they would continue to be picked up in the lymph. In this way he has gone on poisoning and wrecking this poor wretch of a laborer after he himself is dead and in—wherever such people belong! We'll go up now and have an X-ray made and see if anything can be done."

The unfinished lecture broke up and Lancey, Lang and I went up to Glaze's room immediately. As we waited for the elevator Lancey finished explaining to Dr. Lang.

"That nice little set of fingers has now turned to an almost perfect lobster claw, only two fingers of the original five having developed, both with scissorlike claws. His good right hand is to-day nearer a lobster claw than anything else. His speech is gone. His temperature is 93 degrees instead of a normal of 98. His backward leaps when startled are the behavior of a crawfish. And the occipital bones of his head are shrinking day by day. Above all, note his fondness for water, especially on his stump. A crab could not grow a new limb except in a wet place."

We hurried into Glaze's room and on into the bathroom beyond, where he spent so much time. In the tubful of cold water we found Glaze's nude body, doubled and curled up, face far under the water—dead.

"Poor devil," said Lancey, as we extracted the body and laid it upon the bed. "His lobster brain taught him that the only safe place for him was under water, but he lacked the lobster's breathing apparatus. Well, it's better this way, after all."

THE TORTOISE-SHELL CAT

By GREYE LA SPINA

Extract from a letter from Althea Benedict, Pine Valley Academy for Young Ladies, to Mrs. Wordsworth Benedict, New York City:

IN SPITE OF YOUR CARE TO RESERVE A ROOM FOR ME, MISS Annette Lee called me into her office yesterday and begged me to share it with a new girl.

It seems that Vida is the only child of a very old friend of hers, Felix di Monserreau, a rich Louisiana planter. Miss Lee says she thinks I may have a good influence over my new room-mate, but she managed to evade my tactful inquiry as to what Vida's vices might be. She did seem awfully disturbed. She said that she appreciated my nice attitude; and if I found the companionship disturbed me, would I report it to her immediately? She was so agitated she just couldn't look me in the face. I can't imagine what can be the matter with Vida.

So far, my new room-mate appears to be rather nice. Her father has been most generous and our room is the envy of all the other girls. I would have written you earlier, mother, but we've been getting our new things settled.

Vida wants everything to go with her particular style of beauty! She confessed that she was perfectly miserable if she didn't have a background that suited her, and that she knew I wouldn't mind—particularly as she was willing to pay for the decorations. So she has the room decorated in the most stunning fashion, in shades of orange and dull green, with heaps and heaps of down-cushions. She says she loves to lie around on a pile of cushions, like a cat.

I wish you could see her. She's really a type of girl to attract attention anywhere with her dead-white skin, her dark red lips, her black hair and her eyes—. Her eyes are quite the queerest I've ever seen. They are narrow, long, slumbrous, with drooping lids through which she looks at one in her peculiar way. The iris is a kind of pale golden-brown that gives the impression of warm yellow. When dusk comes, I've seen the pupil glowing with some strange iridescence, the iris a narrow yellow rim about it; for all the world, it makes me think of a cat's eye.

Don't forget to tell Cousin Edgar to send me the necklace he promised to bring me from Egypt. I've told the girls about it, and they're dying to see it.

YOUR ALTHEA.

The same to the same:

. . . Studies are going forward nicely. Nothing new, except a couple of rather queer things about my room-mate. I thought I'd better write you first, before saying anything to Miss Lee about it. Perhaps I'm only imagining things,

Vida is certainly a very odd girl, mother. I am beginning to believe that she can see in the dark, with those strange eyes of hers. What makes me think so—you know how I love to change furniture around every little while? The other day I altered the position of everything in the room. Vida wasn't there, and before she came back the "lights-out" bell rang. I meant to stay awake and tell her not to fall over the table that was in front of her bed, but when she did come I was so drowsy that I didn't get a chance to speak to her before she had reached her bed.

And, mother, she threaded her way among those things just as if she could see them perfectly; not a single moment of hesitation. It gave me the most eery feeling. I hid my head under the quilt, for I felt as if she were watching me in the dark. I know you'll laugh when you read this, but I didn't feel like laughing. And I still have an unpleasant feeling about it, for how could Vida walk so rapidly among those things, not one of which was in the same position she had seen them in last, unless she could actually see in the dark?

Last night another odd thing happened. There must have been crumbs in our waste-basket, for we heard a mouse rattling around in it. Just before I could switch on the light I heard Vida bound across the room from her bed. When the light was on, she stood by the waste-basket with that mouse in her hands, and, I can tell you, it was a dead mouse! She looked so strange that I squeaked at her, "Vida!" She jumped, dropped the dead thing and scuttled back to bed. She seemed quite cross because I had put on the light, and I think she cried afterward in the dark, although I can't be sure of it.

Mother, does it seem uncanny to you? I wonder if this night-sight is what Miss Annette referred to? I hate to say anything, for after all, what's the harm in it?

. . . When is Cousin Edgar going to send that necklace?

The same to the same:

. . . Something happened that I cannot help connecting with Vida. Yet I don't like to go to Miss Annette with it. I'm sure she will smile and tell me that I have an exceptionally lively imagination.

Vida and Natalie Cunningham had a dispute the other day about something or other, and Natalie looked it up and when she found Vida was right, she was sarcastic about it —Natalie, I mean. Vida just looked at her with those strange golden eyes glowing, bit her lip, and remained silent.

When we were alone afterward, Vida said to me, "Do you know, Althea, I'm afraid something unpleasant is going to happen to Natalie?"

I must have looked surprised, for she went on hastily:

"There's some kind of invisible guardian watching over me, Althea, that seems to know whenever any one is unkind to me. For years I've observed that punishment is visited on every one who crosses me or troubles me in any way. It has made me almost afraid of having a dispute with any one, for if I permit myself—my real inner-self—to grow disturbed, something always happens to the person at the root of the trouble."

Of course, I hooted at her forebodings. I told her she was superstitious and silly. But, mother, that night Natalie Cunningham lost her favorite ring, a stunning emerald. It was stolen right off her dressing-table five minutes after Natalie turned off her light. She got up again to unlock the door for her room-mate, put on the light, and—the ring wasn't where she'd left it.

The door was still locked; the window was open, but it was a third-story window, as most of the dormitory windows in our building are, and there is no balcony under it.

Mysterious, wasn't it? Our floor monitor, Miss Poore, declared that Natalie must have dropped her ring on the floor, but Natalie has hunted and hunted. The ring certainly isn't in her room. Who took it? How? It frightened Natalie so that she is afraid to be alone in her room without a light.

The odd thing about it is the way that Vida looked at me when the girls told us about it. She actually wants me to believe that her "invisible guardian" stole the ring to punish Natalie for having been sarcastic to her. Did you ever?

I wonder if poor Vida is—well, just a bit flighty, mother? How about that necklace?

The same to the same:

. . . I'm so excited that I can't write coherently. All the school is in an uproar over what took place last night. I am more disturbed than the rest, for I am beginning to have a suspicion that Vida is right when she says that unpleasant things happen to people who cross her. It makes me nervous, for fear she may get provoked at me for something. I don't know whether or not I ought to report the whole thing to Miss Annette; I'm afraid she'll think I'm romancing. Won't you please write me and tell me what to do?

Yesterday morning Vida's old colored mammy, Jinny, who is in Pine Valley in order to be near her charge, came up for Vida's laundry. Miss Poore came in while Vida was putting her soiled things together, and offered to help sort them over.

Mammy Jinny gave a kind of convulsive shiver. She looked up at Vida, staring hard at her for a moment. Vida stared back in a queer, fixed way. Then my room-mate's eyes flashed yellow fire. She told Miss Poore in a kind of fury that she'd better mind her own business and not stick her old-maid nose into other people's private concerns.

Miss Poore was wild. (You can't blame her. It was really nasty of Vida.) She took Vida by the shoulders and shook her hard. Vida didn't resist, but she looked at the floor monitor with such an expression of malice that Miss Poore actually stepped back in dismay.

"I'm sorry for you, Miss Poore," said Vida to her. "I'm afraid you are going to suffer severely for laying your hands on me. I'd save you if I could—but I can't."

Miss Poore went out of the room without answering. Vida gave the laundry to Mammy Jinny, who insisted upon taking laundry-bag and all. After the old colored woman had gone, Vida flung herself on her bed and cried for an hour. She said she was crying because she was sorry for Miss Poore. I failed at the time to see any significance in her remark, until after last night—.

About two o'clock this morning, the whole floor was awakened by the most terrible screams coming from Miss Poore's room. I sprang out of bed and rushed into the hall where I met the other girls, all pouring out of their rooms. We rushed to Miss Poore's room and she finally got the door open to let us in.

Mother, she was a sight! Face, hands, arms, were all covered with blood from bites and scratches. She was hysterical, and no wonder. She declared that some kind of wild animal had jumped in at her window and attacked her in the dark. The queer thing is, how did that creature—if there was one—get into her room and then out again before we opened the hall door? Her window was open, but it is a third-story one and there is no tree near by from which an animal could have sprung into her room.

She is in such a condition this morning that Miss Annette told us in chapel she would have to leave the school to recover from the nervous shock incident to the attack. The mystery of it is the only topic of conversation to-day, as you can imagine. And now for the odd part of it.

When I got back to my room, there lay Vida, apparently sound asleep. She hadn't been disturbed by all that racket. Some sleeper! I woke her and told her.

Mother, she lay awake the rest of the night, crying and carrying on terribly, declaring it all her fault, although she couldn't help it. Her statement was rather confusing. She insisted it was her "invisible guardian" who had attacked Miss Poore, but she begged me not to tell any one. Her advice was superfluous; if I went to Miss Annette with such a statement, she'd think either Vida was crazy or I was simple.

I tried to sleep, but I can tell you I left the light on. And I wasn't the only one; all the girls had lights in their rooms the rest of the night.

The coincidences are strange, aren't they, mother? Natalie displeases Vida and has her emerald ring mysteriously stolen. Miss Poore displeases Vida and gets scratched and bitten. But even a coincidence can't explain why a wild-cat should bite Miss Poore on Vida's behalf, can it?

Do please write me soon and tell me what I ought to do about informing Miss Annette.

The same to the same:

I took your advice and told Miss Annette. She said she must trust my discretion not to let the other girls know anything she told me, and then admitted that Vida has been followed by this reputation in every school she's been in, until her father couldn't enter her in some schools. Something unpleasant always happens to any person who displeases Vida di Monserreau. And although she disclaims having done anything, yet she declares it is done for her.

Miss Annette asked me if I wanted to have my room to myself. I thought that Vida really hadn't done anything to me, and she had certainly made our room the nicest in school. I decided to let her stay on, and Miss Annette thanked me so heartily that I was actually embarrassed.

. . . Why didn't you tell me Cousin Edgar was coming down? I couldn't imagine who it was when I was called to the reception room to see a gentleman. Imagine my surprise!

He gave me the chain, mother, and it's perfectly precious! Have you seen it? It's tiny carved cats with their tails in their mouths, and the pendant is a great jade cat with topaz eyes. The girls are wild over it, and Vida particularly is simply crazy about it. She asked me if Cousin Edgar couldn't get her one like it.

Cousin Edgar said a rather funny thing. He clasped the chain about my neck and declared that I must promise not to take it off without his permission. Now, why do you suppose he did that? When I asked him, he just shrugged his shoulders and said something about your having shown him my letters. What have my letters to do with my promising not to take off the cat-chain?

Yesterday he came over to take me driving. When he came into the reception room, he thrust out his chin in that odd way of his and said abruptly: "There's a cat in the room. Thought Miss Annette didn't allow pet animals."

I knew there couldn't be one, but he insisted and began to look about the room. And then—the oddest thing, mother! We came upon Vida di Monserreau, asleep in a big armchair by the fireplace. She had crouched on her knees, with her hands out on the arm of the chair and her chin on her outstretched hands, for all the world like a comfortable pussy-cat.

I said to Cousin Edgar: "Here's your cat," and laughed.

He looked at Vida closely. Then he said softly to me, "Althea, you are speaking more to the point than is your wont." (You know how he loves to tease me, mother.) "Introduce me to the pussy," said he.

I woke Vida. She was terribly embarrassed to have been seen in such an unconventional pose, but she told me afterward that she liked Cousin Edgar more than any other man she'd ever met. I think he liked her, too, although, of course, he didn't say much to me about it.

Vida asked him, almost at once, if he hadn't got another cat-chain like mine. She'd taken a tremendous fancy to it, she said.

"Perhaps you can prevail upon Althea to give you hers. If you can, I'll get her something else to take its place."

At this suggestion of his, Vida turned imploring eyes upon me. Mother, I was disturbed. I thought of what had happened to Natalie and to Miss Poore, and I wondered if something horrible would happen to me if I refused to give Vida my chain. So I just put it to her point-blank.

"What will happen to me if I don't give my chain to you, Vida?"

"Nothing to you, Althea, darling. I could never be really angry at you," she whispered.

"Then please don't ask me to give up my chain," I begged.

I looked back as I went from the room with Cousin Edgar,

and her eyes were on me in the most wistful way. Poor Vida!

. . . I wonder what the attraction is? Cousin Edgar is remaining here for an indefinite visit, he says. I do hope he hasn't fallen in love with Alma Henning: I simply cannot bear that girl. I suppose he won't ask my advice, though, if he has fallen in love with one of the girls. Belle Bragg is wild over him, and Natalie thinks him scrumptious.

He has old Peter with him and is stopping at the little hotel in Pine Valley.

The same to the same:

. . . I suppose I ought to tell you some things I've hardly dared write before because they are so—well, so extraordinary. I've been afraid you might think something the matter with my brain, because I'd been studying too hard. Cousin Edgar says it is in good condition and my head straight on my shoulders, and to write you the whole thing, exactly what I thought about it.

Mother, there *is* something uncanny about Vida di Monserreau. I told you how cat-like she was at times, and how she loves sitting in the dark, or prowling about the room in the dark.

The other day I came into the room ten minutes before lights-out. The room was empty when I turned on the light. But as I went to my desk, a great tortoise-shell cat was stretching itself lazily in the armchair where Vida loves to sit, near the window.

Like a flash Miss Poore's experience passed through my mind and I started for the door. As I got to the hall, I turned around, and—mother, believe me or not—there wasn't a sign of a cat. But sitting in the armchair, staring at me with those queer yellow eyes of hers, was Vida di Monserreau. I sat down on a chair near the door and breathed hard for a moment. Then I said, "My gracious, Vida, how you startled me! I didn't see you when I came in. What happened to the cat?"

"Cat?" says she, yawning. "What cat?" She stretched her arms lazily and settled herself comfortably on the cushions.

I can tell you I felt queer. My eyes had played me a very strange trick, making me see a striped black-and-yellow cat where Vida was sitting. I felt it best to say no more to her for fear she might think me out of my mind. But the more I think about it, the more I am convinced that there was a cat.

And if I did see a cat, stretching and yawning in the armchair, where, if you please, was Vida when I was looking at the cat? And where did the animal get to? (I looked everywhere before I'd go to bed, although I didn't tell Vida what for. I pretended I'd mislaid my gym slippers that were all the time in my locker. I could feel her yellow eyes on me while I peeped under the beds and around.)

When I happened to mention the incident to Cousin Edgar, he told me not to forget that I'd promised not to remove the chain he'd given me. He said something about its being a talisman to ward off evil influences.

Now, mother, don't write and tell me not to study so hard! Cousin Edgar doesn't think I'm crazy or delirious, so I guess you needn't.

The same to the same:

. . . This morning Cousin Edgar called me on the telephone to ask if anything had been stolen from one of the girls last night. There had. Grace Dreene had lost a locket and chain. Cousin Edgar asked if the locket had her initials on it in chip diamonds! How did he know? I'll tell you.

Last night he was sleepless, so he took a walk up here. The moon was shining directly on my side of the dormitory and he distinctly saw a great tortoise-shell cat come out of what he thought was my room.

There is a very narrow ledge around the building, under the windows, about three inches wide. The cat walked along that ledge until it reached Grace's window, where it jumped in. After a moment it came out with something glittering in its mouth!

Cousin Edgar hissed, "Scat!" The cat hesitated, startled, and the thing went flashing from its mouth to the ground. Cousin Edgar watched it go back to my window, then he picked up the article. It was Grace's locket and chain. The cat had stolen it from Grace's room! Did you ever hear of anything so queer, mother? I've read of monkeys and jack-daws—but a cat!

Cousin Edgar mailed the chain to Grace. Fancy the astonishment of the girls when the stolen thing came back through the mail!

But what do you make of it? The cat came out of, and went back into my room! The things I do think are so extraordinary that I'm afraid to say them, even to myself.

From Captain Edgar Benedict's notebook:

After having found out all I could from Althea about the strange facts in this most interesting case, I determined to follow the only clue that presented itself, *i.e.,* the old colored mammy. It seems that she called regularly every Tuesday, so I made it a point to linger near the academy on a Tuesday morning, and was rewarded by seeing the old woman appear bright and early for her young mistress's laundry.

She is a queer character. Far from being the decrepit old creature I had been led to expect by Althea's description, she is a tall, handsome mulatto woman with flashing eyes that hold a strange magnetism in their direct, unblinking gaze. Her face is deeply lined with wrinkles that to my opinion have been etched by the character of her thoughts rather than by the hand of time. She carries herself humbly when in the presence of academy people, but I have seen her, once out of sight of the school, straighten up that gaunt form and throw her head back proudly, altering her dragging walk into a brisk and lively stride.

She carried the young lady's fresh laundry into the academy and in half an hour came out laden with the soiled laundry, which she had in an embroidered laundry-bag. Once out of sight of the school, she broke into a rapid, swinging walk, and I had much ado to keep her in sight. She reached Pine Valley and made for the negro quarters, where she entered a house that I noted carefully.

As I wanted very much to get a personal impression, I knocked at her door, and inquired if she could do my laundry work. She stared at me, pride in those black eyes of hers. Then she said very curtly that she did washing for one person only, and shut the door in my face. There is a fierce, implacable atmosphere about that old black woman. I would dislike tremendously to arouse her hatred. . . . Just got back from a night-visit to Mammy Jinny's cabin. Fortunately, when I got there, she had left a full inch of space between the window-frame and the lower edge of the window-shade. Through it I got a fine view of the old witch—for witch she certainly is, and somehow involved in the mysterious happenings at the academy.

It is not the first time I have watched a witch's incantations. But I have never before had such a strong personal interest in them.

The old negress pulled out the laundry from the bag, and with it tumbled a flashing emerald ring! That must have been the ring of Natalie Cunningham. How did it get into Vida di Monserreau's soiled laundry, unless put there by Vida herself? Is Vida an accomplice or an innocent victim?

Mammy Jinny now drew from her bosom a stocking, and shook out of it as fine a collection of rings, brooches, bracelets, chains, as I've ever seen outside a jeweler's shop. She laid the emerald ring with them and sat staring at her plunder. After a while, she pushed it back into its hiding-place. Then she began to pace the dirt floor of her squalid cabin.

As she walked, she muttered. Sometimes she wrung her hands. Fragments of her words drifted to my ears, as I listened.

"My baby Vida—my little Missy! Forgive me, missy! But you must pay for your father's crime. I cannot forgive him!"

All at once she flung herself down before the hearth, for all the world like a great cat and began to stare unblinkingly into the smoldering embers. By my watch, she remained in that posture absolutely motionless for fully two hours, during which I honestly wished I were elsewhere; there was something about her tense attitude that conveyed a baleful significance to my intuition. I knew that she was projecting her mental powers to accomplish her black purposes, like the evil old witch she was. It was hardly an agreeable situation for me, but I dared not move until she herself began to stir.

I have an idea that the witch, the tortoise-shell cat, and the odd Vida are more closely connected than might seem credible. I must take Althea somewhat into my confidence.

. . . My plan worked perfectly. Vida was very happy to possess the cat-chain and easily agreed not to take it off. Last night I kept watch over the old negress, and Althea—at my request—watched Vida. Vida slept peacefully through the very hours when I watched Mammy Jinny sweating and working her incantations in vain.

. . . I am on the right track. Althea tells me that Mammy Jinny came into the academy and ordered Vida to take off the cat-chain. Vida refused with what seemed natural indignation. Mammy Jinny told her the chain was "bad voodoo." Vida stood firm. The old negress was so furious that when she left, she forgot to bow herself, and strode away, full height, much to Vida's astonishment.

. . . Althea has been carrying out my further directions with a cleverness and tact that does her credit. She snipped one of the links in the chain when Vida wasn't looking, and Vida has asked me to have it repaired, as my cousin suggested. To-night Vida will be without the protection of the chain. I have instructed Althea to do her part, and I shall myself watch the old witch.

. . . All last night Mammy Jinny worked her spells. They were successful this time. Althea has told me what happened.

Althea saw the cat steal from Vida's bed to the window, and return with a stolen bracelet in its mouth. It dropped the article into Vida's laundry-bag. Then, as Althea expressed it, the cat sprang into Vida's bed, and—there lay Vida, peacefully sleeping! No wonder Althea couldn't close her eyes the rest of the night.

When one of the girl's chums came in to say a bracelet was missing, Althea had it ready to return. She said she had picked it up in the hall.

I am going to put a stop to the whole business. It is voodoo, pure and simple, with a taint of the devil that is unpleasant, to say the last. Whatever the old negress's intentions, she must not attempt to carry them out by means of an innocent young white girl who has somehow fallen under her dominant will-power. If I cannot put a quick stop to it, I shall tell Vida di Monserreau exactly what she has to fear and provide her with a talisman.

Last night was certainly a thrilling one from start to finish. I sent old Peter to remain outside Mammy Jinny's cabin, for I wanted a full report of her actions. I myself, with Miss Annette's kind coöperation, hung a stout rope-ladder from Althea's window while the two inmates of the room were in the gymnasium, and covered the top with pillows to conceal it from prying eyes.

At about one-thirty A.M. the great cat came out of Althea's window—left open for this purpose—and went out upon the narrow ledge. It made me hold my breath. (What if it had fallen? The thought makes me shudder yet.) It disappeared within another open window, and I went quickly under the window and called to Althea that it was the fifth window. She closed hers at once and went to Belle Bragg's room, where the cat had gone in.

Both girls saw it go out of the window. Then Belle looked at her dressing-table and found her wrist-watch missing. Althea said she thought one of the girls had borrowed it and would bring it back in the morning. Then Belle closed her window—a vain precaution—and Althea returned to her own room.

Meantime, I had mounted the ladder quietly until I was directly under Althea's window, where I braced myself strongly for what I had in mind would follow.

The cat found the window closed. It beat with its fore-paws at the pane in a pitiful manner.

I reached up and tossed the repaired cat-chain about its neck. Although I had rather anticipated what followed, it made me gasp, for it was the limp, unconscious body of Vida di Monserreau that I supported in my arms!

Althea opened the window and between us we got the poor girl on to her bed. I warned Althea to be silent, and was off to find old Peter and get his report.

I was thoroughly provoked when I found he was not on watch outside the cabin as I had expected him to be. Then I peered under the window-shade. What I saw was my old black Peter, squatting on the floor before the hearth, his arm about that old witch and her head resting on his shoulder!

I *was* furious! I gave a thundering rap at the door. Peter let me in. But the old scoundrel, instead of seeming shamed and guilty, met me with a broad grin that showed his white teeth from ear to ear. To my further astonishment, Mammy Jinny rose to her full height with a grin that matched his.

It took my breath away. I demanded an explanation. Between them, it was mighty hard to find out the truth, for it was a long story that went back to the young girlhood of the old negress.

She and Peter were slaves, owned by Vida's grandfather. When a valuable ring was missing, the old man charged Peter with the theft, and sold him into a distant state where he could never hope to see his wife again. Jinny knew the facts but what good would it have done her to have told them? She might have received a whipping. She knew that her young master had given the ring to a white girl whom he was courting on the sly.

Jinny appealed to "young marse." He laughed in her face. She determined then to be revenged. Concealing her hatred, she demanded and received the care of Vida, when "young marse's" wife died in child-birth.

From that time on, Mammy Jinny worked out her plans, using her knowledge of voodoo, until she had so bent the child's will to hers that Vida was absolutely responsive to the old negress's thoughts. How she performed the apparent metamorphosis I had seen, she would not tell, however, but only looked at me defiantly out of her proud eyes.

Mammy's idea of revenge seems to have been to fasten the disgrace of theft upon Vida di Monserreau, thus shaming "young marse." Her methods of accomplishing her end are, like all methods of black magic, better left undisclosed to the general public.

As old Peter has long owed me loyalty, since I saved his life years ago, I had little difficulty in persuading him to take his wife to Jamaica, from which place they were originally brought, and where Peter in later years returned, in hope of meeting Jinny there once more. They will be out of Vida's life henceforth.

This does not mean that Vida is to go unprotected. I shall take care of that, with the permission of her father. But I do not believe that old Jinny will ever again crouch in invocation to the Evil Powers to bring the tortoise-shell cat into materialization at Vida's expense.

THE HOUSE OF HORROR

By SEABURY QUINN

"MORBLEU, FRIEND TROWBRIDGE, HAVE A CARE," JULES DE Grandin warned as my lurching motor-car almost ran into the brimming ditch beside the rain-soaked road.

I wrenched the steering wheel viciously and swore softly under my breath as I leaned forward, striving vainly to pierce the curtains of rain which shut us in.

"No use, old fellow," I confessed, turning to my companion, "we're lost; that's all there is to it."

"Ha," he laughed shortly, "do you just begin to discover that fact, my friend? *Parbleu,* I have known it this last half-hour."

Throttling my engine down, I crept along the concrete roadway, peering through my streaming windshield and storm curtains for some familiar landmark, but nothing but blackness, wet and impenetrable, met my eyes.

Two hours before, answering an insistent 'phone call, de Grandin and I had left the security of my warm office to administer a dose of toxin antitoxin to an Italian laborer's child who lay, choking with diphtheria, in a hut at the workmen's settlement where the new branch of the railroad was being put through. The cold, driving rain and the Stygian darkness of the night had misled me when I made the detour around the railway cut, and for the past hour and a half I had been feeling my way over unfamiliar roads as futilely as a lost child wandering in the woods.

"Grâce à Dieu," de Grandin exclaimed, seizing my arm with both his small, strong hands, "a light! See, there it

shines in the night. Come, let us go to it. Even the meanest hovel is preferable to this so villainous rain."

I peeped through a joint in the curtains and saw a faint, intermittent light flickering through the driving rain some two hundred yards away.

"All right," I acquiesced, climbing from the car, "we've lost so much time already we probably couldn't do anything for the Vivianti child, and maybe these people can put us on the right road, anyway."

Plunging through puddles like miniature lakes, soaked by the wind-driven rain, barking our shins again and again on invisible obstacles, we made for the light, finally drawing up to a large, square house of red brick fronted by an imposing white-pillared porch. Light streamed out through the fanlight over the white door and from the two tall windows flanking the portal.

"*Parbleu,* a house of circumstance, this," de Grandin commented, mounting the porch and banging lustily at the polished brass knocker.

I wrinkled my forehead in thought while he rattled the knocker a second time. "Strange, I can't remember this place," I muttered. "I thought I knew every building within thirty miles, but this is a new one—"

"Ah bah!" de Grandin interrupted. "Always you must be casting a wet blanket on the parade, Friend Trowbridge. First, you insist on losing us in the midst of a *sacré* rainstorm, then when I, Jules de Grandin, find us a shelter from the weather, you must needs waste time in wondering why it is you know not the place. *Morbleu,* you will refuse shelter because you have never been presented to the master of the house, if I do not watch you, I fear."

"But I ought to know the place, de Grandin," I protested. "It's certainly imposing enough to—"

My defense was cut short by the sharp click of a lock, and the wide, white door swung inward before us.

We strode over the threshold, removing our dripping hats as we did so, and turned to address the person who had opened the door.

"Why—" I began, and stared about me in open-mouthed surprise.

"Name of a little blue man!" said Jules de Grandin, and added his incredulous stare to mine.

As far as we could see, we were alone in the mansion's imposing hall. Straight before us, perhaps for forty feet, ran a corridor of parquetry flooring, covered here and there by rich-hued Oriental rugs. White-paneled walls, adorned with oil paintings of imposing-looking individuals, rose for eighteen feet or so to a beautifully frescoed ceiling, and a graceful, curving staircase swept upward from the farther end of the room. Candles in cut glass sconces lighted the high-ceiled apartment, the hospitable glow from a log fire burning under the high, white marble mantel lent an air of homely coziness to the place, but of anything living, human or animal, there was no faintest trace or sign.

Click! Behind us, the heavy outer door swung to silently on well-oiled hinges and the automatic lock latched firmly.

"Death of my life!" de Grandin murmured, reaching for the door's silver-plated knob and giving it a vigorous twist. "*Par la moustache du diable,* Friend Trowbridge, it is locked! Truly, perhaps it had been better if we had remained outside in the rain!"

"Not at all, I assure you, my dear sir," a rich, mellow voice answered him from the curve of the stairs. "Your arrival was nothing less than providential, gentlemen."

Coming toward us, walking heavily with the aid of a stout cane, was an unusually handsome man attired in pyjamas and dressing gown, a sort of nightcap of flowered silk on his white head, slippers of softest Morocco on his feet.

"You are a physician, sir?" he asked, glancing inquiringly at the medicine case in my hand.

"Yes," I answered. "I am Dr. Samuel Trowbridge, from

Harrisonville, and this is Dr. Jules de Grandin, of Paris, who is my guest."

"Ah," replied our host, "I am very, very glad to welcome you to Marston Hall, gentlemen. It so happens that one—er—my daughter, is quite ill, and I have been unable to obtain medical aid for her on account of my infirmities and the lack of a telephone. If I may trespass on your charity to attend my poor child, I shall be delighted to have you as my guests for the night. If you will lay aside your coats"—he paused expectantly. "Ah, thank you"—as we hung our dripping garments over a chair—"you will come this way, please?"

We followed him up the broad stairs and down an upper corridor to a tastefully furnished chamber where a young girl—fifteen years of age, perhaps—lay propped up with a pile of diminutive pillows.

"Anabel, Anabel, my love, here are two doctors to see you," the old gentleman called softly.

The girl moved her fair head with a weary, peevish motion and whimpered softly in her sleep, but gave no further recognition of our presence.

"And what have been her symptoms, if you please, *Monsieur?*" de Grandin asked as he rolled back the cuffs of his jacket and prepared to make an examination.

"Sleep," replied our host, "just sleep. Some time ago she suffered from influenza, lately she has been given to fits of protracted slumber from which I cannot waken her. I fear she may have contracted sleeping sickness, sir. I am told it sometimes follows influenza."

"H'm." De Grandin passed his small, pliable hands rapidly over the girl's cheeks in the region of the ears, felt rapidly along her neck over the jugular vein, then raised a puzzled glance to me. "Have you some laudanum and aconite in your bag, Friend Trowbridge?" he asked.

"There's some morphine," I answered, "and aconite; but no laudanum."

"No matter," he waved his hand impatiently, bustling over to the medicine case and extracting two small phials from it. "No matter, this will do as well. Some water, if you please, *Monsieur,*" he turned to the father, a medicine bottle in each hand.

"But de Grandin"—I began, when a sudden kick from one of his slender, heavily-shod feet nearly broke my shin—"de Grandin, do you think that's the proper medication?" I finished lamely.

"Oh, *mais oui,* undoubtedly," he replied. "Nothing else would do in this case. Water, if you please, *Monsieur,*" he repeated, again addressing the father.

I stared at him in ill-disguised amazement as he extracted a pellet from each of the bottles and quickly ground them to powder while the old gentleman filled a tumbler with water from the porcelain pitcher which stood on the chintz-draped wash-stand in the corner of the chamber. He was as familiar with the arrangement of my medicine case as I was, I knew, and knew that my phials were arranged by numbers instead of being labeled. Deliberately, I saw, he had passed over the morphine and aconite, and had chosen two bottles of plain, unmedicated sugar of milk pills. What his object was I had no idea, but I watched him measure out four teaspoonfuls of water, dissolve the powder in it, and pour the sham medication down the unconscious girl's throat.

"Good," he proclaimed as he washed the glass with meticulous care. "She will rest easily until the morning, *Monsieur.* When daylight comes we shall decide on further treatment. Will you now permit that we retire?" He bowed politely to the master of the house, who returned his courtesy and led us to a comfortably furnished room farther down the corridor.

"See here, de Grandin," I demanded when our host had wished us a pleasant good-night and closed the door upon us, "what was your idea in giving that child an impotent dose like that—?"

"S-s-sh!" he cut me short with a fierce whisper. "That young girl, *mon ami,* is no more suffering from encephalitis than you or I. There is no characteristic swelling of the face or neck, no diagnostic hardening of the jugular vein. Her temperature was a bit subnormal, it is true—but upon her breath I detected the odor of chloral hydrate. For some reason, good I hope, but bad I fear, she is drugged, and I thought it best to play the fool and pretend I believed the man's statements. *Pardieu,* the fool who knows himself no fool has an immense advantage over the fool who believes him one, my friend."

"But—"

"But me no buts, Friend Trowbridge; remember how the door of this house opened with none to touch it, recall how it closed behind us in the same way, and observe this, if you will." Stepping softly, he crossed the room, pulled aside the chintz curtains at the window and tapped lightly on the frame which held the thick, plate glass panes. *"Regardez vous,"* he ordered, tapping the frame a second time.

Like every other window I had seen in the house, this one was of the casement type, small panes of heavy glass being sunk into latticelike frames. Under de Grandin's direction I tapped the latter, and found them not painted wood, as I had supposed, but stoutly welded and bolted metal. Also, to my surprise, I found the turnbuckles for opening the casement were only dummies, the metal frames being actually securely bolted to the stone sills. To all intents, we were as firmly incarcerated as though serving a sentence in the state penitentiary.

"The door—" I began, but he shook his head.

Obeying his gesture, I crossed the room and turned the handle lightly. It twisted under the pressure of my fingers, but, though we had heard no warning click or bolt, the door itself was as firmly fastened as though nailed shut.

"Wh—why," I asked stupidly, "what's it all mean, de Grandin?"

"Je ne sais quoi," he answered with a shrug, "but one thing I know: I do like not this house, Friend Trowbridge. I—"

Above the hissing of the rain against the windows and the howl of the sea-wind about the gables, there suddenly rose a scream, wire-edged with inarticulate terror, freighted with utter, transcendental anguish of body and soul.

"Cordieu!" He threw up his head like a hound hearing the call of the pack from far away. "Did you hear it, too, Friend Trowbridge?"

"Of course," I answered, every nerve in my body trembling in horripilation with the echo of the hopeless wail.

"Pardieu," he repeated, "I like this house less than ever, now! Come, let us move this dresser before our door. It is safer that we sleep behind barricades this night, I think."

We blocked the door, and I was soon sound asleep.

"Trowbridge, Trowbridge, my friend"—de Grandin drove a sharp elbow into my ribs—"wake up, I beseech you. Name of a green goat, you lie like one dead, save for your so abominable snoring!"

"Eh?" I answered sleepily, thrusting myself deeper beneath the voluminous bedclothes. Despite the unusual occurrences of the night I was tired to the point of exhaustion, and fairly drunken with sleep.

"Up; arise, my friend," he ordered, shaking me excitedly. "The coast is clear, I think, and it is high time we did some exploring."

"Rats!" I scoffed, disinclined to leave my comfortable couch. "What's the use of wandering about a strange house to gratify a few unfounded suspicions? The girl might have been given a dose of chloral hydrate, but the chances are her father thought he was helping her when he gave it. As for those trick devices for opening and locking doors, the old man apparently lives here alone and has installed these mechanical aids to lessen his work. He has to hobble around with a cane, you know."

"Ah!" my companion assented sarcastically. "And that scream we heard, did he install that as an aid to his infirmities, also?"

"Perhaps the girl woke up with a nightmare," I hazarded, but he made an impatient gesture.

"Perhaps the moon is composed of green cheese, also," he replied. "Up, up and dress, my friend. This house should be investigated while yet there is time. Attend me: But five minutes ago, through this very window, I did observe *Monsieur,* our host, attired in a raincoat, depart from his own front door, and without his cane. *Parbleu,* he did skip as agilely as any boy, I assure you. Even now he is almost at the spot where we abandoned your automobile. What he intends doing there I know not. What I intend doing I know full well. Do you accompany me or not?"

"Oh, I suppose so," I agreed, crawling from the bed and slipping into my clothes. "How are you going to get past that locked door?"

He flashed me one of his sudden smiles, shooting the points of his little blond mustache upward like the horns of an inverted crescent. "Observe," he ordered, displaying a short length of thin wire. "In the days when woman's hair was still her crowning glory, what mighty deeds a lady could encompass with a hairpin! *Pardieu,* there was one little grisette in Paris who showed me some tricks in the days before the war! Regard me, if you please."

Deftly he thrust the pliable loop of wire into the keyhole, twisting it tentatively back and forth, at length pulling it out and regarding it carefully. *"Très bien,"* he muttered as he reached into an inside pocket, bringing out a heavier bit of wire.

"See," he displayed the finer wire, "with this I take an impression of that lock's tumblers, now"—quickly he bent the heavier wire to conform to the waved outline of the lighter loop—*"voilà,* I have a key!"

And he had. The lock gave readily to the pressure of his

improvised key, and we stood in the long, dark hall, staring about us half curiously, half fearfully.

"This way, if you please," de Grandin ordered; "first we will look in upon *la jeunesse,* to see how it goes with her."

We walked on tiptoe down the corridor, entered the chamber where the girl lay, and approached the bed.

She was lying with her hands folded upon her breast in the manner of those composed for their final rest, her wide, periwinkle-blue eyes staring sightlessly before her, the short, tightly-curled ringlets of her blond, bobbed hair surrounding her drawn, pallid face like a golden nimbus encircling the ivory features of a saint in some carved ikon.

My companion approached the bed softly, placing one hand on the girl's wrist with professional precision. "Temperature low, pulse weak," he murmured, checking off her symtoms. "Complexion pale to the point of lividity—ha, now for the eyes; sleeping her pupils should have been contracted, while they should now be dilate—*Dieu de Dieu!* Trowbridge, my friend, come here.

"Look," he commanded, pointing to the apathetic girl's face. "Those eyes—*grand Dieu,* those eyes! It is sacrilege, nothing less."

I looked into the girl's face, then started back with a half-suppressed cry of horror. Asleep, as she had been when we first saw her, the child had been pretty to the point of loveliness. Her features were small and regular, clean-cut as those of a face in a cameo, the tendrils of her light-yellow hair had lent her a dainty, ethereal charm comparable to that of a Dresden china shepherdess. It had needed but the raising of her delicate, long-lashed eyelids to give her face the animation of some laughing sprite playing truant from fairyland.

Her lids were raised now, but the eyes they unveiled were no clear, joyous windows of a tranquil soul. Rather, they were the peepholes of a spirit in torment. The irises were a lovely shade of blue, it is true, but the optics themselves were things of horror. Rolling grotesquely to right and left, they peered futilely in opposite directions, lending to her sweet, pale face the half-ludicrous, wholly hideous expression of a bloating frog.

"Good heavens!" I exclaimed, turning from the deformed girl with a feeling of disgust akin to nausea; "what a terrible affliction!"

De Grandin made no reply, but bent over the girl's still form, gazing intently at her malformed eyes. "It is not natural," he announced. "The muscles have been tampered with, and tampered with by some one who is a master hand at surgery. Will you get me your syringe and some strychnine, Friend Trowbridge? This poor one is still unconscious."

I hastened to our bedroom and returned with the hypodermic and stimulant, then stood beside him, watching eagerly, as he administered a strong injection.

The girl's narrow chest fluttered as the powerful drug took effect, and the pale lids dropped for a second over her repulsive eyes. Then, with a sob which was half moan, she attempted to raise herself on her elbow, fell back again, and, with apparent effort, gasped, "The mirror, let me have the mirror! Oh, tell me it isn't true; tell me it was a trick of some sort. Oh, the horrible thing I saw in the glass couldn't have been I. Was it?"

"Tiens, ma petite," de Grandin replied, "but you speak in riddles. What is it you would know?"

"He—he," the girl faltered weakly, forcing her trembling lips to frame the words—"that horrible old man showed me a mirror a little while ago and said the face in it was mine. Oh, it was horrible, horrible!"

"Eh? What is this?" de Grandin demanded on a rising note. " 'He'? 'Horrible old man'? Are you not his daughter? Is he not your father?"

"No," the girl gasped, so low her denial was scarcely audible. "I was driving home from Mackettsdale last—oh, I forget when it was, but it was at night—and my tires punctured. I—I think there must have been glass on the road, for the shoes were cut to ribbons. I saw the light in this house and came to ask for help. An old man—oh, I thought he was so nice and kind!—let me in and said he was all alone here and about to eat dinner, and asked me to join him. I ate some—some—oh, I don't remember what it was—and the next thing I knew he was standing by my bed, holding a mirror up to me and telling me it was my face I saw in the glass. Oh, please, *please,* tell me it was some terrible trick he played on me. I'm not truly hideous, am I?"

"Morbleu!" de Grandin muttered softly, tugging at the ends of his mustache. "What is all this?"

To the girl he said: "But of course not. You are like a flower, *Mademoiselle.* A little flower that dances in the wind. You—"

"And my eyes, they aren't—they aren't"—she interrupted with piteous eagerness—"please tell me they aren't—"

"Mais non, ma chère," he assured her. "Your eyes are like the *pervenche* that mirrors the sky in springtime. They are—"

"Let—let me see the mirror, please," she interrupted in an anxious whisper. "I'd like to see for myself, if you—oh, I feel all weak inside—" She lapsed back against the pillow, her lids mercifully veiling the hideously distorted eyes and restoring her face to tranquil beauty.

"Cordieu!" de Grandin breathed. "The chloral reasserted itself none too soon for Jules de Grandin's comfort, Friend Trowbridge. Sooner would I have gone to the rack than have shown that pitiful child her face in a mirror."

"But what's it all mean?" I asked. "She says she came here, and—"

"And the rest remains for us to find out, I think," he replied evenly. "Come, we lose time, and to lose time is to be caught, my friend."

De Grandin led the way down the hall, peering eagerly

into each door we passed in search of the owner's chamber, but before his quest was satisfied he stopped abruptly at the head of the stairs. "Observe, Friend Trowbridge," he ordered, pointing a carefully manicured forefinger to a pair of buttons, one white, one black, set in the wall. "Unless I am more mistaken than I think I am, we have here the key to the situation—or at least to the front door."

He pushed vigorously at the white button, then ran to the curve of the stairs to note the result.

Sure enough, the heavy door swung open on its hinges of cast bronze, letting gusts of rain drive into the lower hall.

"Pardieu," he ejaculated, "we have here the open sesame; let us see if we possess the closing secret as well! Press the black button, Trowbridge, my friend, while I watch."

I did his bidding, and a delighted exclamation told me the door had closed.

"Now what?" I asked, joining him on the stairway.

"U'm," he pulled first one, then the other end of his diminutive mustache meditatively; "the house possesses its attractions, Friend Trowbridge, but I believe it would be well if we went out to observe what our friend, *le vieillard horrible,* does. I like not to have one who shows young girls their disfigured faces in mirrors near our conveyance."

Slipping into our raincoats we opened the door, taking care to place a wad of paper on the sill to prevent its closing tightly enough to latch, and scurried out into the storm.

As we left the shelter of the porch a shaft of indistinct light shone through the rain, as my car was swung from the highway and headed toward a depression to the left of the house.

"Parbleu, he is a thief, this one!" de Grandin exclaimed excitedly. *"Hola, Monsieur!"* He ran forward, swinging his arms like a pair of semaphores. "What sort of business is it you make with our *auto?"*

The wailing of the storm tore the words from his lips and

hurled them away, but the little Frenchman was not to be thwarted. *"Pardieu,"* he gasped, bending his head against the wind-driven rain, "I will stop the scoundrel if—*nom d'un coq,* he has done it!"

Even as he spoke, the old man flung open the car's forward door and leaped, allowing the machine to go crashing down a low, steep embankment into a lake of slimy swamp-mud.

For a moment the vandal stood contemplating his work, then burst into a peal of wild laughter more malignant than any profanity.

"Parbleu, robber! *Apache!* You shall laugh from the other side of your mouth!" de Grandin promised, as he made for the old man.

But the other seemed oblivious of our presence. Still chuckling at his work, he turned toward the house, stopped short as a sudden heavy gust of wind shook the trees along the roadway, then started forward with a yell of terror as a great branch, torn bodily from a towering oak tree came crashing toward the earth.

He might as well have attempted to dodge a meteorite. Like an arrow from the bow of divine justice, the great timber hurtled down, pinning his frail body to the ground like a worm beneath a laborer's brogan.

"Trowbridge, my friend," de Grandin observed matter-of-factly, "observe the evil effects of stealing motor-cars."

We lifted the heavy bough from the prostrate man and turned him over on his back. De Grandin on one side, I on the other, we made a hasty examination, arriving at the same finding simultaneously. His spinal column was snapped like a pipestem.

"You have some last statement to make, *Monsieur?"* de Grandin asked curtly. "If so, you had best be about it, your time is short."

"Y-yes," the stricken man replied weakly. "I—I meant to kill you, for you might have hit upon my secret. As it is, you may publish it to the world, that all may know what it means to offend a Marston. In my room you will find the documents. My—my pets—are—in—the—cellar. She—was—to—have—been—one—of—them." The pauses between his words became longer and longer, his voice grew weaker with each labored syllable. As he whispered the last sentence painfully there was a gurgling sound, and a tiny stream of blood welled up at the corner of his mouth. His narrow chest rose and fell once with a convulsive movement, then his jaw dropped limply. He was dead.

"Oh, ho," de Grandin remarked, "it is a hemorrhage which finished him. A broken rib piercing his lung. U'm? I should have guessed it. Come, my friend, let us carry him to the house, then see what it was he meant by that talk of documents and pets. A pest upon this fellow for dying with his riddle half explained! Did he not know that Jules de Grandin cannot resist the challenge of a riddle? *Parbleu,* we will solve this mystery, *Monsieur le Mort,* if we have to hold an autopsy to do so!"

"Oh, for heaven's sake, hush, de Grandin," I besought, shocked at his heartlessness. "The man is dead."

"Ah bah!" he returned scornfully. "Dead or not, did he not steal your motor-car?"

We laid our gruesome burden on the hall couch and mounted the stairs to the second floor. With de Grandin in the lead we found the dead man's room and began a systematic search for the papers he had mentioned, almost with his last breath. After some time my companion unearthed a thick, leather-bound portfolio from the lower drawer of a beautiful old mahogany highboy, and spread its wide leaves open on the white-counterpaned bed.

"Ah," he drew forth several papers and held them to the light, "we begin to make the progress, Friend Trowbridge. What is this?"

He held out a newspaper clipping cracked from long folding and yellowed with age. It read:

ACTRESS JILTS SURGEON'S CRIPPLED SON ON EVE OF WEDDING

Declaring she could not stand the sight of his deformity, and that she had engaged herself to him only in a moment of thoughtless pity, Dora Lee, well-known variety actress, last night repudiated her promise to marry John Biersfield Marston, Jr., hopelessly crippled son of Dr. John Biersfield Marston, the well-known surgeon and expert osteologist. Neither the abandoned bridegroom nor his father could be seen by reporters from the *Planet* last night.

"Very good," de Grandin nodded, "we need go no farther with that account. A young woman, it would seem, once broke her promise to marry a cripple, and, judging from this paper's date, that was in 1896. Here is another, what do you make of it?"

The clipping he handed me read as follows:

SURGEON'S SON A SUICIDE

Still sitting in the wheel-chair from which he has not moved during his waking hours since he was hopelessly crippled while playing polo in England ten years ago, John Biersfield Marston, son of the famous surgeon of the same name, was found in his bedroom this morning by his valet. A rubber hose was connected with a gas jet, the other end being held in the young man's mouth.

Young Marston was jilted by Dora Lee, well-known vaudeville actress, on the day before the date set for their wedding, one month ago. He is reported to have been extremely low-spirited since his desertion by his fiancée.

Dr. Marston, the bereaved father, when seen by reporters from the *Planet* this morning, declared the actress was responsible for his son's death and announced his intention of holding her accountable. When asked if legal proceedings were contemplated, he declined further information.

"So?" de Grandin nodded shortly. "Now this one, if you please."

The third clipping was brief to the point of curtness:

WELL-KNOWN SURGEON RETIRES

> Dr. John Biersfield Marston, widely known throughout this section of the country as an expert in operations concerning the bones, has announced his intention of retiring from practice. His house has been sold, and he will move from the city.

"The record is clear so far," de Grandin asserted, studying the first clipping with raised eyebrows, "but—*morbleu,* my friend, look, look at this picture. This Dora Lee, of whom does she remind you? Eh?"

I took the clipping again and looked intently at the illustration of the article announcing young Marston's broken engagement. The woman in the picture was young and inclined to be overdressed in the voluminous, fluffy mode of the days before the Spanish-American War.

"U'm, no one whom I know—" I began, but halted abruptly as a sudden likeness struck me. Despite the towering pompadour arrangement of her blond hair and the unbecoming straw sailor hat above the coiffure, the woman in the picture bore a certain resemblance to the disfigured girl we had seen a half-hour before.

The Frenchman saw recognition dawn in my face, and nodded agreement. "But of course," he said. "Now, the question is, is this young girl whose eyes are so out of alignment a relative of this Dora Lee, or is the resemblance a coincidence, and if so, what lies behind it? *Hein?*"

"I don't know," I admitted, "but there must be some connection——"

"Connection? Of course there is a connection," de Grandin affirmed, rummaging deeper in the portfolio. "A-a-ah!

What is this? *Nom d'un nom,* Friend Trowbridge, I think I smell the daylight! Look!"

He held a full-page story from one of the sensational New York dailies before him, his eyes glued to the flowing type and crude, coarse-screened half-tones of half a dozen young women which composed the article.

"WHAT HAS BECOME OF THE MISSING GIRLS?" I read in bold-faced type across the top of the page.

"Are sinister, unseen hands reaching out from the darkness to seize our girls from palace and hovel, shop, stage and office?" the article asked rhetorically. "Where are Ellen Munro and Dorothy Sawyer and Phyllis Bouchet and three other lovely light-haired girls who have walked into oblivion during the past year?"

I read to the end the sensational account of the girls' disappearances. The cases seemed fairly similar; each of the vanished young women had failed to return to her home and had never been accounted for in any manner, and in no instance, according to the newspaper, had there been any assignable reason for voluntary departure.

"*Parbleu,* but he was stupid, even for a journalist!" de Grandin asserted as I completed my inspection of the story. "Why, I wager even my good Friend Trowbridge has already noticed one important fact which this writer has treated as though it were as commonplace as the nose on his face."

"Sorry to disappoint you, old chap," I answered, "but it looks to me as though the reporter had covered the case from every possible angle."

"Ah? So?" he replied sarcastically. "*Morbleu,* we shall have to consult the oculist in your behalf when we return home, my friend. Look, look, I beseech you, upon the pictures of these so totally absent and unaccounted for young women, *cher ami,* and tell me if you do not observe a certain likeness among them, not only a resemblance to each other, but to that Mademoiselle Lee who jilted the son of Dr. Marston? Can you see it, now I have pointed it out?"

"No—wh-why, yes,—yes, of course!" I responded, running my eye over the pictures accompanying the story. "By the Lord Harry, de Grandin, you're right; you might almost say there is a family resemblance between these girls! You've put your finger on it, I do believe."

"Hélas, no!" he answered with a shrug. "I have put my finger on nothing as yet, my friend. I reach, I grope, I feel about me like a blind man tormented by a crowd of naughty little boys, but nothing do the poor fingers of my mind encounter. Pah! Jules de Grandin, you are one great fool! Think, think, stupid one!"

He seated himself on the edge of the bed, cupping his face in his hands and leaning forward till his elbows rested on his knees.

Suddenly he sprang erect, one of his elfish smiles passing across his small, regular features. *"Nom d'un chat rouge,* my friend, I have it—I have it!" he announced. "The pets—the pets that old stealer of motor-cars spoke of! They are in the basement! *Pardieu,* we will see those pets, *cher* Trowbridge; with our four collective eyes we will see them. Did not that so execrable stealer declare she was to have been one of them? Now, in the name of Satan and brimstone, whom could he have meant by 'she' if not that unfortunate child with eyes like *la grenouille?* Eh?"

"Why——" I began, but he waved me forward.

"Come, come; let us go," he urged. "I am impatient, I am restless, I am not to be restrained. We shall investigate and see for ourselves what sort of pets are kept by one who shows young girls their deformed faces in mirrors and—*parbleu!*—steals motor-cars from my friends."

Hurrying down the main stairway, we hunted about for the cellar entrance, finally located the door and, holding above our heads a pair of candles from the hall, began descending a flight of rickety steps into a pitch-black basement rock-walled and, judging by its damp, moldy odor, unfloored save by the bare, moist earth beneath the house.

"Parbleu, the dungeons of the château at Carcassonne are more cheerful than this," de Grandin commented as he paused at the stairs' foot, holding his candle aloft to make a better inspection of the dismal place.

I suppressed a shudder of mingled chill and apprehension as I stared at the blank stone walls, unpierced by windows or other openings of any sort, and made ready to retrace my steps. "Nothing here," I announced. "You can see that with half an eye. The place is as empty as——"

"Perhaps, Friend Trowbridge," he agreed, "but Jules de Grandin does not look with half an eye. He uses both eyes, and uses them more than once if his first glance does not prove sufficient. Behold that bit of wood on the earth yonder. What do you make of it?"

"U'm—a piece of flooring, maybe," I hazarded.

"Maybe, yes, maybe no," he answered. "Let us see."

Crossing the cellar, he bent above the planks, then turned to me with a satisfied smile. "Flooring does not ordinarily have ring-bolts in it, my friend," he remarked, bending to seize the iron ring which was made fast to the boards by a stout staple.

"Ha!" As he heaved upward the planks came away from the black earth, disclosing a board-lined well about three feet square and of uncertain depth. An almost vertical ladder of two-by-four timbers led downward from the trap-door to the well's impenetrable blackness.

"Allons, we descend," he commented, turning about and setting his foot on the topmost rung of the ladder.

"Don't be a fool," I advised. "You don't know what's down there."

"True"—his head was level with the floor as he answered—"but I shall know, with luck, in a few moments. Do you come?"

I sighed with vexation as I prepared to follow him.

At the ladder's foot he paused, raising his candle and looking about inquiringly. Directly before us was a passageway through the earth, ceiled with heavy planks and shored up with timbers like the lateral workings of a primitive mine.

"Ah, the plot shows complications," he murmured, stepping briskly into the dark tunnel. "Do you come, Friend Trowbridge?"

I followed, wondering what manner of thing might be at the end of the black, musty passage, but nothing but fungus-grown timbers and walls of moist, black earth met my questing gaze.

De Grandin preceded me by some paces, and, I suppose, we had gone fifteen feet through the passage when a gasp of mingled surprise and horror from my companion brought me beside him in two long strides. Fastened with nails to the timbers at each side of the tunnel were a number of white, glistening objects, objects which, because of their very familiarity, denied their identity to my wondering eyes. There was no mistaking the things; even a layman could not have failed to recognize them for what they were. I, as a physician, knew them even better. To the right of the passage hung fourteen perfectly articulated skeletons of human legs, complete from foot to ilium, gleaming white and ghostly in the flickering light of the candles.

"Good heavens!" I exclaimed.

"Sang du diable!" Jules de Grandin commented. "Behold what is there, my friend," he pointed to the opposite wall. Fourteen bony arms, complete from hand to shoulder-joint, hung pendulously from the tunnel's upright timbers.

"Pardieu," de Grandin muttered, "I have known men who collected stuffed birds and dried insects; I have known those who stored away Egyptian mummies—even the skulls of men long dead—but never before have I seen a collection of arms and legs! *Parbleu,* he was *caduo*—mad as a hatter, this one, or I am much mistaken!"

"So these were his pets?" I answered. "Yes, the man was undoubtedly mad to keep such a collection, and in a place like this. Poor fellow——"

"Nom d'un canon!" de Grandin broke in; "what was that?"

From the darkness before us there came a queer, inarticulate sound, such as a man might make attempting to speak with a mouth half-filled with food, and, as though the noise had wakened an echo slumbering in the cavern, the sound was repeated, multiplied again and again till it resembled the babbling of half a dozen overgrown infants—or an equal number of full-grown imbeciles.

"Onward!" Responding to the challenge of the unknown like a warrior obeying the trumpet's call to charge, de Grandin dashed toward the strange noise, swung about, flashing his candle this side and that, then:

"Nom de Dieu de nom de Dieu!" he almost shrieked. "Look, Friend Trowbridge, look and say that you see what I see, or have I, too, gone mad?"

Lined up against the wall was a series of seven small wooden boxes, each with a door composed of upright slats before it, similar in construction to the coops in which country folk pen brooding hens—and no larger. In each of the hutches huddled an object the like of which I had never before seen, even in the terrors of nightmare.

The things had the torsos of human beings, though hideously shrunken from starvation and incrusted with scales of filth, but there all resemblance to mankind ceased. From shoulders and waist there twisted flaccid tentacles of unsupported flesh, the upper ones terminating in flat, paddlelike flippers which had some remote resemblance to hands, the lower ones ending in almost shapeless stubs which resembled feet only in that each had a fringe of five shriveled, unsupported protuberances of withered flesh.

On scrawny necks were balanced caricatures of faces, flat, noseless, chinless countenances with horrible crossed or divergent eyes, mouths widened almost beyond resemblance to buccal orifices, and—horror of horrors!—elongated, *split* tongues protruding several inches from the lips and wagging impotently in vain efforts to form words.

"Satan, thou art outdone!" de Grandin cried as he held his candle before a scrap of paper decorating one of the cages after the manner of a sign before an animal's den at the Zoo. "Observe!" he ordered, pointing a shaking finger at the notice.

I looked, then recoiled, sick with horror. The paper bore the picture and name of Ellen Munro, one of the girls mentioned as missing in the newspaper article we had found in the dead man's bedroom.

Beneath the photograph was scribbled in an irregular hand: "Paid 1-25-97."

Sick at heart we walked down the line of pens. Each was labeled with the picture of a young and pretty girl with the notation, "Paid," followed by a date. Every girl named as missing in the newspaper was represented in the cages.

Last of all, in a coop somewhat smaller than the rest, we found a body more terribly mutilated than any. This was marked with the photograph and name of Dora Lee. Beneath her name was the date of her "payment," written in bold red figures.

"*Parbleu,* what are we to do, my friend?" de Grandin asked in an hysterical whisper. "We cannot return these poor ones to the world, that would be the worst form of cruelty; yet—yet I shrink from the act of mercy I know they would ask me to perform if they could speak."

"Let's go up," I begged. "We must think this thing over, de Grandin, and if I stay here any longer I shall faint."

"*Bien,*" he agreed, and turned to follow me from the cavern of horrors.

"It is to consider," he began as we reached the upper hall once more. "If we give those so pitiful ones the stroke of mercy we are murderers before the law, yet what service could we render them by bringing them once more into the world? Our choice is a hard one, my friend."

I nodded.

"*Morbleu,* but he was clever, that one," the Frenchman continued, half to me, half to himself. "What a surgeon! Fourteen instances of Wyeth's amputation of the hip and as many more of the shoulder—and every patient lived, lived to suffer the tortures of that hell-hole down there! But it is marvelous! None but a madman could have done it.

"Bethink you, Friend Trowbridge. Think how the mighty man of medicine brooded over the suicide of his crippled son, meditating hatred and vengeance for the heartless woman who had jilted him. Then—snap! went his great mentality, and from hating one woman he fell to hating all, to plotting vengeance against the many for the sin of the one. And, *cordieu,* what a vengeance! How he must have laid his plans to secure his victims; how he must have worked to prepare that hell-under-the-earth to house those poor, broken bodies which were his handiwork, and how he must have drawn upon the great surgical skill which was his, even in his madness, to transform those once lovely ones into the visions of horror we have just beheld! Horror of horrors! To remove the bones and let the girls still live!"

He rose, pacing impatiently across the hall. "What to do? What to do?" he demanded, striking his open hands against his forehead.

I followed his nervous steps with my eyes, but my brain was too numbed by the hideous things I had just seen to be able to respond to his question.

I looked hopelessly past him at the angle of the wall by the great fireplace, rubbed my eyes and looked again. Slowly, but surely, the wall was declining from the perpendicular.

"De Grandin," I shouted, glad of some new phenomenon to command my thoughts, "the wall—the wall's leaning!"

"Eh, the wall?" he queried. "*Pardieu,* yes! It is the rain;

the foundations are undermined. Quick, quick, my friend! To the cellars, or those unfortunate ones are undone!"

We scrambled down the stairs leading to the basement, but already the earth floor was sopping with water. The well leading to the madman's subcellar was more than half full of bubbling, earthy ooze.

"Mary, have pity!" de Grandin exclaimed. "Like rats in a trap, they did die. God rest their tired souls"—he shrugged his shoulders as he turned to retrace his steps—"it is better so. Now, Friend Trowbridge, do you hasten aloft and bring down that young girl from the room above. We must run for it if we do not wish to be crushed under the falling timbers of this house of abominations!"

The storm had spent itself and a red, springtime sun was peeping over the horizon as de Grandin and I trudged up my front steps with the mutilated girl stumbling wearily between us.

"Put her to bed, my excellent one," de Grandin ordered Nora, my housekeeper, who came to meet us enveloped in righteous indignation and an outing flannel nightgown. "*Parbleu,* she has had many troubles!"

In the study, a glass of steaming whisky and hot water in one hand, a vile-smelling French cigarette in the other, he faced me across the desk. "How was it you knew not that house, my friend?" he demanded.

I grinned sheepishly. "I took the wrong turning at the detour," I explained, "and got on the Yerbysville Road. It's just recently been hard-surfaced, and I haven't used it for years because it was always impassable. Thinking we were on the Andover Pike all the while, I never connected the place with the old Olmsted Mansion I'd seen hundreds of times from the road."

"Ah, yes," he agreed, nodding thoughtfully, "a little turn from the right way, and—pouf!—what a distance we have to retrace."

"Now, about the girl upstairs," I began, but he waved the question aside.

"The mad one had but begun his devil's work on her," he replied. "I, Jules de Grandin, will operate on her eyes and make them as straight as before, nor will I accept one penny for my work. Meantime, we must find her kindred and notify them she is safe and in good hands.

"And now"—he handed me his empty tumbler—"a little more whisky, if you please, Friend Trowbridge."

THE COFFIN OF LISSA

By AUGUST W. DERLETH

THE HORROR OF THE SENTENCE OVERWHELMED ME; IT FELL upon me as the black cloak of night descending on the earth absorbed the light—so it heralded the expiration of my life. I was dazed, speechless with the portent of the verdict. The black-robed judges seemed blurred to my sight as I rose and was taken from the chamber to make room for another poor wretch. Outside, night had fallen, and the murk of the darkness still further depressed my sunken spirits. Through the pall of gloom I could discern no ray of hope. I was doomed! Doomed to die by torture, the slow torture of the iron coffin! The final words of the inquisitors reverberated hollowly in the chambers of my benumbed mind.

Slowly the first shock passed, and slowly I became conscious of my surroundings. My captors were leading me through a long passageway. A few candles glimmered feebly in their brackets at the end of the ill-lighted corridor. In a few moments I faced the iron door of the torture chamber. As the heavy door creaked backward on its rusty hinges, the gleam of the flickering candles cast fitful, menacing shadows on the dreaded coffin in the center of the chamber. The sight filled me with renewed horror, and I was seized with a fierce desire for freedom. But the futile struggle that I essayed was immediately frustrated by my guards, whose strength far exceeded mine. I was roughly thrown into the instrument of torture, from which the lid had been removed. Suddenly my head struck something unyielding and I lapsed into unconsciousness.

From then on I knew but hazily what occurred. When I awoke, my sight encountered nought save Stygian darkness. For a space I lay quiet, summoning to my aid all my faculties. Try as I might I could not pierce the blackness. It now seemed to swirl and eddy before my eyes, and often I closed them for the relief of immovable darkness. Now suddenly I bethought myself of moving my arms. But the attempt resulted in a sharp pain at the juncture of arm and shoulder. This, thought I, could be caused by no other agency than the clamps that I had so often heard of from witnesses of an execution. At that preclusion to my efforts the remembrance of the proceedings of some time past came upon me like a huge wave of the ocean and swept away all the remnants of thoughts that I had been collecting, leaving nothing but fear, stark terror, despair. I realized where I was and with the realization came the thought of unhindered death. I was in the terrible iron coffin of Lissa, from which no man had ever escaped! I began to breathe heavily, and I could feel cold beads of sweat on my brow. I raved, I shouted in rage, I swore terrible oaths, oaths of vengeance against Torquemada, the Grand Inquisitor. But my exertions were too much for me and I was forced to sink back in exhaustion.

Shortly after, a reaction set in and I lay quiet, contemplating my untimely end. I strained my ears for any sounds that might meet them. For a space I heard nought save my irregular breathing, then another sound impinged upon my ears. It was a soft padding sound, a very soft sound, scarcely audible. I listened attentively and attempted to find what occasioned it. It stopped at intervals; it resumed almost at once. Then no sound reached me for some little time, but suddenly I felt a sharp, stinging sensation in my right hand. I strove to draw it toward me, but the sharp pain in my shoulder was augmented with each movement of my arm. I groaned aloud. My arms had been drawn through apertures in the sides of the coffin; they had been chained to the stone floor *for the rats to gnaw upon!*

Again and again I shrieked, but the more often I did so, the more acutely did I realize the utter futility of my efforts. I should not be heard here, so far underground; even if I were heard, no one would liberate me. I sighed, and once more sank back to my rough bed exhausted. The rats were gone now, frightened, no doubt, by my wild screams of terror. But poignantly I realized that they must eventually return. I lowered my eyelids and began to mumble a silent prayer, but I was rudely interrupted.

A new sound, a sound fraught with more dangers and horrors than any I had heard heretofore, reached my ears. A light sound, barely coherent—yet it was there. A creaking sound, slow, in truth, and not continuous, but its portent flung me again into the wildest throes of terror. The sound of the slow, sure descent of the coffin lid! This was the climax of the ghastly tortures I was to undergo. I raised my head to find if I could touch the oncoming lid. But I could not, and the clawing pain in my shoulders as the steel clamps sank into my flesh, caused me to sink back again as quickly as I could. The lid, then, was some distance away, and I had a few hours of grace.

The certainty of death threw open the gates to my memory. I thought of my mistress and of my innocent children, and I sobbed despondently. I traversed and retraversed my entire life from the beginning of my miserable existence to this experience of horror. Gradually my sobs quieted and I had recourse in my God.

For about the space of a glass of sand I lay imperturbably, my lips moving in prayer. Then I became cognizant of the proximity of the lid. I did not again endeavor to reach the cover with my head after my former racking experience, but I resorted to another means of finding its proximity. I summoned what feeble strength I had left and forcibly blew air upward. At once I felt a draft on my face; the air had returned at the propinquity of the lid. At this discovery I sought to compose the feeling of haunting alarm which rose within me, but hardly had I attempted to do so, when a biting sensation in my hands and arms acquainted me with the return of the rats, increased in number. I shrieked and screamed to scare them off, but to no avail, for they attacked me as before.

Simultaneously with these dire occurrences a revolting nausea took possession of my senses. The air had become so foul that it oppressed me with its obnoxious poison. Cold sweat stood out in great beads upon my forehead. All my strength had deserted me; I could no longer even sob, and my breathing became more and more difficult as the lid came down. My imagination began to conjure up before me horrible visions. I believe that I saw Torquemada laughing delightedly at my sorry plight; I imagined Satan grinning at me, watching greedily for my soul. There were others, too, horrible faces leering at me through the gloom. I shut my eyes but I could not shut out these damnable sights. They grew upon me, they assumed ghastly proportions, their faces twisted into horrible gargoylesque counterparts; gradually they merged into a vague, indistinct, grotesque mass, and were swirled away by the eddying darkness.

I could feel the lid now, lightly at first, for it advanced but slowly. A space passed, and the pressure began to pain me. Then came to me a last great power, and I shouted and raved, swearing horribly, until the sweat rolled down my cheeks in great drops. The pressure became more and more pronounced, the air more obnoxious, the gnawing more persistent, the racking pain in my shoulders more torturous with each twitch, and at length I became oblivious of all.

What am I doing here? Was I not in the iron coffin? Have I died and come to life?

The sun casts long patches of light upon the stone floor of my cell, and forms a network of conflicting shadows with the aid of the heavy bars at my window. My clothes are torn, bedraggled. I lack three fingers of the right hand, and one and a half of another of the left.

Why is my food reached toward me at the end of a pole? Why is the door of this room never opened? Why does my keeper hurl disgusting epithets at me every time he nears me? What is the meaning of all this? Why am I called such unbearable, bestial names? Above all, why am I so unjustly called that which is most oft repeated, that which, of all, I deserve the least?

"Lunatic!"

At this word there comes upon me again that horrible nausea that attacked me in the coffin of Lissa, and I shriek in terror as those memories surge over me like the resistless waves of ocean. And as my screams reverberate down the corridor, answering screams come from other cells—and my keeper laughs and shouts filthy curses at me.

SWAMP HORROR

By WILL SMITH AND R. J. ROBBINS

MAYHAP IT WAS THE INFLUENCE OF THE MOON'S RAYS playing on my recumbent form—or was it a subtle stealing of that eery sound into the innermost recesses of my subconscious mind? I had suddenly awakened from a profound slumber, every nerve atingle with the premonition of evil. It was as if a ghostly touch on my brow had called me from the enshrouding incubus of sleep and brought me up all standing with fright! The whole atmosphere seemed surcharged with an electric something that still lingers in my memory. Cursing myself for a timid fool I crossed to the window, through which the moonlight streamed in sickly fashion. And now, as I gazed out upon the vista of gray field and ink-black wood I became conscious of a strange stillness, a complete silencing of all the familiar sounds of nature, becoming with each moment more oppressive. Hark! What was that? Reverberating over the distances, horribly loud, came a frenzied, screeching cry!

As I stood at the open window, wildly straining my ears, it came again. This time the cry had almost a human quality, but there had also crept into it a suggestion of eeriness that made my flesh tingle all over, and a tremor ran over my spine.

Now I am not a coward, and since early childhood I have never feared the dark nor anything which might lurk under its cover. Still, to an essentially city-bred man such an occurrence as this was bound to have a fear-inspiring flavor. I had always, indeed, detested anything rural, even before I suffered the frightful experience I am about to relate; had always entertained for the woods and swamps a nameless, unreasoning fear. It was in response to that same fear that I had migrated from the ancestral residence at the tender age of sixteen, getting a job as errand boy in the near-by city. After this I had held down several minor jobs until I had finally found my métier in telegraphy. It was the latter occupation that was earning me my living when the awful horror of the swamp took place.

That morning Sam Falton, operator and general factotum at my home town station, had started the ball rolling by engaging me in some small talk on the wire. Both being desirous of learning the Phillips press code, we had, for practice, been couching every possible word of our conversation in that language. Apparently he had decided to sign off for the time being when he gave a signal for me to hold the wire a moment. His next words gave me a severe jolt.

Literally, they were, "Ml man js ca in ses u btr cm ses trs smg myx ab it ur dad bn msg nry a wk." These words, unintelligible to the reader, were sufficient to cause me to demand leave of absence for an indefinite period. Translated, they are: "Mail man just came in. Says you better come. Says there's something mysterious about it; your dad been missing nearly a week!"

I had about decided to go back to bed when I heard the sound repeated again and again. It was nearer this time and sounded like the wail of some creature in a frenzy of torture. At times it would end in a long-drawn-out, strangling, rattling howl that made my blood run cold.

Could this have anything to do with my father's disappearance? The sounds might have been made by madman or beast, or by something altogether unearthly. My mind, ever used to quick decisions, was instantly made up. I resolved to see.

The night was hot and humid, and in the hollows a heavy ground fog was beginning to manifest itself, and I suspected that before sun-up the air would be pretty chilly. Plainly, time was short, so I contented myself with a pair of trousers, a sleeveless jersey and a pair of tennis shoes which lay at hand. Snatching a hastily lighted lantern, I dashed out into the pulsing night.

The sounds had evidently issued from a stretch of forest about a quarter mile to the rear of the house, and toward this I made my way. The ground fog had by this time become quite thick, so that at times I had to grope my way through it. Nature had resumed all her various discordant notes. As I entered the forest the odor of decayed vegetation and mould smote my nostrils. The lantern, a relic of bygone days, cast a feeble circle of light which but served to intensify the surrounding gloom. My thoughts, as I struggled through the underbrush and thickets, were anything but cheerful.

At times fantastically formed roots took on the appearance of serpents ever waiting to drag me down. That I did not fall on more than one occasion was more a result of good luck than of agility on my part. I must have proceeded into the depths of the woods for at least a mile when suddenly the fearful cry came again, now in a direction more to my left and somewhat nearer. I shivered and grasped the lantern more tightly, meantime cursing the folly that had sent me on this wild quest unarmed. Then again the cry—fearsomely close!

At this juncture, grown careless of the terrain beneath my feet, I suddenly stumbled violently over a rotting log lying directly in my path. I remember taking a desperate grip on the lantern, which barely prevented it from flying from my hand, when—a most unearthly scream resounded in the bushes not ten feet away, and a huge body dashed against me, brushing me flat and extinguishing the lantern. Before it died the flame flared up into momentary brilliancy, giving me a passing glimpse of a great, wolf-like creature with blood-slavering jaws and terrible glistening fangs!

I struck my head as I fell, and my senses reeled.

I have no distinct recollection of my return to the house. I must have lain unconscious in the forest for some time, for it was nearly dawn when I finally got up and somehow made my way out. Once in bed I dropped again into oblivion, and did not awake until some hours later.

Since my father had had no hired man, and mother had died long years before, there was no one to call me or prepare the meals. When I finally found the ambition to arise and dress, my first act was to get together a meal, for I intended to cover a lot of ground during the day and felt that my stomach should be well fortified. Had I known what lay ahead of me I doubt if I could have eaten anything!

I had about finished my bacon and coffee when I was aroused from a momentary abstraction by a sound from the outside. A quick glance around the premises revealing nothing, I was about to give up the search when I heard it again; but this time it was a low moan, and of a character which I recognized. Hurrying to the back shed I threw open the door. There, brilliantly limned in the shaft of sunlight that streamed in, lay the still form of a huge wolfhound!

I started back aghast. Could this gaunt creature be our good old Fang, the pet with whom father and I had used to spend so many happy hours, and who had greeted me with such rough joy only yesterday? Yes, it was indeed he, for at my call the faithful fellow struggled feebly to his feet, and, swaying drunkenly, wagged a heroic tail.

But to what a terrible state the animal had been reduced! His whole form was wasted to a painful thinness. The skin, hairless in patches, was nearly white, colorless. The poor creature seemed to be suffering from what I could attribute to no other cause than such a weakness as is caused by a heavy loss of blood. And yet, minutely examining every inch of the slackened skin, I could find not a scratch, *no visible wound whatever!*

I lost no time in feeding the dog and did my poor best at doctoring him. My efforts, aided no doubt by the vitality of his ancient wild ancestry, were sufficiently successful to enable the animal after a while to recover enough strength to walk without difficulty, and even to run and fetch sticks. But I knew well that it would be many days before he could regain the robust sturdiness of the day before.

What, I kept wondering, could have been the agency that had brought Fang to this pitiful condition? What could have drained his veins so completely without leaving a single mark? Where had he been the night before, and what frightful thing could have reduced him to the state of abject fear that caused him to dash so madly through the forest uttering those agonized, strangled screams? For I was convinced that the creature I had encountered last night under such terrifying circumstances was none other than Fang, his really monstrous size enlarged in my terror-stricken eyes to gigantic proportions.

But I could swear to the blood I had seen dripping from the beast's jaws. Whence had that come?

The horrible answer to all these questions was vouchsafed me that very day.

It being by now early afternoon, I realized that if I were to search for my father to-day, I should have to start at once. As I locked up the house preparatory to setting out I tried to recall to mind the general topography of the region.

The farm, which has been in the possession of our family more than a century, is of considerable extent, and is made up mostly of timberland and swamp, there being only a few acres of open land. Directly to the rear of the house is a large forest tract, some parts of which have not been penetrated by men for years. Beyond this is an almost unexplored waste known as Marvin's Swamp.

Legend has it that Old Man Marvin, who owned the farm before it came into my family, died in this vicinity under mysterious circumstances, and it is thought that his bones found their last resting place at the bottom of the morass. The only clue to his fate was furnished by his ancient shotgun and a few bloodstains found near a stagnant pool in the depths of the marsh. I shudder as I recall the terrible solution I myself was enabled to furnish to this mystery of long ago!

In starting on the search my footsteps followed almost without deviation the course I had pursued the previous night, but this time I was not alone. The great wolfhound was now my guide, and I soon discovered he was following a scent. Indeed, I had considerable difficulty at times in keeping up with him, so great was his evident desire to lead me to a definite spot.

This forest tract is in itself extensive, and is pretty wild. My father had never allowed any one to hunt here except members of the family and, as a result, the place abounded with partridges, squirrels, rabbits and other small game. Occasionally even, I would get a glimpse of a deer or a fox as it leapt away at my approach. Everywhere was the odor of pine, hemlock and decaying vegetation. The silence of the place was so profound that the smallest sound was immediately noticeable, and even the snapping of twigs under foot and the breaking of dead branches as I made my way through the thickets served to keep my nerves continually on edge. At length we had penetrated to the other side of the forest, and I found myself at the edge of Marvin's Swamp. Somehow, call it premonition or what you will, a cold shiver passed up my spine as I gazed upon this dreary stretch, and I glanced around apprehensively.

Nothing appeared within my field of vision, which could possibly be alarming, so after a brief hesitation I followed the big wolfhound on the trail. Within a few minutes I could see that we were heading toward the vilest part of the great morass, and again that strange presentiment of evil came over me. The ground was getting softer now, and small sink-holes became more and more numerous. For an hour we pushed on, the way becoming more difficult every minute. The vegetation here grew very rankly, and had become almost entirely aquatic. Cat-o'-nine-tails were now in evidence everywhere, especially about the spot where the dog now impatiently awaited me. This spot was at what marked the center of Marvin's Swamp—a small stream of almost stagnant water known as Dead River.

The name is rather a dignity, for Dead River is in reality little more than an arm of the main pool of the swamp. Its course had once been traced back and found to extend through the worst part of the region for about a mile and thence into the hills, where its only source was found to be a series of small springs. At the bank of this repulsive waterway I stopped and began to examine the locality closely. Finally I found what I had been looking for, namely, a multitude of footprints in the soft mud. A glance at these was enough to convince me as to who had made the tracks, but such evidence was as nothing to that which now met my eye. For a little to the right of the trail, half hidden in a tuft of rank grass into which it had evidently been unwittingly dropped, lay father's familiar old hunting knife! I bowed my head; all hope had left me.

But I had little time to stand here sadly musing, for the strange behavior of the dog now claimed my attention. He stood a little way ahead of me along the bank, trembling from head to drooping tail; first whining beseechingly back at me, then snarling with a sort of frightened ferocity as he gazed ahead to where the trail led into a dark, evil-looking glade. Absently dropping the knife into a trousers' pocket, I hastened to follow his fear-halted lead; and my quest came to an abrupt end!

The glade—what a hideous spot it was! The river at this point was but a desolation of cat-o'-nine-tails, rank growths and green, slimy water. Little green lizards basked dreamily on rotting logs and swam lazily about in the stagnant pool. Brilliant-colored dragon-flies poised for a breathless instant over foul, exotic lilies, only to dart away into black, hot aisles of the swamp. Leeches were everywhere, and now and again a water snake came zigzagging among the lily pads in search of prey. More noisome still, the bottom of the pool and its filthy banks were littered with all kinds of dead creatures—all sizes of bodies, from those of tiny squirrels up to the carcasses of bob-cats and even deer. Not one of them bore a visible wound, and every one was almost colorless. Those soaking in the murky water were bloated into gross exaggerations of their proper sizes, but those on the banks were dry, shriveled, shrunken things! All this I noted as in a wondering dream, the while I gazed on the body of my father.

It lay on the bank with one leg dangling in the water, the limbs weirdly contorted, as though the man had succumbed only after a terrific struggle. Nearly demoralized, I flew frantically at the body, seizing it by the shoulders and yanking it clear of the horrible pool. A hasty examination sufficed to show that father had met the same mysterious fate that had taken toll of so many lives in this hateful place.

I had barely made the discovery when I was completely undone by a distant, long-drawn-out howl—the frightened bay of the wolfhound. His mission accomplished, he had promptly deserted, leaving me alone with my dead.

I was not long to wonder why!

What was the terrible fate that could strike down a man in the sanguine glow of physical strength and activity and leave this shriveled white, bloodless death? And that, too, without leaving a single mark on the husk of a body! To be sure, the clothing was covered with dried blood-stains, but whence had the blood come? Was there not some tiny wound which I in my first frantic pawing of the corpse had overlooked—perhaps the two little purple holes which I shudderingly remembered were supposed to be the mark of venomous snake bites? I stooped again, and, clenching my jaws to still my chattering teeth, began a careful search of the drained thing that had been my father. And as the fruitless quest went on there came again that hush, that awed stilling of the myriad sounds of this rank nature about me.

I became conscious of each noise, as it were, when it had ceased to beat its note on my ears. The shrilling of the frogs first dropped out of nature's discordant symphony, to be followed by the chirp of the crickets, the various low bird-twitterings and rustlings, and other sounds, most of them to me fearsomely unidentified. Now all that remained was the droning of bees, punctuated at longish intervals by the mournful *sol do-do-do-lo-do-o-o*—of a far-away swamp robin.

Now, after one dismally long-drawn-out call, the bird became silent, and the only sound left in the steamy, fetid swamp world was that bee-hum. This now seemed slowly to increase in volume until finally the very air became charged and volatile with its menace. At last I could endure the deafening sound no longer and, ear-drums bursting with the throbbing, zooming waves—smothered in them, overwhelmed—I toppled over in a black faint.

I was destined soon to bless that fainting fall, for I was to realize it had saved me from a fate worthy the ingenuity of a thousand fiends—the same ravaged death that had claimed my father.

Of course I could not have lain unconscious more than a minute or two, but at the time it seemed ages before I opened my eyes—opened them to a sun-drenched, somehow less fearful world—to find myself sprawled on my back, evidently in a little depression. Of this hollow, the bottom seemed covered with some wet, sticky substance, which to my not over-critical bones made a rather pleasant couch.

Nature had resumed her normal note, and I became gratefully conscious that the horrible droning of bees was no longer in evidence. As I again closed my eyes in response to a certain feeling of lassitude that ground me, I wondered if it had been a sound from the outside world or if it had come from within me. Dreamily revolving the affair in my mind, I was inclined to believe the whole thing—the hush, the drumming in my ears and the fainting—had been caused by the gradual weakening of my faculties. But then how to account for that weakening?

The mystery was getting too deep for me, and I almost decided to give it all up and flee from this hellish swamp, sending some one in after father's body. At any rate, I could not lie long dreaming in this soft bed. Lazily I opened my eyes; wearily I stretched out an arm; limply I let it fall at my side: and then, screeching with all my poor strength, I leapt to my feet. My outflung arm had dropped with a sirupy splash in what was revealed to my popping eyes as thickening, dark red blood!

And now began the horror—ugh! an experience so incredibly, grotesquely horrid that recollection of its lewd details now halts my pen and imbues me with stark nausea. If I had disliked and distrusted the woods and waste places before, my feeling was nothing compared to the seething, loathing hate that grips me now at the mention of that dread word, swamp.

Reeling giddily, my unmanning utterly completed by the sickening realization that I had been lolling so softly in a bed of blood, I had time only to clutch at a low-hanging vine for support before the things—oh, those fat, slime-sweating, crawling *things*—came on! There seemed to be hundreds of them—snail-shaped things as large as dogs—hemming me in on every side. With a slow, irresistible purpose they advanced in a horrible silence. As they closed in, their silence became broken by a nasty, greasy sound as of molasses being lazily lifted and stirred with a million sticks. Now they were upon me, and I ran amuck!

I leapt on the nearest and tried to scuff them into the earth; I beat them foolishly with my fists; I sought to hug them off my heaving chest; I rolled over and over them; I tore at their filthy bodies with my teeth; the while I uttered one tortured shriek after another. But in my unarmed state I was no match for the horde, and the things continued in their deadly purpose, bearing me down and beginning to fasten themselves on to every part of me. At last my frenzied yells were stilled by a clammy body laid across the whole lower half of my face; and now my eyes, rolling in dumb agony, encountered the foulest scene of all, and I understood.

The blood-filled hollow in which I had been lying! Crowding around all sides of it like pigs at a trough were a dozen of the monsters, greedily and with many blubbery swilling sounds absorbing the clotting gore!

Now I knew the fate that had befallen father, had taken old Marvin years before, had claimed the deer and other animals, had dragged at Fang when he had searched out father's body, and now bade fair to add me to those other letted cadavers. Yes, I could see it all now, could understand anything in this rank world of evil growths.

Bloodsuckers! That's what they were! Great, fat, overgrown leeches; spawned of the filth and grown here to this morbid size by centuries of breeding and interbreeding in the lushness. Oh, the horror that swept me!

It was when the obscene feast drew to a close that I thanked God for the fall I had taken a few minutes before when I had fainted, for there was now revealed in the bottom of the depression the empty sacklike body of one of the gigantic leeches. Evidently the scout of the main herd, it had stolen and fastened itself to my back as I stooped over the remains of my father. Its slow sapping of my life's blood had caused the humming in my ears and finally the deathly faint which had saved my life and been the thing's undoing. For in falling I had landed on my back on a jagged bit of stone which had pierced and emptied the creature, filling my resting place with blood.

The sharp tip of the rock now protruded through the flattened carcass and became my inspiration. What did it suggest to me? I was fast sinking into a soft, black oblivion and could not think—did not care to, particularly. Now another slimy body drew along my head and settled itself in such a way as to cover my eyes, shutting out the scene completely. Still the memory of that rock sliver persisted and disturbed me, vaguely. What did it remind me of, anyway? Well, I didn't know—never mind. But yes, I *did* know! Now I had it—a knife! Father's knife, in my pocket!

Gone in a breath was that deathly languor. I became imbued with the strength of desperation. I heaved, I threshed—one hand came clear. Lifting the arm, almost unmindful of the weight of a monster still clinging to it, I worked my hand between two foul bodies into my pocket. And now I drew it out, clutching that blessed knife!

Butchery! Blood!

My first kill was the bloated thing that lay across my scalp and eyes. But what a flood of gore now cascaded over me, filling hair, ears and eyes! Blinking an eye, I plunged the knife into the stinking monster that blocked my mouth—and was again soaked in a green-streaked red deluge. My mouth free, I found strength once more to yell, but now a note of battle and triumph in the cry!

Slashing and hacking, I gained my feet. Now I seemed to swim in a sea of blood, as sinking the knife to the hilt again and again, I finally freed my legs. And even as I had used my mouth the instant I had cleared it, so now I used my legs. Stumbling, groping, crying, laughing I ran.

THE PARASITIC HAND

By R. ANTHONY

(*NOTES FROM THE DIARY OF DR. BURNSTRUM*)

I. THE EXTERNAL HAND

JUNE 6, 1925.—THIS MORNING I ENCOUNTERED THE strangest case of my twenty years of practice. John Pendleton, a young real estate agent of Cassia City, requested a physical examination, particularly of a growth on his left side. After he had stripped I saw that he had a bandage taped to his side.

Upon removal of the bandage the growth proved to be a *completely formed right hand,* its base (or wrist) fastened at the curve of the eleventh rib, directly beneath the armpit. The hand was slightly open, the palm turned outward and upward. In size it was that of a babe's several months old.

"How long have you had this?" I asked Pendleton.

"Always, as far back as I can remember," he answered. "I was born with it, so I was told. But it wasn't always the same size."

I looked up in surprise. "Not the same size? What do you mean?"

He hesitated and flushed. "Well, it—it was——" He made a quick gesture and added energetically, "Doctor, don't think me a fool, or an imaginative idiot. I am a college man and not given to silly imaginings. It's the truth I am telling you, remember! That hand used to be small, very small.

But in the last three months *this hand has been growing steadily.* And you see its present size!"

A parasitic hand it was, clearly so. I knew the thing, for I had seen such structures before. But a growing hand! And growing after the host had reached maturity! That seemed impossible.

By accident I placed an index finger against the palm of the hand. Immediately its fingers closed upon my fore-fingers and *gripped it firmly.* Here was surprise! Usually these parasitic growths are inactive, without nerves and provided with a very scant blood supply. But the grip of this parasitic hand was firm and strong, like that of a babe. It took considerable effort to release my finger, so tenacious was the grip.

And after I had freed myself, it continued to close and open, much like a small babe's, and finally made an infant fist.

Pendleton nodded as he observed the experiment. "That's what it does to me," he said. "But only since the last six weeks. It never did that before then. Now it's a nuisance. It clutches at everything I put on—at my underwear, my shirt, my pajamas. The only way I can keep it from pulling and tearing at my clothes is to bandage it and tape it fast to my body. Even then I feel it wriggle and clutch at things. It's bothered me a lot. What does this thing mean, doctor?"

"Well——" I hesitated.

"Go ahead, doctor," Pendleton urged. "I've been told that it's a sort of parasite. But I don't understand exactly. How the deuce can an extra hand be a parasite? Why should a hand grow from my side? Remember, I was born with it!"

"You probably were a twin," I explained, "at least in the early stages of your embryonic life. In fact, you and the twin probably came from a single egg. Identical twins, you know, come from a single fertilized egg. Sometimes such twins are equally developed; more often one twin is better developed than the other. What it means is that the twins compete with each other during embryonic and fetal life, and one may develop at the expense of the other. As a matter of fact, *one twin may absorb the other,* sometimes completely so, sometimes leaving a few traces such as a hand or foot. Apparently you absorbed your twin nearly completely. This hand is all that is left of him."

"Well, I'll be hanged!" Pendleton ejaculated in wonderment. "But I clearly see how that is possible and that your explanation fits. But look here, doctor! Then in a way I must be two personalities merged in one body—myself and the other twin." He paused and his eyes grew wide with some astonishing thought. "Doctor! Do you—do you suppose that the personality, the soul, of the other twin is still intact and is now trying to establish itself in this growing hand?"

"Of course not," I said firmly.

But while I photographed him and bandaged the hand the idea suggested by his question kept revolving in my mind. I may as well put down my ideas of the matter:

If the interpretation of twins is correct, then Pendleton is the autosite and the hand is all that is left of the parasite. But what became of the personality, the soul of the parasite, when its body was merged into that of the stronger twin, the autosite? If we allow it entity, then the fact that the parasitic hand, after being dormant for twenty-three years, is now growing, would seem to indicate that the parasite was dominated by Pendleton until he had attained his full development, and that now the dormant personality of the other twin is asserting itself and trying to establish its own proper self. A strange theory! Yet it seems to fit! How else account for the growth?

June 7, 1925.—I have the general photographs and the X-rays before me. The X-rays show that the hand is completely formed, all carpals, metacarpals and phalanges being clear and of proper shape. A rudiment of radius and ulna are present, but fade away near the point of attachment of the hand. The muscles and fasciæ of the hand are attached to the intercostal muscles below the eleventh rib. Blood supply from an intercostal artery. A doubtful spot may be a ganglion for the nerve supply.

June 15, 1925.—Pendleton in again to-day, after a week's absence from town. At my question, "How is the hand getting on?" he answered shortly, "See for yourself, doctor."

He stripped, and I proceeded to remove the tape and bandages.

I started back when I saw the hand. "Why, it has grown!" I exclaimed. "It seems twice as large as last week. Like that of a child of five or six years!"

Pendleton nodded grimly. "That's why I told you to see for yourself, doctor! I wanted you to be sure about that fact. What are you going to do with it?"

"Remove it," I said firmly. "This week! It should not be a very serious matter."

A queer look came into Pendleton's eyes. "You don't suppose that in removing this—er—this—what is left of my twin, we would be—or—doing murder?"

I smiled at the fancy. "No, hardly. You may liken this hand to a tumor. Removal of a tumor does not constitute murder, does it? A tumor is a parasitic growth. This hand is a parasitic growth. We remove parasitic growths before they become too dangerous. Murder?"

"Well, no," he said. "But I had a crazy dream about it the other night," he added apologetically. "I dreamed I saw my twin and that he said, 'You have had your share of life at my expense. Now I want my own. Don't you dare tamper with things. I'm going to have my way.' And then I woke up."

"Rather obvious," I commented. "A natural sequence of our conversation of twin entities, or rather, of one twin overcoming the other. Nothing to it, my boy." I patted him on the shoulder. "What do you say about three days from now? That will give you time to prepare. Not a serious operation, you understand. But it is good to be prepared."

He assented, and after taking a few more photographs I dismissed him.

July 21, 1925.—San Francisco, Calif. A telegram just received from Pendleton: "Come back to operate. Urgent." The illness and death of my father had called me to California before I could operate on Pendleton. And the disposition of the estate required a longer absence than contemplated.

I wired back, "On way in two days. Expect me by twenty-fifth."

July 26, 1925.—Back in Cassia City. Pendleton met me at the station this afternoon. He looked pale and thin and haunted. Despite the heat he was shivering. "Thank God you have come, doctor!" he cried. "I am going insane."

I looked at him curiously. "You don't mean that the hand——"

"It's—it's growing, doctor!" His eyes held a wild and frightened look. "It is larger—and a *part of the forearm has grown out!*"

I stared at him in unbelief. "Hardly possible," I said.

"But it is, doctor," he insisted. "Doctor, you haven't known me for a fool. This thing has given me no rest for a month. It is always twisting and pulling, as if it were trying to reach into me for something. It's driving me mad!" Cold terror was in his voice.

The taxi stopped at my office and we hurried in. Pendleton stripped quickly and jerked off the bandages. "There!"

He was right. The hand had grown and now was the size of that of a vigorous boy of fourteen or fifteen. But, in addition, the *lower half of a forearm had grown out!*

July 27, 1925.—Removed the parasitic hand from Pendleton's side this morning. Would not repeat the operation for a million dollars. It was a terrifying experience.

General and local anæsthetics used. But while P. responded excellently, the parasitic hand remained active; in fact, it seemed to be animated with a fighting spirit. It seized the wrist of one of the surgical nurses during the preliminaries and held it in a relentless grip, so that she fainted in horror.

Later, when I proceeded to make the first incision, it seized my wrist and with remarkable force tried to direct the scalpel *toward Pendleton's heart.* Only by dropping the scalpel did I avoid stabbing P. to death.

I then applied anæsthetics to the hand itself, with no appreciable results. Finally, in desperation, I pushed a wad of cotton into the hand, threw a loop around its wrist and had one of the nurses hold it taut. By thus misleading and misdirecting its efforts I was able to proceed. (How silly these words sound, as if I had been dealing with a separate entity! And yet that seems to be the only plausible assumption that would help to explain.)

Throughout the operation the hand kept up its writhing and clutching motions. As I made the final cut it jerked loose from my hand, fell to the floor and then fastened around the ankle of the chief surgical nurse. In horror she dropped the instruments, screaming hysterically, and ran out of the operating room and fainted in the hallway.

I darted after her and removed the fiendish hand. Even then it kept up its autonomous struggle. It was with a feeling of relief that I dropped it into a jar filled with preservative and returned to complete my work on Pendleton.

I was careful to remove all traces of the attaching structures, and also treated the vestiges with X-rays to destroy all rudiments of the growth.

The operation, though simple, and normally requiring perhaps half an hour, lasted nearly four hours, because of the constant interference of the parasitic hand. Brent, the interne in charge of the anæsthesia, the three nurses and I were complete wrecks at the end of the ordeal. After we wheeled the operating table from the room and turned the patient over to the special nurse, we found that the nurses had fallen to the floor, either in a faint or exhausted.

Brent looked over the room. "Rather like a shambles to-day," he remarked in ghoulish humor.

I nodded and dropped into a chair, and knew no more. I believe I fainted also.

August 10, 1925.—Pendleton dismissed from the hospital to-day. Only a circular scar indicates the position of the parasitic hand.

II. THE INTERNAL HAND

March 5, 1926.—Pendleton dropped in this morning. He looked worried and thoughtful.

"You're not sleeping well, my boy," I told him.

"You wouldn't sleep well, either, doctor, if you felt something clawing within you."

I manifested surprise. "What do you mean?"

He smiled wearily. "Exactly what I said. Something clawing and pulling within me. And right at the place where that hand was removed."

"Hm!" I muttered. "That sounds rather curious."

"Call it crazy, but I know what it is like! It is as if a hand were gripping lightly, shoving things aside, pulling at me, as if somebody—doctor, *that hand is coming back!*"

I looked sharply at him. No, he did not look silly. Of course, like other physicians, I knew that the imagination can produce astonishing delusions. But Pendleton did not seem to me to be of that sort.

"Strip and get up on the examining table," I ordered tersely.

With a sigh he obeyed. I could find little. The circular scar showed signs of disappearing. Below it the abdomen seemed faintly distended, but not enough to be symptomatic. The stethoscope revealed only the normal sounds, and palpation was similarly uninforming.

"Let's see what an X-ray will show," I suggested.

March 6, 1926.—Just examined the X-ray prints. Nothing important indicated, no signs of congestion as in a tumorous growth.

I went back through the files for the X-rays taken last June. Comparison showed that some of the internal organs had been displaced. The stomach, for one, was pushed to the right a distance of nearly two inches.

This discovery surprised me, and in my astonishment I dropped the print. I bent down to pick it up, and jerked back in amazement. For from a distance I saw what had escaped me in a closer view; *a hand was outlined within the body,* to the left of the stomach.

I picked up the print and examined it carefully. No, it was not a positive structure. It was merely that certain structures had been pushed aside and that the vacated portion had the outline of a hand. No evidence of actual entity, only the handlike outline.

A puzzling case! Is Pendleton right in saying that the hand had returned? But it isn't an actual structure. A phantom, then?

March 15, 1926.—Pendleton complains of internal pains and difficulty in breathing. I have prescribed sedatives.

March 20, 1926.—Pendleton ordered to the hospital last night. Another X-ray taken, with orders to rush. Just examined the plate. The hand-shaped space has increased in size and has pushed upward. The technician called my attention to it. So she has noticed it, too! But there is no sign of a tumor. Just an absence of structures, an outline of a hand. What to do?

March 22, 1926.—Pendleton suffering and in agony. "It's reaching for my heart!" he groaned. "Can't you do something, doctor?"

I gave him a strong sedative. After that I discussed with Brent the chances of an operation. But operate for what?

After that I went to the surgery and told the nurses of

the possibility of operating on P. in a day or two. Miss Cummings, the chief surgical nurse, and her two assistants paled at the announcement, and then did something rather unethical. They refused.

"No," said Miss C., with a shiver. "No, doctor! I can't work with you on that case. I should faint with terror."

Her two assistants expressed themselves similarly.

"Please, doctor! Don't ask me," said Miss Cummings. "I'll—I'll never forget how—how that—that *thing* seized my ankle." She collapsed at the recollection and began to cry softly.

"Do you wish Pendleton to die without a chance?" I asked gravely. "I must do something, I am afraid, but I do not know what to do. I do not know what is troubling him. He is suffering, that is evident. The X-rays tell too little. As it is, I must proceed on a pure guess. I do not know what I'll find. But it is Pendleton's only chance. That is, if you will do your duty."

"Duty!" The appeal to duty was effective. Miss Cummings smiled faintly and said in a low voice, "Very well, doctor! I'll try!"

Her assistants nodded in fearful assent.

March 23, 1926.—The climax came this morning. I was making the rounds of the patients and stopped in Pendleton's room. He had slept quietly last night, he said. "Still, I feel queer, doctor! As if things had come to a decision. Sort of ready for the final battle. It's going for my heart, I know, trying to take my life for its own. Can't you do something, doctor?"

I reassured him and remarked that we would probably operate on him to-morrow.

"Thank God!" he muttered. "I don't think I can stand this much longer. Do you think you can rid me of this—whatever it is?"

"I hope so," I answered. "In fact," I added, quite contrary to my actual belief, "I feel sure that I can. I've been studying up this matter and know something definite now."

My fabulation gave him confidence and he seemed more cheerful. So I left him and went down the corridor to see other patients.

Scarcely ten minutes later I heard a fearful scream, a choking cry of "Help!"

I rushed into the hallway and saw the nurses making for Pendleton's room. But they stopped at his door and shrank back.

I ran up and pushed them aside.

Pendleton was in a turmoil, his bed a cyclone of whirling sheets and blankets. He was twisting, tumbling and bounding up and down, his groans fearful to hear.

Just a few seconds! Then the sheets were whipped aside and I saw Pendleton. His face was red, eyes blood-shot and staring glassily, the mouth wide open, chin pendent, and tongue protruding.

"He's—he's—got me!" he gasped. His body rocked uncertainly; his lips moved in a rotary motion; there was a final "A-a-aah-h-h!"; then he snapped erect, and fell over on his side.

Pendleton was dead. I tried restoratives, but it was no use. The coroner, Dr. Bidwinkle, performed the autopsy, in which I helped him. We found the abdominal organs pushed aside as indicated in the X-rays. Just above this the diaphragm was ruptured, the lung shoved aside, the pericardium ripped open. The heart was contracted and furrowed, as if *a fully grown hand had squeezed it until it stopped beating.*

Dr. Bidwinkle was astounded. "Of all the crazy things!" he muttered.

So I told him of the case and also showed him the photographs. "Hell!" he exclaimed, after I had concluded. "You and I, Burnstrum, don't know it all! I think you're right, but we can't afford to expose ourselves to possible ridicule. Your X-rays and witnesses wouldn't convince one out of ten physicians. There are some people that you simply can't convince! So why bother? Here's what I propose to put down on the certificate: 'Death from hemorrhage induced by internal rupture.' Do you agree?"

"Yes, it will be better that way," I said. "But kindly note this!" I added, turning to Pendleton's body. I reached over and placed the fingers of my hand—the right hand—into the impressions or furrows of Pendleton's heart. *The fingers and thumb fitted the grooves.*

THE DEATH CRESCENTS OF KOTI

BY ROMEO POOLE

OUR PREPARATIONS FOR SLEEP IN THE TROPICAL NIGHT having been completed, Dr. Seego stood back and surveyed his invention with pardonable pride. Out of slender bars of angle steel made for the purpose he had fashioned a cage near the top of a big hardwood tree, a shelter large enough to support two folding cots, one on each side of the tree trunk, and furnished with a steel ladder in lieu of a stairway. When the panels of fine screen were set in place we had a sleeping gallery proof against all animals, insects and birds, and high enough above the ground to be cool and airy.

"Bugs may come and bugs may go," commented the doctor, "but we'll be as safe in that conning tower as a dollar in the U. S. Mint."

"Unless," joked Mark Frissian, "some of your friend Siwaloo's devils come to visit you."

"I'll take a chance on any scrub South Pacific devil opening that Yale lock," responded the doctor.

"Who's sharing your tree-top nest to-night, Doc?" asked Frissian, without any showing of envy.

"Mace was the first applicant."

Frissian turned to me. "You've got the makings of a real explorer in you," he said jovially. "I'm not afraid, but I'll take my chances on a good sleep aboard the *Magpie* the first night. If you fellows find it so delightful here after a trial, we can set up more bird cages to-morrow." And he and

Phelan, with the two black laborers, returned to the boat landing.

Dr. Seego had conceived this expedition to Koti Island to observe the odd race of Polynesian savages who occupied the place. Having been here previously himself, he knew the lay of the land and boasted a personal acquaintance with old Siwaloo, chief of the colony. The uncanny resemblance between all Polynesian languages made it easy for the doctor to master the dialect of Koti, and he held a long conference with the aged chief promptly upon landing.

When we two had ascended to our screened dwelling that night, Seego drew the steel ladder up until the bottom end was out of reach of the ground. Noting my surprise, the doctor explained.

"Frissian tried to kid us about the devils on the island," he said, "but he didn't know there was more truth than poetry in his suggestion. When I last saw this place four years ago there were nearly twenty-five hundred people here; to-day, old Siwaloo tells me, his colony numbers a scant hundred and fifty."

"The result of disease?" I suggested.

"Apparently not. The people are being killed off by some agency they don't understand; and I'll have to confess that at present I don't understand it either. You've noticed that this cliff we are on is roughly V-shaped. The inside of the V is all rock formation, and the people live in caves, partly natural and partly chiseled in the face of the cliff. The only approach to these caves is by the trail we came up on. You noticed, of course, that it winds back and forth from level to level, giving access to all the cliff dwellings, and it is guarded every night. Yet something manages to elude the guards, get into caves far up the cliff, and inflict fatal injuries on the occupants. Lately this plague has fallen on so many of the men, especially the young men, that there is little life left in the colony."

"Aren't the victims able to explain what has happened?" I asked.

"They are usually delirious or dead when discovered. I haven't had time to go over the case thoroughly with Siwaloo, but so far it has me baffled about as completely as it has him. We'll get the whole story to-morrow, and see what we can do for the old man."

We smoked in silence for a few minutes, the sparse jungle around us being almost devoid of animal life, when there came a distinct vibration in our tree, as if a weight had landed against it. We strained our ears for a sound, and at last there came a furtive scratching and the faintest rustling like a rubber raincoat as the thing climbed upward toward us. The trap-door through which we had entered was closed beneath our feet, and the doctor, anxious for a look at the would-be intruder, stooped to open it. At the first click of the latch, however, the thing abruptly ceased to scratch, and only the faint, sudden vibration of the tree told us that it had leaped without pausing to study the consequences. We never heard it light. A flock of sleepy birds in the nearest tree, some fifty yards away, stirred themselves and squawked plaintively, and then all was silent.

This incident, with its mysterious ending, gave both of us plenty of food for shuddering reflection. There was no near-by tree to which a thing of that evident size could have leaped; yet it hadn't dropped. Was it a huge bird? Birds do not light low on a tree and climb, especially into a strange nest with a human scent. A monkey? No monkey could have landed silently from so high a jump.

My sleep was much troubled by visions of creeping monsters that came through the walls of our shelter, and I was impatient as a child to hear the savages' description of their mysterious enemy, which we got the next forenoon.

"There is a tradition of my fathers," said the venerable Siwaloo, stroking his long white beard, "that the other part of this land, around yonder ancient volcano across the river, was once inhabited by a puny race of people not like ourselves. They neither ate, nor drank, nor slept as we do. They were smaller than our people, and not good fighters with spear or knife. In short, we could not enjoy any kind of companionship with these weaklings.

"As it was not a pleasure to continue fighting year after year with these people, and as we did not want their wives or other possessions, my fathers destroyed the spindling race, as we would do to-day in a like case. If one is to live in Koti, either he must be strong, to take care of himself with club and spear, or he must be pleasing or useful. My fathers killed all these brown-skinned people because they were neither.

"So far, all was right. But now that a scourge has come upon us, we can only say that these worthless pests have returned from the dark world as devils seeking to destroy our good race.

"My people can deal with snakes, with monkeys, with tigers if need be, but we know not the ways of devils, and we are helpless. Perhaps they go through the solid rock, or make themselves unseen to our sentries. We guard our trail; yet they go where they will on that same trail to do their killing. We fasten our doors with staves and thongs blessed by all the gods, and they are found open, with death inside. If the wise Americans know aught of the ways of devils, and can drive out this curse, we will repay them well in any such goods as we have, especially wives, of which we have now far too many for the remaining men."

"Chief Siwaloo," said the doctor, "could not these things climb to the top of your cliff and descend by ropes to your doors, there to do their work and then go either up or down on the same ropes?"

"The cliff," said the chief, "cannot be climbed by anything alive except at one or two points, and these are closely guarded day and night. The broad wall that faces the sea is covered with small bush, but not my hardiest soldier will try to climb it to-day, although hundreds have tried in other years. The cliff is of soft rock, that cracks off in great flat pieces, like the scales of fish. The little green bushes feed on the wet surface, and having no long roots they will not support the weight of half a man. So, even if one were small enough to trust his weight to these little bushes, somewhere up the bluff the rock must give way, and death be the answer. That side guards itself, my friend.

"And there have been no ropes. There is a scream in the night. Two minutes are gone before the nearest of us can get out to look, and nothing is to be seen. If there were ropes, some one above or below must see them in front of his door, but there is nothing.

"The victims rave about the vision of a devil in a long, flapping coat going out the door. Perhaps they see something—perhaps it is only their idea of a devil, learned from white sailors. I do not know. Surely no man would wear a long cloak in Koti. Nor would man leave the sign of the three half-moons on every victim.

"If you doubt my belief of devils, sir Americans, but follow me, and you shall see the latest victim, whose body is not yet given to the ground."

We went with him into the vault-like cave where the body of the lost warrior lay in state. On the cheek were three crescent-shaped marks, each probably half an inch long, the concave sides of the crescents facing each other. The cuts had been badly infected, and in anything but a savage, death might have resulted from the filth alone. The victims, Siwaloo told us, had all been marked exactly alike. On some exposed part of the face or body there always appeared those three little crescent-shaped cuts, and the strongest victim rarely lived longer than sunrise after a night attack.

"Yonder old volcano," warned the chief, as we were leaving him, "is a place of strange things. My people have thought that these devils might dwell there, and they have tried to hunt them out, seeking in the dark save at the mountain's base. They never found anything alive, but even so they returned sickened, and some died within a day or two.

"Such was all the success we had in the black cave. As for the old crater itself, we think it is the home of the king of all devils. The inside walls of the crater are much the same as the face of this cliff, and they cannot be scaled safely. My men dread to go near its edge for fear of spells, although the bravest have ventured there at times without learning anything. Strange cries seem to come from far down in the crater, and our goats and dogs that have prowled too near its edge at night have disappeared, not to return. My white friends must be protected by most powerful gods if they would go near the volcano at either top or bottom, or you will never return."

There was a suggestion from Phelan that some of us take a turn at watchman duty upon the face of the cliff, but the doctor vetoed it. "We would be just as helpless as old Siwaloo is, or more so," he said. "The trouble comes only on dark nights, and we might see something if we had our searchlight thrown on the cliff at the right time. The weather is clear now, and they won't be bothered to-night. To-morrow we'll have a look at the cave that troubles our black friend so."

The principal barrier that prevented Siwaloo's people from exploring that fearful cave seemed to be that it was dark and they had no lights except crude fish-oil lanterns or pine knots, which the draft through the cave soon blew out. Hence when the four of us, Dr. Seego, Frissian, Phelan and I, entered the place we were armed with a storage battery and a 250-watt electric light.

The bottom of the cave was virtually all rock, but at intervals there were black, moldy pools of mud, emitting a vile odor.

"Here," said Seego, "is probably where our barefooted friends from across the river met their fate. Poking around here in the dark, they could easily get scratched and skinned, and if I'm not mistaken that mud is dangerous." And he took up a sample in a little bottle.

From the first we had been conscious of a noise that seemed too loud to be caused by the wind; and after a twenty-minute climb up a well-worn trail on the rock bottom, we came out upon the edge of an underground stream that roared through the rocky cavern like a freight train through a tunnel. The cave at this point opened into a large space, probably forty or fifty feet high above the surface of the water, and although there was apparently no way of crossing the stream there was plentiful evidence of human workmanship in the subterranean cavern.

Crude scaffolds had been built up the rocky walls on each side of the stream, so that one could climb high up above the water. These structures were of sticks not much larger than a broomstick, and were put together in the most crude and awkward ways. They were not strong enough to hold the weight of one grown man at any point, yet every stick was worn on the top as if from continual climbing up the framework.

Here was work beyond the intelligence of any known animal—yet not strong enough for human use. What could the answer be? Did men labor to make a climbing place for monkeys? And how did anything cross that stream to do the same work on the other side?

We sought for a long time for some means of proceeding, but as none became apparent, the doctor decided to come again and bring steel material from the ship with which to construct some sort of a bridge.

On board the *Magpie,* Seego analyzed the mud from the cave. After half an hour's work he came out on deck where Frissian and the rest of us were planning the bridge work.

"Anything in the mud?" hailed Frissian.

"Plenty. Arsenic, antimony and sulphate of mercury from the rocks; bacteria enough to pollute the Pacific Ocean, and traces of picrotoxin from cocculus berries, which must have been carried in from the outside. Nature did her worst on that mud, and whoever finished the job certainly was thorough."

Four of us were now using the "bird cages" for sleeping, on account of their coolness, and as we threaded our way up the path to the top of the cliff old Siwaloo came out of his royal cave-dwelling with much trouble written in his wrinkled face, inquiring if we had made any progress against the mysterious killers.

"We know little as yet, friend Siwaloo," replied the doctor, speaking the savage's dialect, "but I believe I can overcome the poison of these devils. In three days, or four, perhaps we may find their stronghold and try other means upon them. So, if the weather remain cloudless, as now, your colony may not suffer another single loss."

"Clear weather the gods are giving us," said Siwaloo, "but your goodness has not reckoned with yonder smoke." He pointed across the river toward a small volcanic hill beyond the one in which we had explored. A thin stream of smoke drifted upward from the summit of the hill, and the slow but steady wind brought it across the land, so that the sky was somewhat darkened.

"The smoke has always been with us," explained the old chief, "and we have given it no notice, any more than a thunderstorm or a summer rain, for the hill does nothing but smoke. But now, when the wind comes this way, it makes dark nights for the three-moon devils to work in, that is why we dread to see the smoke coming. By the end of another watch the moon will be hidden and—death may come among us again."

Seego pondered this a long time. "Chief Siwaloo, is there any one family more likely to be attacked than others?"

"Yes. It has always been the way of my people for the warriors to decorate the doors of their caves with the teeth of wild animals. This is an honor to our gods, and we cannot stop it, even though it guide these demons who come to destroy us. A warrior of Koti would rather die than forego this sign of his bravery. And it seems that the three-moon things notice these signs, for they always strike at my best fighters.

"The four brothers Banota were good fighters and brave, hence they had the largest animal teeth and the most of them. Half a year ago the devils singled them out for death, and now there is but one Banota. And with every dark night—who knows what may happen to him? Every family of fighting men has suffered the same way, until to-day I am king of a colony of women, and almost without any army."

At this Seego lapsed into English, shutting out Siwaloo from the conversation, and briefly translated for us.

"Boys, you can all see as well as I can the kind of intelligence that is doing this killing, or directing it. How they get here, or how they escape, is another story, but no animal ever read the signs on a cave door, nor cared whether it killed men or women. Whoever does this is interested in making the colony powerless; hence their preference for fighting men.

"I'd like to know more about these spooky things, what they are and how they work, before I come to loggerheads with them; but on the contrary there are reasons why I'd like to trap some of them to-night, if it can be done. I hate to see Siwaloo's people wiped off the earth without a chance to save themselves; and half a dozen of his men may be killed to-night. In the second place, it's an absolute certainty that the killers are not armed with guns or any civilized weapons, and they can't be dangerous in the least beyond the reach of their claws. We know to a certainty that they use mud out of the cave for poison, and if the worst came to the worst I believe I could save a victim after he had been attacked."

"Well, what's the idea, Doc?" asked Frissian. "Do you propose for one of us to go and sleep with the last of the Banota boys?"

"You're a rotten humorist, Mark," commented the doctor. "No, I don't think brother Banota's cave is any place for safe and sound sleeping on dark nights. But I am game to fix up a net of fine cables and lay for the midnight callers, wherever Siwaloo thinks they may drop in. What do you say?"

"Doc," replied Frissian, "in the eighteen years we've followed this gentle game I don't believe you can look back and recall a time when I've balked at anything because it was dangerous. But I don't believe we're prepared to make a success of your idea to-night. It's late, and we'd have to plan our trap as well as make it, and I don't think we ought to tackle the job."

"On the contrary," said Seego, "I've done most of the engineering in my head already. It's nothing but an extra-strong monkey-snare. And we'll have a big light in the cave to keep the thing from surprising us."

In the end, of course, the indomitable Swede doctor had his way, and we scurried about as fast as possible to bring up the materials from the ship.

Long before the witching hour arrived, we had fitted out three of the best-decorated caves with nets of fine steel cable, hung so that they could be dropped quickly, and so arranged that should we capture any catlike monstrosity we could keep aloof from its claws and teeth. We also had lights, wired to substantial batteries, which the islanders feared only a little less than the three-moon devils.

The last of the Banotas pleaded for a chance to be in at the finish. He was marked for death, he said, and it was his ambition to die fighting. Seego had no objections except the fear that the gallant Banota might get excited and hurt some one in case of a capture. However, he finally exacted a promise from the warrior not to do anything rash, and we all assumed our appointed places.

The soldiers' caves were all large, as befits prominent men, and we had ample room to stretch out and await what might happen. Dr. Seego and I with Banota and a black deck-hand from the yacht, took up the vigil in Banota's cave, while Frissian and Phelan made their ambush in another. A third cave had a net with an automatic trap and alarm, but no occupant. As the last fish-oil lamp was put out, leaving us in the humid blackness of a tropical night, the adventure took on a decidedly creepy aspect, and I doubt very much that the most benighted savages in the colony were any worse scared than I was.

Hours came and went, hours that we counted by our radium-faced watches, and which otherwise might have been mistaken for centuries. One o'clock came, and no disturbance. Two o'clock dragged by on leaden feet. Sleep tugged at our eyes.

A scratch on the rock landing in front of the cave entrance, and every nerve was on edge. A rustling sound, as of a rubber raincoat. The inky blackness of the door grew denser.

Slowly something moved toward the center of the cave, where Banota usually slept. I could sense the big savage stiffening in his corner for a spring at the intruder—a spring that dared death in its most terrible form. Seego's hand moved, and like a shot down came the weighted net and a blinding flash of white light.

Something blackish-gray tore and twisted helplessly inside the net, unable to escape or to reach any of us, for it was secured in the middle of the cave like a fly on a spider web.

Clouds of dust, the only enemy we were not prepared for, rose and blanketed the scene at the same time the sudden light blinded our eyes. In the midst of the confusion big Banota, goaded to fury at the proximity of what he supposed to be his enemy, sprang barehanded toward the squirming mass in the net, bent on finishing the matter hand to hand.

The doctor, to save Banota's life, loosened the wire that led toward the back of the cave and attempted to swing the thing nearer to the door until he could crowd between Banota and the captive, for he did not want either one destroyed.

But instantly everything went wrong. In the space of a second Banota let out a yell of pain, the doctor made a false move with the cables, and the thing we had trapped jerked itself free and went out the cave door like a black shadow, the rest of us plunging helplessly out after it. But of course it was gone.

Our searchlight did not illuminate the outside, but savages with pine knots and oil torches were swarming toward the scene of action from both up and down the trail, and none had met or seen anything.

The next minute the gallant Banota began to groan, and sank down upon the rocky trail in a deathly sickness. Seego turned the bright light on the man, and there, upon one stalwart black leg, was the sign of the three crescents.

There was no delay now. Whipping out that ever ready first-aid kit, the doctor opened and cauterized the wound, and then administered a hypodermic of strychnine, followed by a stiff drink of brandy. Before we left the savage colony at dawn, we had the satisfaction of having beaten the plague on at least one ground, for Banota showed a marked improvement; and his complete recovery in the next three days gave the colony much cause for rejoicing.

We had failed to trap the clawing thing that was destroying Siwaloo's army, we had not learned whether it was beast or human, nor how it made its amazing escapes; but we had analyzed its venom and exposed its place of living, in addition to beating it out of one victim.

These factors all added to our enthusiasm for finishing the job of exploring in that black cave across the river, and we worked like beavers during the next three days, throwing a curious sort of suspension bridge across that tempestuous underground stream. Frissian was a master engineer in tight places, and by nightfall of the third day the steel framework rested firmly on both sides of the stream. The work of exploring the unknown portion was to proceed the next day.

Uncanny as the project was, there was no restraining a single member of our party from going through the perilous cave next morning. Seego in the lead, as usual, followed by two of our own black men from the *Magpie,* then Frissian and I with two more blacks, and the rest of our party bringing up the rear, we crossed the narrow foot-bridge that had been thrown up, and entered the upper end of the cave, that dwelling place of silent, terrible danger which no man could define.

The passage here led steadily upward, and the footing was dry and not unpleasant. The continuous draft of air from above lessened one's inclination to feel faint, and we were as alert and full of adventure as schoolboys when we finally came upon the first signs of what we sought.

Our bridging work had knocked out a considerable part of the crazy scaffolding we found in the cavern, and here, on the floor of the passageway, we found little piles of hardwood sticks of a size and length suitable for rebuilding the work. Whatever these murderous cavern ghouls were, they had evidently started to repair their handiwork when something interrupted them and caused them to drop the bundles of sticks in the passage.

We all helped ourselves to samples of these sticks, and carried along one or two apiece, trying to learn how they had been cut, and where; and our curiosity in this line proved valuable a few minutes later. Beyond this spot, the passage suddenly opened into a wide underground space that must have covered several acres, for our searchlights did not reach its farthest limits. Daylight, somewhat subdued, came in from somewhere ahead of us, and occasional deposits of phosphorus made a ghostly light in dim corners and crevices, but we still had to use our artificial light to see our way.

The spacious cavern was somewhere near level on the bottom, although uneven and strewn with rock formations of all shapes and sizes. Above was a "ceiling" that varied in height from twenty to sixty or seventy feet, seamed with great fissures large enough for a man to crawl in, and festooned with sickly-looking cave vegetation.

There was no sign of the strange inhabitants as we pressed forward toward that light space ahead, the doctor and Frissian being determined to investigate the source of the light. Finally we came under a large hole in the rocky roof, and after a little calculating learned that this opened above into the bottom of the ancient crater. The bottom of the crater had an area of an acre or more, and this flue, by some agency or freak of chance, was walled about so that the heavy rains could not drain into it, otherwise they would have drowned out all forms of life in a day during the wet season.

The last eruption of that old volcano, which occurred before human history began, had left this subterranean space well concealed and self-guarded from above and below; a fit home for midnight prowlers. But where were the things that dwelt there?

Our answer came soon enough.

We paid but little attention to the rocky formation above our heads, although we kept a sharp enough lookout for the clawing things that occupied the place, when all at once there was a whirring sound behind our backs, and something like a huge vampire bat shot down from a fissure in the roof and darted at the face of the doctor, who stood a little apart from the rest of us, and not so much in the light. He was taken entirely by surprise, and had only time to swing up his hand in self-defense as the thing reached him. A black streak and a rustling sound were all that our senses perceived, as the thing dashed at the doctor, dropped to the ground and scurried away into the deeper darkness before a light could be trained on it.

The doctor jerked at his first-aid kit with his left hand, shaking his right vigorously. "Give me a hand, somebody—he's gaffed me—see his sign?"

We gathered around somewhat terror-stricken as Frissian, under the doctor's directions, proceeded to cleanse and cauterize the wounds in Seego's right hand—three little crescents that faced each other. "Don't waste the silver nitrate," warned the doctor; "this may not be the last of the trouble."

A general desire to get back toward our sturdy little suspension bridge began to manifest itself all through our party, and presently we started back toward the entrance. Phelan limbered up his automatic pistol and counted his shells ruefully. "Twenty little shots," he said, shaking his head. "Let's hope they don't travel in swarms."

Shuddering in spite of myself at the sight we had just witnessed, I made sure that my own good revolver was accessible and then suggested that a few of the cave-dwellers' sticks might also come in handy. Following this idea, every member of the party proceeded to load his pockets with stones and select a good, knotty club. We were perhaps twenty yards from the end of the narrow passage that led down and out when the deadly attack came.

With no warning except that faint swishing sound, a fleet of the black things suddenly descended from their hiding places in the fissured roof and charged us. Squealing, clawing, with rubbery wings flapping like huge bats, they sought to inflict their poisonous trade-marks on our bodies.

The light flashed in erratic circles in an effort to illuminate the scene, but owing to its funnel-shaped hood it was of little use, and we fought in virtual darkness with the death-dealing and inscrutable things. I forgot my revolver, and seizing my club in both hands, I swung it with all my strength toward a shadow that hurtled toward me. There was a gratifying contact with a bony skull, and the thing dropped, still and unresisting, at my feet.

I struck wildly at another that landed just behind the fallen one, and the thing dodged backward with a squeal of rage. Why didn't it fly away, as it had come, I wondered? But, as events took shape, in the perilous minutes that followed, the reason became clear.

The things could not fly—they could only volplane downward. Defying death in his pause of a few seconds, Frissian finally tore the metal funnel off the searchlight, and it threw a comforting glow in every direction. Pistols barked, and flapping, swishing things fell to the ground helpless, or scrambled away, leaving a trail of blood. And still we knew not what they were, nor did we dare stop fighting for a second to learn, for more than one member of our party was already marked for death with those filthy hypodermics. We must reach the passageway before we stopped for idle questions.

At last the things stopped descending, and we guessed that they had all come down. They were still lurking in the dark corners, however, and we did not feel safe by any means. One consolation, however, was ours. On the bottom they could move no faster than ourselves, and they were at the mercy of our clubs. There came a truce, and our two leaders snatched the first-aid kit and called for the injured men. Of the fourteen that composed the party, only five were uninjured by those poisonous claws, and, treat as we would, there was no escaping the poisonous effects from the very first minute, even though the lives were saved in the long run.

For a full minute not one of the attackers appeared, and for the first time I approached one of the prostrate things for a closer inspection. As I came within reach, however, it came to life enough to reach toward my leg with a muddy claw. In a transport of revenge I brought my empty revolver down with a sounding crack on the head, and had the pleasure of hearing its puny skull split under the blow. Then I turned it over and looked at its face.

It was human! A human bat!

Between its emaciated arms and its bony legs there stretched a membrane of black skin like the wing of a bat, except different in formation, for the bat's wings are on its elongated fingers, while these stretched from arm to leg, like the flaps on a so-called flying squirrel. The rubbery membrane covered two of the original five fingers, leaving three fingers and three toes on each limb available for use. It was hard to draw any distinction between the fingers and toes, for both had those wicked, horny, clawlike nails, which carried the charge of poison for their victims.

I stretched the body out at full length. Although it was nearly five feet tall it could not have weighed more than thirty or forty pounds at the most. The emaciated body was not much larger than the robust doctor's upper arm, while the limbs were mere pipe-stems.

The face was indescribable. The eyes were small and weak, from a life spent in semi-darkness; the teeth were small, discolored and sharp-pointed; and the whole head, from generations of climbing and sailing, was canted upward like that of a bird, which impression was heightened by the long pointed nose. The bat-man's facial expression, if there could be an expression on that wizened and wrinkled barb, was one of pure animal ferocity.

In the sickening revelations of the last few minutes I almost forgot the necessity of escaping rapidly, when Seego's sharp reminder brought us all into line. The doctor was weak and sick from the poison, but his dominant mind was not harmed, and he was fully aware of our danger. With all the wounds treated, we hastened toward the exit, keeping a sharp lookout in all directions.

Evidently the things that had fought with us were in no hurry to renew the combat, for we were not pursued. Just as we were about to enter the narrow passage a ray of light thrown across the rocky ceiling above disclosed one of the largest bat-men hiding in a great crack, hanging on by fingers and toes like an animal. Phelan, walking beside me, waited not for orders. His automatic cracked, and the bat-man fell to the ground, with a jagged hole in one wing. Another leaped from almost the same spot, and for the first time we had a chance to observe how they made such enormous distances. They leaned downward as far as possible, then sprang with their wiry legs; and the force of gravity, thus supplemented, carried them for long stretches.

As the wounded pigmy struck the ground it was stunned by the fall, and Frissian, quick to seize the opportunity, tore off his own belt and proceeded to tie the dwarf's limbs securely; after which he slung the puny thing on his back and we proceeded unhindered down through the passageway.

As we at last emerged into daylight the dwarf "came to" and began to struggle. Frissian dropped it hastily on the ground. "Be quiet, my hearty," he said, addressing the bat-man, "while I manicure your nails." And, drawing the bonds tighter than ever, he proceeded to empty the thing's claws of mud, washing them out with creek water. The captive offered no further resistance as we marched in triumph back to Siwaloo with our story and our prize.

"Doc," suddenly asked Frissian, as we paused for a minute's rest on our return trip, "what do you think of the old chief's story about the origin of his devils now? Are these the people they thought they exterminated, coming back to get even?"

After a long pause the doctor answered. "It's a fine, plausible tradition, except for one thing. That, if there's any truth in it, it's half a million years old. You'll all have to abide by your own guesses."

The old savage chief was delighted beyond all words to learn the real truth about his enemies, and he was no slower than we were to understand now how the things had come down from the top of the cliff, done their killing, and then volplaned on downward, crossing the little river at the foot of the cliff before landing. We could all comprehend, too, how they had climbed up the cliff on the side that "guarded itself." Somewhere there was a safe route for the diminutive things to climb to the top, and they were able to experiment until they found it, for what did a few falls mean to men with wings?

As we were planning our departure Seego announced his decision to take the winged dwarf back to the United States with him. "It may be involuntary servitude," he said, facetiously, "to carry a human being around a strange country without his consent, but if he objects to it I shall prefer charges of first-degree murder against him. With a blow-out patch on that punctured wing he will be able to give flying exhibitions at the museums. Maybe we'll have time to go back and bring his wife, if he will identify the lady."

We were sitting around Siwaloo's "council house," a spacious cavern where many people could be entertained, enjoying the old chief's reactions at the opportunity to study his erstwhile enemy from the volcano, while the bat-man, secured to a ring in the wall, sat hunched up and disconsolate amid the merriment, like a diminutive Samson at the Philistine feast.

Siwaloo besought us to remain and destroy the whole colony of poison pests across the river, and shook his head sadly when we tried to explain our prejudice against wholesale murder.

"Let it be as my white friends say, then," concluded the old man, "but at least give us a supply of your medicine, that we may cure our injured men. We would also beg one of your bottled lights, but we have not the knowledge to make it burn, and will have to do without it. And we shall deal with the little men according to the custom of Koti."

He had stepped backward as he spoke, until he was close to the captive bat-man, who had seemed harmless since being deprived of his poison. But now, in a sudden blind fury, the pigmy leaped at Siwaloo's throat, clawing with his three available limbs like a trapped wildcat. It was but the work of a second for the old chief to seize the creature by the neck and snap its puny spine in two, although his face and arms were covered with ugly gashes when the skirmish ended.

Seego, deprived of his unique exhibit, walked to the door of the cave and gazed meditatively across the river toward the old volcano, and we immediately surmised that he was planning another excursion into the cave to replace his lost prisoner. I arose and went out beside him, and even as we stood thus there came a sickening shudder in Mother Earth, and the cliff on which we stood moved perceptibly. Another eruption was in progress, and what its results might be no one knew.

There was a storm of excitement, Seego snapping out sharp orders, and the savages scattering about like madmen in their fright, for the experience was all new to them. We tore down the winding trail, abandoning everything we possessed in our rush for the wharf and the safety of the *Magpie's* deck. The trembling was not repeated, but as we gained the safety of the vessel at last and looked back toward the hill wherein dwelt the flying men, we saw the ancient crater belch forth a great, solid mass of yellow smoke—a deadly gas which no living thing, even a microbe, could survive in; and as we steamed away we knew that, while Siwaloo's people were probably in no danger, the race of bat-men had been wiped out of existence, and Koti would see no more death crescents.

THE BEAST

By PAUL BENTON

HOW SHALL I PUT DOWN MY STORY, SO WEIRD AND unbelievable, on paper that it may convince any who reads it, should it ever be read? Even as I consider it calmly, freeing my mind from the sudden chill dread that seizes me as I think of that terrible and curious moment, it seems a wild figment of the imagination, a strange optical illusion for which tired nerves and lack of sleep are responsible. And then as I get it figured out in this conventional fashion its utter reality suddenly grips me again, and down falls my fine fabric of logic. Of course, I should know that such a thing cannot be, is impossible. In reply I can only set down helplessly but obstinately, that it is. As for the scientific side of the question I know nothing and frankly care nothing. Again I can only repeat that I saw it.

Sometimes when I think of that man walking the streets, mingling with human beings, speaking, being spoken to—I could rush to the window and scream a warning into the night.

I care not whether these pages be read. I may destroy them myself if I am not myself destroyed. For the moment it suffices that I must have some confidant in the matter, even if it be only a sheet of paper. It may seem a strange proceeding, but then all my actions have been strange of late—for two days—yes, two days, although it seems as though two centuries could scarcely have passed more slowly. Only the night before last? Correct, according to my calendar. But then I have not slept, which makes a difference.

When did I first meet Walter Strong? It must have been two, no, three years ago. He was then what, God help us both, he is to-day. A careful, courteous gentleman, polished, cultured, engaging in manner, with a nice perception in all those minor delicacies of human intercourse which are the savor of life. One could no more imagine his doing an inconsiderate or thoughtless act than—I know not what. He was—I use the past tense advisedly—one of those rare beings to whom ugliness in any form brings a pain almost physical.

I came to know him well. We were intimates, our tastes and feelings inclining us to the same things. He was frequently at my house; I often visited him in his place in Madison Avenue, half studio, half apartment. He painted casually but well, an excellent amateur. He turned up in New York from London, I believe, with good letters of introduction. He claimed to be English, and quite possibly he is. His was the casual claim of a casual man.

Although Mrs. Lukyns' dinner was but forty-eight hours ago I cannot recall any marked characteristic of the meal. It was good, I suppose, and the usual run of artistic and near-artistic folk were there who always come to Mrs. Lukyns' dinners. The thing happened after dinner, and here I had best pause a moment to arrange every incident methodically in my mind.

First Strong was talking to our hostess. I stood with them for a moment and the talk was of some new book, I forget which one. Then Strong moved away and sat down by Betty Ives in one of those S-shaped chairs. I was left alone as Mrs. Lukyns strolled away with Wildrow, the new professor. I walked over to the fireplace and stood facing the room, and owing to the position of his chair I could see Strong clearly. The light on his face was excellent, as he was seated within the radius of a big lamp on the center table.

I was standing there, smoking and wondering idly what

a man like Strong could find to talk to Betty Ives about. My temperature was normal. I was feeling slightly fatigued but otherwise in excellent condition. There was absolutely nothing abnormal in the surroundings or in myself, physically or mentally.

Then——

As God is my witness, I saw the soul of Walter Strong. And the horror of it was and is that it was not the soul of a man; not that of a human being. It was that of a wild beast.

I do not have to shut my eyes to visualize it now. The man's body had faded into a faint but perfectly distinct outline. And within it was something which appeared to be a sort of a panther. Written down, this appears to be absurd, sounds like sheer raving, yet I am telling what I saw and nothing more. The face was a mask of horror, a grinning, hateful thing.

For a moment—it must have been but a moment, since evidently no one noticed anything strange in my behavior—I stood staring. Then with an effort which took every ounce of physical strength I looked away.

When my eyes in a few seconds turned back instinctively to where Strong was seated there was nothing unusual about his appearance at first, but when our eyes crossed, he was staring fixedly at me. There came into his face, hitherto so invariably calm, gentle, almost too expressionless, a look of the most ghastly malignancy I have ever seen a human countenance express. It cannot be described accurately, nor are there words to do credit to the hate, fear and bitterness in the man's face. It was the soul speaking. We were challenging each other across a great chasm, the chasm of our surroundings. Had we been alone I have no doubt he would have sprung at my throat. All the beast within him was clamoring for an outlet.

I looked away again, almost physically sick this time. Lukyns was the first to notice my condition.

"How pale you are; are you ill?" he asked in a low voice, coming up to where I stood.

"No," I replied, and my voice sounded strange and hoarse as though forced by my will through a great empty distance. I told him, heaven knows what conventional lie. I only remember I fairly fled, but quietly enough.

How long I wandered aimlessly through the streets I have no idea. I remember dismissing the cab which Lukyns had called, as soon as we had turned the corner. Then I walked rapidly ahead, striving to settle my problem.

For indeed a very real and terrible problem confronts me which I have so far been unable to solve. What am I to do about Strong? It is unbearable that he should continue to live free and unhampered, unsuspected, unwatched, until the thing culminates in some frightful tragedy. Looking at the question coldly, I suppose he should be confined somewhere. Scientists should be able to observe him, make daily notes, psychological tests, and try to solve this strange problem of identity. But of course that is impossible, quite impossible.

I am bound hand and foot by the incredulity of humanity. I should be marked down as a lunatic. I should be lucky to escape the asylum. I wrestle through the long hours with the problem and find no solution. I can write no more now, but must drive my tired brain afresh.

June 3, 1911. I am leaving to-morrow and have come to two definite conclusions which I am convinced, despite their contradictory nature, are true. Strong is afraid of me, and I am afraid of Strong.

The second I know to be correct. I have felt fear before, but that which I felt when I saw Strong's beastlike glare fixed on me that night was the cause of my physical repugnance primarily. It was a fear so great that I did not recognize it as fear at first—not indeed until, seated in my library with doors and windows locked, I seemed to see those malevolent eyes fixed on me from a dark corner. Since that moment it has never left me. Sleeping, I dream of it, and awake to find the sweat running down my face, my lips rough and dry, and my limbs twitching as though in an ague. Waking, I see constantly before me the man's face as it appeared to me at that moment.

As for my first conclusion, I am driven to it. In this morning's paper I read that Walter Strong, "the society painter," sailed at 11 o'clock last night on the *Lusitania.* The reporter declared Mr. Strong was going to Paris to study "the new art of Picabia." Fool! He is going because in his beast soul he fears me. I am a man and his master! He fears to meet me. But I shall give him no rest. We are pitted against each other by fate, the primeval foes of the world—Man and Beast. Fear him? Yes, I do. But he fears me more and cannot conquer his fear because he cannot conquer his soul. I am sailing on the French line for Havre to-morrow.

June 6, 1911. On Board S.S. La Tôuraine. At Sea. This brisk air is doing me good. Then, too, as the days pass I am feeling stronger in my conviction of his fear. And while I cannot account for it now, there must be some subtle, deep-rooted reason for it. Evidently he had no idea of the strength of his position but fled in panic, trusting that I might be content to let things drift along casually as long as he kept out of the way. But I am not doing so. I cannot quite analyze the feeling that pervades me these days. I think of little, I dream of little, save this pursuit which is beginning. I feel, despite what has happened to throw my normal, easy-going life, with its daily work and recreation, out of gear, a strange lightness of spirit, a certain almost fierce exultation, when I think of my quarry, for as such I now regard Strong. Sometimes I walk the boat deck at night wondering whether he is walking the deck of the *Lusitania,* out there somewhere ahead of us, churning him toward England, France, what? I wonder what his thoughts are. Does he sometimes, when the deck is vacant, astonish some amazed sailor by raising his head and snarling beastlike at the moon? Does it seem a relief to him when alone in his cabin to take out the pent-up emotions of a day of civilized repression by hurling himself upon the pillows in his berth, worrying them with frantic teeth, eager for the taste of blood?

Or perhaps he does not dare relax for a moment from that iron self-control which has carried him through so many years of civilized intercourse, his secret undiscovered.

It is all a speculation to me, fascinating in interest, which daily loses more and more of its horror.

There is a famous man on board, Emile Le Saunier, the psychologist. He is most approachable for a scientist, and as he sits at my table we have struck up a walking and talking acquaintance which bids fair to become more. I welcome it as it gives me healthful recreation from my own thoughts. I was interested in getting his impression of some aspects of my case, and to-day as we were doing our constitutional I asked him how he thought a sudden and terrible revelation might affect such a man as myself. He replied, "You have been a man of action?"

"Yes," I answered, "to some extent. I have lived in the wilds where one's existence hinges upon one's ability to withstand nature."

He considered the problem for some minutes, now and then glancing at me as we strode along the deck, quick glances from iron-gray eyes under bushy brows. At length he said slowly, "Very interesting. A sudden and terrible revelation, eh? *Mon ami,* I think you would go back, revert—you understand me?"

"Atavism?" I asked.

"Hm—well, yes. You are the strong type; the physical lies near the surface in you. The repression of civilization we may all drop like—like some big snake dropping his old skin. But some of us drop it sooner than others. Of that type, I think you, Monsieur Hadley. My opinion, knowing you so slightly, may be hasty. If you think me wrong, you will pardon me, I trust. I am but answering your question."

Later, at dinner, he presented me to his daughter, a charming slip of a girl about seventeen, I should judge, of exquisite but undeveloped beauty.

At Sea, June 11, 1911. We shall land in a few hours and I shall go to Paris at once. Somehow I feel sure that I'll find my man without much difficulty. There is no reason for this, but I have given up reason as a guide and shall follow instinct blindly. After all, what has poor old sober reason to do with a wild affair like this? If I had listened to reason, I should have stayed quietly at home. I was standing up in the bow this morning, immersed in my thoughts, gazing at but hardly seeing the frantic bobbing of a little trawler in the choppy channel sea, when I became aware that some one was speaking to me. I turned and found Cecile Le Saunier standing at my elbow. She made a lovely picture with her golden curls tossing and her eyes sparkling like the foam-crested waves. I stammered an awkward enough "good morning," for indeed I must have looked strange glaring out across the waters with unseeing eyes.

"Oh, Monsieur Hadley, did I disturb you?"

"No, indeed, nor would I have objected."

"The water and the sky seem particularly beautiful this morning, do they not, *Monsieur?*" she went on in quaint precise English. "But then probably I feel that way because I'm to see France again in another half-hour. Papa says we should be within sight of the coast then. Won't that be glorious?" She laughed and clapped her hands.

Somehow the vision of her has haunted me all day. Perhaps more than I care to admit. She is a charming child, astonishingly mature along certain lines, yet as fresh and unspoiled as the clean sea wind; young but already fascinating and giving the promise of a rare and wonderful womanhood. Before we landed, Le Saunier asked me to visit them at Les Roches, their place in Normandy. Pretty name. I don't know whether I shall go.

Paris, June 18, 1911. Damnation! I have been here a week and discovered nothing. Not a clew, not a trace. Strong is well known here. I have unearthed a dozen acquaintances. But none of them has seen him for several years. However, I shall stay here. My hunter's instinct, if I can call it that, tells me that this is the place to be.

Paris, June 21, 1911. Something terrible has happened. This can't go on. I'm all right again now, and looking back I wonder at moments whether it is not imagination—no, damn it! That theory won't hold water. If I am to beat this malignant thing that has come into my life, I've got to be frank with myself first of all. Last night I was tired, too tired to go out for my dinner, and ordered a cutlet and a bottle of wine in my room. I was reading, with the book propped up against the sugar bowl, the cutlet brown and appetizing on the plate in front of me. Suddenly the most violent desire I ever experienced—and I have experienced the normal number of passions—swept over me with a force I can only describe as sickening. I wanted, longed, ached, to snatch up that meat, tear it with my teeth, worry it, suck out its juices. I came near doing it, too. My head went down toward the plate as though some one had pushed it violently; my hands clenched like claws, the fingers clutching.

With a supreme effort of the will, I raised my head and caught sight of my face in the big mirror on the other side of the room. It was a perfect mask of bestiality. My groping hand came in contact with the wine glass which I had just filled, and with a sudden impulse of sanity I raised the glass and flung the wine in my face.

The shock brought me to my senses. Just as soon as I could change my soaked shirt and coat I fled from the room, took a taxicab and passed the rest of the evening on the *terrasse* of the Café de la Paix. Then went home and slept normally.

Now, what in God's name can a man make out of a thing like that?

Paris, June 23, 1911. Things are approaching a climax. I believe I am in the most frightful danger, yet the fear this arouses in me only strengthens my determination to find Strong—find and kill him. . . . Therein, as I reason it, lies my one chance of salvation.

I stumbled on the explanation quite by accident. I ran across Brownson in the Tuileries. He has been here for years enjoying himself and painting. He asked me to dinner, and the explanation came from him, quite unconsciously, while we were eating.

"Do you remember, or did you ever know Donaldson?" he asked.

I replied I had never heard of him.

"Well, he lived here, in the Rue Bellechasse, with a charming chap, English I think; Strong his name was—Walter Strong."

He sipped his coffee and lighted his cigar with maddening deliberation, moving the match from side to side, until it burned exactly even. I controlled my face and patience with an effort.

"Yes," I said finally, "go on."

"No haste, no haste. Story'll keep. Never hurry a good cigar. Well, where was I? Oh, yes, this chap Strong. One morning after the two, who were great friends, had been living together for about a year, Strong came home early, found Donaldson reading, rather irritable at being disturbed, and went to bed. Later, he told the police, he was awakened by some one moving in the next room, the living room of the flat. Said it sounded as though the fellow was on his hands and knees, and then a moment later he heard some one sniffing, like an animal, you know, at the keyhole. Then, according to his story, he got up, switched on the light and found young Donaldson crouching on the hearth rug on all fours, snarling at him—stark, staring mad, you know. They took him to Charenton. He's there yet, I guess. A perfectly hellish thing. He's never spoken a word or shown a human trait since that night. He's simply a beast."

For a moment an agony of terror fell upon me, similar to that I experienced when Strong was revealed to me in New York, but so infinitely greater that I shall not attempt to describe it accurately. It must have affected my appearance, as Brownson looked across the table with a frightened expression.

"Good Lord, man," he said, "are you ill?"

"No," I lied, swallowing my liqueur at a gulp; "but that yarn of yours—it's too damned horrible!"

So I must, must, must—God! I've got to find Strong and kill him. I've been warned. I'll not succumb like a weakling. The law holds as innocent men who kill to save their lives. But I am fighting for far more than life.

Paris, July 1, 1913. If an irreligious man with death in his heart can thank his Maker sincerely, I should do so. Here am I back in Paris, more than two years after this long and bitter chase, a hunt never before, I believe, duplicated in history. I am alive, sick in body and soul, after passing through experiences I firmly believe no man before me ever has undergone.

I suppose Strong thinks me dead, as well he might after the last glimpse he caught of me, floating helpless in the current of the Zambezi. And incidentally the upsetting of my canoe which saved him is the cause of my setting down these past experiences now, since I lost the note-books containing the full account of my wanderings. My first book left at the Crédit Lyonnais here when I followed Strong from Russia to Manchuria, tells the story, I perceive, of my early fears and hates and hopes, bringing it up to the time I discovered Strong could influence me mentally, even from a great distance.

Taking up the thread, it is sufficient to say I got trace of him in Berlin and followed his trail on the next train, only to miss my man by a matter of hours. For a time, the scent was lost. Finally, I heard of him in Vienna and chased him from there through Poland, Russia, and, in the midst of a frozen Balkan winter, nearly ran him to earth in Sofia. But some malign influence seemed to be operating against me. My train was delayed and I caught a glimpse of him on a train bound for Russia, as my own rolled into the Sofia station. Then, afterward, in the station restaurant, I had another attack. I clung to the table and swayed in my chair, then mercifully fainted. Mental overstimulus, the doctor called it.

Through Russia, I followed into Siberia and Manchuria, and finally to China. Early this year, he fled to Africa. As usual, it was a touch-and-go affair. His steamer sailed from Bombay at nine in the morning and my train from the north got in at ten. He had two weeks' start.

I lost the trail, following to Capetown, to find he had left the steamer at Zanzibar. I followed and was told he had struck into the interior. I followed, making the lone trek to the top of Tanganyika. Down the mighty lake, I followed. I felt that surely we should meet in this great unknown and fight out our primitive battle here in the wilderness. He struck the Zambezi and went up-stream, heading for the West Coast. I followed, mad with exultation.

Scarcely sleeping, traveling as never African traveler went before, I pushed on. My men fell exhausted. I hired new bearers—we lost the trail—I raged like a madman, sleepless and tireless for two days, until we were on the spoor of his safari again.

Finally, we headed him off. Mohammed Abdul, good old villain, and myself left our men, got ahead of him, and struck the river. We got a canoe, left what little remained of our outfit and drove down-stream. We were not far above the mighty cataract, Victoria, when we sighted his canoes coming up. Then he turned, and fled down-stream. He had six paddles going to our two; fear moved his as hate did mine.

We gained as he sheered toward the south bank to avoid the death pull of the current.

Then, even as I was sighting my rifle, came the accident. A log crashed into us, driven by the full force of the stream. It smashed our frail dugout like a shell.

Mohammed, whom I picked up starving in Peshawar, saved my life that day. Not only on that day, but on many another, during the long journey south to civilization.

Yes, Strong must think me dead. Few men escape the current of the Zambezi above Victoria.

So, here I am again, my strength gone, my hope nearly so. Thank God! I have had no attack of animalism; it might succeed, I fear. I have been too long alone, removed from my kind. I need something—I can't say exactly what. I must get rest.

Paris, July 4, 1913. The problem is solved. To-day, sunning myself on the *terrasse* of a café in the Boulevard des Italiens, I met Dr. Le Saunier, as hale and hearty, and delicately kind, as I knew him on the *Touraine* two years ago. Nothing would do but that I must tell him where I got the tan that even the African fever pallor cannot wear away. I told him I had been hunting in Africa, and of my sickness. Well, then, I must come down to Normandy, to Les Roches; eat apples; listen to Cecile play on the harp; read; loaf; enjoy myself. I accepted, and am to motor down with him in the morning. But I must not neglect my quest. Last night, I had a slight attack. I called Mohammed, who placed his hands on my shoulders, called me Bahadur, and bade me remember that I was a man. He is a great help to me. I have long since told him all my story. Orientals can understand such things. I believe he regards Strong as an evil spirit, with some sort of magical powers. A sort of demon.

Château des Roches, July 5, 1913. We came down from Paris this morning. It was a beautiful trip. This countryside is charming, and to me, fresh from the horrors of that terrible journeying in Africa, doubly so. The old château, a long, low building, modern but built around the shell of an old Norman fortress, is delightful. Cecile Le Saunier was at the door to meet us. Her father had wired ahead. It seems impossible that two years could have done as much for any one. I can't quite describe her. She is like a flame. Between lunch and dinner she showed a dozen different moods and phases, all delightful.

After dinner, we gathered in the salon, the doctor, Cecile and myself, and I was called upon for an account of my African wanderings, obliged to account for Mohammed, and a dozen other things, and before we knew it, midnight was well past. It was good, good, to be able to sit in a civilized room talking to my own sort of people again after so long. I even forgot Strong, and as I write this and pause for a moment to look out into the cool, dark night, through the long window, my pursuit and the events leading up to it seem strangely unreal.

But I cannot forget the poor lad in Charenton asylum—the boy who howls nightly at the moon from behind his barred windows.

Château des Roches, July 6, 1913. Cecile and I walked to Verneuil, the nearby town, this morning. She wished me to see the historic old place. We walked around the grass-grown, moss-covered battlements and she told me of the battle fought here in the Hundred Years' War.

Les Roches, July 14, 1913. It has been a great day for Cecile. We have had a *célébration civique*. There have been speeches in the town by various dignitaries, official and other, including Dr. Le Saunier. Then, they all came to lunch at Les Roches. The men, old and young, rave about Cecile, and the younger ones are worried by my presence at the château. Indeed, in the rare moments when I permit myself to think of the future instead of merely taking what the present has to offer, I am worried myself. I wish I could go to Le Saunier with the problem. However, he might be excused for thinking me a lunatic. He is working tremendously just now on a new book. To-day, he told me the researches for it had been going on for more than fifteen years. It is something about the psychology of the abnormal. I would be an interesting specimen for him.

Les Roches, July 17, 1913. Rather disjointed affair, this journal of mine, but I have never, since the beginning, put anything in it unless something had happened worth putting in. The question before me now is whether to drop my quest and risk any possible consequences or leave Les Roches. I love Cecile. I dare no longer disguise this to myself by calling it dallying or resting. I have been staying on here for two weeks now simply because I love her and have loved her from the first. Can I remain longer without letting her know it? And can I let her know it? No! A hundred times, no! A menace hangs over me day and night, and God alone knows what the final result will be. In the meantime, until I have freed myself of Walter Strong, I am not my own master but the slave of forces of which I am ignorant. I have made my decision. I shall go to-morrow. I feel ill to-night. For two days my African malaria has been getting worse. These tropical troubles are hard to shake off. But I shall go to Paris to-morrow, and resume the trail, hurry the pursuit, rush it with all the old fervor, and then hurry back. Cecile, I know, will wait.

Les Roches, July 18, 1913. Just a few lines before I slip this into my bag. My hand is trembling and I feel worse than since I won to Cape Town. I saw Cecile this morning after breakfast and told her I must leave for Paris to-day. She started and paled, and—curse me for a fool!—I had her in my arms, choking and crying and whispering things I had no right to say. I am wildly, feverishly glad, yet hate myself for a cowardly scoundrel.

She asked suddenly, "But, *chéri,* why are you going, since you love me?"

It was a terrible moment. Every instinct, every nerve, prompted me to stay. Finally, I managed to say, "Sweetheart"—Lord, but it was good to call her by that good old English name!—"I have work to do and for the present it must be secret, even from you. See, I am frank. I must do it, and have delayed too long already, dearest. I cannot tell you what it is, but will when it is finished. Can you trust me, be silent about our love until you hear from me? Can you, dearest?"

She suddenly caught me by the shoulders, swung me around facing her with a force I did not think she possessed, and looked long into my face. Her eyes were full, first of a great questioning which gradually turned to such love and trust that my heart pounded madly. She answered simply, "*Bien.* Kiss me and go."

To kiss and to leave! She is wonderful, inspiring in her passion of fearless love and trust.

Les Roches, July 25, 1913. I hardly know how to tell what has happened. Strong is here at Les Roches, and I am here, and Cecile, all the dramatis personæ of my tragedy. I have been ill. In fact, this is my first day out of bed, and the first chance I have had to put anything down in my journal. The other morning as I was preparing to leave, I was knocked out by my old African fever and until yesterday was in a state halfway between consciousness and oblivion. It appears from what Cecile tells me that Strong came here the day I was taken ill. In the mere fact of his staying after he found I was in the house, I read a menace. The man, or beast, or whatever he is, must be as tired as I of this everlasting chase and resolved to bring it to an end. He probably counts on my physical weakness as an aid in overcoming my soul. I haven't seen him yet, but have no doubt that Cecile is the attraction which brought him to this quiet corner. I understand they met in Paris at some affair or other a few months ago.

Well, I shall welcome him—I, too, am tired—so weary.

After dinner. I have met him. He is suave and charming as ever, but to me as beastlike. When he looked at Cecile, he came nearer his death than at any time since that day on the Zambezi. I could read the beast in his look, and some fine, subtle communication between us made me aware that she could do so too. Anyway, I can easily see that although we retained our respective poses it is a situation which cannot continue. The strain is too great. I was overcome by weakness before the end of the dinner and had to be helped up here where I am writing what very possibly will be the last words I shall set down in this matter. For the impression is very strong upon me that something will happen to-night.

Midnight. Here I am back at my desk. This little book seems to have a fascination for me. I have read over the whole story since I sat down to write these words and the extraordinary and unaccountable adventure seems madder than ever. I can think only in bits. I am filled with boiling and contradicting emotions. My love for Cecile which surges hotly through my veins; my hatred for him; my fear which is with me always; a certain wild and reckless gayety in the adventure; then again and running through everything else, Cecile, my darling, my golden girl, there is the thought of you and everything you mean to me—no, decidedly I am not myself, although I possess apparently a cold power of detached introspection. The feeling of doom that prevailed in me just after dinner has increased tremendously and I am sure that the inevitable conflict will occur soon. The thought of what I have at stake makes me wonder if ever mortal man fought for more—love, life, reason, liberty, all hang here in the scales, and I sit scribbling disconnected sentences. But then—what can I do? I can't search out the man and kill him in his bed—I can't! . . . hark! . . . some one is coming toward this room . . . now he has passed the end of the corridor. . . . I can't hear anything but I know it's true. . . . Aaah! . . . the hair on the back of my neck is rising. . . . God! like a dog's or any other kind of a beast . . . the door-knob is turning . . . slowly . . . slowly. . . .

From the Diary of Mlle. Cecile Le Saunier

July 26, 1913. Now that it is all over, can I write of it calmly?—yet, I wish to do so. Papa says nothing save novels should be written with emotion. It spoils calm thought. But it was tremendous; even now, I can only begin to picture to myself the terrible and frightful peril from which Robert has been saved . . . that I should have saved him seems too good to be true, nor do I yet know exactly how I did so, but he insists that had I not been drawn to his room that particular moment he would have lost his great fight and would be now—what I can hardly bear to write, or think—what that other man, no, not a man, that *thing* is. Of course, Father explains it all in the only possible manner.

I must tell my story consecutively, however. To begin with, after that horrible dinner last night, I went to my room early. I could not sleep from worry about Robert, but, finally, after reading some proofs for papa, I went to bed but still could not sleep. My love for Robert has become so great a thing that it possesses my entire being and I thought of him constantly. There was something tapping, tapping, tapping, at the back of my brain as I lay there in the darkness. I tried at first to ignore it and sleep. Then, realizing this was impossible, I attempted to solve the message I felt was being carried to me subconsciously. At first I had no success. I merely felt some one was trying to tell me something. It was horrible. As though some poor dumb animal was trying to make me understand a desperate need by half-articulate noises. I suffered for the suffering I felt, but did not, could not, understand.

Then suddenly I did understand, and for a moment was transfixed by icy fear. I swear I read that message which had been hammering at my brain as clearly as though the words had been printed before my eyes. Robert was calling,

calling: "Cecile, Cecile, save me. Help!" Just those words, over and over again.

I didn't think coherently after that. Everything was instinct. I jumped out of bed and without even putting on a robe dashed down the corridor toward Robert's room. My one thought was to protect what I loved. I came to the door, and there, I remember, I paused to listen a moment.

From within came sounds, a subdued sort of growling, now and then a word spoken low, and then that growling again—like some great, malignant beast—and then, suddenly, as I stood transfixed with horror in front of the door, came a great cry from Robert: "Cecile, oh God, Cecile!"

I rushed at the door-handle and tugged; the door flew open; and there I saw Robert standing on the far side of the table on which lay his writing things, one hand thrown up as though to ward off a blow, his head half bowed while the fingers of the hand with which he was shielding his face were slowly, but horribly, transforming themselves into claws, were opening and shutting, curved like talons.

In front of him, his back turned to me, on the other side of the table from Robert, stood that man, and even as I looked it seemed to me that I could see, within the man, a great beast sitting, snarling—then I screamed at Robert. I don't know what I said but he raised his head and saw me standing there. Then he seemed to grow in height, his fingers stopped that horrible clutching, his arms fell to his sides, and for a moment the two men stood there glaring at each other.

Suddenly, Robert turned to his dressing table and seized a heavy whip lying there. It was the one we used for Bruno, the St. Bernard.

All the time, it could have been but a few seconds that this was occurring—I mean, since I opened the door—the beast had been saying in a low voice, which had in it that horrible growl, the sound I had noticed when standing in the corridor:

"You're a beast, Hadley, howl—you're a beast—howl, damn you, howl!"

But when Robert turned back toward him with the whip in his hand, his voice suddenly changed and took on a note of terror, the growl in it changed to a whine.

"Don't," he screamed, "don't!"

But Robert raised the whip and brought it down, again and again, lashing his face, his neck, his back, with short, cruel strokes, exclaiming: "You animal! You're not worth shooting. Down, beast! Down!"

And as he lashed, the *thing* suddenly groveled at his feet, howling horribly, and turning up to him a tortured face from which all semblance of humanity had fled—he looked and was all animal. Then, rapidly as a flash, he turned and, running on all fours, passed by me, standing in the door, and disappeared from the corridor, snapping his teeth as he ran.

I had turned to watch him, and when I looked back at Robert he was tottering, gripping the table with both hands to support himself, his face ghastly. I rushed to him, and as I put my arms around him, he sank down and fainted, but before he lost consciousness, he whispered as I was bending over him: "We were too strong for him, darling. Love, that's the difference. Thank God, you came in time!"

I looked up just as Father came running up the corridor into the room.

HIS WIFE

By ZITA INEZ PONDER

I FOUND THE FOLLOWING NARRATIVE AMONG MY FATHER'S papers when sorting them after his death in 1904. It occurred to me that it might be interesting to others besides my family circle, so now for the first time I make it public.

We often used to wonder why he went to Hampstead regularly on a certain date every year. He would never satisfy our curiosity or relate how he came to possess the splendid diamond ring which he wore on his little finger. Often and often he would look at it, shake his head and sigh, "God alone knows the tragedies you have seen. God alone knows!"

The following document explained everything except his reluctance to disclose the extraordinary adventure during his life.

I am a successful business man, retired, and living in a comfortable house with an affectionate wife and family. Few men, perhaps, are as happy and contented as I, but in the early days of my career, life was by no means a bed of roses nor my lot an enviable one. What I have to relate will disclose how my fortunes began to change.

While quite a young man I fell on bad times. My master, a joiner, died, and in consequence I was thrown out of work, friendless and penniless. My bed became any door step which was sheltered from the wind. Sometimes I slept in the old Adelphi Arches near the Strand—they were more comfortable than the open street.

In my search for work in the outlying parts of London, night would often overtake me unawares, then any place was good enough to rest my aching limbs.

One bitterly cold night in the middle of February I was stranded out at Hampstead. Walking along a lane in the hope of finding a high hedge under which to shelter, I suddenly became aware that footsteps were behind me. I walked on, but in spite of my quickening pace I was overtaken and looked up to find a man at my side.

"A very cold night," the stranger observed, as he settled down to my pace.

In the moonlight I could see his features clearly. He was a most extraordinary figure, dressed in clothes fashionable about forty years earlier. His mouth and chin were hidden under a heavy beard, his hair was plaited in a pigtail. His frame was enormous, and well covered in spite of his age, which I reckoned to be about sixty.

I was terribly lonely and heartsick and was glad to have some one to talk to.

"It is cold, damn cold, sir," I answered.

As we walked he looked me up and down with his strange bright eyes, which seemed to penetrate me to my marrow.

"Where are you bound for, young man?" he inquired.

I shrugged my shoulders. "Nowhere in particular, sir, I am trying to find a high hedge to sleep under."

"Had anything to eat?" he asked abruptly.

I shook my head. "No, sir, I have been looking for work and haven't a penny."

He looked at me again in a way that made me feel uncomfortable, though I could not for the life of me have said why. Then he put a hand on my arm.

"Would you like to come along and have a meal with my wife and me? My house is quite near. She was fond of young men. You can stay the night if you like."

He spoke jerkily and started to whistle, and his manner of speech puzzled me. But the offer sounded good to a youth who was tired and hungry, so I accepted with alacrity.

"Very well, we go down here," and he turned off to the right along a lane which seemed to lead nowhere. We had not gone far, however, when a large detached house loomed into sight. On reaching it my companion took a key from his pocket, unlocked the front door, and invited me to enter.

As we crossed the threshold I suddenly became conscious of a feeling of foreboding and nausea which quickly increased to suspicion and fear as I saw him carefully relock the door and drop the key in his pocket. There was something in his manner which made me feel distrustful of him and made my flesh creep. Without a word he struck a lucifer match and lit a lamp standing on the hall table. By its light I looked around me, and saw that at one time or another the house had been very sumptuously furnished. The carpet on the floor and stairway, the splendid pictures on the walls, spoke of luxury and wealth, but everything was now covered with dust and dirt. The whole place smelt of mold.

The stranger led the way down some stairs leading to the basement. Following him I could feel my heart was beating wildly. What was to be the upshot of this strange adventure?

On reaching the bottom of the stairs he unlocked another door and stood on one side for me to pass. Hardly knowing what to expect I entered what appeared to be a cellar fitted up as a bed sitting-room with a table laid for two standing in the center. To my surprise the floor was of earth with no carpet on it.

"Cheerful little hole, is it not?" my companion remarked, showing his teeth for the first time in a broad grin as he placed the lamp upon the table. There was something in those teeth which sent cold shivers down my spine, but I managed to smile and agree with him.

"Sit down, young man," he commanded, "while I get supper ready."

I sat down on the edge of a bed, which was set on one side of the room, holding my hat between my knees. He busied himself getting food out of a cupboard, which stood by an obviously home-made fireplace. A log was smoldering upon the hearth, and smoking abominably.

He placed a dish of cold potatoes, a half shoulder of mutton and a loaf of bread upon the table, setting an extra knife and fork. Then he came and sat down beside me.

"What kind of work do you do, young man?" he asked, without as much as a suggestion that we should start supper.

"I am a joiner, sir," I answered.

"How excellent," he cried, rubbing his hands together. "You are just the man I have been looking for for years."

"Indeed, sir?" I answered, becoming more and more amazed.

"Yes. My wife needs a large chest."

"What kind of a chest?" I inquired against my will.

"A big one to keep her things together in."

I nodded. "Well, sir, if you would care to give me the wood and tell me how it is to be made, I will make it for you. I cannot polish it though, as I have not learned that part of the trade."

My host laughed. "Oh! She will not mind it being unpolished, so long as it is strong and light." He then seized my arm and peered into my face. "By the way, young man, what do you think of women?"

"I think—" I answered, stammering a little, "I think they are most agreeable creatures, sir."

He laughed again. "Then you will get on well with her," he chuckled. Then he relapsed into silence and still made no effort to call his wife.

"Have you been married long, sir?" I ventured at length by way of conversation.

He nodded. "Yes, long enough to know all there is to know about women."

He spoke rather fiercely, then suddenly turned on me in such a manner as to make me jump.

"Have you any money, young man?"

"Not a penny in the world, sir," I answered nervously.

"Do you want some?" he almost shouted.

"It—would—help—me a good—deal, sir," I stammered, now thoroughly frightened.

"Money does not make happiness, young man," he hissed as his strange eyes bored me through and through.

"No, sir, but it helps towards it," I replied, wondering what he was going to say or do next.

He got up suddenly and walked across the room to the cupboard. Taking out a small box he brought it to my side.

"Look in here, young man."

He lifted the lid and the sight of the contents made me gasp with amazement. The box was full of gold coins and unset gems. The stranger chuckled evilly at my surprise, his eyes gleaming with the peculiar light which made me feel so nervous and uncomfortable.

"That lot is worth well over a thousand pounds," he said, glaring at me.

I nodded. "I am sure it is, sir."

He took a handful out and let them fall back into the box.

"Many a man has been murdered for less. Would you murder me for them?"

His question appalled me and I was surprised into silence. He mistook the meaning of my not answering, and burst into a loud fit of laughter. Then he became suddenly quite serious, frowning on me most unpleasantly.

"Ah! you would! I am not surprised. Money is a great temptation to the poor."

"God forbid!" I stammered. "Nothing was further from my thoughts, sir. You startled me by your question."

I was beginning to be more than nervous at this queer man's behavior.

He looked at me for a moment and laughed again. "I do not believe you would. Here, take them. They will do you more good than they ever will me."

He thrust the box into my hands and I sat holding it,

hardly knowing what to do or say. Here was a fortune: enough for me to start a business of my own. Should I keep it? I looked up at the man and saw that his clothes were almost as ragged as mine. Then I recognized his gift must have been prompted by an impulsive compassion for my sorry condition in spite of his own needs. I felt tears of gratitude come into my eyes as I handed the box back to him, stammering:

"No—no—sir, I could not think of taking all this; if you could spare me a guinea I should be very grateful."

The stranger stared at me with a look of bewilderment upon his face. "You are the first young man who has refused them—you must be very honest. Take them. Do as I tell you, young man, take the gold and gems. I want the box. It has sentimental value for me. Come, I will take no refusal."

In spite of my protests he began hastily to stuff the valuables into my pockets. When he had finished he closed the lid and kissed the box reverently.

"Poor little box. Did I not send a Valentine in you? My gift wrapped in loving thoughts."

He shook his head and sighed as he walked towards the cupboard and placed the box upon a shelf. In spite of my strange fear for my host I felt sorry—unaccountably sorry for him, and wondered who had received the Valentine, the memory of which made him sigh.

Coming towards me the stranger laid his hands upon my shoulders and grinned into my face, making me feel uncomfortable again.

"Now you are rich, boy!"

"Yes, sir, thanks to you," I answered.

He threw back his head and laughed uproariously. It sounded like a bellow in that vault-like cellar, and I felt cold shivers run up and down my spine.

"Few people have ever thanked me for anything since I was a young man, and since then I have changed a good deal.

I was a doctor once. A very wealthy one. My family was wealthy—that gold and those gems belonged to them. I inherited them when I was twenty. How old are you, boy?"

"Twenty, sir, last December," I answered, wishing very heartily I could have something to eat before answering his questions.

"Well, young man, make better use of your youth than I did." He spoke a little grimly.

I did not know what to say, but just sat looking at him. He smiled a little sadly: "I wasted mine."

"Indeed, sir?"

I hoped to hear what his trouble had been, but he did not pursue the subject further, and I began to wonder about his wife, why she did not appear and why they chose such an uncomfortable room to live in. Suddenly he spoke

"Do you smoke, boy?"

"No, sir," I answered.

"Quite right, it is a very bad habit, but it soothes one."

He walked away and, picking up a churchwarden pipe which was leaning against the fireplace, proceeded to fill it in silence. I had not noticed how quiet everything was until he stood there looking at me. I had been too puzzled and excited to notice anything more than the man, his queer ways and gift. The stillness made me feel creepy. It lasted such a long time. He lighted his pipe and stood with his back to the fire, staring at me as if trying to fathom my thoughts.

I kept looking at the food on the table. I was so hungry that I could have almost parted with some of the wealth in my pockets for some of the bread and meat. Then my host took out his watch. Looking at it, he raised his eyebrows.

"Humph, it is time for supper. I will go and fetch my wife."

"Is she an invalid?" I ventured.

He glared at me rather like an animal at bay as he answered.

"She cannot walk. I have to carry her everywhere. Will you excuse me?"

I nodded. He lit another lamp, and picking it up left the room.

When he had gone I sat puzzling upon my good fortune and the strange man. Then I got up and began to wander about the room. It had such a strange sickening smell. I could not at first remember where I had experienced a similar odor; then in a flash it came to me. As a child I had played hide and seek in a disused churchyard, and had hidden in the tumbledown vaults. It was there that I had smelled that moldy, rotten odor. I broke out in a cold perspiration as a great, undefined fear struck me. The other young men—who had taken the gems; what had happened to them? I wanted to get out into the open air—away from the stranger and his horrible bright eyes. I got up and moved toward the door, then I remembered the front door was locked. I turned back and sat on the bed again, wondering what I should do. It seemed ungrateful to flee from the house of a person who had befriended me because of a fear which had no definite proof to confirm it. The man was odd in his ways, but that was nothing to go by. I had nowhere to go and he offered me shelter. There had been very few people who had ever offered to help me, and now that some one had taken compassion on me, I wanted to run away. I decided I could not leave. It would be ungrateful and mean. No, I would stay and see what happened.

The stranger had not been gone long when I heard him coming down the stairs. He was talking very gently to some one and I was reassured for the moment.

"My love, I have brought home a young man to see you—you will love him like you loved Charles Wynton—and the other young men. He is a good-looking young man—an honest young man, my dear—he is a joiner—he will make you the pretty box I have promised you for so long. Come, my love, and be introduced."

I rose to my feet, preparing my best bow for the lady to whom the strange conversation was addressed. My host kicked open the door and entered, carrying a woman clad in much the same period as himself. But—Oh, my God! shall I ever forget that sight!

It was a corpse —a mummy. The face made me feel sick. It was parched and withered, the hair—a bright golden color —hung in thick profusion from the ghastly head. There was a terrible black cavern where the mouth should have been, and to add to its hideousness two glass eyes stared vacantly at me. Below the hem of the dress there hung two stumps devoid of feet. The dried, stick-like arms had no hands. The whole thing was falling to pieces.

As I stared in horror-struck amazement a portion of one arm fell to the ground. I think I shrieked. The stranger's request for a box, "to keep his wife's things together in," came to my mind. This was the reason he wanted that chest!

The terrible stranger must have seen the fear and horror that I felt upon my face, for he kicked the door to quickly and locked it with one hand, slipping the key in his pocket. Seeing him do this I realized that I should have to fight for my life. He was mad! Terribly mad!

He laid his ghastly burden down, propping it up against a chair, where the frightful, unmoving eyes glared straight before it with unwavering intensity. I flung myself upon the door as the madman moved from it, and tugged at the handle wildly. My heart was beating enough to choke me and a cold bath of sweat broke out all over my body. I heard a movement at my back and swung round to see the stranger coming towards me, with a slow, cat-like tread.

"No, no, young man, you must not go. You must have supper with my wife and me," he hissed through his fast set teeth.

"Let me out! Let me out!" I shrieked.

"Don't go, young man; it is years since we have had a

companion at table. My wife likes young men." The stranger smiled grimly as he spoke.

I felt a terrible faintness coming over me, but something in my brain kept saying, "You must not faint, you will die if you do." I pulled myself together and tugged at the door, again to no purpose, and the dreadful man began to speak rapidly and fiercely.

"You can't get out—you can't get out! Listen! I want to warn you. Warn you of the wiles of women. You are an honest young man as I was until I married this woman." He pointed to the mummy. "Look at her!"

I had seen enough of that dreadful thing without wanting to look again.

"Once she was young and beautiful. I believed her honest, like myself. I loved her, trusted her, worshiped at her feet as if she were a goddess; slaved for her, showered affection and all the worldly goods I possessed upon her; prayed for her happiness, prayed to God to make me worthy of her. She gave me kisses for kisses, loving words and sweet caress, and—" he flung out his arms. "All lies! All lies!! Young man!"

I stood looking at him in horror, not knowing what to do. There was no means of escape except through the door, and that was locked—the key in the madman's pocket. He began to walk up and down the room waving his arms about and laughing wildly as he talked.

"She was giving birth to a child and in her agony she called on a name that was not mine! Charles Wynton—my friend—my bosom companion. She had an untimely travail in this house and there was none near to help her, save myself. I questioned her. Do you hear, young man, I questioned her?"

I nodded mutely.

"She told me all; how Wynton—Wynton, my friend, made love to her—while I was working to give her the luxuries that are a good wife's due! She begged my forgiveness, while I sat with my head buried in my hands trying to recover from the terrible blow. My love—my darling—the glorious flower of my life! As I sat by her side sobbing, she died—my beloved—she died—Do you hear, young man? She died!"

I nodded again, and I saw that tears were running down his face.

"The people tried to rob me of her body, but I tricked them. In the secret hours of the night I had a pauper's body brought from the hospital. I unscrewed her coffin and took my darling out and placed the pauper in her place. I hid her dear body beneath my bed, and in secret preserved it. I hate her!—yet I love her."

As if drawn by some memory of love he crossed to the awful mummy. "See, I kiss her dear mouth!"

To my horror I watched him lay his lips upon where the mouth should have been. I shuddered at the sight. It made me feel sick to see him fondling the dreadful thing's hair and arms, kissing it and talking all the while.

"The dear, sweet mouth that lied to me, that spoke false sweetness." Suddenly he flung round to me.

"I swore that a man should die for her—an honest young man—for every month she labored for a false one."

Then I knew my fears were justified—the smell—the other young men—the awful man came toward me, and I flattened myself against the door looking round me for some means of defense. There was nothing—only the knives on the table, and the madman stood between them and me. I realized that nothing but my own fists could save me, should the need arise. Slowly he came toward me, watching me as a cat does a mouse. Suddenly he sprang upon me, crying:

"Beneath this floor lie eight young men, and now you die." His voice rose to a shriek.

He caught me by the throat. I was trembling with fear and horror, but God gave me strength and I hit him full between the eyes. He fell to the floor with blood streaming down his face. He rose again immediately, and snatching a knife from the table leapt upon me again, upsetting the lamp. It fell with a crash to the floor and the oil caught fire. For a few moments we swayed to and fro. He was as strong as a lion and as nimble as a cat. He got a strangulation grip about my throat and for a moment I thought my life was ended, for while he kept his left hand about my throat he raised his right to strike. Somehow I managed to get the knife from him and then felled him to the floor.

In falling he knocked over the remains of his wife. They toppled over him. He remained still—and I knew he was insensible. Trembling all over I knelt down by his side and began to grope for the keys. I found them. With a sob of relief I sprang up and unlocked the cellar door with all speed. The flames were creeping near the mummy as I fled from that chamber of horrors. I took the stairs at a leap and a bound and reached the front door. I had hardly got the key in the lock before I heard the terrible madman shriek. He had recovered!

"Darling! My darling Margaret!" I heard him cry. "My ninth sacrifice has escaped me. Courage, my sweet, thou shalt be avenged!"

I heard him pounding up the stairs and waited no longer, but fled away from that gruesome house as fast as my young legs would carry me. As I tore down the lane I heard the madman following me, shrieking, "Come back! Come back!"

I came to a gate in a field and vaulting over it flung myself down in the shadow of a hedge. I heard him running by, panting and whimpering, "Margaret! Margaret!" and held my breath until his footsteps were out of hearing. Then I crept along the sides of the hedges until at last I came to an Inn called "The Spaniards." Rousing the innkeeper with difficulty, I called for a bed and a stiff glass of brandy. The spirit steadied my nerves to some extent and I went to my room, but not to sleep, for the sound of the madman's voice was ringing in my ears.

No dawn have I ever so gladly welcomed. Going into the Inn parlor for breakfast I saw two men enter by the front door bearing the body of a man—that of the stranger. My heart almost stopped. The host came hurrying up, and catching sight of the corpse gave a cry of surprise.

"My God! If it isn't Sir Joseph," he exclaimed.

The bearers nodded, and one of them spoke.

"We found 'im lying on the London Road, as stiff as a pikestaff, an' we thought we'd better bring 'im in 'ere. I went up to 'is 'ouse to see if I could get any 'elp, but it was burnt to the ground."

The landlord shook his head dismally. "Poor soul, I suppose he must have been going for help to put out the fire. He was a queer man." He turned to me. "Do you know, sir, he's lived in that house for thirty years, an absolute hermit with never a soul to talk to or help him. He was a famous surgeon once. But after his wife died—poor soul, he never got over it!"

"Indeed?" I replied, trying to hide my nervousness.

The landlord followed me into the parlor, and hovered round the table.

"There's queer tales told about Sir Joseph," he volunteered, as I began my breakfast. "They say there were strange doings at his house. People have told of shrieks and laughter more fit for hell than for a human place. No one near here would dare pass down that lane at night. They say a man went down once and came back, raving of a dead woman and staring eyes. . . ."

I could bear no more. With a mumbled word of apology I flung my reckoning on the table and ran from the Inn.

I wanted to get away from that district which had held such a night of terror for me. I went to London where I founded the now famous business of William Vanstone's, the furnishers and cabinet makers, on the money the poor madman gave me.

I go to the site of his house every year, in spite of the awful experience I had there, and murmur a prayer for his soul's happiness in the world where all betrayals are forgotten.

LAOCOON

By BASSETT MORGAN

AS THE LITTLE TRADING SCHOONER DREW NEARER THE shadowy fringes of the island, the talk on deck fell to silence. The tropic beauty of Papua was strangely repellent. Willoughby, who had impulsively answered the offer of Professor Denham to spend a year or so helping the scientist in his investigation in deep sea lore off these shores at a salary of three thousand dollars a year, rather regretted his acceptance. He felt as if mysterious tentacles of miasmic jungle swamps breathed poison in the perfume-laden off-shore wind. It was like the breath of a black panther. He took Professor Denham's letter from his pocket and read it again.

Five years before, Willoughby had been a student under Professor Denham in the University of California, and had gained a name for himself as a football star. He had regretted the circumstances which prompted Professor Denham to resign the chair of science under the storm of ridicule and protest resulting when a newspaper featured the scientist's assertion that sea-serpents really existed. The article was illustrated by a cartoon of Professor Denham and Chueng Ching, a Chinese student, who was his especial protégé and devoted to Denham, in the coils of a serpent labeled "Public Opinion," depicting the agony of the Laocoon. There was the account of class experiments in transplanting the brain of one rat to the head of another, and of the practical joke perpetrated by a student assistant in substituting the brain of a female rat for that of a male, which led to riotous speculation on the campus as to the outcome of the experiment.

Willoughby had been sorry for Professor Denham. It was, however, the three thousand dollars salary that decided him to accept Denham's offer and take the next steamer from San Francisco east, reëmbarking on a trading schooner for Papua, and Denham was to send a boat to take him to his own habitation.

The letter, which he reread within sight of landing, had emphasized the necessity of "a strong fearless man, without nerves." Willoughby interpreted the phrase with a new meaning, now that he recognized the repellent fascination of Papua.

He had no sooner stepped ashore than a Chinese in oil-stained dungarees approached him and spoke: "You allee samee Mista Will'bee, you come 'long my boat."

He had scant time to bid farewell to his acquaintances of the trading vessel when he was led to a launch lying on water so clear that she seemed to be floating on air. Her propeller churned foam and she careened a little as they rounded the point; then for hours the launch raced along the coast, where jungles brooded and river mouths showed no banks, but only trees rooted in swamp. Fighting a loneliness he could not analyze, Willoughby watched sea gardens beneath and tried to reason away a lowering depression. The Chinese ignored his tentative approaches to conversation by unbroken and stoical silence.

In the late afternoon, with her engines slowed to half-speed, the launch entered a lagoon, where echoes of her pulsations disturbed boobies on the wreck of an old ship pronged on coral spurs. The lagoon water held gaudy little fish scattering like sparks between skeleton-white roots of drowned trees. Sea life had made the wreck its prey. White decay crept up her sides and she was rooted to abysmal depths by weed. A small wharf sagged under forest creepers with tendrils trailing in the sea. The planks creaked alarmingly as Willoughby trod them following the boatman, and met the shrill hum of insects. The heat was like a furnace blast. He was aware of a throb like *tic-douloureux,* pulsing incessantly, as if on distant hills the heat had a voice.

What had once been a path leading from the wharf was now overgrown. The Chinese, lathered with sweat, slashed with a knife at trailing vines. Orchids quivered like flames. The incessant hum of insects rose in loud crescendo, but as they progressed the trail became less confused with looped lianas. Sunlight filtered through branches overhead. And ever nearer came that slow beat of sound, touching nerve centers as insistently as the insect humming irritated the ear-drums.

Then the jungle was ended and Willoughby saw a bamboo palisade enclosing ground that had once been cleared and under cultivation; yet the jungle, beaten back, had swarmed again, choking the garden, creeping over the palisade and the crushed coral walk which led to a substantial dwelling with nipa-thatched roof and a vine-covered pergola leading to shore rocks which rose abruptly at one side. It was then that Willoughby understood that diapason of sound, the shock of outer seas breaking in subterranean caverns.

The Chinese who had guided him did not enter the gate, but darted beside the palisade. Willoughby heard no sign of human presence save the "shir-rr" of his boot-soles on the coral. Then a Chinese wearing the white ducks of a house-boy appeared in a doorway cut through luxuriant bougain-villea vines purple with bloom. He stood staring at Willoughby, with his hands twisting together. For a moment Willoughby felt again that sense of helplessness bred by the jungle, the fear of encroaching death.

"Tell your boss-man that Willoughby is here," he said.

He followed the Chinese into the house. The large living room was shaded and cool. Chinese matting covered the floor. Sea-grass chairs offered ease. There were wall cases filled with labeled specimens of sea denizens, a table holding a typewriter and notebook and some loose pages of script. The house was clean and orderly, yet he still felt as if the jungle lay too close for safety.

"Boss-man, he come bimeby," ventured the Chinese plaintively.

"Where's Chueng Ching?" Willoughby knew the Chinese student had accompanied Denham to his retreat and, it was rumored, provided funds for the scientist.

"Him gone long time. I not know much." The reply brought a grimace from the house-boy, as of apprehension.

"You got one piecee ship, I go out 'longside," he added plaintively, then darted back at the sound of steps, as Professor Denham entered.

Willoughby was shocked at the change in him. Denham's skin seemed stretched over his bones, his eyes shone like those of a madman, the hand extended to Willoughby felt cold and lifeless as that of a corpse in spite of tropic heat.

"Glad you arrived, Willoughby," he said. "You've come too late to see Chueng Ching to-day, but he'll be here tomorrow. We'll eat, then you can rest. You'll excuse me if I write a few notes right away. I've just come from Chueng Ching and I must get them down at once."

Willoughby was a little surprised, but he followed the house-boy to a room with a bed screened by netting, took off his shoes, collar and coat and dropped on the cotton covering and dozed. He was wakened by the clink of dishes. In the living room a table was set for two, but Denham did not appear.

The house-boy hovered near, serving Willoughby eagerly, and when the coffee was brought voiced again his wistful plea, "You got one piecee ship, I go out 'longside."

He seemed to hang on Willoughby's answer. Plainly the Chinese was in the grip of fear, and the white man remembered again the encroaching jungle and the derelict rooted to sea gardens. He wished Denham would return, and went on the porch to look for his host. He did not mind the lack of courtesy, but the silence and oppression were affecting his nerves. Tropic night had fallen, the mosquitoes were vicious. Beyond the murmur of sea caverns he heard nothing, and returned to the house, to look at the specimens in wall cases, then to reach the typewriter stand where he glanced at a sheet still in the carrier. Without consciousness of reading something not intended for him, Willoughby glanced at the typing in view:

"There is now no doubt but the physical coarseness of the beast has absorbed the fine mentality of Chueng Ching. I fed him double the usual amount of chicken yesterday, and he was in a fine rage for more. His roarings are bestial. The pool was lashed to foam by his fury. And I am assured that his rage was directed toward me, his friend and companion. It is scarcely a year since he was sorrowful at the thought that I should die before he died and leave him alone. Now he is all brute and I am punished. He no longer heeds my voice . . ."

As if the writer had been interrupted at his task, the sentence was left unfinished. Willoughby read with mingled rage and horror. Evidently Chueng Ching had gone insane and he had been hired to care for a madman. He resented it. Yet he was virtually a prisoner on the island unless he could find the boatman who brought him. He stood a moment, wondering what to do. The little house-boy lingered near him constantly without giving the impression of watching, but shook his head when Willoughby demanded to see Denham.

"No can do," he said plaintively.

Willoughby went through the curtained doorway into a room evidently belonging to Chueng Ching, to judge by the embroidered tapestries moving in the draft. Chests of carved teak stood between wall cases. A table held metal tubes, with sealed ends and addressed to the Royal College at Pekin. Willoughby heard the squawking of hens and ran outside into the pergola of vines. A lantern stood beside a bamboo coop and Professor Denham was wringing the neck of a hen and tossing it on the ground while he reached for others. He looked at Willoughby, and it seemed to him that Denham's eyes held mingled fear and madness.

Then he heard the sound of water threshed as if by storm, although there was no wind and not a leaf of the vines stirred.

"Chueng Ching," said Denham. "Hungry again. Such gluttony. I wish you'd arrived earlier, but it's difficult to see him at night. Go into the house, Willoughby, and read those notes you'll find. I'll return presently and tell you all about him."

Denham gathered the slaughtered hens and darted down the vine-covered passageway of the pergola. There was the sound of an iron door banged shut, the repeated noise of water threshed violently, and Willoughby returned to the house, where he took up the typed script, arranged the pages according to numbers and glanced over them. Fear, horror, fascination held him. He forgot where he was. He was unaware of the house-boy standing mute near his chair, seeking companionship in a fear that was sapping his life. Willoughby sat on the edge of his chair, hair slowly rising, scalp prickly, his palms moist with cold sweat.

"I have now the evidence that ocean depths are a desert of ice-cold water with no living organism; soundless, still, dark nothingness. A ship sinking to those depths would cease to be, ground into molecules on the ocean bed. The silence must be fearful. But greatest satisfaction of all, is the proving of my theory that sea-serpents, as they are popularly called, do exist, and that their armor of scales and longevity has preserved some of them to this day. The cavern pool is an ideal spot for such a sea denizen to lurk. Chueng Ching told me that he had heard rumors of this haunted cavern, when we were both in California, and he is as delighted as I, that we have found the thing, and my years of research are rewarded. . . .

"It is three months since I added to this diary. Chueng Ching is despondent. The white spot which he tells me has been spreading for a year is only too plainly evidence of leprosy. Chueng Ching is accursed, doomed to a lingering death, a tragedy for both of us. He feels it keenly because we have found what we sought, and for him there will not be time to pursue the study of the sea-serpent. We spoke, last night, of the restrictions of man's limited span of life, the pity that we are not given enough years, even centuries, for research. One envies the sea-serpent, which is undoubtedly older than whales, older than the sequoias of California, much older than the Christian era. To judge by his length and the size of his armor plates, our dragon is centuries old. I said to Chueng Ching that I wished I could inhabit his body, and not only live indefinitely but also explore the ocean depths, learn his manner of living and perhaps find his relatives. Chueng Ching seemed startled rather than amused. . . .

"Two months later. This morning Chueng Ching asked a terrific thing of me. He pleaded the growing decay of his flesh. His fingers are already numb. He believes that I could give him the magnificent body and strength of our sea-serpent, a thought suggested no doubt by those experimental tamperings of mine in college surgery, substituting the brains of one rodent for those of another. But I could not do such a thing. Chueng Ching is a man, a brother to me, a fine mentality, a higher organism."

Willoughby ripped open his shirt, longing for a cooling breath on his skin. The shadow of the house-boy fell across his feet; the brown hands were twisting mutely. The page he had just read fell to the floor, and he seized the next.

"Chueng Ching has worked out an arrangement by which he is confident we can manage the operation. The steel net will confine the sea-serpent, a collar of steel will hold his head while I shoot ether from a spray gun. The bench, the instrument, the cauterants, are ready. Only, I am afraid.

If it were not that Chueng Ching's fingers and toes are already sloughing away, I could not do this thing. He pleads all day, and moans all night. To-morrow I shall be alone save for the house-boy Wi Wo and the boatman who is hired to call here at regular intervals."

There was the rustling of the page which Willoughby crushed in tense fingers as he took it up, and the sound of his heavy breathing.

"Chueng Ching wakened with a great fear, although he assures me that he went under the anæsthetic not only reconciled but even rejoicing in a resurrection of which he felt surer than I did. He felt no pain, only fear and the sense of a great weight dragging him down. No doubt the serpent body is not yet under control of nerve telegraphy of the mind. I attribute his fear to the same cause. Time will cure both troubles. To-day, I made out the first of his attempts to communicate with me. There is no doubt he speaks, but I scarce understand his words, roared in that tremendous voice. I spent hours with him, and had Wi Wo fetch my meals. I asked questions to which he could reply by a nod or shake of his great crested head. What a pity those fools who ridiculed my assertions that sea-dragons do exist, cannot see this triumph!

"The vitality of Chueng Ching's body is prodigious. He revived quickly from the ether. The leprous shell of my poor friend is in the ocean depths, sewn in canvas, weighed with iron. The sea will sing a requiem. But Chueng Ching is now invulnerable and magnificent. Nothing could harm that marvelously constructed coat of mail unless it is some device of man, the destroyer."

Willoughby lifted his head and brushed his hand across his eyes. He was entering into horror that chilled his flesh, a nightmare he could not and would not believe. He abominated the crime of Denham, yet was fascinated.

"He will not take meat, yet we fed the sea-serpent he now inhabits, at regular intervals, on raw flesh. But since the change Chueng Ching will not touch it. No doubt the higher mentality of an æsthete has subjugated the beast body. To-day I prepared another roll of notes for the Royal College of Pekin, a rare collection of data which will receive consideration from Chinese savants that I could not wrest from my own people. Chueng Ching and I have proved the existence of sea-dragons and the ability of science through martyrdom to penetrate to the mysteries beneath the waters."

Willoughby mopped his face. Wi Wo held a tray toward him and he took a bottle it held and poured himself a peg of brandy, then seized the next page.

"Chueng Ching is timid of the dark. His fear throttles our investigations. And much that he would impart is lost through my faulty understanding of his articulation. The curse of Babel rings down the ages. He breaks into Cantonese in his endeavor to enlighten me. The finer details would be invaluable but I hoped too greatly. I cannot understand his fear, and his rather pathetic regret at the loneliness he will find when I am dead. But one thing comforts me, he is taking food and prefers rather undercooked chicken and pork. I must keep a stock on hand, as his appetite is prodigious. . . .

"Six months since I last wrote these notes. Chueng Ching has furnished me with priceless specimens and data of the ocean depths, the notes of which I seal daily in metal tubes to be sent to Pekin. But I notice a change in him. While at first he was afraid of the depths, he now goes fearlessly and remains for a longer period each time. The silence down there must be fearful, but he seems to like exploring, and has even identified geographic indentations of continent shores, and recognizes the chill of polar seas . . .

"Three months from my last entry. Another period of change has come over Chueng Ching. The little fish spewed from his jaws are spoiled by carelessness. Things are not going so well. There is a change of temperament and his articulation is thick. For a time he spoke clearly although in a voice like a church organ. Now he roars in sullen rage when I refuse to feed him before I obtain an account of his wanderings. I believe it was a mistake to feed him flesh. Better to have left him to find sea-food only. I wonder if the brute body is in ascendance, or if meeting other monsters of his own kind has upset him. He would know no means of communication with them, and no methods of defense, but what a spectacle it would be to view a battle of sea-dragons! I wish it had been my lot to change from a human to this saurian. I am past middle age and the passions which plague a younger man. Chueng Ching, who in his human shape was vowed to celibacy and had devoted his life to science, is seeking a mate. He was never more lucid than when he roared to me that he had found a sweetie, the college slang of old days for a sweetheart, and demanded more food for strength he would need to fight off other males of his kind. With great sorrow, I must admit the end is in sight. He is indifferent to our researches and I gained nothing to-day but the account of this female sea-dragon, which seems coy and exhibits greater speed and endurance than Chueng Ching, as they tear through the depths, circling islands, lashing a riot of phosphorescence in the night. Oh, to see them! To find another and change from this body hampering me to a saurian like Chueng Ching!"

Cold sweat broke out on Willoughby's forehead as he took the last sheet from the typewriter, and reread the bit which had fascinated him a little while before.

He understood perfectly what Denham had written, of the change over this *thing*. The brute body had conquered the mind of Chueng Ching. The ferocity of the sea-dragon was in ascendance. He had turned on Denham, no longer obeying the voice of the scientist. The remainder of the page held no less of horror, a prophetic intimation of Denham's fear.

"Chueng Ching is a fiend. He struck at me to-day with

open jaws. I have sealed the complete notes to date, and addressed the results of my researches to the Royal College at Pekin, where they will act on the instructions to use the balance of Chueng Ching's wealth to pursue this investigation in case anything should happen to me. But Willoughby has arrived, and I am confident that the skill he displayed in the science class can be enhanced by practice so that he can perform the operation I desire. Chueng Ching laughed when I told him my plan, but promised to entice another male of his kind to the pool where Willoughby and I shall trap him by means of the iron-barred gateway dropped behind this sea-dragon we used as a body for the brain of Chueng Ching. I have not talked to Willoughby about it, but I noticed he seemed as well set up and fit as in college days. His reward shall be a share of Chueng Ching's wealth, and the fame of . . ."

Willoughby crushed the sheet in his hand, every nerve in his body on edge, his breathing sounding loud in the silence. The chair crashed over as he rose and stared past Wi Wo at the curtained doorway. The embroidered dragons seemed to move with malignant life. And a more terrible dragon inhabited this place, the Madness which had caught Denham and made of him a priest of more dreadful rites than voodoo of the jungles.

Willoughby realized now for what he had been summoned by the scientist. He must escape or be caught in a trap from which there was no escape. He would find Denham, and tell him that he was going; Denham was at that moment near the pool. Willoughby remembered the chickens he had been killing, and his words: "Chueng Ching, hungry again. Such gluttony!" He remembered the sound as of water threshed by storm. Denham feared the thing, yet he had gone to it again. He might be in danger of his life. Common decency demanded that Willoughby try to save the man. As for remaining under the conditions to be imposed, his body shivered as if with nausea at the thought.

Under the vine-covered pergola, he was startled by the sight of Wi Wo in his white ducks. The hand of the Chinese fell on his arm, the man's teeth chattering like castanets. And above that chattering and Willoughby's breathing, came the sound of water crashing on rocks, threshed under flails of no wind that ever was.

Willoughby stalked down the pergola, gripping his courage in his hand, assuring himself the typing was the fantasy of a madman, and that the worst he would find would be Denham in the violence of insanity brought on by loneliness and the eery mystery of the island. The heelless slippers of Wi Wo shuffled reluctantly as they came near an iron door, with light from beyond shining through the space between heavy bars. Willoughby saw the lantern on the stone floor. Steps led down. There was the crash of waves subsiding gradually, and a low moaning audible.

Willoughby opened the iron door, snatched up the lantern and began to descend the steps. A cool wind swept upward, a smell of sea-wrack and cavern chill. He saw the oily luminance of water where the sea filled a natural cove. It was stirred as by a violent upheaval from beneath. The rock ledge below glistened with minute sea life. He saw something resembling a huge horsecollar slung to iron rings in the cavern roof, and a steel net dependent from ropes, the apparatus of that operation performed on the sea-dragon. Along one side was a litter of things scarcely discernible by the faint lantern light.

With his scalp prickling, Willoughby held the lantern at arm's length, to learn what manner of gigantic bird it was that ran to and fro on the ledge, uttering squawks of fear which the cavern echoed. He saw a heap of dead chickens on the ledge, then a movement of Wi Wo caught his eye. The Chinese was retreating up the steps, backward, his eyes staring at the pool, his hands groping along the rock wall. Willoughby looked again at the pool, straining his vision to see what had thralled Wi Wo and turned his yellow skin green with terror.

It came like gushing light in the depths, stirring the black water, a radiance of glittering unrest, undulating flitter and shadow, faintly phosphorescent; then coils broke a moving swirl in the gloom.

Willoughby turned to run up the steps. The breath of Wi Wo hissed between his teeth. There was the silken slur of water washing the rock, and in another moment Willoughby was crowding the Chinese on the steps, for the water parted and a crested head was upreared, water dripping from fanged jaws, red tongue quivering, large glassy eyes regarding the two men on the steps with malevolent glaring. Coils of a serpent body upreared. Willoughby saw the great scales like iridescent metal plates. There was that threshing hiss of water, tremendous in the cavern walls. Willoughby's heart was pounding in his throat and wrist. Fear paralyzed him.

Then he screamed. From that great throat came a roar that swelled and boomed, and in that sound Willoughby heard unmistakably the name of "Denham" howled in wrath.

His own scream seemed to be echoed by the flapping white thing on the ledge. For the first time he realized that he had lost the chance for what he came to do: to save Denham. That was Denham—that mad disheveled thing clad in white ducks which was bent nearly double, waving its coat-tail over its head. It stood erect, laughing horribly.

"Chueng Ching," it called, "did you bring your sea-dragon? See, Willoughby is here, Willoughby who will make me invulnerable so we can rove the deeps together . . ."

The rest was drowned in that howl of the sea-dragon, a burst of laughter boomed through a gigantic throat, and the crested head swooped at Denham. The sea leaped, a wave shot by those armored coils crashed up the steps and over

Willoughby. The lantern fell from his numbed fingers, the sea was in his mouth.

Then he felt the hands of Wi Wo clutching him. They were crouched in a heap on the steps. The pool was dark and the seas fell quiet. Willoughby felt his way a few steps lower and saw the outer archway of the cove. Dawn had bloomed, early tropic dawn shone silver. The ledge was empty. Denham had disappeared.

Willoughby turned and pushing the terrified Chinese before him went up the steps, clanging and bolting the iron door.

He strode through the house, looked at the sealed tube of notes addressed ready to send, and at the typed account of Denham's crime. Then he went to the porch.

A voice at his shoulder startled him: "You got one piecee ship, I go out 'long you." The plaintive wail was chattered through quivering lips.

"Come on," snapped Willoughby and ran down the path.

Along the palisade sauntered the Chinese boatman. Willoughby took money from his pocket and offered it.

"Take us back to the port," he commanded. "Quick!"

THE LIFE SERUM

By PAUL S. POWERS

I HAVE FOUND THE SECRET OF ETERNAL LIFE, YET MY BODY has been buried for three years. As far as I know I shall live forever, and shall wander through the dim ages of the future when my body is dust. I never died.

Perhaps I am at your elbow as you read, for I am invisible, though I can see you and hear your words. I am able to follow you, even though you close the door at your back. While I can mingle with those who were once my fellows, my shout in your ear would be as useless as my trying to move a sheet of paper on your desk. Fourth dimension? Perhaps. I don't know.

Dr. Biuret would be the most famous man in your world to-day, had he not died that day. Together we had plotted and calculated until failure seemed impossible, but Death himself stepped into the laboratory unexpectedly, and brought our experiment to a terrible ending. Even now I can see Biuret's horribly discolored face writhing under the agony of the liquid fire. Since then I have wished that his fate had overtaken me also. There are things more awful than death, and it is a strange thing to see your own corpse lowered into the tomb.

About four years ago, a short time after I graduated from medical college, I met Dr. Biuret and soon became his assistant. I had my own way to make; I needed the money; and Biuret was a fascinating man. The work was decidedly complex, and though I understood the task that was given me, I at no time knew what my employer was working upon.

He had hinted that he was after a new anæsthetic, and as Biuret had been a specialist along this line I did not ask further. Biuret was very well known to the medical profession, although some of his earlier experiments were so daring that he had become an object of derision among the other physicians. It was known that he was attempting to perfect a so-called "Panacea of Life," and although some of his results were startling, his discoveries were laughed down, and Biuret retired to work out his problem in seclusion. At no time did he violate the ethics of the profession, yet his work was so amazing—so unbelievable—that coöperation with other scientists was impossible. He needed an assistant, and it was in this capacity that I grew to know his methods, even if I never quite understood the composition of the strange chemical he compounded.

Dr. Biuret was very human. Rather shamefacedly, he told me that it was his own very healthy fear of death that determined his lifework.

"Since I was a small child," he said, "I have had a morbid fear of death. And now, after years of study and investigation, I know no more about it than I did. That is the reason it seems terrible to me."

I wonder if he knows more about it now!

The doctor was a trifle past fifty, and he literally lived in his office and laboratory on Thirty-ninth Street. After I had worked with him for a few months, his habits became mine, also, and I turned my back on the world, absorbed in what I knew to be the impossible. It is impossible, isn't it, to tear oneself away from the body? For a long time I thought my wanderings a dream—a rather pleasant nightmare—but now I know it to be true. And Dr. Biuret is dead.

I was skeptical at first. The contents of the scientist's bottles and vials puzzled me, and for a time I thought him mad. What is the use of compounding Indian hemp, the medical name for which is *Cannabis Indica,* chloral, and a host of other narcotic drugs, with extracts of pineal and other brain glands? I couldn't see the object. The scientist haphazardly threw together enough drugs to poison a city, poured in solutions and powders the nature of which I only guessed, and then started all over again. I was set to work at tasks that seemed foolish to me, and for the first few weeks my time was taken up mixing some of the more familiar chemicals used by the doctor. Some of the materials I was warned not to touch. "Not that there is any special secret attached to them," Biuret said, "but for the reason that some of them are extremely dangerous, even with expert handling."

It was some time before I wormed the object of his search from him. We were sitting at the laboratory table before his test-tubes, when our talk wandered to the subject of the mind.

"You know that it is a strange thing," remarked Biuret, "but it is a known fact that the mind, or consciousness, is a product of the cerebral cortex. You yourself are the child of this part of your brain, as I am the child of mine. Isn't it strange that the product of a living thing should die with it?"

I agreed with him, and added that when death took, he took all. As I spoke the words a strange look crept over the doctor's face, and his lips quivered with excitement.

"That seems to be the case," he cried, *"as far as we know.* We do know, however, that the mind develops through the five senses, and through these senses alone. The baby, when born, has no mind and no consciousness. Can the mind exist after the senses, which are destroyed by death, are gone? There are theories and always will be theories, but I'm going to prove it. I'm developing a drug with the power of tearing the mind from the body—*before death!*"

"What?" I gasped. "You don't mean to say we've been wasting our time on such a wild scheme as that?"

Biuret nervously drew out a cigarette and lit it.

"And why not?" he challenged. "That's the only way to find out, and science has been making progress in solving the unknown since early centuries. I tell you, man, it's important, and we haven't been wasting time."

Important! It was more than that, if he was successful; but I had no idea that it was anything other than a mad and impossible undertaking. I told him so. The idea of Biuret throwing away his energy on a thing like that angered me. I added that I did not care to work at this foolishness any longer.

"I'm sorry," sighed my employer. "You've been invaluable to me, and your knowledge of chemistry and materia medica has made our work run smoothly during the time you've been here. I suppose you thought I was working on a new local anæsthetic, if the few hints I dropped did not go astray. I wish I had told you all from the first, and if you'll listen now I'll try to explain something of what I am trying to get at."

He told me something of the composition of the strange drugs he was using. Of course I understood chloral, cannabis, hyoscin and a few more of them, but most of the drugs were new to medical science. Some had, indeed, been discovered before, but their uses were unknown. And the brain glands! At this time the profession was just beginning to know the use and purpose of some of them. I wonder how soon it will be before they know all.

"This compound," summed up the doctor, "which I believe I have perfected, will take the mind away from the body—do what delirium fails to do. Delirium, which of course only deranges the mind, enables it to function abnormally. My compound will detach the mind completely from the body, without distorting its functioning."

"The name for which is death!" I smiled.

"The name for which is eternal life," corrected Biuret. "It is true that an overdose of this would mean death, for most drugs are poisons, but if you will remain with me long enough to see the end of my experiments you'll see for yourself. To-morrow we will test it out."

My curiosity got the better of me, and I agreed.

The rest of that day, and the following evening, we worked to devise a chemical antagonist—an antidote. It would be nearer the truth to say that Biuret worked upon it—I helped, knowing scarce more than I had already known. Finally, Biuret seemed satisfied.

"It will work," he said. "Both of them will work. The antidote should be perfect, and we will need it to make the experiments—to call the mind back to the body."

I concealed a superior smile.

"What's the idea of the cannabis, for instance?" I asked.

"That's a curious drug, isn't it?" sparkled Biuret, enthusiastically. "And it has properties unguessed of by most experimenters. Of course the symptoms following a large dose are well known; before its narcotic action takes place and the patient slips into unconsciousness, there is a strange prolongation of time—and a sense of double consciousness. Indian hemp is a well known but little used drug, and it is an important drug in my compound. When hemp is mixed with other hypnotics, such as chloral and opium in small amounts, the effect is—well, you shall see."

This was interesting, but I was not greatly impressed. Already I had doomed Biuret's wild plan to failure, but I was willing to give him a trial to make good. That evening we talked late, after we had finished dabbling in chemicals, and I thought that my companion was laboring under an intense excitement. We talked of death, that mysterious phenomenon that strikes soon or late, and Biuret spoke of his theories in an awed whisper. Soon I, also, entered into the spirit of the thing and discussed the unknown as easily as he. Biuret told of a happening of a few years ago. He had made an enemy, he said, while studying in Austria. The man, a doctor, had threatened Biuret's life and had threatened to track him across the world. Biuret told me something of the quarrel—there was a woman in it, the other doctor's wife—a fact that astonished me. Biuret had a past, evidently.

"There was really nothing to it," murmured Biuret. "Nothing wrong, I mean. Sometimes I think that Dr. Laster's mind must have become unbalanced. But, be that as it may, I'll confess that I'm afraid. Not that I fear Laster, but that I fear death. Since that day I have led the life of a recluse, and his threat has hounded me. I have a feeling that something is going to happen. Laster has a powerful and revengeful mind, and he will not stop at anything."

I wonder if this was Biuret's reason for wanting to solve the mystery of life and death. Somehow, after I had learned this chapter in his life, the man seemed more human than ever. He had been threatened, and he feared the thing known as death, as a child fears the dark—but then, who does not? There was, however, nothing childlike about his amazing deductions, and to me, his knowledge seemed boundless. Since that evening I believe he had me hypnotized, and unknown to myself, I could not have left Biuret's laboratories had I wished it.

The next day we spent in looking for a suitable subject for the experiments. As a rule such individuals are not hard to find; almost any derelict will allow himself to be experimented upon for a substantial fee, but we were unsuccessful in our search. I believe Biuret searched only half-heartedly, for in a way it would be a breach of medical ethics to have tried his formula on a human being while its effects were unknown. If anything should happen, Biuret could be held for murder. The same day, Biuret made a proposal.

"See here," he said, after an hour's restless pacing in his office. "You can handle this thing all right. Try it on me—I'll take the chance."

In vain I argued the matter. But there seemed to be no other way, and, as the doctor said, he had enough confidence in his own invention to try it himself. That evening we did try out the formula—cautiously I gave him a few minims of the solution with a hypodermic needle, and waited nervously for the results. There were none. Beyond a feeling of drowsiness and languor, Biuret confessed that he felt no effects at all. The formula was a failure.

"Give me a larger dose," commanded Biuret, impatiently.

I refused. While the effects upon the scientist had been negligible, I knew that the solution held enough chloral and hyoscin to make a large dose unsafe, and I told him so.

"We'll get that formula right if it takes a year!" muttered the doctor. "There can't be much between failure and success, in this case. I tell you, it's got to come out right! Bring me the test-tubes!"

I obeyed. It was strange that the thought of leaving him did not at this time enter my mind. For a month I worked with him, and then we seemed no farther along than before. Even Biuret's hopes were beginning to fade and I believe he would have given up the idea, had not a letter arrived at his office one morning.

I saw him open it. Carelessly, a trifle impatiently, he slit open the envelope, which (I noticed) bore a foreign postage stamp. Then I thought I saw his face pale as he took in the contents, which he seemed to read in one hasty glance. For a moment he sat at his desk, holding the paper in hands that trembled a little. He turned to me with a faint smile, and handed the letter across to me.

Just two words: "Congratulations," and "Laster," which seemed to be the signature.

"What does it mean?" I asked in astonishment.

"It means," said Biuret, moistening his lips, "that I must perfect my formula."

He laughed, as if it were a jest, but I noticed that his knees nearly gave way when he rose and staggered toward the cluttered laboratory table. Was this, then, proof for that wild story Biuret had told to me the month before? At the time I had given it little thought, supposing that Biuret had rather overstated the matter, and that the danger from this strange enemy was largely a product of my associate's brooding mind. But this was real. Biuret's fear was not feigned. The danger was there.

"He congratulated me," mused the scientist, picking up the concise letter again. "He must have heard of my—experiment," he added bitterly.

"Do you mean that this fellow actually will take your life?"

"He will if I leave it in his way," smiled Biuret. Then his face sobered. "He's a paranoiac, and is dangerous because he is educated. A fancied injury, years ago, made me the object of his insane hatred. But come—let's forget about it, and set to work."

We did so, but I saw that Biuret did not forget it. I believe his dread hastened our work to a successful conclusion. Late that evening Biuret checked up, and his face told me that he was satisfied enough to give his solution another trial. The compound of chemicals and drugs was not far different from the one we had tested before, although they were in different proportions. He had added, also, an extract from the left lobe of the pituitary gland in the brain. Its place in the compound I could not guess.

"We will try it to-morrow—no, to-night!" cried Biuret.

He rolled up his sleeve, and although there was a couch in the next room, stretched himself out on the dissecting table. He seemed willing—nay, eager—that the hypodermic needle enter his tissues.

"Intravenously, this time," he ordered, meaning that I should inject the liquid directly into a vein. "One reason for our failure before was, I think, that the active principle was destroyed in the tissues before it reached the brain."

I diluted the liquid several times and poured a portion of it into a large glass syringe. This I hooked up to a tube with a needle attached, for in operations of this kind extreme care must be taken that the solution does not flow too rapidly into the vein. I also knew that should I allow an air bubble to enter the tube, it might mean instant death to Biuret, when it reached his heart. Of course I had been schooled in such things, yet I confess I was not nearly as cool as Biuret, who was reclining at his ease on the dissecting table and actually smoking a cigarette.

"And this is the man who fears death!" I muttered, as I thrust the needle into the fleshy part of the doctor's forearm.

I elevated the syringe and let the solution flow into the vein, which I knew I had pierced, from the spurt of venous blood that had entered the tube. No word or expression of pain had Biuret uttered, and I watched him closely. For a moment or two nothing happened—thirty seconds passed. Then I saw Biuret's body suddenly stiffen. The cigarette dropped from his nerveless hand. His face had become tinged with the bluish danger signal—cyanosis. Before I could stop the injection of the rest of the drug he had become unconscious. His face was a peculiar leaden color, the jaw had dropped to an absurd angle. The eyes remained open and fixed in a peculiar stare that reminded me of the glass eyes of a puppet.

In an agony of haste I gave him powerful stimulants. A hypodermic of strychnine, to support the heart, followed by another. But it was too late—there were no signs of life, and respiration and the heart action had ceased. Dissolution had already taken place. Biuret was dead!

Was this, then, the result of our experiments? Biuret had sought life, and found death. Or was this his plan after all—suicide, to escape the fear that was haunting him? Desperately I sought to bring back life to the doctor's body—with horror I found that it was cold as ice. I tried every test I knew, all the while chanting the hideous phrase: "Biuret is dead and I have killed him." Every test I used told me that Biuret had been dead for some ten minutes, and finally I thought of the telephone—I must notify the police. At that moment I thought of Dr. Biuret's antidote, and as a last resort I injected a large dose at the base of the cerebrum, as Biuret had told me the week before. Hopeless!

It was no use—Biuret was dead. There was no effect—five minutes passed—anxious minutes in which I cursed and prayed by turns. If the fiendish formula would work, why not the antidote? Then, as I watched, a change came over the face of the corpse. It was a miracle the like of which no man has ever seen, for I watched life slowly pulse back into the ghastly face of a cadaver. The eyelids trembled faintly, the blue tint faded away and normal color took its place. I could feel Biuret's pulse warm under my fingers. His heart was beating—Biuret lived! Whether I fainted then I do not know, but with a sigh of relief I groped for the table and found darkness.

When I regained consciousness I found Biuret shaking me by the shoulder. I sipped the brandy he had given me, and stared at him as if he had been a ghost. A few minutes before he had been stretched out in death—his soul had fled—yet here he was, his hand grasping my shoulder.

"Brace up—everything is all right," he was saying.

Biuret was smiling, though still a trifle pale. I could make no answer—the shock I had received still numbed my brain.

"I was standing beside you all during the time you were working over my body," said Biuret. "Worried—weren't you?"

He looked at me with another chuckle.

"For a moment I thought you were going to forget all about the antidote. I saw you rush to the telephone."

"What!" I gasped. "You don't mean to say you—saw me? That's impossible! Why, the telephone is in the next room."

"I followed you there," Biuret murmured.

I was conscious of a headache. Either I was mad, or Biuret was delirious. But how did he know that I had hesitated at the telephone, in the next room, when I had nearly decided to call the police?

"Go to bed and get some sleep," directed the scientist. "Don't puzzle your head over this. I'll explain all about it in the morning—forget it."

I tried to take his advice, but the few hours of sleep I snatched from wakefulness were haunted by terrible visions and nightmares. I awoke unrefreshed the next morning, and when I reached the doctor's office I found him there before me. He too, had not slept, he said. Enthusiastic as a small boy with a new toy, he had paced the office floor all night.

At once he went into an explanation, which, however, left me as mystified as before. The drug, he told me, had acted as he had hoped. As he lost consciousness he regained it in a new form and was able to follow me about as he pleased, and could see my every move.

"Yet my body *was* dead," said Biuret. "Not dead in the way of complete physical death—but dead all the same, for the vital forces had ceased. Still my blood did not congeal, though the heart had stopped, nor did rigor mortis set in."

"All the signs I knew pointed to death," I agreed. "Under such circumstances any coroner would sign a death certificate, and any undertaking parlor accept your body."

The more I thought of this miracle—what else was it? —the more fascinated I became. Biuret had come out of it unscathed, why not—

"Biuret," I said, calmly. "I want to try this thing."

The doctor seemed a little astonished for a moment, then he wrung my hand as though I had gained greatly in his estimation.

"That's the spirit, lad," he cried. "I hesitated to ask you —but I wanted to be on the other end of the experiment once. You shall take it—and when you've *returned* you must tell me what you experienced."

But, nevertheless, I was somewhat uneasy. While Biuret

was preparing my arm for the needle, I thought of the terrible change that had come upon him the evening before. What if things should fail—this time? However, I kept my fears to myself, and took my place on the dissecting table. I would have much preferred the couch in the other room.

There was a little twinge of pain in the region of my forearm. Biuret had evidently inserted the needle. I resolutely turned my face away and stared at the ceiling. A lone fly was buzzing aimlessly about the skylight.

I could feel my arm swell, as the liquid distended the vein. The tingling sensation reached my elbow, and I was conscious of a desire to rub my shoulder, but refrained. Still, I felt as usual. The fly at the skylight had alighted on the glass and was bathing himself in the morning sun. As I watched it, a strange feeling stole over me. A feeling of content—of sleepy languor.

It seemed as if a soft hand had been laid across my brain. This was not bad at all. I wondered—

Lights flashed before my eyes, yet I did not close them. Sleepy as I was, the act of closing them seemed to require too much effort. The lights floated before me in an endless procession, and as things grew dark, the flashes grew more brilliant.

Suddenly—crash! Something seemed to snap within my skull. It was as if something icy cold had writhed about my brain. I wanted to cry out—to scream, but I could not stir a muscle. Then something seemed to wrench away from my consciousness, and I found myself by Biuret's side, staring down at my gruesome body.

Ordinarily I should have been horrified at such a spectacle, had such a thing been possible; but now it seemed the most natural thing in the world. A novelty, it is true, but a very pleasant novelty. I moved about. I had no body, but I could think—see—hear. I needed no body. That terrible thing on the dissecting table was of no use to me now. I tried to speak to Biuret, but I could make no sound. His eyes were fastened anxiously upon my corpse, and from time to time he felt my pulse and shook his head. I noticed that my jaw had fallen and that the whites of my eyes were showing where the pupil and iris should have been. God! Did I look like that thing—in life? My face was distorted as if in terrible pain, yet I felt no pain. I moved freely about the room and then I—or shall I say my consciousness?—moved *through* the closed door into the adjoining room.

When I came back I saw that Biuret was nervously fingering the syringe containing the antidote. At this time I made an astonishing discovery. Anywhere I wished to go I could go. In a twinkling I was there. I thought intensely of the street below, and instantly I found myself in the avenue outside Biuret's office. People were passing to and fro, yet no one paid the slightest attention to me. They could not see me.

Then, as I wandered in the street, drinking in this indescribable sensation, a blackness, a faintness enveloped me. I was in the dark again, an empty vacuum, and then—

My eyelids fluttered, and I opened them with difficulty. In a haze I saw Biuret bending over me. I was lying again on the dissecting table. My ears were ringing and for a few minutes I was overcome with nausea, but soon I was myself again, I sat up as if nothing had happened—as if I had been asleep.

In a few broken sentences I told the delighted Biuret of my strange experience.

"It worked again," almost shouted the doctor, wringing my hand in excitement. "It will work. We have succeeded. The secret will shock the world!"

"But how do you account for it?" I asked, smiling feebly at his enthusiasm.

"How does one account for electricity—or radium—or the X-ray?" countered the scientist. "We have discovered something new, that is all, and greater than any of them."

We had, indeed. It was unbelievable, yet it was true—

I knew it to be no hoax. Biuret had reason for enthusiasm, and I, too, was impatient to break the news to the world.

The rest of the day we spent in the laboratory, where Biuret compounded several vials of his elixir, and also a quantity of the antidote, which was very similar in composition to the new drug itself. However, chemical antagonists to the various drugs in the "elixir of life" were included in the antidote, and the extract of a different brain gland. I wish I could give the chemical formula here for both of them, but I might as well attempt to give you the formula for electricity.

The same evening, Biuret tried the mixture again, I, of course, administering it. The results were the same—the terrible process of death on the dissecting table, followed by what Biuret termed the "return." This time I let a full forty-five minutes elapse before I called him back with the antidote.

However, his awakening was not as rapid as it was the first time. I was compelled to give him several doses of stimulants before he "snapped out of it." He was pale, and I thought there was a tense, haunted look on his face when his eyes finally opened. It was as though he had just awakened from a terrible dream.

"Are you all right, Biuret, old man?" I asked, when he seemed able to speak.

There seemed to be a look of fear on his face, and he answered with difficulty.

"I saw—Laster!" he cried, staring at me with eyes that seemed to look beyond me.

"Laster!" I exclaimed. "You saw him? Where?"

"I don't know where I had wandered," Biuret whispered in an awed voice. "But it was Laster—he must be here in the city. I saw him quite plainly, and then . . . you called me back. I was safe then, for Laster could not have touched me, could not have seen me."

Biuret glanced nervously out of the window. He seemed to be in a state of extreme restlessness, and although the rather disagreeable effects of the drugs he had taken had not yet worn off, he lit a cigarette and smoked feverishly. Then he turned to me with a sudden idea.

"I say! Put me under that again—will you? I can't have Laster creeping up on me unexpectedly. I must find just where he is, and discover his plans if possible."

I told him that to do so would mean death; that another dose so soon after the other would certainly be disastrous. Biuret agreed, and stared moodily at the floor.

"You must let me give it to you, then," he said finally.

"But how could I find him? Why, I've never seen him!"

"Don't you understand?" snapped Biuret. "When freed from your body you can go where you like and see what you like. I will describe him to you. Then, if you concentrate, you won't fail to find him. That's the way my system works—don't you see? Laster is the one man in the world, as far as I know, with acid splashed over the left side of his face. He's a small man—foreign. And the acid burns—remember those! You will see him, even as I saw him, by *thinking of him.* That's the secret of my drug—if there is any. Quick—to the table!"

Rather against my will, I took my place on the table. Biuret hastily made ready a solution, and I bared my arm for the second time. I had scarcely time to think before I felt the quick sharp pain of the needle.

He must have given me a larger dose, this time. Either that, or I was becoming accustomed to the drug. The lights danced as before—bells seemed to ring in my ears, and then with a rending noise my brain seemed to collapse. Again I felt that dreadful shock. Again I stood staring down at my lifeless body. I was free.

What was it now, that Biuret had told me about the little man . . . the acid-scarred man? Biuret was staring at the thing on the table—the shell that had been myself. Could I find Dr. Laster for him? I tried to propel my being through space, with Biuret's description of him still ringing in my ears, but I could not stir. That was strange. I seemed to be pulled as if by an unseen force toward the office door—then I heard footsteps. Some one was clumping up the stairway!

I looked at Biuret. He had risen to his feet and his face had paled. He stared at the door as if Death himself had laid fingers on the latch. I heard a knock.

"Come in," answered Biuret in a low frightened voice.

The door opened, and at the sight of the man who stood there Biuret uttered a short despairing cry.

"Laster!"

There he was; the man of mystery. For a moment he stood silent, his face distorted in a sardonic smile. With horror I saw that the whole of one side of his face was hideously disfigured with acid.

"Biuret!"

The visitor closed the door behind him; Biuret seemed rooted in his tracks. Laster smiled again—one side of his face twisting into a leer. Then he advanced into the room and looked about. His glance fell upon my body on the table.

"Ah, I see that we are alone," said Laster. "That is fortunate. I'm sure that the cadaver won't be interested in this little—er—scene."

For the first time I saw that Laster held his right hand in his coat pocket. Biuret made no sound, nor did he move. He stood there like a man of ice—white and rigid. Laster's expression had changed. He, too, had grown pale—but from fury, not from fear.

"Look at my face!" he fairly screamed. "Look at it—it's your work! You made the woman do it—that hag of hell! First she cursed me with her beauty, and then burned my face into that of a beast. And now—"

The hand flashed from the pocket, and I caught a glimpse of a bottle. Biuret saw it too, and with understanding came panic. He made a dash toward the drawer in the desk, but he never reached the revolver. Too late! The acid splashed into Biuret's face in a burning Niagara. Strange to say, Biuret made no sound. With the agony came blindness, for his face was bathed in it, but he stood upright, his hands at his sides. Biuret's face was being slowly cooked. The nitric acid was eating rapidly into his very brain!

I could do nothing—I was helpless, though I could see it all. Laster gloated at the spectacle as if it were an entertainment, and finally drew a revolver from his pocket. I felt a sense of relief. After all—the man was merciful!

I heard a report—I could not bear to look, and then another. Why two? Yes. . . . Laster must have been quite insane, for his body lay across that of Biuret, a hole in the temple. They were dead, both dead, and I—yes, I was dead, too.

The coroner said so, and the police surgeon. What a stir that affair caused! It was a mystery that was never solved . . . the mystery of the three dead men. But then I am not dead.

The antidote? Dr. Biuret's "junk" was dumped into the sink by his successor, after the excitement had died down. My body has been under ground a long time now. I'm just a wanderer, and I suppose I shall always be such, even after the men who knew Biuret are dead and forgotten.

For a time I wished that I could go mad. There are things worse than death, and perhaps madness would bring forgetfulness. If I could only have died with my body! At least it would mean peace. It's lonesome to see and hear, and yet remain unseen and unheard. Some day Biuret's secret may be rediscovered, and then perhaps I'll have company. Until then . . . farewell.

THE GIRDLE

BY JOSEPH McCORD

THE POOL OF MOTTLED LIGHT ON THE TABLE-TOP HAD drifted over to where Sir John's clawlike fingers, emerging from the silk sleeve of his dressing robe, drummed slowly on the black oak.

Carson, erect on the hearth rug, had ignored the chair indicated by the fingers and was filled with a sudden resentment as he sensed the indifferent weariness of their tapping. And this old man was Pelham's father! It was all so different than he had pictured. There was no fathoming the expression of that masklike face with its impenetrable stare, settled in the cushioned depths of the wheel chair.

The heels of Carson's boots came together with a suggestion of military stiffness, and he spoke curtly: "I confess I don't understand."

And his host replied, in a curiously dry voice: "Perhaps it is not altogether necessary that you should."

The words carried a studied courtesy, but their veiled irony was not lost on the officer.

"Granted. But Pelham was my friend—if he was your son—and I am here only because he asked—"

"Of course," interrupted Sir John. "Spare me the formula, if you will. He's dead. It was arranged you should come and tell me how well he died. He was to perform the same service for you, no doubt, had the circumstances been reversed. The Pelhams always die well. It's in the breed. If you insist, however—"

Carson choked back his resentment.

"There were circumstances that make it seem necessary—and yet—"

"Pray get on."

"Then I'll make it short." Carson advanced a little nearer the table. "It was in a little hut I last saw him—alive. Enemy ground, newly occupied it was, and here was this hut in a small clearing. It might have been a woodcutter's and it was empty, save for some heavier furniture.

"Several of us were poking about its one room, then Pel started up a crazy ladder at one end leading to a small loft. I heard him moving around and scratching matches, then he was quiet. I walked over near the ladder and hailed him.

" 'Nothing up here but an old chest,' he came back, 'and empty at that.' Then I heard him laugh. 'Somebody left me a Dutch Sam Browne—thought the cursed thing was a snake—felt cold!'

"I heard the lid of the chest fall, then Pel started down into the room. Part-way, he turned and faced me. He had the end of a belt in each hand, holding it behind him as if he were going to wear it. I didn't notice that, though. All I saw was his face—the way he looked."

"The way he looked," prompted Sir John, as the younger man stared at him soberly. "And, pray how did he look?"

Carson seemed to pull himself together with an effort. "That's exactly what I have to tell you. I'll try to." He seated himself on the edge of the table, one booted foot swinging nervously. "Why, it was his eyes, I think—yes, that's what it was. There was something in them that shouldn't ever be in a man's eyes. You've seen a dog that was vicious and a coward—all at the same time. He wants to go at your throat and something holds him for the moment." He drew a long breath. "It was like that," he decided.

Sir John was watching one of his visitor's hands; it had

gripped the edge of the table and the knuckles were white. The boot was motionless, tense.

"As you say, like a dog. Well?"

At the quiet words, the younger man relaxed. "Yes, sir," he agreed gratefully. Then: "I spoke to him, and he never answered. He came on down the ladder, slowly—still facing us. The others were drawing up behind me—I could feel them. We all watched Pel. It wasn't that he just moved slowly either—it was something different. Slinking! I think that's the way to say it. And he watched us—never blinked. No one said a word.

"When Pel's feet hit the floor, he began moving toward the door—it had come shut. He backed to it and began feeling for the latch with one hand, holding the belt all the time. He kicked the door open with his heel.

"Then I knew we were losing him—if you can understand what I mean—knew he'd got to be saved—from something!"

Carson's voice was curiously strained.

"I wanted to stop him—I tell you I did want to! I tried. I started for him."

"And the belt?" interposed Sir John, quietly.

"The belt," echoed the other man dully. "Oh, yes. He held it all the while—I just told you that."

"But he escaped."

"He did. I had scarcely moved. He gave a dreadful sort of cry and leaped out of the doorway—backward. We rushed it then. But he had made the trees and we could hear him crashing through the undergrowth, as though there hadn't been a boche within a hundred miles of us. That's how he went."

The heavy silence that followed was broken only by a coal falling in the grate. With a long sigh, Carson raised his head. He fumbled a packet of cigarettes, thrust one between his lips, but made no move to light it.

"I am waiting," came the voice from the chair.

"Waiting?"

"Come, come! You tell me my son is dead. If I recollect, you mentioned gallantry. So far, you have suggested desertion. The details."

"Oh, yes. The details. But you won't believe them. One would have to have seen."

"Have the kindness." Sir John leaned back wearily among his cushions and closed his eyes.

"Well. It was the third evening after that—I think it was the third. There had been an advance, a lot of machine-gun work. It was growing dark, I remember. Harvey, my sergeant, came up and asked if he could speak to me. 'I've seen Lieutenant Pelham,' he whispered queerly.

" 'He's dead?' I said. I knew he was dead.

" 'Yes, he's dead, sir,' says Harvey, 'but there's something queer about him. Will you have a look?'

"He led the way and I followed."

Carson's voice was becoming strained again. Sir John leaned forward and stared steadily into his eyes.

"We came to a little open place. There was some light there—enough to see the dreadfullest group God ever bunched in one place!

"First of all, I saw Pel—sitting with his back against a little tree, chin on his knees. He was staring straight to the front—dead. But around him! Five German infantrymen—dead too. Dragged into a sort of semicircle. And they weren't shot and they weren't gassed—nothing like that. Every one had his throat torn! Torn!"

Carson leaned close to the old man; his voice shrilled as he demanded, almost piteously, "You hear me, can't you?"

"They would be—torn," said Sir John Pelham very quietly. "Finish your story."

The officer pulled himself together with an effort. "It makes it easier, having you understand. I've seen men—"

He thrust the fingers of one hand into the collar of his tunic, as though it choked him. "I've seen men, sir, meet death in a thousand ways—but not, not that way! And Pel wasn't marked at all—I looked."

The father leaned forward in his chair, but the gesture of interest was not reflected in his impassive face.

"What of the belt?"

"He wasn't wearing it, but the thing was there—lying at his feet. And it was coiled!"

"Show it to me."

"Why, I—yes, I took it. I don't know why. I dropped it in my kit bag—next day I got mine. I'm just out of the hospital by a month. Otherwise I'd have been here sooner."

With an unexpected clutch at the wheels of his chair, Sir John was close to the table, one white hand extended.

"Give it me."

An instant's hesitation, then Carson slowly pulled a paper-wrapped object from his pocket, laid it easily on the table.

"It's in there," he muttered. "I don't like the damned thing."

With deft fingers the baronet loosened the paper, shook the contents on the table.

There lay the leathern belt, coiled compactly. In the waning light it was of a pale brown color, thin and very flexible. On the other end was a metal clasp, its surface cut with marks that might or might not have been characters. There was a reading lens lying near and Sir John used it to study the coiled strap. He examined it grimly, from many angles, without once touching it. Finished, he leaned back in his chair and thoughtfully tapped the palm of his hand with the lens.

"Captain Carson."

"Sir."

"Attend most carefully to what I say—follow my instructions exactly. Take that belt in one hand only. Carry it to the hearth—lay it directly on the coals. When it is burned, quite burned, you may tell me."

Carson got slowly to his feet. With a hand that hesitated

and was none too steady, he reached for the coiled belt, lifted it a few inches from the table. At his touch, seemingly, the coil loosened; it started to unroll. He caught at it with both hands.

For a fraction of a second his body seemed caught in a strained tension. Then he began backing away from the table, noiselessly, furtively. With an end of the belt in each hand, he shifted his eyes to Sir John and they glowed with a strange, sinister light. From his sagging jaw came his tongue, licking.

Screaming an oath, Sir John Pelham flung the reading lens with all his frail strength full into that distorted face.

"Drop it!" he bawled savagely. "Jarvis!"

At the call an elderly man-servant came hurrying. He saw his master supporting himself on the arms of the chair, trembling with the exertion, and staring curiously at the uniformed visitor. Carson was swaying unsteadily, one hand pressed against his face, blood trickling from between his fingers. At his feet lay the belt and the shattered lens. Jarvis saw all this and took his post near Sir John, waiting his orders.

"Jarvis."

"Yes, sir," said the man-servant evenly.

Sir John sank back wearily.

"The tongs, Jarvis. Fetch the tongs. Pick up that strap. Only the tongs, mind you—don't touch it with your hands. So. Now lay it on the coals—hold it down hard."

The three watched the burning in deep silence, watched the belt writhe and twist in the heat, scorch with flame, fall in charred fragments.

"Jarvis."

"Yes, sir."

"Lights, then brandy for our guest. You may bring things and patch that cut for him." To Carson: "Sit down, man, and pull yourself together. I regret I was obliged to strike you, but, under the circumstances, you will agree it was quite necessary, I think."

"I don't understand," muttered Carson dully. He slumped weakly into a near-by chair. "I'm—I felt—I don't know." His voice trailed off; his chin sagged on his breast.

"You don't wish to eat, by any chance?"

"What made you ask that? God, no! I couldn't eat—I only—"

But Jarvis was offering him the brandy.

"None for me," said Sir John shortly. "But you may help me over to the far case—I am looking for a book."

In a few moments, Jarvis had wheeled him back to the table and he was turning the pages of a small book he had found. It was bound in parchment and bore evidence of great age. Carson shiveringly helped himself to another drink, as his host turned the crackling pages until he found what he sought. Tracing the lines with a lean forefinger, he read silently for a moment, then looked shrewdly at his guest.

"This may interest you, Captain. Read here," and he indicated the place.

Carson slowly deciphered the strange script of the hand-printed page:

> Another means wherethrough men have become were-wolves is that they in som mannere getten a belt or girdel maked of human skin. By an autentyke cronicle a yoman hadde such a girdel which he kept locken in a cheste secrely. It so felle on a day that he let the cheste un-locken and his litel sone getteth the girdel and girteth his midel with it. In a minute the childe was transmewed into a mervilously wilde beste but the yoman fortuned to enter the house and with spede he remewed the girdel and so cured his sone who sayde he remembered naught save a ravissing apepetyt.

The book slipped from Carson's nerveless fingers. Wide-eyed he stared into Sir John's impassive face.

When he could find the words: "God! You never mean —you couldn't mean—"

"I was in hopes," mused the old man, "you know, I was quite in hopes you would feel hungry."

BAT'S BELFRY

By AUGUST W. DERLETH

The following letter was found among the papers of the late Sir Harry Everett Barclay, of Charing Cross, London.

June 10, 1925.

My dear Marc:—

Having received no answer to my card, I can only surmise that it did not reach you. I am writing from my summer home here on the moor, a very secluded place. I am fondling the hope that you will give me a pleasant surprise by dropping in on me soon (as you hinted you might), for this is just the kind of house that would intrigue you. It is very similar to the Baskerville home which Sir Arthur Conan Doyle describes in his *Hound of the Baskervilles.* Vague rumors have it that the place is the abode of evil spirits, which idea I promptly and emphatically pooh-poohed. You know that I am but slightly interested in the spiritual world, and that it is in wizardry that I delight. The thought that this quiet little building in the heart of England's peaceful moors should be the home of a multitude of evil spirits seems very foolish to me. However, the surroundings are exceedingly healthful and the house itself is partly an antique, which arouses my interest in archæology. So you see there is enough to divert my attention from these foolish rumors. Leon, my valet, is here with me, and so is old Mortimer. You remember Mortimer, who always prepared such excellent bachelor dinners for us?

I have been here just twelve days, and I have explored

this old house from cellar to garret. In the latter I brought to light an aged trunk, which I searched, and in which I found nine old books, several of whose title pages were torn away. One of the books, which I took to the small garret window, I finally distinguished as *Dracula* by Bram Stoker, and this I at once decided was one of the first editions of the book ever printed.

At the cessation of the first three days a typical English fog descended with a vengeance upon the moor. At the first indication of this prank of the elements, which threatened completely to obscure the beautiful weather of the past, I had hauled out all the discoveries I had made in the garret of this building. Bram Stoker's *Dracula* I have already mentioned. There is also a book on the Black Art by De Rochas. Three books, by Orfilo, Swedenborg, and Cagliostro, I have laid temporarily aside. Then there are also Strindberg's *The Inferno,* Blavatsky's *Secret Doctrine,* Poe's *Eureka,* and Flammarion's *Atmosphere.* You, my dear friend, may well imagine with what excitement these books filled me, for you know I am inclined toward sorcery. Orfilo, you know, was but a chemist and physiologist; Swedenborg and Strindberg, two who might be called mystics; Poe, whose *Eureka* did not aid me much in the path of witchcraft, nevertheless fascinated me; but the remaining five were as gold to me. Cagliostro, court magician of France; Madame Blavatsky, the priestess of Isis and of the Occult Doctrine; *Dracula,* with all its vampires; Flammarion's *Atmosphere,* with its diagnosis of the Gods of peoples; and De Rochas, of whom all I can say is to quote from August Strindberg's *The Inferno,* the following: "I do not excuse myself, and only ask the reader to remember this fact, in case he should ever feel inclined to practice magic, especially those forms of it called wizardry, or more properly witchcraft: that its reality has been placed beyond all doubt by De Rochas."

Truly, my friend, I wondered, for I had good reason to

do so, what manner of man had resided here before my coming, who should be so fascinated by Poe, Orfilo, Strindberg, and De Rochas—four different types of authors. Fog or no fog, I determined to find out. There is not another dwelling near here and the nearest source of information is a village some miles away. This is rather odd, for this moor does not seem an undesirable place for a summer home. I stored the books away, and after informing my valet of my intentions to walk some miles to the village, I started out. I had not gone far, when Leon decided to accompany me, leaving Mortimer alone in the fog-surrounded house.

Leon and I established very little in the town. After a conversation with one of the grocers in the village, the only communicative person that we accosted, we found that the man who had last occupied the house was a Baronet Lohrville. It seemed that the people held the late baronet in awe, for they hesitated to speak of him. This grocer related a tale concerning the disappearance of four girls one dark night some years ago. Popular belief had and still has it that the baronet kidnaped them. This idea seems utterly ludicrous to me, for the superstitious villagers cannot substantiate their suspicions. By the way, this merchant also informed us that the Lohrville home is called the "Bat's Belfry." Personally I can see no connection between the residence and the ascribed title, as I have not noticed any bats around during my sojourn here.

My meditations on this matter were rudely interrupted by Mortimer, who complained of bats in the cellar—a rather queer coincidence. He said that he continually felt them brushing against his cheeks and that he feared they would become entangled in his hair. Of course, Leon and I went down to look for them, but we could not see any of them. However, Leon stated that one struck him, which I doubt. It is just possible that sudden drafts of air may have been the cause of the delusions.

This incident, Marc, was just the forerunner of the odd

things that have been occurring since then. I am about to enumerate the most important of these incidents to you, and I hope you will be able to explain them.

Three days ago activities started in earnest. At that date Mortimer came to me and breathlessly informed me that no light could be kept in the cellar. Leon and I investigated and found that under no circumstances could a lamp or match be kept lit in the cellar, just as Mortimer had said. My only explanation of this is that it is due to the air currents in the cellar, which seemed disturbed. It is true a flashlight could be kept alight, but even that seemed dimmed. I cannot attempt to explain the latter fact.

Yesterday, Leon, who is a devout Catholic, took a few drops from a flask of holy water, which he continually carries with him, and descended into the cellar with the firm intention of driving out, if there were therein ensconced, any evil spirits. On the bottom of the steps I noticed, some time ago, a large stone tablet. As Leon came down the steps a large drop of the blessed fluid fell on this tablet. The drop of water actually sizzled while Leon muttered some incantations, in the midst of which he suddenly stopped and fled precipitantly, mumbling that the cellar was incontestably the very entrance to hell, guarded by the fiend incarnate, himself! I confess to you, my dear Marc, that I was astounded at this remarkable occurrence.

Last night, while the three of us sat together in the spacious drawing-room of this building, the lamp was blown out. I say "blown out" because there is no doubt that it was, and by some superhuman agency. There was not a breath of air stirring outside, yet I, who was sitting just across from the lamp, felt a cool draft. No one else noticed this draft. It was just as if some one directly opposite me had blown forcibly at the lamp, or as if the wing of a powerful bird had passed by it.

There can be no doubt there is something radically wrong

in this house, and I am determined to find out what it is, regardless of consequences.

(Here the letter terminates abruptly, as if it were to be completed at a later date.)

The two doctors bending over the body of Sir Harry Barclay in Lohrville Manor at last ceased their examinations.

"I cannot account for this astounding loss of blood, Dr. Mordaunt."

"Neither can I, Dr. Greene. He is so devoid of blood that some supernatural agency must have kept him alive!" He laughed lightly.

"About this loss of blood—I was figuring on internal hemorrhages as the cause, but there are absolutely no signs of anything of the sort. According to the expression of his features, which is too horrible for even me to gaze at—"

"And me."

"—he died from some terrible fear of something, or else he witnessed some horrifying scene."

"Most likely the latter."

"I think we had better pronounce death due to internal hemorrhage and apoplexy."

"I agree."

"Then we shall do so."

The physicians bent over the open book on the table. Suddenly Dr. Greene straightened up and his hand delved into his pocket and came out with a match.

"Here is a match, Dr. Mordaunt. Scratch it and apply the flame to that book and say nothing to any one."

"It is for the best."

Excerpts from the journal of Sir Harry E. Barclay, found beside his body in Lohrville Manor on July 17, 1925.

June 25.—Last night I had a curious nightmare. I dreamed that I met a beautiful girl in the wood around my father's castle in Lancaster. Without knowing why, we embraced, our lips meeting and remaining in the position for at least half an hour! Queer dream that! I must have had another nightmare of a different nature, although I cannot recall it, for, upon looking in the mirror this morning, I found my face devoid of all color—rather drawn.

Later.—Leon has told me that he had a similar dream, and as he is a confirmed misogynist, I cannot interpret it. Strange that it should be so parallel to mine in every way.

June 29.—Mortimer came to me early this morning and said he would not stay another instant, for he had certainly seen a ghost last night. A handsome old man, he said. He seemed horrified that the old man had kissed him. He must have dreamed it. I persuaded him to stay on these grounds and solemnly told him to say nothing about it. Leon remarked that the dream had returned in every particular to him the preceding night, and that he was not feeling well. I advised him to see a doctor, but he roundly refused to do so. He said, referring to the horrible nightmare (as he termed it), that to-night he would sprinkle a few drops of holy water on himself and that (he stated) would drive away any evil influence, if there were any, connected with his dreams. Strange that he should attribute everything to evil entities!

Later.—I made some inquiries to-day and I find that the description of the Baronet Lohrville fits to every detail the "ghost" of Mortimer's dream. I also learned that several small children disappeared from the countryside during the life of the last of the Lohrvilles;—not that they should be connected, but it seems the ignorant people ascribe their vanishing to the baronet.

June 30.—Leon claims he did not have the dream (which, by the way, revisited me last night), because of the potent effect of the holy water.

July 1.—Mortimer has left. He says he cannot live in the same house with the devil. It seems he must have actually seen the ghost of old Lohrville, although Leon scoffs at the idea.

July 4.—I had the same dream again last night. I felt very ill this morning, but was able to dispel the feeling easily during the day. Leon has used all the holy water, but as to-morrow is Sunday he will get some at the village parish when he attends mass.

July 5.—I tried to procure the services of another chef this morning in the village, but I am all at sea. No one in the town will enter the house, not even for one hundred pounds a week, they declare! I shall be forced to get along without one or send to London.

Leon experienced a misfortune to-day. Riding home after mass, almost all his holy water spilled from the bottle, and later the bottle, containing the remainder of it, fell to the ground and broke. Leon, nonplused, remarked that he would get another as soon as possible from the parish priest.

July 6.—Both of us had the dream again last night. I feel rather weak, and Leon does, too. Leon went to a doctor, who asked him whether he had been cut, or severely injured so as to cause a heavy loss of blood, or if he had suffered from internal hemorrhages. Leon said no, and the doctor prescribed raw onions and some other things for Leon to eat. Leon forgot his holy water.

July 9.—The dream again. Leon had a different nightmare—about an old man, who, he said, bit him. I asked him to show me where the man had bitten him in his dream, and when he loosened his collar to show me, sure enough, there were two tiny punctures on his throat. He and I are both feeling miserably weak.

July 15.—Leon left me to-day. I am firmly convinced that he went suddenly mad, for this morning he evinced an intense desire to invade the cellar again. He said that something seemed to draw him. I did not stop him, and some time later, as I was engrossed in a volume of Wells, he came shrieking up the cellar steps and dashed madly through the room in which I sat. I ran after him and, cornering him in his room, forcibly detained him. I asked for an explanation and all he could do was moan over and over.

"Mon Dieu, Monsieur, leave this accursed place at once. Leave it, *Monsieur,* I beg of you. *Le diable—le diable!"* At length he dashed away from me and ran at top speed from the house, I after him. In the road I shouted after him, and all I could catch of the words wafted back to me by the wind, were: *"Lamais—le diable—Mon—Dieu—tablet—Book of Thoth."* All very significant words, *"Le diable"* and *"Mon Dieu"*—"the devil" and "my God"—I paid little attention to. But Lamais was a species of female vampire known intimately to a few select sorcerers only, and the *Book of Thoth* was the Egyptian book of magic. For a few minutes I entertained the rather wild fancy that the *Book of Thoth* was ensconced somewhere in this building, and as I racked my brains for a suitable connection between "tablet" and *Book of Thoth* I at last became convinced that the book lay beneath the tablet at the foot of the cellar steps. I am going down to investigate.

July 16.—I have it! The *Book of Thoth!* It was below the stone tablet as I thought. The spirits guarding it evidently did not wish me to disturb its resting place, for they roused the air currents to a semblance of a gale while I worked to get the stone away. The book is secured by a heavy lock of antique pattern.

I had the dream again last night, but in addition I could almost swear that I saw the ghosts of old Lohrville and four beautiful girls. What a coincidence! I am very weak to-day, hardly able to walk around. There is no doubt that this house is infested, not by bats, but by vampires! Lamais! If I could only find their corpses I would drive sharp stakes through them.

Later.—I made a new and shocking discovery to-day. I went down to the place where the tablet lay, and another rock below the cavity wherein the *Book of Thoth* had lain gave way below me and I found myself in a vault with about a score of skeletons—all of little children! If this house *is* inhabited by vampires, it is only too obvious that these skeletons are those of their unfortunate victims. However, I firmly believe that there is another cavern somewhere below, wherein the bodies of the vampires are hidden.

Later.—I have been looking over the book by De Rochas and I have hit upon an excellent plan to discover the bodies of the vampires! I shall use the *Book of Thoth* to summon the vampires before me and force them to reveal the hiding place of their voluptuous bodies! De Rochas says that it can be done.

Nine o'clock.—As the conditions are excellent at this time I am going to start to summon the vampires. Some one is passing and I hope he or she does not interrupt me in my work or tell any one in the town to look in here. The book, as I mentioned before, is secured by a heavy seal, and I had trouble to loosen it. At last I succeeded in breaking it and I opened the book to find the place I need in my work of conjuring up the vampires. I found it and I am beginning my incantations. The atmosphere in the room is changing slowly and it is becoming intolerably dark. The air currents in the room are swirling angrily, and the lamp has gone out . . . I am confident that the vampires will appear soon.

I am correct. There are some shades materializing in the room. They are becoming more distinct . . . there are five of them, four females and one male. Their features are very distinct. . . . They are casting covert glances in my direction. . . . Now they are glaring malevolently at me.

Good God! I have forgotten to place myself in a magic circle and I greatly fear the vampires will attack me! I am only too correct. They are moving in my direction. My God! . . . But stay! They are halting! The old baronet is gazing at me with his glittering eyes fiery with hate. The four female vampires smile voluptuously upon me.

Now, if ever, is my chance to break their evil spell.

Prayer? But I cannot pray! I am forever banished from the sight of God for calling upon Satan to aid me. But even for that I cannot pray . . . I am hypnotized by the malefic leer disfiguring the countenance of the baronet. There is a sinister gleam in the eyes of the four beautiful ghouls. They glide toward me, arms outstretched. Their sinuous, obnoxious forms are before me; their crimson lips curved in a diabolically triumphant smile. I cannot bear to see the soft caress of their tongues on their red lips. I am resisting with all the power of my will, but what is one mere will against an infernal horde of ghouls?

God! Their foul presence taints my very soul! The baronet is moving forward. His mordacious propinquity casts a reviling sensation of obscenity about me. If I cannot appeal to God I must implore Satan to grant me time to construct the magic circle.

I cannot tolerate their virulence . . . I endeavored to rise but I could not do so . . . I am no longer master of my own will! The vampires are leering demonically at me . . . I am doomed to die . . . and yet to live forever in the ranks of the Undead.

Their faces are approaching closer to mine and soon I shall sink into oblivion . . . but anything is better than this . . . to see the malignant Undead around me. . . . A sharp, stinging sensation in my throat . . . My God! . . . it is— . . .

THE SEA-THING

By FRANK BELKNAP LONG, Jr.

July 16.—We are caught in one of the great calms. There is water in the well, and our food is nearly gone. Everything is hid from view by the fog. I confess that I am a hopeless coward. The situation appalls me. What an expressive word is *despair*. I shall write it large—DESPAIR. Luckily a flying fish came scudding over the rails this morning.

July 17.—The fog has lifted, but there is no relief in sight, and the water in the well has risen several inches. The seven of us worked on the pumps all night. Thompson seemed surly and inclined to rebel. He is a man to be envied. He still retains his egoism and he fancies himself a very shrewd and important person. I hadn't the heart to be angry with him. Poor devil! He doesn't know how near we are to the rocks. I speak figuratively, of course. We are at present in the open sea, a thousand miles from land, and our rudder has gone by the board. We drift aimlessly. A fine situation, truly, for the skipper of the *Octopus!* Three months ago I had a full crew and full sails, and now . . . Cholera isn't pleasant! Damn it all, cholera is *not* pleasant.

July 18.—I have given up all hope. By working desperately we are able to keep the water in the well from rising, but our food has given out. We have pumped and cursed on empty stomachs for fifteen hours. Bullen collapsed. He collapsed like the *others,* but thank God, his face didn't turn black. We are done with the cholera now. I'll stake my reputation on that. My prompt disposal of the bodies nipped the cholera in the bud. In the bud, did I say? Ha! When a man loses three-fourths of his crew he can't think straight. The cholera really ran its course. It couldn't have lasted much longer. I wish to heaven that it had taken the rest of us.

July 19.—It was funny. Another flying fish came aboard to-day, and Tommy Wells made a dive for it. He dived after it head first, with arms akimbo, like a man just awakening from some crazy dream, and he slid along the planks. But he got the fish. He caught it between his two hands and bit into it, and finally disposed of it, bones and all. "That was a devilish thing to do," said Thompson. Big Johnny Boeltzig cursed horribly. I felt rather light in the head, and I didn't say anything. But I was a bit put out. We could have divided the flying fish up, but as I say, it was funny.

July 20.—Our case is desperate. There isn't a breath of air stirring and Boeltzig has joined Bullen. They are both below, unable to move an arm between them, and Bullen is very near death. Curiously enough, though, the five of us are able to keep the water down. But we are tired—tired.

July 21.—We have one thing to be thankful for. The water has not risen an inch in twelve hours—and we didn't pump. We are too tired to pump. We lay about on the decks and cursed and made faces at the sky, and we never mentioned food. But Thompson's tongue stuck out queerly. "Put that rag in your mouth," I shouted. It was a coarse remark to make to a starving man, but I was suffering acutely. Why do I continue to write in this log?

July 22.—We are saved! Who could have anticipated such glorious good luck? A boatload of provisions and a jolly companion to cheer us up. He claims that he is the sole survivor of the *Princess Clara.* You have undoubtedly heard of the *Princess.* A finer brig never put out from 'Frisco. And she's gone. A hurricane and a leak did for her. Six or seven got away in the long boat, but my friend (I call him that, because he has saved us all)—my friend threw them overboard. They died first, of course. Get that straight. They died from fright or from drinking salt water, and my friend didn't like the company of corpses. So he just naturally disposed of them. That's his story, and I accept it at its face value. I'm not a man to go poking about and asking questions. It's enough that he's brought us provisions and jolly companionship. We were growing weary of each other—we seven. He calls himself Francis de la Vega.

July 24.—De Vegie (we call him that) has been with us now for three days. He has the run of the ship, and I have given him the mate's cabin. The mate has no further need for a cabin, since he spends his nights on the ocean floor. A splendid chap, the mate. He was the first to go. But I mustn't rake up old ashes. De Vegie is tall and amazingly lean, and I never saw a paler man. His face is drawn and haggard, and his eyes large—and they consume you. There is something devastating about his eyes. Sometimes they seem a hundred years old. His forehead is high, and as yellow and dry as parchment, and his nose is curved like a scimitar. Strangely enough, he reminds me of Poe's Usher. I say strangely enough, because the man has nothing but his appearance in common with the aristocratic neurotic of Poe's tale. He is boyish, gay and utterly free from gloom. His manner is ingenuous and charming. He is all smiles and assurance. And he tells stories that are almost Rabelaisian in their frank, coarse humor. He possesses a remarkable knowledge of medicine, or perhaps I should say, of healing, since he uses no drugs. But he has completely restored Bullen and Big Johnny Boeltzig. The eight of us make a jolly crew. He has given us new life, new confidence. His presence is a delight to us. There is one thing curious about him. His hands are cold and almost lifeless. There is no blood in them. I never before saw such hands on a human being. And the nails are astonishingly long.

July 27.—De Vegie has kept more to himself. He remained locked in his cabin this morning, and answered my anxious questions through the keyhole. But I was too busy to show surprise. There was a curious chill in the air, which promised wind, and Thompson, Wells and I worked desperately to get up the topgallants and strengthen the weather leaches. The rest were too tired to work and I did not press them. I have no desire to reassert my authority just yet. The first sign of a breeze will increase the crew's morale, and then I hope to regain my old power of discipline.

July 28.—I am worried about De Vegie. This morning he came on deck looking so drawn and haggard that I left the taffrail where I had been standing with one hand grasping the weather vang and crossed the deck to comfort him. His eyes looked appealingly into mine. "Couldn't sleep all night," he said. "The ship tosses so. The great calms certainly make a ship roll."

"They do," I replied. "But you don't notice the roll so much on deck. If you wish, you may carry your bedding up and sleep with the boys on the planks. But don't be startled if a flying fish flops in your face."

De Vegie smiled. "Thanks," he said. "The idea appeals to me. I'll act on it to-night."

July 29.—A breeze is surely coming soon. All of the signs point to it. I have been working frantically on a miserable substitute for a rudder. I think that I shall be able to steer fairly well in a pinch, but I hope the breeze doesn't come until we are better prepared.

De Vegie slept on the planks with the crew last night, and this morning he looks ten years younger. His cheeks are flushed and full, and the greenish hollows have disappeared from under his eyes. But Thompson isn't well. He complains of pains in his chest, and once or twice he spat blood. He is abnormally pale.

July 30.—Still no breeze. Thompson is sick unto death. He lies in his cabin and groans, and I can do nothing for him. His pallor is genuinely alarming. Even his lips are bloodless. He complains of noises in his ears. And De Vegie has shown his first gleam of ill-nature. "I can do nothing for him," he says and shrugs his shoulders. His eyes smolder when he speaks, and I discern for the first time a hard cruelty in the man. He is not what he pretends to be!

July 31.—Thompson died this morning, and De Vegie actually gloated over his death. What does it mean? Why such a sudden change in a man who owes everything to our generosity? It is true that his coming supplied us with food, but we snatched him from the very maws of the sea. That is ingratitude for you! Human beings are utterly despicable and I have lost faith in them. De Vegie does not differ from the rest. He gloats over the misfortunes of others. He actually smiled when I read the burial service and dropped poor Thompson into the sea. Imagine it!

August 1.—There is still no wind. I should welcome any sort of breeze after what I *felt* to-day. There is something unnatural about this ship. Even the cook has noticed it. "It ain't natural," he said, "for a ship to smell like this. And that De Vegie fellow's cabin. Phew! It not only stunk, but—"

I laid my hand over his mouth. "You're an idiot," I shouted. "De Vegie's all right. I don't know what made him smile yesterday when I shipped off poor Thompson, but he isn't a bad sort." I lowered my voice: "He never complains, and his companionship is jolly stimulating. The boys couldn't get along without him. You have a feeling that he knows more than ten ordinary men whenever he opens his mouth to tell one of his amazing yarns. And that tale of the Spanish Inquisition that he frightened Boeltzig with yesterday morning was so real, so vivid—"

"I allus distrusted him," said the perverse fool. I grimaced and remarked coolly that nothing could be more absurd than the prejudices of a lazy son of a sea-cook. But I must confess that the smell of De Vegie's cabin did horrify me. I had entered it while De Vegie was on deck, and the stench nearly laid me on my back. The place smelt like a hellish charnel-house. The odor of decaying shell-fish mingled with a peculiarly offensive and acrid smell that in some indefinable way suggested newly-shed blood. There was no sign, however, of anything amiss in the cabin. I was so horrified that I left almost immediately, slamming the door with a bang. To-night I shall drink heavily. Oh, I shall get gloriously drunk! I shall make a fool of myself, but what does it matter?

August 2.—De Vegie has grown hard and cynical. He curses my men and refuses to speak to me. This morning little Tommy Wells went below and lay down. He was as white as a squid's belly. Something told me to examine him. I commanded him to strip, and I searched his entire body for signs of discoloration. I thought that possibly the cholera had taken a new form. Like influenza, cholera may manifest itself in curious and amazing ways. I had never read of cholera draining the blood from a man, but I wasn't taking any chances. Well, it wasn't cholera. It was a bite. Something had bitten him in the chest. A round, circular discoloration disfigured the center of his chest, and in the very middle were two sharp incisions, from which blood and pus trickled ominously. I didn't like it. Neither did Tommy. When he saw the wound he sat up very stiff and straight, and asked me if I knew any tropic insects capable of such devilry.

"There are no insects a thousand miles from land," I shouted. "Don't be such an incredible imbecile!"

Tommy looked at me reproachfully. "Flies," he said. "They're often found on board. You know that just as well as I do. This stinking hold would breed 'em big as whales. It couldn't have been anything else. I didn't feel it at all—didn't even know that I had the bite."

"There's something more than flies in this, Tommy," I said. "The thing that bit you came out of the sea. Ever see a lamprey's wound on a fish, Tommy?"

"Did I ever see a man walking with his legs!" snapped Tommy. "But how could a lamprey get me? I didn't sleep on the bottom of the sea. I slept on deck, and I was covered up. I suppose your lamprey climbed over the rail, and walked about, and finally decided that I would make a good, juicy meal. Then I dare say he lifted the blankets, and crawled under my shirt and fed until morning. He would be wise enough, of course, to get away and over the side before daybreak. Is that your theory, captain?"

I was curiously impatient with the boy. His levity had somehow stung me. "It's a better theory than your flies," I responded.

Tommy smiled grimly, and turned over in his bunk.

August 3.—To-night I went down into the pit. Something *walks* at night in this ship. "The pestilence that walketh at nightfall"—I wonder if the Hebrew prophet saw what I *felt.* I awoke from a heavy sleep, and something that does *not* sleep was standing above my bed. The cabin was wrapped in a velvety darkness, and I could see nothing, not even a shadow. But I heard it gulp. And I smelt—the odor of decay was so strong that it stung my nostrils. And I heard the thing above me gulp. It didn't breathe or whisper or cry out, but it simply *gulped.* I tried to rise, but it laid its hand on my head and forced me back. And its hand was slimy, like the hand of a frog.

August 4.—An unaccountable incident occurred on deck to-day. I am obliged to believe that De Vegie is insane. "Red" Walker was working on the braces, and his hand accidentally slipped. He cut himself badly. The blood ran down his arm, and we all feared that he had severed an artery. His under lip trembled, but he didn't complain or cry out. He simply walked with unsteady steps toward the forecastle, while he sought to stanch the flow of blood with his uninjured hand. De Vegie was standing above the lee scuppers, and the sight somehow startled him. He threw up his arms and ran straight for "Red." "Red" saw him coming, and stopped, puzzled and a little hopeful. He recalled De Vegie's power of healing. In a moment De Vegie had seized upon the injured arm. He gripped it forcefully and *put it under his shirt.* He held "Red" Walker's wrist against his chest, and he seemed horribly excited. His eyes bulged. His cheeks turned gray, and balls of sweat accumulated on his forehead. De Vegie was making a tremendous effort to achieve something—but we couldn't guess what. The situation was uncanny. I stepped forward to interfere, but when I reached them they were free of each other, and "Red" was examining his arm with horror and amazement. "There's no blood in it," he groaned. "And, my God, it's as cold as ice!" De Vegie scowled. "I didn't expect gratitude," he said dryly, "but you have no right to complain. I've fixed your wrist for you. It won't bleed again—for some time!"

I could only stare. Is De Vegie mad, or has he mastered some monstrous system of healing?

August 5.—"Red" Walker is dead. I disposed of his body this morning. It was white and rigid, and I noticed an extraordinary discoloration above the wound on his wrist. From the elbow down, his arm was bright green. I cannot explain it. Blood-poisoning, perhaps—but I do not like De Vegie. I no longer trust him. His presence has become obnoxious to me.

Something walked again to-night. It bent above my head, and I heard it gulp.

August 6.—I am stunned, frightened. Who could have dreamed, who could have expected? The thing is so incredible, so hideous, so utterly outside human experience!

I found the book in the ship's library. It was one of forty water-soaked volumes. It was a very ancient book, and the leaves were yellow and the cover eaten away at the corners. It was dated 1823. But that is not strange. Books one hundred years old are not uncommon on clipper ships that should have been scuttled before the beginning of this century.

I had poked among the absurd books out of curiosity, incidentally seeking something to read that would lift me above a gruesome world of sea and sky and walking pestilence.

I turned the pages of the little book rapidly, and laughed at the ridiculous lore that graced its soiled yellow pages. It was a miscellany, bearing the title, *A Winter's Evening,* and the incongruity of such a book among such surroundings amused and delighted me. And then I discovered the following passage, and I had no longer any desire to laugh:

> According to Father Feyjoo, in the month of June, 1674, some young men were walking by the seaside in Bilboa, when one of them, named Francis de la Vega, suddenly leaped into the sea and disappeared presently.
>
> About five years afterwards, some fishermen in the environs of Cadiz perceived the figure of a man swimming and sometimes plunging under the water. It is said that his body was entirely covered with scales. They also added that different parts of his body were as hard as shagreen. Father Feyjoo adds many philosophic reflections on the existence of this phenomenon, and on the means by which a man may be enabled to live at the bottom of the sea!

August 7.—This morning I showed Tommy Wells the miscellany. He read it slowly and his face actually turned yellow. His small blue eyes narrowed. "We must act at once," he said.

Later—We have made our plans. Tommy and I are to bunk together to-night. We have automatics—and a sharp knife. The knife, we feel, will be necessary. This morning Tommy and I discussed vampirism. "A stake or knife must be driven through the heart," said Tommy. "But a sea-vampire, Tommy," I responded, "is—is different." Tommy shrugged, to conceal the horror and uncertainty in his tired brain. We *are resolved to do everything possible.*

August 8.—It is over! Poor Tommy is gone, but De Vegie will trouble us no more. I am dazed, horrified—but I must write it all. It is a duty I owe to Tommy. He would want it on record. Tommy was always methodical, and he insisted on regulations. I must put it in the log, to please Tommy.

We were awake in our bunks when the door opened. We heard the door creak on its hinges. Something unutterable had entered the room. We could hear the thing gulp. Tommy gripped my arm, and I got ready to strike a match. I waited until its soft, slimy approach became unbearable. I waited until it stood at the foot of my bunk and until its green, glassy eyes were vaguely discernible in the almost total blackness. It was watching me, and I realized that it could see in the dark. I lit the match. My hand shook frightfully, but I carried the match to the tallow wick, and then—it sprang.

But it didn't spring at me. It went higher, and it got Tommy about the neck. I could hear him choke and gasp. In passing me the thing had knocked the match from my fingers, and we were once more in total darkness. I had seen something long and green and slimy going upward, and I had heard Tommy's frightful scream. But I saw and heard nothing else for the space of thirty or forty seconds. I was unable to move or think. I sat on the edge of my bunk, and my heart came up in my throat and flopped over.

I was conscious of two objects struggling and gasping on the floor. I heard a gulping and a low moaning, and then the night was loud with Tommy's screams. He shrieked, and shrieked, and shrieked. And between the screams there came a torrent of jumbled nouns and adjectives. "Green—eyes! Ugh! Ooze! Mouth! Wet!"

I finally got out another match and struck it. I kept my eyes averted, and carried the match rapidly to the candle-wick. I knew that if my eyes fastened upon the thing on the floor I should drop the match. I waited until the wick flared, and then—I looked!

Something was on top of Tommy. It covered him, and seemed apparently about to absorb him. In its evil, distorted features and long-nailed hands, I recognized a caricature of De Vegie. But the evil in the man had sprouted. It had turned him into a jellyish, fishy monstrosity. His legs and arms actually *gave*. They were like nothing in this world under the sun and moon and stars. They lengthened, and enveloped and choked Tommy. But the worst of all, the body of the thing was covered with greenish scales, and it had pink suckers on its chest. The suckers were lustily at work on poor Tommy.

The suckers were draining Tommy dry. His screams kept getting louder and louder. And he muttered pathetic invocations and shameless blasphemies. And his scared eyes watched me. There was a challenge and a mute appeal in them.

I thought of the revolver in my bunk. I turned, and my fingers sought frantically for the weapon. At length I found it. I gripped the butt, and leveled it. I leveled it at Tommy and the thing on the floor.

I fired at Tommy and the thing. I had no intention of sparing Tommy. I knew that Tommy would not want that. The appeal in Tommy's suffering eyes was unmistakable. After that, objects refused to retain their identity in my sight. They coalesced and separated and came together again. The objects on the floor merged with the table and chairs and bunk-ends.

I have a vague recollection of carrying two bodies on deck and dumping them overboard. I remember that one body was long and slimy and strangely heavy. The other was amazingly light. Before I carried the long heavy body on deck I drove a knife through its heart. I think that the blood spurted out and spattered my arms and legs. But the memory of this occurrence is more vague than the shadow of a dream. Did the long green body groan when I stabbed it, and did a look of ineffable happiness and gratitude come into its eyes? Did the small body also speak to me before I carried it on deck? Did I later go into De Vegie's cabin and breathe the fresh clean air that blew through it? I cannot answer these questions, but I do not think that they require an answer.

August 9.—A breeze! A breeze! The great calm is broken and all hands are busy forward. I thank God that by to-night we shall be headed toward 'Frisco.

THE HORROR ON THE LINKS

By SEABURY QUINN

IT MUST HAVE BEEN PAST MIDNIGHT WHEN THE SKIRLING of my bedroom telephone bell wakened me, for I could see the moon well down toward the western horizon as I looked through the window while reaching for the instrument.

"Dr. Trowbridge," came an excited feminine voice through the receiver, "this is Mrs. Maitland. Can you come right over? Something terrible has happened to Paul!"

"Eh?" I answered, half asleep. "What's wrong?"

"We—we don't know," she replied jerkily. "He's unconscious. You know, he'd been to the dance at the country club with Gladys Phillips. We'd all been in bed hours when we heard some one banging on the front door. Mr. Maitland went down, and when he opened the door, Paul fell into the hall. Oh, doctor, he's been terribly hurt! Won't you please come right over?"

Physician's sleep is like a park—public property. With a sigh I climbed out of bed and into my clothes, cranked my superannuated motor to life and set out for the Maitland house.

Young Maitland lay on his bed, his eyes closed, teeth tight clenched, his face set in an expression of unutterable dread, even in his unconsciousness. Across his shoulders and on the back of his arms I found several long incised wounds, as though his flesh had been raked by a sharp, pronged instrument.

I sterilized and bandaged the cuts, and applied restoratives, wondering what sort of encounter had produced such hurts.

"Help, help! Oh, God, help!" the lad muttered thickly, like a person trying to call out in a nightmare. "Oh, oh, it's got me; it's—" his words gave way to a gurgling, inarticulate cry of fear, and he sat bolt upright in bed, staring about with vacant, fear-filmed eyes.

"Easy, easy, young fellow," I soothed. "Lie back, now; take it easy, you're all right, you're home in bed."

He looked uncomprehendingly at me a moment, then fell to babbling inanely. "The ape-thing—the ape-thing!" he screamed in a frenzy. "It's got me! Open the door; for God's sake, open the door!"

"Here," I ordered gruffly as I drove my hypodermic into his arm. "None o' that. You quiet down."

The opiate took effect almost immediately, and I left him with his parents while I returned to catch up the raveled ends of my interrupted sleep.

Headlines shrieked at me from the front page of the paper lying beside my grapefruit at breakfast:

SUPER FIEND SOUGHT IN GIRL'S SLAYING

BODY OF YOUNG WOMAN FOUND NEAR SEDGEMOOR COUNTRY CLUB MYSTIFIES POLICE—CRIMINAL PERVERT BLAMED FOR KILLING—ARREST IS IMMINENT

Almost entirely denuded of clothing, marred by a score of terrible wounds, her face battered nearly past recognition and her neck broken, the body of pretty Sarah Humphries, nineteen, a waitress in the employ of the Sedgemoor Country Club, was found lying in one of the bunkers of the club's golf course by John Burroughs, a green keeper, early this morning. Miss Humphries, who had been employed at the clubhouse for three months, completed her

> duties shortly before midnight, and, according to statements of fellow workers, declared she was going to take a short cut across the links to the Andover Road, where she could get a tram to the city. Her body, terribly mutilated, was found about twenty-five yards from the road on the golf course this morning.
>
> Between the golf links and the Andover Road is a dense growth of trees, and it is thought the young woman was attacked while walking along the path through the woods to the road. Deputy Coroner Nesbett, who examined the body, gave his opinion that she had been dead about five hours when found. She had not been criminally assaulted.
>
> Several suspicious characters have been seen in the neighborhood of the club's grounds recently, and the police are checking up on their movements. An early arrest is expected.

"There's two gintlemen to see ye, sor," Nora, my housekeeper, interrupted my perusal of the paper. " 'Tis Sergeant Costello an' a Frinchman, or Eyetalyun, or sumpin. They do be warntin' ter ax ye some questions about th' murther of th' pore little Humphries gurl."

"Ask *me* about the murder?" I protested. "Why, the first I knew of it was when I looked at this paper, and I'm not through reading the account of the crime yet."

"That's all right, Dr. Trowbridge," Detective Sergeant Costello answered with a laugh as he entered the dining-room. "We don't figure on arresting you; but we'd like to ask you some questions, if you don't mind. This is Professor de Grandin, of the Paris police. He's been doing some work for his department over here, an' when this murder broke, he offered the chief his help. We'll be needin' it, too, I'm thinkin'. Professor de Grandin, Dr. Trowbridge," he waved an introductory hand from one to the other of us.

The professor bowed stiffly from the hips, in continental fashion, then extended his hand with a friendly smile. He was a perfect example of the rare French blond type, rather under medium height, but with a military erectness of carriage which made him look several inches taller than he actually was. His light blue eyes were small and exceedingly deep-set, and would have been humorous had it not been for the curious cold directness of their gaze. With his wide mouth, light mustache waxed at the ends in two perfectly horizontal points, and those twinkling, stock-taking eyes, he reminded me of an alert tom-cat. Like a cat's, too, was his lithe, noiseless step as he crossed the room to shake hands.

"I fear Monsieur Costello gives you the misapprehension, doctor," he said in a pleasant voice, almost devoid of accent. "It is most true I am connected with the *Service de Sûreté,* but not as a vocation. My principal work is at the University of Paris and St. Lazare Hospital; at present I combine my vocation of savant with my avocation of criminologist. You see—"

"Why," I interrupted, grasping his hand, "you are Professor Jules de Grandin, author of *Accentuated Evolution?*"

He shrugged deprecatingly. "Yes, I am he," he admitted with a smile; "but at present our inquiries lie in another field. You have a patient, one young Monsieur Paul Maitland, is it not? He was set upon last night in the Andover Road?"

"I have a patient named Paul Maitland," I admitted, "but I don't know where he received his injuries."

"Nor do we," he answered with a smile, "but we shall inquire. You will go with us while we question him? No?"

"Why, yes," I acquiesced. "I should be looking in on him this morning, anyhow."

"And now, Monsieur," Professor de Grandin began when introductions had been completed, "you will please to tell us what happened last night to you. Yes?"

Paul looked uncomfortably from one of us to the other and swallowed nervously. "I don't like to think of it," he confessed, "much less talk about it; but here's the truth, believe it or not:

"I took Gladys home from the club about eleven o'clock, for she had developed a headache. After I'd said good night to her I decided to go home and turn in, and had got nearly here when I reached in my pocket for a cigarette. My case was gone, and I remembered laying it on a window ledge just before my last dance.

"The Mater gave me that case last birthday, and I didn't want to lose it, so, instead of telephoning the club and asking one of the fellows to slip it in his pocket, like a fool, I decided to drive back for it.

"You know—or at least Dr. Trowbridge and Sergeant Costello do—the Andover Road dips down in a little valley and curves over by the edge of the golf course between the eighth and ninth holes. I was just in that part of the road nearest the links when I heard a woman scream twice—it really wasn't two screams, more like one and a half, for her second cry was shut off almost before it started.

"I had a gun in my pocket, a little .22 automatic—good thing I did, too—so I snatched it out and drew up at the roadside, leaving my engine running. That was lucky, too, believe me.

"I ran into the woods, yelling at the top of my voice, and there in the path I saw something dark, like a woman's body, lying. I started toward it when there was a rustling in the trees overhead and—*plop!*—something dropped right into the path in front of me.

"Gentlemen, I don't know what it was, but I know it wasn't anything human. It wasn't quite as tall as I, but looked about twice as broad, and its hands hung down—clear down to the ground.

"I yelled, 'Hey, what're you doin'?' and pointed my gun at it, and it didn't answer, just started jumping up and down, bouncing with its feet and hands on the ground at once. I tell you, it gave me the horrors.

" 'Get out of it!' I yelled again, 'or I'll blow your head off.' Next moment—I was so nervous and excited I didn't really know what I was doing—I let fly with the pistol, right in the thing's face.

"That came near being my last shot, too. Believe me or not, that thing, whatever it was, reached out, snatched the gun out of my hand and *broke it.* Yes, sir, snapped that pistol in two with its bare hands as easily as I could break a match stick.

"And then it was on me. I felt one of its hands go clear over my shoulder, from breast to back in a single clutch, and it pulled me toward it. Ugh! It was hairy, sir. Hairy as an ape!"

"*Morbleu!* Yes? And then?" de Grandin murmured eagerly.

"Then I lunged out with all my might and kicked it on the shins. It released its grip a second, and I beat it. Ran as I never did on the quarter-mile track, jumped into the car and took off down the road with everything wide open. But I got these gashes in my back and arms before I got into the roadster. He made three or four grabs for me, and every one of 'em took the flesh away where his nails raked me. By the time I got home I was almost crazy with fright and pain and loss of blood. I remember kicking and banging on the door and yelling for the folks to open, and then I went out like a light."

The boy paused and regarded us seriously. "I know you think I'm the biggest liar out of jail," he announced; "but I've been telling you the absolute, honest-to-goodness truth."

Costello looked skeptical, but de Grandin nodded eagerly, affirmatively. "But, of course, you speak truth," he replied. "Now tell me, young Monsieur, if you can, this *poilu,* this hairy one, how was he dressed?"

"Um," Paul wrinkled his brow in an effort at remembrance. "I can't say surely, for it was dark in the woods and I was pretty much excited, but—I—think he was in evening clothes. Yes; I'd swear to it. I saw his white shirt bosom."

"Ah," muttered de Grandin softly. "A hairy thing, a fellow who leaps up and down like a jumping-jack or an ape in his anger, and in evening clothes. It is to think, *mes amis.*"

"I'll say it is," Costello agreed. "What sort o' affair did they have out at th' club last night, young feller?"

"Dr. Trowbridge is wanted on the 'phone, please," a maid announced from the door. "You can take it on this one, if you wish, sir; it's connected with the main line."

I picked up the instrument from young Maitland's bedside table and called, "Hello, Dr. Trowbridge speaking."

"This is Mrs. Comstock, doctor," a voice informed me. "Your housekeeper told us you were at Mrs. Maitland's. Can you come to my house, please? Mr. Manly, my daughter's fiancé, was hurt last night."

"Hurt last night?" I repeated.

"Yes, out by the country club."

"Very well, I'll be over shortly," I answered, then held out my hand to de Grandin.

"Sorry to have to run away," I apologized, "but another man was hurt at the club last night."

"Ah?" he replied interrogatively. "That club, it is an unfortunate place. May I accompany you, doctor? This other man, he may tell us something also."

"Very well," I agreed, "I'll be pleased to have your company."

Young Manly's injury proved to be a gunshot wound inflicted by a small caliber weapon, and was located in the left shoulder. He was very reticent concerning its cause, and neither de Grandin nor I felt inclined to inquire too insistently, for Mrs. Comstock hovered about the sickroom from our entrance until the treatment was concluded.

"Nom d'un petit porc!" de Grandin muttered as we left the Comstock residence. "He is close-mouth, that one. Al-

most, it would seem—pah! I talk the rot. Let us get to the morgue, *cher docteur*. You shall drive me there in your motor and tell me what it is you see. Ofttimes you gentlemen of the general practice see things which we specialists overlook because of the mental blinders of our specialties. *N'est-ce pas?*"

In the cold, uncharitable light of the city mortuary we viewed the remains of poor little Sarah Humphries. As the newspaper had said, she was disfigured by twenty or more wounds, running, for the most part, in converging lines down her shoulders and arms, deeply incised, deep enough to reveal the bone where skin and flesh had been completely shorn through in places. On her throat and neck were five distinct livid patches, one some three inches in size, roughly square, the other four extending in parallel lines almost completely around her neck, terminating in deeply pitted scars, as though the talons of some predatory beast had been sunk into her flesh. But the most terrifying item of the grisly sight was the poor girl's face. Repeated blows had reduced her once pretty features to an empurpled level, bits of sand and fine gravel still bedded in the cuticle told how her countenance must have been ground into the earth with terrific force. Never, since my days as emergency hospital interne, had I seen so sickening an array of injuries on a single body.

"Eh, what do you see, my friend?" the little Frenchman demanded in a raucous whisper. "You think—what?"

"It's terrible"—I began, but he interrupted impatiently.

"But, of course. One does not expect the beautiful at the morgue. I ask what you see, not for your æsthetic impressions. *Pardieu!*"

"If you want to know what interests me most," I answered, "it is those wounds on her shoulder and arms. Except in degree, they are exactly like those which I treated on young Maitland last night."

"Ah—yes?" de Grandin responded, his little blue eyes

dancing with excitement, his cat's-whisker mustache bristling more fiercely than ever. "Name of a little blue man! We begin to make progress. Now,"—he touched the lividities on the dead girl's throat daintily with the tip of one well manicured nail—"these marks, do they tell you anything?"

I shook my head. "Possibly the bruise left by some sort of garrote," I hazarded. "They are too long and thick for fingerprints; besides, there's no thumb mark."

"Ha, ha," he laughed mirthlessly. "No thumb mark, do you say? My dear sir, had there been a thumb mark, I should have been all at sea. These marks, they are the stigmata of truth on the young Monsieur Maitland's story. When were you last at the zoo, eh?"

"At the zoo?" I echoed stupidly.

"But, of course, have you never noted the quadrumana, how they take hold? My dear sir, it would, perhaps, not be too great an exaggeration to say the thumb is the difference between man and monkey. Man and the chimpanzee grasp an object with the fingers, using the thumb as a fulcrum. The gorilla, the orang-utan, the gibbon, he is a fool, he knows not how to use his thumb. Now see"—again he indicated the bruises—"this large patch, that represents the heel of the hand, these encircling lines, they are the fingers, these wounds, they are nail prints. Name of an old one-eyed tomcat! It was truth the young Maitland told. It was an ape which accosted him in the *bois*. An ape in evening clothes! What think you from that, *hein?*"

"God knows," I answered helplessly. "I give up."

"Qui, Monsieur le Docteur," de Grandin lapsed into his native tongue in his earnestness, "truly, God does know. But I, do I give up? Me, I am like your so splendid Paul Jones, I have but commenced to fight!"

He turned abruptly from the dead girl and, seizing my elbow, urged me from the morgue. "No more, no more now," he declared. "You have your mission of help to the sick to perform, and I have my work, also, to do. If you will take me once more to your charming suburb I will leave you to your duties while I pursue mine, and, if the imposition is not too great, I will dwell at your house while on this case. You consent? Good!"

"Until to-night, then," he hailed as he leaped agilely from the car at the village limits. "I shall attempt to be at the house before you have—how do you say?—hit into the straw? *Bien, au revoir, cher ami.*"

It was somewhere about eight o'clock when de Grandin returned to my house, laden with almost enough bundles to tax a motor truck's capacity. "Great Scott, Professor," I exclaimed as he laid his parcels on a convenient chair and gave me a grin which sent the waxed points of his mustache shooting upwards like a miniature pair of horns, "have you been buying out the town?"

"Almost," he admitted as he seated himself and lit a vile-smelling French cigarette. "I have talked much with the grocer, the druggist, the garage keeper and the tobacconist, and at each place I make purchases. I am, for the time, a new resident of your so pleasant suburb, anxious to find out about my neighbors and my new home. I have talk, talk, talk. I have milled over much wordy chaff, *hélas!* But from it I have extracted some good meal, *grâce à dieu!*"

He fixed his curiously unwinking cat-stare on me and asked: "You have a Monsieur Kalmar resident here, have you not?"

"Yes," I replied, "I believe we have."

"And you can tell me of him?"—he paused, raising eyebrows questioningly.

"No," I answered, "I'm afraid I can't. He's lived here about a year, and kept very much to himself. As far as I know, he has made friends with no one in the village, and has been visited by no one but the tradesmen. I've been given to understand he is a scientist of some sort, and took the old Means place, out on the Andover Road, so that he could pursue his experiments undisturbed."

"Ah, yes, I see," de Grandin tapped his cigarette case thoughtfully with his finger tips, "that much I have already gathered from my talks this day. Now tell me, if you can, is this Monsieur All-Unknown a friend of the young Manly's—the gentleman whose wound from gunshot you treated this morning?"

"Not that I know," I replied. "I've never seen them together. Manly is a queer, moody sort of chap, never has much to say to any one. How Millicent Comstock came to fall in love with him I've no idea. He rides well, and is highly thought of by her mother, but those are about the only qualifications he has as a husband that I've been able to see."

"He is very strong, eh?" de Grandin queried.

"I don't know," I had to confess.

"Well, then," he returned, "listen at me. You think de Grandin is a fool, eh? Perhaps yes; perhaps no. This day I make other business besides talk. I go to that Comstock lady's house and reconnoiter. In an ash-can I find one pair of patent leather dress shoes, much scratched. I grease the palm of a servant and find out they are that Monsieur Manly's. I also look farther and find one white linen dress shirt, with blood on it. It is torn about the cuffs and split at the shoulder, that shirt. It, too, I find, belong to Monsieur Manly. I am like a Jewish second-hand man when I talk with that servant of Madam Comstock—I buy from him that shirt and those shoes. Behold!"

Undoing a parcel, he exhibited a pair of dress shoes and a shirt, as though they were curios of priceless value. "In Paris we have ways of making the inanimate talk," he asserted as he thrust his hand into his pocket and drew forth a bit of folded paper. "That shirt and those shoes I put through the third degree, and I find this." Opening the paper he disclosed three coarse, dull-brown hairs, varying from a half-inch to three inches in length.

I examined them curiously. From their appearance they might have been from a man's head, for they were too long and insufficiently curved to be body-hairs, but their texture seemed too harsh for human growth.

"Uh," I commented noncommittally.

"Um," he mocked. "You cannot classify them, eh? No?"

"No," I admitted. "They are entirely too coarse to have come from Manly's head. Besides, they are almost black; his hair is a distinct brown."

"My friend," de Grandin leaned forward suddenly, staring me straight in the eyes, "those hairs, I have seen such before. So have you, but you do not recognize. *They are from a gorilla!*"

"Impossible!" I jerked back. "How could a gorilla's hair get on Manly's shirt?"

"Not on," he corrected, still gazing directly at me. "They were *in* it, below the neck line, where a bullet had torn through the linen and wounded him. The hairs were embedded in the dried blood. Look at this garment"—he held the shirt before me for inspection—"behold how it is split. It has been upon a body too big for it. Monsieur Trowbridge, that shirt was worn by the thing—the monster—which killed that pitiful girl dead on the links last night, which attacked the young Maitland a few minutes later—and which got this paint from the side of Madam Comstock's house on these shoes when it climbed that house last night.

"You start, you stare? You say to yourself, 'De Grandin, he is *caduc*—mad?' Listen, I prove each step in the ladder:

"This morning, while you examine Monsieur Manly's wound, I examine him and his room. On his window sill I note a few scrapes—such scrapes as one who drags his legs and feet might make climbing over the window ledge. I look out at the window, and on the white-painted side of the house I find fresh paint-scratches. Too, also, I find marks on the painted iron pipe which carry the water from the roof down in rainy weather. That pipe runs down the corner of the house, near Manly's window, but too far away for a man to reach it from the sill. But if that man have arms as long as my leg, what then? Ah, he could make the reach most easy.

"Now, when I buy these shoes, that shirt from the Comstock servant, I note the paint on the shoe, and the scratch also thereon. I compare the paint on the shoe with the paint on the house-sides. He are the same.

"I note that shirt, how he are blood-stained, how he are all burst, as though the man who wear him suddenly grow great and break him out. I find the beast-hairs in the blood-stain on the shirt. I take that shirt to the laundry and ask the excellent *Chinois,* 'Whose shirt are this?'

"He reply, 'Not know.'

"I say, 'You are liar, but I give you this'—I show him a bill of ten dollair—'to tell the truth.'

"He take my bill and smile like summer as he reply, 'Mr. Manly's.' *Voilà!* You see?"

"No, I'll be hanged if I do," I denied.

He bent forward again, speaking with rapid earnestness: "That servant, he tell me more. Last night the young Manly was nervous—what you call ill at ease. He complain of headache, of backache—he feel r-r-rotten. He go to bed early, and his *amoureuse,* she go without him to the country club dance. The old madam, she, too, go to bed.

"The young man, he go for walk, because he cannot sleep, he tell that servant that this morning. But the servant, he was up with the toothache all night, and while he hear the young man come in after midnight, *he did not hear him leave.*

"Now, what do you think? A policeman of the motorcycle tell me he see the young Manly come from that Monsieur Kalmar's house, staggering like one drunk. He wonders, that policeman, if Monsieur Kalmar keep so much to himself because he are a legger-of-the-boot? Eh? What now, *cher docteur?* You say what?

"Damn it!" I exploded. "You're piecing up the silliest nonsense-story I ever heard, de Grandin. One of us is crazy as hell, and I don't think it's I!"

"Neither of us is crazy, *mon vieux,*" he returned gravely, "but men have gone mad with knowing what I know, and madder yet with suspect what I am beginning to suspect. Will you drive me past the house of Monsieur Kalmar?"

A few minutes' run carried us out to the lonely house occupied by the eccentric old man whose year's residence near the village had been a twelve months' mystery.

"Ah, ha," de Grandin exclaimed as we passed the place, "he works late, this one. Observe, the light burns in his workshop."

Sure enough, from a window at the rear of the house a shaft of electric light cut the evening shadows, and, as we stopped the car and gazed, we could see Kalmar's bent form, swathed in a laboratory apron, passing and repassing the window as he shuffled nervously back and forth across the room.

"Let us go," de Grandin suggested, turning from his silent contemplation of the worker. "While we drive back I will tell you a story.

"Before the war which racked the world, there came to Paris from the University of Vienna one Doctor Beneckendorff. As a man he was intolerable, as a scholar he was incomparable. The knowledge of the greatest savants concerning organic evolution and comparative anatomy were but as children's A B C to that one. With my own two eyes I have seen him perform experiments which, in an age less tolerant of learning—perhaps in your own America, with its so curious laws against the teaching of scientific truth—would have brought him to the stake as a wizard.

"But science is God's tool, my friend, and it is not meant

that man should play at being God. That man, he went too far. We had to restrain him in prison."

"Yes?" I answered, not particularly interested in the narrative. "What did he do?"

"Eh, what did he not do?" de Grandin replied. "Children of the poor were found missing at night. They were nowhere. The gendarmes' search narrowed to the laboratory of this Beneckendorff, and there they found not the poor infants, but a half-score ape-creatures, not wholly human, not wholly simian, but partaking horribly of the appearance of each, with fur and handlike feet, but with the face of something which had once been of mankind. They were dead, those poor ones, fortunately for them.

"He proved mad, like the bug of June, as you Americans say, but ah, my friend, what a mentality, what a fine brain gone bad!

"We shut him up for the safety of the public, and for the safety of the race we burned his notebooks and destroyed the serums with which he had injected the human babies to turn them into apes."

"Impossible!" I exclaimed.

"Incredible, yes," de Grandin admitted, "but not, unfortunately, impossible—for him. His secret entered the madhouse with him; but in the turbulent days of war when the *Boche* thundered at the gates of Paris, he escaped."

"Good God!" I cried. "You mean to say, de Grandin, this mad fiend, this maker of monsters, is loose on the world?"

He shrugged his shoulders with Gallic fatalism. "Perhaps. All trace of him has vanished, though there are reports he was later seen in the Congo Belgique."

"But—"

"Ah, no, I ramble on like a fool. Of what connection is this remembrance of mine with the case of Sarah Humphries? *Pardieu,* none!

"One favor, Monsieur, if you please; let me accompany

you once more when you attend the young Manly. I would have a one minute's talk with Madame Comstock. Perhaps—"

His voice trailed off into silence.

Mrs. Cornelia Comstock was a lady of imposing physique and even more imposing manner. She was wont to receive respectful and ceremonious consideration from society reporters, her fellow club members, even from solicitors for "causes." But to de Grandin she was simply a woman who had information which he desired. Prefacing his inquiry with the sort of bow none but a Frenchman can achieve, he began directly:

"Madame Comstock, do you, or did you ever, know one Dr. Beneckendorff?"

Mrs. Comstock, who was used to dominating her husband, her daughter and all mankind in general, drew herself stiffly erect and directed a withering gaze at him.

"My good man—" she began, as though he were an overcharging taxi driver, but the Frenchman met her cold eyes with eyes equally cold and uncompromising.

"You will answer my questions, please," he told her. "Primarily I represent the Republic of France; but I also represent humanity. Once more, please, did you ever know a Dr. Beneckendorff?"

Mrs. Comstock's imperious glance lowered before de Grandin's unwinking stare, and her thin lips twitched slightly as she replied, "Yes."

"Ah. We make progress. When did you know him—in what circumstances? Believe me, you may speak in confidence before me and Dr. Trowbridge, but please to speak frankly. The importance is great."

"I knew Otto Beneckendorff many years ago," the lady answered in a low voice. "He had just come to this country from Europe, and was teaching science at the university near which I lived as a girl. We—we were engaged."

"Ah? So. And your betrothal was broken. For what reason, please?"

Looking at her, I could scarcely recognize the community's social dictator in Mrs. Cornelia Comstock as she regarded de Grandin with wondering, frightened eyes. She shivered, as though she felt a sudden draft of chilled air, before answering. "He—he was impossible, sir. We had vivisectionists, even in those days—but this man seemed to torture poor, helpless animals for the love of it. I gave him back his ring when he boasted of one of his experiments to me. He seemed to enjoy telling how the poor beast suffered before it died."

"Eh bien," de Grandin shot me a meaning glance, as though I, too, followed the thread his examination unraveled, "we do progress. Good. Your betrothal, then, was broken. He left you, this so cruel experimenter. Did he leave in friendship?" He leaned forward, waxed cat-mustache bristling, as he awaited her reply in breathless eagerness.

Mrs. Comstock looked like one on the verge of fainting as she almost whispered: "No, no; he left me with a terrible threat. I remember his very words—can I ever forget them? He said, 'I go from you; but I shall return. Nothing but death can cheat me. I shall bring on you and yours a horror such as no man has known since the days before Adam.' "

De Grandin almost danced as she finished speaking. "Ah, ha," he exclaimed, "the explanation is ours! The mystery is almost solved. Thank you, Madame. If you will tell me one more little thing, I shall retire and trouble you no more:

"Your daughter, she is betrothed to one Monsieur Manly. Tell me, I beg, when and where did she meet this young man?"

"I introduced them," the lady replied with a return of something of her frigid manner. "Mr. Manly came to my husband with letters of introduction from an old schoolmate of his—a fellow student at the university—in Capetown."

"Eh?" de Grandin almost shrieked. "Capetown, do you say? Capetown, South Africa? *Nom d'un petit bonhomme!* From Capetown! When was this, Madame, please?"

"A year ago. Why—"

"And Monsieur Manley, he has lived with you how long?" the question shut off her offended protest half uttered.

"Mr. Manly is *stopping* with us," she answered icily. "He is to marry my daughter, Millicent, next month. Really, sir, I fail to see what interest the Republic of France, which you represent, and humanity, which you also claim to represent, can have in my private affairs. If—"

"And this Capetown friend," de Grandin interrupted feverishly. "Tell me, his name was what, and his business?"

"I—"

"Tell me!" he cried impatiently, extending his slender hands as though to choke the answer from her. *"Nom d'un fusil!* I must know. At once!"

"We do not know his street and number," Mrs. Comstock replied. "His name is Alexander Findlay, and he is a diamond factor."

"Ah, ah! *Bien.* Thank you, Madame. You have been most kind," said de Grandin, and he struck his heels together and bowed as though hinged at the hips.

It was past midnight when the 'phone rang insistently. "Western Union speaking," a girl's voice announced over the wire. "Cablegram for Dr. de Grandin. Ready?"

"Yes," I answered, seizing the pencil and pad beside the instrument. "Read it, please."

" 'No person by name Alexander Findlay, diamond factor, known here; no record of such person in last five years. Signed, Burlingame, Inspector of Police.'

"The cable is from Capetown, South Africa," she added as I finished jotting down her dictation.

"Very good," I replied. "Forward a typed confirmation in the morning, please."

Then I went to de Grandin's room with the message.

"Mille tonnerres!" he shouted, flinging the covers back, as I read him the cablegram: "de Grandin, he is a fool, *hein?* Listen—" he leaped from the bed and raced across the room to where his coat hung over a chair. Extracting a black leather notebook, almost as large as a desk dictionary, he thumbed its pages rapidly, finally found the entry he sought. "Behold! This Monsieur Kalmar, whom no one knows about, he have lived here ten months and twenty-six days. I have it from that so stupid real estate broker who think I ask information for a directory of scientists.

"That young Monsieur Manly, he have known those Comstocks for 'about a year.' He bring them a letter of introduction from a schoolmate of Monsieur Comstock who are unknown to the Capetown police. *Pardieu!* Hereafter Jules de Grandin he sleep all day and prowl all night. To-morrow, Monsieur, you shall introduce me to the gun merchant. I desire to possess one Winchester rifle."

The time drifted by, de Grandin going, gun in hand, each night to his lonely vigil; but no developments in the mystery of the Humphries murder or the attack on Paul Maitland were reported.

The date for Millicent Comstock's wedding approached, and the big mansion was filled to overflowing with boisterous young folks; still de Grandin continued to invert the time, sleeping by day, patrolling by night.

Two nights before the marriage day he accosted me as he came downstairs. "Trowbridge, my friend, you have been most patient with me. If you will come to-night, I think, perhaps, I can show you some result."

"All right," I agreed, "I haven't the slightest idea what all this folderol is about, but I'm willing to be convinced."

At his request I got out my car and drove to within a block of the Comstock house, parking the machine in a small copse of trees where it would be readily accessible, yet effectually concealed.

"My friend," de Grandin began as we skirted the Comstock lawn, keeping well hidden in the shadows, "I am not certain of what I do. I am like one who walks an unfamiliar path with a hoodwink on his eyes; yet my brain tell me I follow no false road. No man knows what part Tanit, the Moon Goddess, plays in the affairs of men, even to-day, when her name is forgotten by all but dusty-dry antiquaries. This we know, however; at the entrance of life our appearance is governed, in the matter of days, by the phase of the moon. You, as a physician with obstetrical knowledge, know that. Too, when the time to go approach, the crisis of disease is often governed by the moon's phase. Why this is we know not; that it is we know full well. Suppose, then, the cellular organization of a body be violently, unnaturally changed, and nature's whole force be exerted toward a readjustment. Is it not reasonable to suppose that the moon, which affects childbirth and death, might have some force to apply in such a case?"

"I daresay," I conceded, "but I don't follow you. Just what is it you expect, or suspect, de Grandin?"

"Nothing," he answered. "I suspect nothing, I affirm nothing, I deny nothing. I am agnostic, but I am hopeful. If events prove me a doting fool, making a great, black *lutin* of my own shadow, no one will be happier than I. But he who prepares for the worst is most agreeably disappointed if the best occurs."

He touched my elbow. "Here we rest awhile," he murmured, squatting in the shadow of a small clump of dwarf pines. "That light, it is in the window of Mademoiselle Millicent's room, *n'est-ce pas?*"

"Yes," I confirmed, wondering if I were on a fool's errand with a lunatic for company.

The merrymaking inside the house was wearing to a close

as we took our station; within half an hour the mansion was shrouded in quiet darkness.

De Grandin fidgeted nervously, fussing with the lock of his gun, ejecting and reinserting cartridges, playing a devil's tattoo on the barrel with his long, tapering fingers.

Almost like a floodlight turned on the scene, the moon's radiance suddenly deluged the house, grounds and surroundings with silver as the wind swept aside a veil of clouds. "Ah," de Grandin muttered, "now we shall see what we shall see—perhaps."

As though his words had been a cue, there echoed from the house before us a scream of such wild, bewildered terror as few men have been unfortunate enough to hear. In the course of twenty years' active practice of medicine I had heard almost every sort of cry that physical anguish can wring from tortured flesh, but never anything like this. Fear—stark, hideous fear—played on the vocal cords of the screamer like a madman twanging a harp, bringing forth a symphony of terror that stopped the breath, hot and sulphurous, in my throat, and sent an itching tingle through my scalp.

"A-a-ah!" de Grandin exclaimed in a rising tone as he grasped his rifle and stared fixedly at the house. "*Grand Dieu,* grant he comes forth. Only that, and I shall be content."

Light flashed inside the house. The patter of terrified feet sounded among the babel of wondering, questioning voices, but the scream was not repeated.

"A-a-ah!" de Grandin breathed again, his voice razor-edged with excitement. "Look, my friend, *Le Gorille!* Behold, he comes!"

Emerging from Millicent's window, horrible as a devil from lowest hell, was a great, hairy head set low upon a pair of shoulders which must have been four feet across. An arm which, somehow, reminded me of a giant snake, slipped forth, grasped the cast-iron downspout at the corner of the house, and drew a thickset, misshapen body after it. A leg, tipped with a prehensile, handlike foot, was thrown over the sill, and, like a spider from its lair, the monster leaped from the darkened window and hung a moment to the iron pipe with its sable body silhouetted against the white walls of the house.

But what was that, that white-robed form which hung pendent from the grasp of the beast's free arm? My staring eyes strained across the moonlit night and my mouth went dry with horror.

Like a beautiful, white moth inert in the grasp of the spider, her fair hair unbound and falling like a golden veil before her marble-white face, her night clothing rent into a motley of tatters, Millicent Comstock hung in the creature's grasp.

"Shoot, shoot, man; for God's sake, shoot!" I screamed, but only a whisper, inaudible ten feet away, came from my fear-thickened lips.

"Silence, fool!" de Grandin ground between his teeth, as he pressed his gunstock against his cheek and drew the muzzle in line with the descending brute's body.

Slowly, so slowly it seemed an hour was consumed in the process, the great primate descended the waterpipe, leaping the last fifteen feet of the trip and crouching on the moonlit lawn, its tiny, deep-set eyes glaring malignantly, as though it challenged the world for possession of its prey.

I could hear de Grandin's breath rasping in his nostrils as he sighted his gun and drew the trigger.

A roar like a bursting shell sounded as the smokeless powder's flash burned a gash in the night and a bullet went screaming through the air.

Again de Grandin fired, throwing the magazine mechanism with feverish haste.

The monster staggered drunkenly against the house as the detonation of the first shot sounded. With the second, it dropped Millicent's body to the lawn and uttered a cry which was part roar, part snarl, and, trailing one of its hairy arms helplessly, leaped toward the woods, crossing the grass plot in great, awkward leaps which reminded me, absurdly, of the bouncing of a huge inflated ball.

"Attend Mademoiselle," de Grandin commanded sharply, throwing a fresh cartridge into his firing chamber. "I will see to the hairy one. Have no fear, I have shot his brethren in Africa."

I bent above the girl's huddled body, putting my ear to her breast. Faint but perceptible, I made out a heart-beat, and lifted her in my arms, carrying her toward the house.

"Dr. Trowbridge!" Mrs. Comstock, followed by a throng of frightened, half-clothed guests, met me at the front door. "What has happened? Good heavens, Millicent!" She rushed forward, seizing her daughter's flaccid hands in both her own trembling ones. "Oh, what is it; what is it?"

"Help me get Millicent to bed and get me some smelling salts and some brandy," I commanded, ignoring her questions.

A few minutes later, with restoratives applied and electric pads at her feet and back, the girl showed signs of returning consciousness. "Get out—all of you," I ordered curtly. Hysterical women, even patients' mothers, are no fit occupants for the room when consciousness is regained after profound shock.

Millicent stirred in her faint, rolling her head feebly from side to side and moaning. "Oh, oh, the ape-thing—the ape-thing!" she whimpered in a small, childish voice. It was not till several hours later I realized she used exactly the term Paul Maitland had employed when recovering from his faint.

"All right, dear," I comforted. "It's all right, now. You're safe in bed. Old Dr. Trowbridge is here; he won't let anything hurt you."

She half opened her lovely eyes, saw me sitting beside her, and smiled sleepily in reassurance. Next moment, she was soundly and naturally asleep, both her hands clasping one of mine.

"Doctor, Dr. Trowbridge," Mrs. Comstock whispered from the bedroom door, "we've searched all over the place, and there's no sign of Mr. Manly. Do—do you suppose anything could have happened to him?"

"I think it quite likely something could—and did," I answered, turning from her to smooth her daughter's hair.

"Par la barbe d'un bouc noir!" de Grandin exclaimed as, disheveled, but with a light of exhilaration in his direct blue eyes, he met me in the Comstock hall some two hours later. *"Chère* Madame Comstock, you are to be congratulated. But for my so brave colleague, Dr. Trowbridge, and my own lowly self, your charming daughter had shared the fate of that never-enough-to-be-pitied Sarah Humphries.

"Trowbridge, *mon vieux,* I have not been quite frank with you. I have not told you all. But this thing, it was so incredible, so seemingly impossible, that you would not have believed. Even now, knowing what you know, having seen with your two eyes what you have seen this night, you do not quite believe. *Eh bien,* perhaps it is better so.

"To begin: When this *sacré Beneckendorff* was in the madhouse, he raved continually about his confinement cheating him of his revenge—the revenge he had so long planned against one Madame Comstock of America.

"We French, we are logical, not like you English and Americans. We write down and keep for possible reference even what a madman say. Why not? It may be useful some day.

"Now, friend Trowbridge, I tell you some time ago this Beneckendorff were reported in the Congo Belgique. Yes? But I do not tell you he were reported in charge of a young, half-grown gorilla. No.

"When this *pauvre* Mademoiselle Humphries is killed in that so terrible manner I remember my own African days and I says to me, 'Ah, ha, it looks as if *Monsieur le Gorille*—the gorilla—have been about this place. I ask to know if any such have escape from a circus or zoo from near by or far. All answers are no.

"Then that Sergeant Costello, he bring me to this so splendid savant, Dr. Trowbridge, and with him I go to interview that young Paul Maitland who have encountered much strangeness on the golf links where the young woman was killed.

"And what do he tell me? He relate of a thing that have hair, that jump up and down like an enraged ape and that act like a gorilla, *but wear man's evening clothes. Parbleu!* It is to think! No gorilla have escape, yet what *seems* one is here encountered, wearing the clothes of a man. I search my memory. I remember that madman and the poor infants he turn into monkey-things with his damnable serums.

"I say: 'If he can turn man-children into monkey-things, why not can he turn ape-things into men-things? Eh?'

"I find one Dr. Kalmar live here unknown. I search about and learn a certain man here are seen coming from his place in secret. I also find in this certain man's discarded shirt the hair of a gorilla. *Morbleu!* I think some more, and the thoughts I think are not pleasant thoughts.

"I reason: 'Suppose this serum which make a man-thing of an ape are not permanent? What then? If it are not renewed at times, the man becomes an ape again.' You follow? *Bien.*

"Now the other day, I learn something which make me think some more. This Beneckendorff, he rave against one Madame Comstock. You, Madame Comstock, admit you once knew this Beneckendorff. He have loved you, as he understand love; now he hate you as only he with his diseased, but great, brain, can hate. Is it not against you he plan his devilish scheme? I think so.

"I send a cablegram—never mind who to; Dr. Trowbridge knows that—and I get the answer I expect, but fear.

The man in whose shirt I find those gorilla hairs is no man at all, he is one terrible masquerade of a man. So. Now, I reason, 'Suppose this masquerading monkey-thing do not get his serum as expected, what will he do?' I fear to answer my own question, but I do answer it just the same, and I buy a gun.

"This gun have bullets of soft lead, and I make them still more efficient by cutting a V-shaped notch in each of their heads. When they strike something they spread out for a space you could not cover with your hand.

"*Voilà!*" I take my gun and wait. To-night what I have expect come about. I am ready. I shoot, and each time my bullet strike, it tear a great hole in the body of the man-who-is-an-ape. He drop his prey and seek the shelter his little ape-brain tell him to fly to. He goes to the house of this so unknown Dr. Kalmar. I follow quick.

"The ape are tortured with my bullet wounds. When he reached the house of Kalmar, he is angry, and set upon this Kalmar and tear him to pieces, even as he have killed poor Sarah Humphries before. I, arriving with my gun, I kill the gorilla with one more shot.

"But before I come back here I recognize the dead corpse of that Dr. Kalmar. He are one and the same as that Beneckendorff who have escape from our Paris madhouse.

"I destroy his devil's brews with which he make monkeys of men and men of monkeys. It is better their secret be never known.

"I think the Mademoiselle Humphries were so unfortunate as to meet this man-ape when he were on his way to Kalmar's house, as he had been taught to come. As man, perhaps, he knew not this Kalmar, or, as we know him, Beneckendorff; but as brute this Beneckendorff was the only man he know—his master, the man who brought him from Africa.

"When he find that poor girl, she scream, and his savageness become uppermost—believe me, the gorilla is ten thousand times more savage than the lion—and he tear her to pieces. He also try to tear the young Maitland to pieces; but, luckily for him and for us, he fail, and we get the story which put us on the track.

"Voilà!" It is finished. *Triomphe!* I make my report to the good Sergeant Costello, and show him the bodies at Kalmar's house. Then I return to France. The Ministry of Health, they will be glad to know that Beneckendorff is no more."

"But, Monsieur de Grandin," Mrs. Comstock demanded, "who was this man—or this ape—you killed?"

I held my breath as de Grandin fixed his direct stare on her, then sighed with relief as he replied, "I cannot say, Madame."

"Well"—Mrs. Comstock's natural disputatiousness came to the surface—"I think it's *very queer* you know so much about him; but don't know his name."

"Ah, Madam," he shook his head sadly, "there are very many queer things in life; things which may puzzle even you. I bid you good night."

. . . .

"When the police look for Monsieur Manly—*Mon dieu,* what a name for an ape-thing!—they will be puzzled," he told me as we walked toward my waiting motor. "I must remember to warn Sergeant Costello to enter that disappearance on his books as a case permanently unsolved. No one will ever know the true facts but you, I, and the French Ministry of Health, Trowbridge, my friend. The public, they would not believe, even if we told them."

I wonder if they will?

THE EXPERIMENT OF ERICH WEIGERT

By SEWELL PEASLEE WRIGHT

THE MOMENT I GAZED OUT OVER THE AUDIENCE I SAW HIM. He was seated far back under the balcony that overhung the little auditorium, but even in the heavy shadow I could see his eyes; eyes that seemed alight with cold brilliance, like a diamond in the moonlight.

Although I was more or less accustomed to public speaking, and was very much at home with my subject that evening, "Radio As It Used To Be," something about the unfaltering regard of the man under the balcony confused me. His eyes were on me constantly; every move I made, every gesture, every change in expression, those unwinking blue orbs seemed to register.

I wondered who he was; surely I had never seen him before, nor he me. I caught myself addressing myself to him, and when once his head seemed to nod slightly as though in approval of something I had said, a strange thrill of pleasure tingled along my spine. There was a power in the man; a sort of benign malignancy. I was glad when I finished and could escape from that unwavering regard.

After the meeting broke up he came up toward the stage, where I was chatting with several officers of the radio association responsible for the meeting I had just addressed. They moved away as they noted the stranger's obvious intention to speak to me.

He was a little man, I saw now, not more than five feet

six inches in height, but his shoulders were broad and massive, and his head was larger than mine.

But it was his face that held my gaze. His eyes, as I had said, seemed to burn coldly, with the same chilly, weird blue light of an electric spark. They were deep-set eyes, separated with a thin, sharply beaked nose that somehow seemed repulsively cruel. His mouth was thin and turned down sharply at the corners, two deep wrinkles springing from near the base of his nose accentuating its contour. Above a high forehead that bulged strangely, clung tangled, sparse gray locks.

He smiled ingratiatingly as he drew near, and as he spoke, his voice was surprisingly pleasant.

"Mr. Saylor, I enjoyed your talk very much indeed. For a man of your years you have a very keen insight into radio."

He offered his hand as he spoke, and I took it cordially. For all his unprepossessing appearance, there was a certain appeal about the man; the strength of his personality attracted more than his appearance repelled.

"I've been working with radio for fourteen years now," I replied smiling. "Ham, Marconi 'op,' experimental work for a manufacturer, designing, all that sort of thing. Bound to pick up a little here and there, you know."

"Yes, indeed! A great deal of experience for a young man. You seem—pardon me! I have neglected to introduce myself: Erich Weigert, at your service!" He bowed a quick little, foreign, military bow, heels together. "If you have nothing else in mind, Mr. Saylor, and would be interested, I would like to take you through my own little laboratory this evening."

Erich Weigert! And an invitation to go through his laboratory! It is no wonder that I gasped. I had heard of him as a wealthy, somewhat mysterious recluse with scientific leanings, but I had never seen him before that memorable night.

Weigert's machine soon whisked us out to his residence near the outskirts of the city. Only a few lights were burning as we turned in at the grass-grown drive, but I could make out the house as a massive, square pile, squat and ugly in the moonlight, topped with an octagonal cupola, like some uncouth excrudescence, its panes glaring bleakly over the rather extensive, high-walled grounds that surrounded the place.

The door was opened by a young woman whom a moment later Weigert introduced as his wife. The affection and pride in his voice as he presented me struck me as being the first real feeling that he had evidenced since I had met him.

He had a very real reason for his pride, for his wife was undeniably beautiful. The instant she raised her soft, dark eyes to mine I was struck almost dumb with their remarkable loveliness. I say I was struck almost dumb; I say that because to talk of love at first sight is to bring up visions of youthful exaggerations. It is true that as Vera Weigert and I looked into each other's eyes that night, something was born of that union of glances that never died—that never will die. Call it what you will, for I must on with my story.

I remember but vaguely the trip through the big bare laboratory that Weigert had made of two adjoining rooms at one side of the house. Later I became very well acquainted with the delicate instruments, the generators and transformers and the immense variety of tubes with which the laboratory was equipped, but that night my mind was too full of Vera Weigert. It was not until after Weigert invited me to a chair in front of the big fireplace in the front room, between himself and his wife, that the trend of his conversation began to make an impression on my mind.

"Your remark this evening that the mystery had all gone from radio, despite the fact that radio was doing greater marvels to-day than ever, struck me particularly," Weigert said with a nod of approval, glancing first at me, and then at his wife. "It is true, to-day they hook up eight tubes and hear from one coast to another or perhaps one continent listens to another—with the power of the sending station listed in many thousands of watts. Bah! It is like killing ants with a steam-roller! In the days when we caught the buzz and scratch of spark signals two thousand miles away —and more—with our crystals, silicon, galena, perikon—then there was mystery, romance, to radio. To-day, my barber's wife can twiddle the switches and dials of her set and copy from coast to coast as easily as she can change the records on her phonograph. The scientist, the man with imagination, has left that phase of radio far behind; it is a husk from which all the sweetness has been sucked!"

"True," I nodded. "I find no interest in radio communications now. But, sir, the transmission of photographs by radio—and we are doing that now, you know—fires my imagination. I have been working myself along those lines," I added somewhat timidly, for Erich Weigert had a terrific force of personality that made me feel very young beside him. "Perhaps the day is not so far off when we shall be able to broadcast moving pictures as well as the music to accompany them!"

"Aber! Aber! That is but a step!" broke in Weigert, interrupting me with sudden and unexpected violence. "First code, then speech, then pictures. Good! A start, perhaps, but—not more than a start, Mr. Saylor!" He dropped his voice until it was little more than an insinuating whisper, and his eyes gleamed with indescribable earnestness. *"Thought!* That's the thing; the transmission of thought! Through the ages they have tried it. Some have claimed to have perfected it, but it was never so. Between two particular individuals, perhaps; but it has never been made a science. Radio *can* make it a science, Mr. Saylor; radio and *I!*"

I think he would have said more, but his wife deftly changed the subject, and Weigert allowed himself to be led by the soft leash of her voice. As for me, I was in a sort of uneasy paradise to be there beside her, to listen to her sweet voice, and the rest of the evening flew by far too quickly.

For days after two voices ruled my brain. One was her soft "Good night, Mr. Saylor!" and the other was Erich Weigert's cordial invitation to return to talk radio again some other night very soon. Should I go? Or should I heed the warning that my inner self shrieked in my mental ears? Should I place myself as one side of a triangle? And such a triangle! It was very evident that Weigert was wildly in love with his young wife, and with his temperament and personality—but why prolong the debate that raged in my mind? You know, if you have ever been a man, and young, how it was decided. I went—went not once but many times.

I think that Erich Weigert had a real affection for me; I could follow him along the lesser-trodden paths of radio research and could even lead him into some of the ramifications of the great science. My ideas, or at least many of them, agreed with his own. And to the man who had cut himself off from the rest of the world that he might devote himself to his work, I suppose I was a welcome contact point with the outside.

It was the love that waxed and grew between Vera and myself that caused me the most concern. There was that between us that made every moment near her a bitter paradise; a joyous hell. And that she responded to my passion with a love as great as my own, I had only to look into her eyes to see.

A quick pressure of her hand, a touch on the arm in passing; little things, yet they were all we had. And they were enough to drive me to any madness.

One night Weigert excused himself for a moment, to fetch something from the laboratory. As he disappeared through the heavy curtains her eyes met mine, and for a long moment we sat, drinking deep of the forbidden draft. Then, compelled by a force greater than the will of either of us, we rose to our feet and an instant later I had her in my arms, my lips crushed on hers.

I thought that I caught out of the corner of my eyes, a movement of the curtains across the door, and she detected my sudden start.

"What is it, dear?" she whispered.

"Nothing. But I thought the curtains moved just then. It startled me for a moment."

"It might have been him!" she whispered fiercely. "He is a devil! He knows everything. Perhaps—" But before she could finsh we heard his steps coming down the hall, and we hastened to seat ourselves.

Evidently Weigert had not been spying on us, for he was his normal self when he entered the room. Intensely jealous though he was, he had never seemed to see the love that was between his wife and me.

I should have read the man better; should have realized that those cold blue eyes missed nothing, and that such a personality could dissemble until—until—

"We have often talked about thought transmission by radio, Saylor. You remember?"

Weigert was talking to me over the 'phone, as we often chatted of an afternoon, when both of us had a little time. There was a certain tenseness in his voice that vaguely excited me.

"Yes," I answered quickly. "Have you—?"

"I think so. I am going to try the experiment to-night. Would you care to be on hand and assist me?"

"I certainly deem it an honor to be asked!"

He chuckled as at some private bit of humor before he replied.

"Will you be on hand at eight sharp, then? I must get to work now; there's a lot to do before to-night. Remember, eight o'clock sharp!"

It was exactly three minutes to eight when Erich Weigert admitted me that night. I showed him my watch, laughingly.

"See how well I obeyed orders?"

"Fine!" he nodded. "We will go directly to the laboratory; I am naturally anxious as to the success of our experiment."

The cold glitter in his eyes and the deepening of the harsh lines that accentuated the habitual sneer on the thin lips had told me at first glance that his nerves were near the breaking point, and as he spoke a vibrant undertone of his voice affirmed the truth of my judgment.

The laboratory, as I have said, was composed of two rooms, but to-night Weigert had pulled tightly shut the sliding doors between them. Before I had time to question him, even had I felt so inclined, he directed my attention to a table in the center of the room. On it was a mass of apparatus, in which I recognized many familiar instruments, although one or two of the devices were utterly foreign to my experience. Four receiving tubes burned near one edge of the tangle.

"Sit down in the chair, Saylor," suggested Weigert. "You're going to act as the receiving agent in this little test, since you so kindly volunteered to help. There; so."

He placed me in a big, overstuffed chair that stood beside the table and directed his attention to the apparatus.

"You see, I have reasoned it out this way," he commented as he worked: "thought is a function of the brain. Therefore"—he turned to me with an odd contrivance in his hand, a collarlike piece of apparatus, attached to some part of the array on the table by two long, flexible wires—"receiving of thought must be by getting in contact with the brain, either directly or through nerves running to the brain. Understand?"

I nodded, only partly understanding, and yet dominated utterly by the intense blue light that flared in his agate-hard blue eyes.

"So! Then we place this little collar of soft chamois

around your neck, buckling it tightly in place," he continued, suiting the action to the word. "That cold sensation you feel at the back is nothing but a plate of heavy silver foil; its function is to conduct to the nerve-cable of your spinal column the thought impulses after they are sufficiently amplified and energized by this apparatus."

For a few minutes he seemed to forget me utterly, and he leaned over the apparatus on the table, inspecting it, testing and adjusting. I watched him curiously, a premonition of evil settling down over me as a cold ocean fog rolls down into the lowlands. I was glad when he finally straightened up and once more spoke.

"Everything seems to be all ready," he said. "I'm not quite sure what current will be needed here, so I'll cut out this potentiometer slowly. You tell me"—and he put his face close to mine and glared down into my eyes—"what you feel."

"But—but the other subject?" I ventured. "Who is transmitting?"

"The other subject," he said curtly, "is in the next room. Keep your mind as free from outside thoughts as you can. Close your eyes. Relax."

In the stillness of the room I could hear the slight scrape of the contact arm over the wires of the potentiometer, but save for a nervous tickle up and down my spine I could feel nothing.

"Not enough, eh?" questioned Weigert, evidently watching my impassive face. I shook my head.

The potentiometer scraped again, and I became aware of a soft warmness in the region directly under the metal plate; a warmth that crept upward until it suffused the whole base of my brain. There was a sort of undulating quality about it that made me dizzy, that seemed to make me reel and sway even as I sat ensconced in the broad arms of the chair.

"It begins to make itself felt?"

I opened my eyes with a little start; his voice seemed to come from some outer world.

Weigert was peering down at me, his blue eyes alight with scientific fervor—or was it something more? He scowled as he saw my eyes open.

"Keep your eyes shut!" he commanded harshly. "How can the experiment succeed if you disobey orders?" I closed my eyes and sank back into the chair, and again the surging heat swept upward into my brain. I heard the potentiometer scrape; more and more. . . .

It is hard to put down in black and white that which sounds so incredible that I myself can hardly believe it. But I shall try.

The pulsation of the warm waves increased; slowly at first and then with a sudden rush. Although my eyes were tightly shut, the impression of great, red, roaring flames swept before me as though my face were buried in a very fountain of fire.

And then, gradually, a thought was born in my mind; not a thought as it springs to the normal, conscious mind, but a thought from without forced itself into my mind and grew there, swelling from an unrecognizable seed to a palpitant growth—and the thought that had been planted in my mind, and that grew there so vividly, as if before some inner eye, was a thought of *love!* Love as boundless as space itself; as real and actual as a mighty block of granite. Love; *love for me!* Soundless, formless words, as intangible and elusive as wisps of mist, swam through my bursting brain; words of affection, endearment, sacrifice, love.

I was aware, too, of another element, as though the picture was shot through with intermittent flashes of red, disrupting light. Pain! Agony! Fear! Despair! These were the things that were marring the beauty of my inward vision. I could feel my face writhe with the beauty and the horror of it all, but it held me enthralled in its mysterious grasp.

I wanted to tear the accursed thing from my throat, to leap up, to cry aloud—

Suddenly, totally, the torture stopped; there were only the warm, throbbing waves of feeling inundating my brain. I opened my eyes and leaped from the chair, cursing.

"What damnable thing is this you have here?" I shouted. "I have been to hell and back again! I should have gone crazy had you not turned it off when you did!"

The eager, curious light went from Erich Weigert's eyes, and in its place came a glint of sardonic amusement.

"I did not turn it off," he said calmly. "But I can imagine why you thought I did." He deftly removed the band around my neck and tossed it carelessly on to the table. "And now—would you not like to see—the other subject; the sender?"

An icy chill gripped my every nerve and sinew; there was something diabolically sinister in the man's face and in the soft tones of his voice.

I nodded dumbly, still dazed from the experiment, and stumbled in his wake to the closed double doors. He slid the doors open and stood aside that I might enter.

On an operating table near the door lay a figure covered with a long white sheet. A faint odor as of an anæsthetic came to my nostrils, but there was something about the absolute, deathly stillness of the supine figure that told me I was in the presence of death itself.

Trembling, the blood draining from my face, I stood and stared at the still figure and at the instrument-littered table beside the operating table. Three small wires from the maze of instruments on the table disappeared under the edge of the sheet; two big transmitting tubes glowed yellowly in the bright light that flooded the room. A dim, horrible idea began to take shape in my mind.

"See!" chuckled Weigert, his voice grating on the silence like the screech of a rusty hinge. "The sending subject!"

He strode forward and tore the sheet from the figure.

I felt my knees tremble beneath me, and I leaned against the wall for support. *There on the table, dressed in a simple white robe, lay the body of Vera Weigert!*

My eyes refused to move from the fearful sight. A spot above either ear had been shaved, and on the scalp thus exposed a red circle with edges—my God!

"Just as the receiving element must work directly upon the nerve trunk," I heard Weigert saying, "the sending must be done, at least with the crude apparatus I have, direct from the emanating source. And that, of course, is—*the brain!* Hence the trephine that seems to strike you as so interesting.

"This little band passes under the head as you see, and presses two silver disks directly upon the brain; or, strictly speaking, upon the *dura mater,* to get the desired contact."

Faster and faster the man spoke—or did my reeling senses imagine that? His voice, from a calm, scientific monotone, rose almost to a shriek.

"There she is, Saylor! Why don't you caress her hand now? Why don't you hold her close and press her lips now? There she is, and with the last spark of her energy she sent you a message, Saylor! What was the message? You won't tell me? It must have been wonderful; wonderful!

"I knew the experiment would be a success! You two loved each other; you were attuned as two human beings seldom are attuned. It was an ideal opportunity to prove that I was right; that thought *could* be transmitted—and to avenge myself upon a faithless wife and a faithless friend!"

I tried to speak, but my dry tongue refused to move from the roof of my mouth. But he saw my throat move, and he chuckled again.

"You would deny it, eh? You— But no matter! Let me tell you how I did it. It will interest you.

"I told her what I was going to do. Told her that if she did not submit, I would take your life as the penalty. And —does this give you pleasure, Saylor?—she consented.

"I gave her scopolamin-morphin as an anæsthetic, for I

knew that would permit her subconscious mind to continue its functioning. Then, carefully—oh, very carefully, for I did not want her to die too soon!—I trephined the skull, just at the fissure of Sylvius, thus locating my electrodes in the sensory area. Very well thought out, was it not?

"I knew that her last thoughts would be of you; thoughts of love for her lover. Strong thoughts, you know; thoughts that would enable my unperfected apparatus to work; to prove that my idea is feasible! Thoughts that would hold over and run constantly through her subconscious mind. Thoughts of love, eh, Saylor? And thoughts of fear, too, perhaps? Ah! I thought I read that in your face, man; and can you blame her? It is not pleasant to die when you are young and very beautiful and in love!"

He paused and drew the tip of his tongue across his thin, bloodless lips.

"And—oh, this was a joke I had not thought of!—you thought I turned it off, did you? You false friend! You fool! You meddler! You heard"—and his voice rose to a shriek like that of a maniac in hell—"I tell you, Saylor, *you heard her die!*"

I shook off the icy grip that had numbed me and leaped for the man, but before I could sink my clutching fingers in his throat, he stopped me at the point of a gun which he flashed from a pocket.

"Back!" he shrieked. "Back! I don't want to kill you; I want you to live and remember—but if you move, I'll shoot to maim. I have my plans all laid for my escape, and—"

Just then I lunged. The gun roared over my head and the stench of the powder smoke swirled in my nostrils. We went down on the floor together in a whirling, flaying heap. The instrument table fell over with a terrific crash, and as I fought I saw out of the corner of my eye a flicker of red flame shoot up as the tangled high-voltage wires hissed their danger signal.

It was over in a few minutes. He was a maniac, and

fought with a maniac's strength, but I was possessed of ten thousand devils! I wrenched the gun from his hand and put it to his head, holding him down with my body and my left arm in a wrestling hold I had learned years ago.

His cold blue eyes looked up into mine, glinting with sardonic amusement.

"And now for the Great Experiment!" he said, panting. "Shoot!"

I glanced up at the still figure on the operating table. The flames were beginning to roar, now, and were licking fiercely at the woodwork. Then I placed the gun directly above his ear, closed my eyes and pulled the trigger.

I never looked back. The papers ran a story of a recluse and his wife trapped in a night fire. The bodies were so burned that they could not detect the holes—both just above the ear.

But *I* know! *I* know! *I*, who heard, or felt, or lived, a woman's dying thoughts, *I* know.

And to-night—now, just as soon as I write the last word of this—I shall know more, for then I shall put the same gun to my head carefully just above the ear, and—pull—the —trigger. . . .

THE HOODED DEATH

By JOEL MARTIN NICHOLS, Jr.

THE OPEN LOG FIRE THREW ONLY A DIM FLICKER INTO THE far end of the room where the window looked out upon the terraces, and yet I was sure that I saw a face there, an evil, yellow face made the more ugly by a broad nose flattened against the pane. For the moment I thought it might be Peronne, the watchman, who had glanced in on his weary rounds about the château, but that would have been directly contrary to my orders and he was not the man to disobey. Moreover, I had explained to him his own peril, pointing out that Brinville, in his present nervous condition, would be more than likely to shoot first and ask questions afterward, were he suddenly confronted with any face not immediately familiar to him.

It angered me to think that Peronne had been so careless as to let this fellow get by him and thus brave us boldly to our faces. Yet I knew I must remain cool and make no false move, for I had no mind to be potted from that window without a chance to defend myself. Calling up as much sleepy indifference as I could muster I shifted about in my chair, letting my hand fall carelessly to my hip where the hard bulge of my pistol lent its reassuring pressure. In an instant that face had faded into the black background of the night. But no, he was watching me clearly from a distance, for his nose was on the glass again when I had once more half-closed my eyes in mock slumber. Where was that careless fool, Peronne?

What move should I make? I could try a shot at him

from my pocket, but there would be several seconds lost in getting at my weapon. If he were so minded he could kill me easily before my finger even touched the trigger. Besides, there was Brinville's condition to be considered. He sat there facing me in his armchair, his Gargantuan figure now limp in the fitful sleep which was all that haunting fear had granted him during those many long months. By his side on a small taboret was his ever-present automatic, the heavy butt ready to his hand. For my own safety I dared make no sudden disturbance, since on two other occasions I had seen him, thus aroused, bound out of his slumber, a raging, fear-maddened animal, ready to grasp and strangle the first living thing at hand. I would not care to be caught in those bone-crushing fingers of his!

It must be that fear prodded him even in his sleep, for at that instant he leaped to his feet with a cry of horror that still rings in my ears.

"It's Cunningham! It's young Cunningham, curse him!"

He was quick for his great size—I suppose fear had made him so. Even quicker than I could have done it from a full-awakened start he had seized the pistol, wheeled about and sent three bullets crashing through the window. But the face had gone the instant before.

"I—I dreamed there was somebody at the window," he muttered, sinking back into his chair.

"Will you take this opiate now?" I asked, pushing toward him the sleeping mixture he had refused the hour before—refused because he feared that the demons of his imagination would come upon him chained in slumber.

He gulped it down and sank back with a sigh. I watched him until his heavy lids had fallen and then I got up and went to the door. Yvonne Marcy was there, but Madame Brinville had not put in her appearance.

"He was dreaming again," I explained hurriedly. "He thought he saw somebody at the window. He had his back to it and couldn't have seen it—but there was a face there this time. Where is Madame, your mother?"

"She would not come," she answered. "She has asked for you several times this evening. You must go to her. But you are so pale, Edward. You are not going out there?"

"I must," said I. "I am beginning to fear that something may have happened to Peronne. He should have heard those shots and come."

I closed the door softly after me. Out in the night the moon lay pale and still on the terraces. Far away on the lower slopes beyond the deserted warden's lodge the Marne swirled swiftly by under the stone-arched bridge leading to the village. I wanted to follow that road—follow it far away toward the warmth and love and life that were there —follow it away from all this behind me, so dank and grim and foreboding.

But there was Yvonne Marcy—and my errand at Brinville's château. I pulled myself together and glanced about for Peronne. He was not there, so I called his name, at first low and then louder, until the stone walls bandied the echo with the trees in the forest and threw it back to me in hollow mockery.

I hurried about the château in the path he should have taken. He was not there. I whistled. I called his name once more. No answer. After a time I went down to the edge of the wood. There were patches of dead white snow there under the trees—sodden, lifeless snow that hid from the light of the sun and rotted the leaves in the thickets. I walked about for a while and then I found footprints. There were Peronne's heavy hobnailed boots. There were two others—quick, light, little men, to judge from the indentation. I followed them as best I could, losing them here in the sodden underbrush, finding them again where the snow lay a soggy blanket upon the moss.

Presently I found him. He had been dragged a short distance and there was blood on the snow. His body was still warm, so I turned him over, but let him drop quickly back when I saw that dripping rent in the back of his jacket. He had gone down there, lured by a crackling of the underbrush, and they had stalked him, those silent prowlers of the night, even as they were stalking Brinville up there in his château!

There was nothing to be done for the poor fellow, and as I could not leave Brinville alone for very long, I walked slowly back, pondering the situation. I had come to this place ten months before as an operative for a firm of international secret service agents. I will not mention the name—suffice it to say they are well known in all quarters where a business is made of knowing such things. They furnish guards and sometimes spies, as the case may be, for those individuals who feel the need of protection from other sources than the local police where protection often entails awkward explanation. As yet I had attained no giddy heights with the firm, being merely a sort of chief watchdog—an office which satisfied all my ambitions in that profession, for I had relished it but little during the five years I had been with the bureau. Indeed, I had been minded several times to abandon it altogether.

Thus I had been sent to this obscure corner of France to eat and sleep at the side of a man whose every waking and sleeping hour was filled with mortal dread—dread of something which the events of this night had shown me were no mere chimera of his imagination.

At the door I paused, a sudden ejaculation of surprise leaping to my lips. The clear moonlight showed it so plainly I wondered why I had missed it before—a long, curved dagger, a species of short Malay kris, embedded in the timber! It was the man at the window! He must have thrown it there as he slunk by, for I could scarcely reach it, though I stand near to six feet. It was not until I pulled it down that I saw it was still wet with blood—the blood of poor Peronne down there in the thicket!

I brought it inside but hid it quickly under my coat, for Yvonne Marcy was there waiting for me and I did not want her to see. She was crying now.

"I cannot stand it any longer, Edward," she sobbed. "Why does mother insist on staying here? She owes him nothing. I believe she hates him just as much as I do, and yet she lingers. Can't you take us away and leave him here?"

"I think it is high time that you both went away," I admitted, speaking to her as casually as I could, though my own nerves were shredding under the strain. "I will speak to her about it to-night. You said she wanted to see me, so I must go. But you must promise me to go up to your room. Lock the door well and remember that I shall be about all night."

She drew nearer and whispered in my ear, "I think she is going mad. I found her again this afternoon listening at that barred door in the east tower—the one he never lets us into. And she has sent all the servants to the village since noon. But you have enough to worry about now. Will you kiss me before I go?"

I gazed after her as she went slowly up the stair. Then I locked the door, looked in at Brinville sleeping in his chair, closed the heavy oaken shutters that guarded the library window, and went up to Madame's room. I found her there as usual, peering morosely into the fire, her heavy, iron-gray hair in disarray, her gaunt body swathed in the folds of a dark velvet dressing gown. She took but one look at me out of her hollow eyes.

"You are ready to take Yvonne away, now?" she asked abruptly.

"Yes," I said. "It is time for you both to go. I should not have hesitated so long as I have. My man, Peronne, was murdered out there to-night. I found this knife sticking in the door. We have tarried too long."

I laid the bloody thing down on the table at her side and stood over her while she examined the handle. "Yes," she said presently, as though with a great weariness, "it is the Gohils. They have come for us—him and me. I do not care. I am ready. But he is afraid now, the coward! Oh, he was brave enough that night in the temple because nobody knew. But you love Yvonne. Perhaps you will not want to marry her when you know."

"What I shall know will make no difference with me concerning her," I answered. "I love—"

"Listen," she cut in; "when he jumped up and fired those shots he shouted Cunningham's name, did he not? Yes, I knew it would be Cunningham or Marcy. Sometimes it is Marcy that he sees, but not so often as Cunningham because he knows that Marcy is dead. So is Cunningham dead, but Cunningham had a brother. His kid brother, he called him. I always thought the kid brother got away. But the river was full of crocodiles."

Until then she had been peering before her into the fire, but now she turned toward me and I saw deep in her eyes a faint flicker of madness.

"Look," she whispered, grasping my arm and peering into the room behind us. "There is the temple again in the jungle. I always see it, but now, to-night, it is clearer. There is a god there, a green god high up on a pedestal of ivory. In his hands a bowl. There are pearls in that bowl—a fortune in pearls tossed in by the priests. A fortune in pearls—and death. The moon is shining through the roof. There are two persons waiting in the shadows. One is Cunningham, the American. The other is Marcy's wife. Cunningham is impatient. The woman is pale, trembling. Another comes in through the arched doorway. Ah, see, it is Brinville! The woman stifles a scream. 'You will have to climb the altar,' says Brinville to the American. 'Marcy has been delayed at the river and sends word not to delay. All is in readiness. Your brother awaits us at the canoe.'

"Cunningham mutters and moves toward the altar. 'Remember you are not to touch the god,' says Brinville. 'Otherwise the curse will be upon you.' He hides a sneer as he says it.

" 'It is a rotten business,' says Cunningham. 'I wish I'd never brought the kid into this.'

"He climbs up the altar. Brinville lays his lips to the ear of Marcy's wife. 'You are a widow now, Marie,' he whispers. 'He died without a murmur. But that accurst brat of a Cunningham got away from me. He heard me in the bushes and began to run. I cut him good in the shoulder as he went by. But he is dead now. I cornered him and ran him into the river. A good morsel for the crocodiles.'

"Brinville is enjoying himself. He relishes such tales as this. He relishes the misery of the woman. She moans softly to herself. She would turn back now but it is too late. 'Tell him to come down,' she whispers hoarsely. 'Tell him to come away. Do not let him die. He has done us no harm. Tell him, for God's sake, not to touch that bowl. I cannot go farther with this. It is not worth it.'

"Brinville seizes her wrist and twists it until she cries out in pain. 'You fool,' he whispers. 'If he comes down from there alive he will know enough to hang us both. Let him go. Not a word.'

"Cunningham on the altar reaches up toward the bowl. But he is not high enough yet. It is a difficult climb and he dare not touch the god, for he is superstitious. He is up one more step now. The woman would scream out a warning, bid him for God's sake not to go farther—bid him keep his hand away from that bowl.

"See, now, there is but one more step necessary and his fingers are on the edge. He climbs again. Now he dips his hand down into it in the darkness. The woman screams, but it is too late. Cunningham cries out. It is a low, fearful cry. He stumbles down from the altar. He holds one hand up in the moonlight. There are four tiny holes there —and blood.

" 'I have been bitten,' he says. 'I think they were cobras. Watch out!'

"In a few minutes he is dead. He has struggled it out in silence there on the floor of the temple, for death sleeps but lightly outside in the village. Unknowing, he protects his murderers even to the end.

"And now Brinville mounts the altar. He is quicker, for he scorns the curse. His hands are on the god in many places. He clings to the throat of it as he thrusts with his foot at the bowl in its outstretched hands. The bowl sways and falls, hurtling down in the moonlight. It strikes the earth. It flies in a thousand pieces. A thousand creamy globules roll out over the temple floor. A thousand pearls—the ransom of a king. But there is something else there—creeping, sliding things that wriggle across the floor toward the woman. She screams, but Brinville is down in a moment. Two padded blows and the cobras are dead. Their work is done."

Her voice had begun in a low whisper, rising to a sort of chanting monotone, but now it broke into a shrill scream as she clutched at me with her clawlike fingers. "I tell you, madman," she shrieked at me, "they brought that curse away with them. They have lived in fear of it all their lives. It has smothered their souls. And now, it comes to take their bodies."

"Madame, Madame," I broke in. "Hush. He will hear you."

Whatever spell Brinville had woven around Marcy's wife in years gone by, it had not yet lost its potency, for she calmed immediately at the mention of his name, and I knew then that she feared him still. "I know," she said, "you are right. He must not hear. I must keep to my purpose, for you are to go away with her to-night. But there is more to be told. Listen: that god—that god of the temple is here under this roof."

"In heaven's name, Madame, hush!"

"It is here, I tell you. Yes, yes, you are right. I must be quiet. He must not know what we are going to do. But it is here. I know because it was only five years ago that he brought it back. Oh, he was cunning! He did not tell me. He sent us away, Yvonne and me. He was gone a year, but when I saw him again his face was tanned. I knew then that he had been back to the temple. I knew that he had brought it here. That was the curse. That was why the American would not touch it. Oh, he is cunning! Brinville was always cunning. He brought it here and now he hides it behind that door in the tower room. He holds the key. It is there. I must seek it. That was the curse."

Her voice dropped again to a whisper. She peered at me cunningly through those haggard eyes of hers. "But we must be careful—very, very careful. You have noticed how he asks that a bowl of warm milk be brought to him every morning? Yes, he pretends to take it to his room and drink it. Yet neither you, nor I, nor anybody here has ever seen that bowl touch his lips. He carries it while you are sleeping to that room in the tower. I know, because I have spied upon him."

Sane or insane, what she said was true! I had never seen Brinville drink from that bowl he ordered each morning.

"Why?" she demanded suddenly. "I can see the question in your eyes. Ah, I will tell you, because it is I who have guessed it. In India I have seen a king cobra drink a whole bowl of warm goat's milk."

"Good heavens—" I broke in, but she cut me off.

"And now they are coming. Those Gohils are here. Or perhaps it is Cunningham's kid brother. Perhaps the crocodiles did not get him. But I think it is the Gohils, for this is a Gohil knife. In the morning, no, it must be now, to-night!—you must take Yvonne out of this—far away from here. She must never know. But first get the keys to that room. He is asleep. Only you can move in that room without awakening him. Will you go?"

What it was in her eyes that was so compelling I do not know, but I answered, "I will do it."

Brinville was sitting there much as I had left him, when I reëntered the library. I walked slowly across the carpet and sat down opposite him for a few minutes. He stirred uneasily in his sleep but did not awake, so keenly attuned, even in slumber, were his acute senses to my presence at his side.

Presently I reached out to the taboret and took his pistol. Emptying the magazine into my pocket, I replaced it carefully at his side. He did not stir. I got to my feet and stood over him. The keys were on a ring at his belt. I knew the exact place, for I had not lived at his side these many long months for nothing. I reached down and ran my fingers slightly around his waist as far as the back of his chair would permit. I touched the keys and they rattled, it seemed to my taut nerves, like a thousand drums. He stirred and groaned, his subconscious mind struggling against the opiate that had dulled his being. The second time I gritted my teeth, slipped my finger under the ring and jerked it loose. They were in my hands! He did not move again.

I met Madame Brinville at the door of the tower room and handed her the ring. There were five keys and it was the third that turned the bolt. She pushed back the door.

It was standing there opposite on its ivory pedestal, its grinning features made the more horribly alive by the rays of the flickering oil lamp overhead—the green god of the Gohils!

I had expected a scream from Marcy's widow but there came from her lips only a gasping rattle. Then, with a little sob, a smothered cry, she ran toward it.

I should have acted quicker—I had no wish to see her

die. She had been punished enough in those fifteen years she had lived with that archfiend back there in the library. I guessed her purpose before she reached it, but I was too late! She was up that pedestal, and before I was halfway across the room had plunged her hand into the open bowl on the knees of the god.

I saw only the heads of the brutes as they struck. I saw her wince once, twice, and then tumble backward. I caught her as she fell. "The cobras," she murmured. "They were there." Then she fainted.

There was a low couch in the room, so I laid her on it. Then I snatched off my coat, stripped shirt and undershirt from my body, twisting the fabric into a rude tourniquet. But it was idle effort. The venom would have struck well into her heart before I could so much as apply it to her arm.

Presently she opened her eyes. They rested on me for a moment and then suddenly shot by toward the door. "Watch out—Brinville," she whispered. I turned slowly and there he was standing in the doorway.

"Now," he said quietly, "I shall kill you both." Out of the depths of my soul there came a deep surge of anger, the suppressed emotion of ten long months. I stepped toward him, while his bulky figure, the god, everything in that room, went red before my eyes.

"You will not have to bother with her," I told him between clenched teeth. "Those snakes of yours have done it for you. As for me—we shall see."

I saw it in his hand then—that big automatic of his. I remembered how carefully I had drawn its teeth, so I threw back my head and laughed. To be sure, I was no match for him physically, and yet my hands yearned for the moment when they should fasten themselves on that big, corded throat of his.

He raised the pistol and brought it to bear across the room. I heard another laugh—a strangely horrible laugh that must have been mine, for his lips were tense, unmoving. But I had laughed too soon! Like a flash the thoughts seared my brain! I had made one fatal mistake after all. There would still be one bullet in the chamber, for he kept it always at cock!

He seemed to gloat over me while he carefully took his aim. My fingers fumbled helplessly for my own weapon, reminding me that I had left it in Madame's room. I felt a choking sensation at the throat. Breath failed me altogether. I knew that I should jump—spring at him—do something—but what?

I saw his finger tighten on the trigger and leaped sidewise. There was a roar as the heavy charge tore open the silence. I heard the crack of the bullet as it drilled past my ear. He had missed me at that distance—Brinville, who practiced daily in the courtyard and boasted, not without reason, of his prowess!

A second later I knew why he had missed, for I saw him reach back into the hall. An instant's struggle out there and he had dragged her into the room. It was Yvonne Marcy who had pushed his arm as he fired.

"So it's you!" he muttered. "The two of you together, then."

He raised the automatic once more, and this time the hammer rapped uselessly against the empty chamber. But he was quick to recover. His big hand shot back and I dodged as the heavy weapon went hurtling past my head. From behind me there came a crash. The girl screamed. I turned just in time to see that green bowl in the hands of the god fly to flinders—just in time to see those two hooded brutes tumble down upon the floor!

The three of us stood there as though fascinated with the sight of it. They coiled themselves quickly and raised their ugly heads, hoods outspread and menacing. I backed away toward Brinville, for I knew the cobra to be a fighter; knew that these two would come for us so long as we remained in reach of their limited vision.

They started for me—I being nearest. Yvonne cried out a warning and I turned, hardly in time to shift quickly as Brinville swooped down upon me. His great fist came crashing down across my naked shoulders—fortunately for me, only a glancing blow, but withal a blow that rocked me from head to heel. I rushed in then and clinched, and the snakes, confused for the moment by the swirl of bodies, paused.

I knew Brinville must be as wary of them as I, so I squirmed out of his grasp when he had me almost cornered. He rushed again and I caught up a chair, driving it in toward his head. He brushed it aside like a straw with his flail-like arms. I saw, then, that there was but one salvation for me—my quickness. He had his great strength, but those ponderous muscles were not so quick as mine.

He rushed again, but this time I was ready for him and rapped him smartly on the chin. It might have been a flea-bite, so little did it bother him, though there was blood on his lips a moment later. Once again he had me nearly boxed in a corner, but this time it was the chair that saved me—the chair shoved in between us by Yvonne Marcy. It held him up only a second. That second was my life. Given a moment's respite, now, I glanced about and saw that the cobras, confused by the turmoil, had crawled forward and stood between us and the door. There would be no egress there!

Again Brinville bore down upon me, attempting to drive me within reach of their fangs, and again I tried to slip under his arm. But I slipped and fell and he had me. Like a gorilla, he wrapped his muscles taut until my ribs seemed to crack under the strain. He could have killed me then and there, had he pressed further, but he was a fiend and the thoughts of a fiend lived in his brain.

"Ah," I heard him mutter in my ear; "the cobras shall have you."

He dragged me toward them, pushing me down upon the floor where they could strike easily and quickly. Of a sudden, a deathly stillness fell upon that room. I lay there, helpless, unable to move a muscle, so chained was I by horror. Those two brutes were not long in taking advantage of it. I heard the soft rustle of their bodies as they glided toward me.

Something had to be done, and quickly. I could make no move in his iron grasp. There came a scream to my ears and I remembered Yvonne—remembered a red scarf she had thrown across her shoulders.

"Quick," I shouted to her, "your scarf! Drag the end of it before their eyes!"

Thank heaven for its generous length and bright color! She, holding the corner of it, dragged it before them and they made after it, faster and faster, yet never quite near enough to strike.

I heard Brinville curse between his clenched lips. And then he made his first mistake. He tried to drag me after them. I managed to wriggle one arm free and drove my knuckles up under his chin until he cried out with the pain of it. I had his head and eyes away from the floor now, and I knew that so long as he could not see the cobras he would not dare draw near to where they were.

Until now I had been fighting coolly. I had boxed him, I had dodged him, I had run away before him. He held me now, so I could do none of these, but I still had my two hands. There was his throat, and my fingers had ached to clamp upon it. One hand was already free. I loosened the other with a desperate wrench that almost stripped the muscles from my shoulder. And then, with a savage joy such as I have never known before or since, I settled them on his throat, shifted them quickly to his chin and pressed back his head.

He groaned and I felt the grip about my waist weaken. Back, back, I pressed that head of his. Could I but bend his spine I would have him! With as much force as I could summon, I pulled back by foot and drove it in against his shins. These tactics worked better than I could have hoped, for he stepped backward and I had him with his knees crumpling under him. Then it was I felt the first savage triumph, felt the sodden strength running out of him like water.

"For God's sake," he gasped between pain-twisted lips, "let me up. I'm through."

"Never while I have the strength, Brinville," I said in his ear. "Come, I will let the cobras have you as you did poor Cunningham."

They were not long in seeking us, those wriggling devils. Closer and yet closer they came. I pushed him down to make it easier for them, and then I laughed long and loud as they struck and struck again. I did not move him until I was sure that the deadly fluid had seeped well in toward his heart. Presently, with the first twist of pain on his face that told me it was working, I threw him down upon them and crushed out their lives with the weight of his body.

He lay there gazing up at me in the abject fear that his kind always has for approaching death. "Take a good look at me, Brinville," I said. "I could have killed you a dozen times during these past ten months. But you were suffering and I wanted to see you suffer. I would have left you for a better death than this, but you yourself have willed it otherwise. I am leaving you here for the Gohils. They will be here for you before the dawn—for you and their god."

"In God's name," he gasped hoarsely, "who are you?"

Then I bent closer to his ear, for I wanted him to take the knowledge with him where he was going.

"Look well at the scar here across my shoulder," I whispered. "I am Cunningham's kid brother."

THE MAN WHO WAS SAVED

By B. W. SLINEY

"ONLY I ESCAPED." THE MAN WHOM THEY HAD FOUND adrift in the dory hung his head. "The others"—the listeners bent nearer to catch his throatily whispered words—"the others . . . it got them—that monstrous, cursed thing!" His eyes rolled back, showing bloodshot whites; his body tensed, and then he shook as with the ague. His attempt to say more resulted in stuttering failure.

"He had better be put to bed," the ship's doctor said. "His nerves are all gone. Heat and thirst and exposure, of course. Hallucinations. He'll come out of it in time."

So they put him in the hospital where he raved for three days. And the things he said caused intense interest on board the freighter *Pacific Belle;* and among the crew lurking fear whispered that some of the things he said were true.

It was a week before he came into his right mind again, and then the fevers and fears which had beset him passed. He was able to talk to the captain, and to tell a coherent story.

"There were seven of us," he said with sad recollection, as he glanced at the ship's officers, who had gathered about him on the poop deck, "who set out in a two-topmaster—the *Scudder.* It belonged to Bob Henry, who was our captain. Just a sort of lark, you know—an idle cruise for the joy of the sea, and the freedom.

"I was mate, for next to Bob, I knew more about handling a ship than the others. And so we sailed along the coast, putting into whatever ports we fancied, and living an idle, ideal life. All of us had long been friends.

"Then we rashly decided to make it across the Pacific, depending on a season of few storms to aid us. We were successful. Honolulu was easy; and from there we headed southward, made the Marquesas, and then we sailed from island group to island group—you know them all—until we made the Philippines.

"There we turned homeward, pointing our course for Guam. But midway to Apia our luck failed, and we were becalmed for days. We had a small auxiliary motor, which we used for a time to make headway, but it got out of order, and we were forced to remain in virtually the same spot for nearly a week. We did not especially mind, for we were in no great hurry, except that it was somewhat monotonous with so very little to do.

"One evening during our becalmed period, just toward sunset, Hal Rooney pointed out a great disturbance of the water some little distance from us. It shot up in sprays, and eddied in a most inexplicable manner, and then it suddenly ceased. We wondered about it for a long time, but no thinking or imagining or deducing on our part could explain the phenomenon.

" 'Possibly,' Bob Henry said, 'it will appear again.'

"And sure enough, it did. The next evening at the same hour we again noted that strange disturbance of the water. We knew that it could not possibly be a whale, nor any other large sea-creature of which we had ever heard, for the tumult was too vast; and the fact that none of us could offer an explanation of the mystery piqued our curiosity.

"The calm continued. The sea floated away from us endlessly, equally on all sides, caught at the edges of the sky, and became one with it. Once in a while a blackfish went blowing by, or an occasional whale. The waters teemed with life. At night the phosphor glow was almost livid, uncannily brilliant. And each evening that same disturbance of the water occurred somewhere in our neighborhood.

"It was with the third appearance that the thing became too much for us. We determined to put out in a dory and investigate the next time it appeared. It did not disappoint us. Again, at sunset, while the sky glowed extravagantly, flaunting an enormous batik at the parting day, the water almost dead ahead of our bows broke into a churning fury. We piled into the dory, which was ready alongside, and made for it, pulling as hard as we could. But before we were able to reach the spot, the maelstrom had ceased, and we gazed into the intense indigo of unruffled water that was nearly five miles deep.

"Following that attempt, we were more determined than ever to find out the nature of the thing. It was an amazingly large patch of sea that it churned, and though the unbroken immensity of the space we were the center of gave us little for comparison, we judged the area to be approximately that of an acre—an unbelievably large expanse to show such agitation in the midst of so glassily calm a sea.

"The next afternoon, just as the sun fell into the sea, splashing all our horizons with myriad tints, a huge whale went lolling by, sounding and coming up with great jets of water cascading over it. I watched with the glasses as it drove powerfully through the water, peacefully taking its time. Suddenly, however, it changed. It displayed signs of confusion, of alarm. First it turned one way, then another, cutting about sharply—and then I very distinctly heard it give a groan of anguish. It was a heart-breaking sound—the cry of a great, helpless animal in mortal distress. Immediately afterward the water surrounding it broke into its daily wild disorder, and the leviathan seemed gripped by a force it could not escape. It struggled violently, throwing its huge bulk about with futile effort. Greater and greater the mêlée became, and then, suddenly, the whale was still.

"We looked at one another, fright in our eyes. It was

tremendous, awful. And then, as we looked again out there, the whale lost all shape and the water became red with gore and blood as it was crushed to a pulp. In but a few minutes it was gone, utterly vanished from view—even the bloodiness of the water cleared—the whirling and splashing ceased, and the sun went down on a still sea. All of us were speechless. It was the most dreadful thing any of us had ever seen."

The speaker paused in his narrative, shaken by the memory of what he had related. The captain and his officers looked at one another with veiled skepticism. The doctor raised an eyebrow. There seemed no doubt of it; the man was insane.

Presently he went on with his wildly impossible yarn. His listeners were attentive, but secretly unbelieving. In time, it was hoped, he might regain his mental balance. In the meanwhile—

"To say that we were shaken would not be half expressing our state of mind. It was so inexplicable, so wildly preposterous! I was for getting away as soon as possible, and so were several of the others. But the rest were keen to learn what the thing was. And, to settle any argument, the calm held unbroken and the motor continued in disrepair, despite our efforts over it.

"For three days, then, the thing did not come to the surface. We had decided that it was some sort of deep-sea creature, some Gargantuan monster that came out of the vast depths of the ocean to feed. But we had never heard of such a thing, save in stories of early navigators' superstitions. We hesitated to believe the thing we had seen—we were afraid to believe it!

"It was now that fear came to us. Hitherto we had been curious, idly speculative, and inclined to laugh. Now our thoughts were interrupted by premonitions of disaster. Flying fish, as they flashed from the surface and splashed into the water about us, startled; and porpoises blundering into our vicinity brought us all on deck. At night, a lost puff of breeze, slatting the rigging against the sails, startled us into alarmed awakening. And though the same subject of possible danger from the unknown out of the deep occupied the mind of each of us, it was never spoken of. But there was in the air a chilling presence of dread.

"I believe we would have left that place had we been able. For the memory of the fate of the whale was ever vivid in our minds. Following the death of the whale, the monster did not rise, however, for three days, as I have said. This gave us some sense of relief, but it was on that third day that the great tragedy occurred.

"I was occupied with fitting a new seat to the dory, which was swung up on deck, and the others were idling, making bets as to the quarter in which the creature would next appear, or if we should see it again.

"I was startled by a scream from one of the men, and immediately after followed the sound of churning water—a sound which sent the very essence of dread all through me and cowed my soul. Somehow I knew we were in the midst of the monster's rise to the surface. I stood and looked over the side. There was a horrible mass of pulsating green matter—a revolting substance that had no definite form, and yet was solid—a writhing, heaving island of the stuff.

"Even as I looked it surged up from the water and rolled over the side of the schooner, turning over on itself, slithering and cascading on the deck. Every one of us was frantic. Some rushed for the aftercabin, but they were cut off by a slimy arm that slid across their path. It spread and lifted with terrorizing rapidity. Two of the men tried to climb a mast; Bob Henry raced toward the bow and fell. An instant later he was covered with the gruesome matter, even before he had a chance to cry out, and was hidden from sight. Hardly knowing what I did, I turned the dory over on myself, dragging Mark Whittmore, the nearest man to me, under with me. Fortunately I had removed all the seats, and there was just room for the two of us as we lay prone.

"Then came darkness and an inconceivably foul odor of decay as the monster mass pushed itself over the dory—a suffocating, interminable darkness, while we were cramped under that flat-bottomed boat, scarce daring to think, even, of the horror that crawled over us. When we thought our lungs would burst for the want of fresh air, light came under the dory once more, and gradually the slithering, churning, swishing of that thing which had boarded us ceased. For a long while, however, we were too frightened to move, but finally our concern for the fate of our companions compelled us to lift the dory.

"The sky glowed with the last rays of the setting sun, and the sea slept beneath it, undisturbed. But the decks of the *Scudder* were wet with a yellow-green, malodorous slime, and silence hung like a pall over the ship.

"We called. There was no answer—not even the mockery of an echo. With consternation seizing us we rushed into the aftercabin, but it was without a person in it. In a panic we ran to the forecastle, and it, too, was suggestively deserted. And nowhere on that ship did we find a soul. Every man, except ourselves, had disappeared. That thing"—his voice broke, and again into his face came that haunting pain —"that thing had got them all!"

For a while he paused, making strong effort to overcome his rising emotion, and the fear that memory brought him. The listeners looked away and were silent; and presently they heard his voice, firmly continuing the tale.

"You cannot conceive of the terror which descended on us after that frightful discovery. Aimlessly, dazedly, we searched the vessel through and through, but we were the only men aboard the *Scudder*. It was a fact that we had to face, but could not bring ourselves to believe.

"Night came quickly, and the moon and stars stared coldly down on us. We decided at length that to remain on the ship would be suicidal, for the calm still hung over the water like a dead thing, and the thought of the unspeakable thing that lived somewhere beneath us was appalling. So we fitted the dory with water and food, and rowed away in the night from that ill-fated ship.

"Then there came interminable days of torture under a malignant sun, and nights of terror of what might lurk in the waters around us. And one morning I awoke to find myself alone in the dory. The day before Mark had talked of insanity, and I believe that he could not face the possibility.

"Now I attained the utmost in despair. I was, I believe, too shocked to think clearly, or I, too, might have gone over the side. From the morning of that discovery, until you picked me up, I was in a coma. Of the passage of time I do not recall.

"And such is my story, gentlemen. You may find it hard to believe. I find it difficult myself, and wonder, sometimes, if it is not an insane conception of diseased imagination. I wish it were. But I am tormented with the reality."

The *Pacific Belle* held her westward course for Manila. The story of the man who had been saved spread among the crew, where it was hotly debated, and quite generally accepted. The officers of the ship, however, avoided the subject, and particularly before the stranger it was never mentioned.

But one morning, just at dawn, a derelict schooner was sighted. The captain, awakened, ordered the *Pacific Belle* hove to while investigation was made. With closer inspection and increasing light it was made out to be the *Scudder* of San Francisco. The man who had been saved was called.

"Yes!" he cried. "Yes! That's the boat—our schooner. But—"

He drooped, swayed. The mate caught him and called one of the crew.

"Take him to his cabin," he said, "and keep him there."

Investigation corroborated the statements the stranger had made. Furthermore, the *Scudder's* papers proved beyond doubt that the man they had aboard came from her. And since there was nothing to indicate that anything else could have possibly driven the men from the ship, their strange passenger's story assumed a verity that even the officers reluctantly admitted.

A short consultation decided the fate of the *Scudder*. Left as she was, derelict, she would have become a serious menace to shipping, and possible salvage value did not warrant the long tow into port. Dynamite was placed amidships and set off.

With a splintering crash the *Scudder* heaved upward and outward, and plunged into the deeps of the ocean. The *Pacific Belle* continued on her way.

Later in the day the captain studied his charts. "Do you think," he asked the mate, at length, "that there is really anything in the fellow's story?"

The mate shrugged. "Such things," he answered readily, "don't happen. He's off, that's all. All the men were gone from the *Scudder,* yes, but I'd hate to accept such an explanation for it."

"The water in this part of the ocean, mister," the captain slowly said, "is five miles deep—as deep as the tallest mountain is high. It's barely possible that there's a lot about things out here that we don't know, or even remotely suspect. However—"

That night, after the swollen moon went down, and after all slept, save the watches and the man who had come aboard from out of the ocean, the *Pacific Belle* plunged into stark, brief terror.

The stranger, affected by again seeing the *Scudder,* had been unable to sleep. After hours of restlessness, he had gone to the bows, where he stared dully across the water. As he stood there, slowly, almost imperceptibly, he felt himself to be afraid.

An odor had come to him, an odor which brought to his mind the horror of his last day aboard the *Scudder*—the sickening, decay-laden odor of the monster from the deep. Then he listened with super-intent ears, and above the vessel's vibration he caught a sound of churning, swirling water. He screamed with a loudness that awoke every one on the *Pacific Belle* as he recognized these things—a scream that brought every one to his feet, anticipating calamity.

He turned from the prow and ran in stumbling haste across the deck and up the ladder to the bridge. The mate was there, alarmed at the cry of horror.

"Mister," he gasped, his mouth dry with panic, "mister! The thing—the monster! Stop the ship! Reverse her, for God's sake!"

The mate laughed with relief, as he recognized the man. He had been in dread of something terrible, and it was only another fit.

"Come, now, old boy!" he said in an effort to comfort. "Better quiet down a bit, don't—"

With another terrible scream the fellow was gone from the bridge. Jerking a preserver from the rail, he leaped free of the *Pacific Belle.*

"Man overboard!" The mate had seen him disappear and gave the alarm as he ran to the bridge controls. But before he reached them the speed of the *Pacific Belle* slackened abruptly, as though it had fouled the meshes of a gigantic net; and then it lost headway altogether. A bright, eerie glow of phosphorescent green lighted the water in a vast area, suddenly bursting into a lurid brilliance which caught the vessel out of the night and revealed its helplessness to the stars.

The glowing green mass surged sweepingly toward the vessel, piled against it, rolled over it, clinging to its sides, flooding its decks. Men who had come out to investigate the shouting and confusion frantically rushed below deck, barricading ports and doors behind them. On his bridge the captain sent useless messages to the engine room. The ship could not move.

Then, slowly, inexorably, as the brilliance of the phosphorescent light lessened, the great mass which was its source began to sink. Gradually it settled, carrying the *Pacific Belle,* fair-sized steamer though she was, down with it. The waves closed over the ship's main deck, touched and submerged the bridge, poured down the funnels, sending clouds of steam hissing into the air, and finally even the tops of the masts disappeared. There had been no time for a wireless message, but a message would have been futile.

Again the waters calmed, but after a half-hour they were torn for a few minutes by a great rush of bubbles to the top, following the caving in, from depth pressure, of the *Pacific Belle's* bulkheads. But after that the surface was never more disturbed by the *Pacific Belle.*

Microcosmic in a terrifying vastness of water, a man floated on a preserver, in the path of a liner that later picked him up. And, as he slowly realized the irony of his second escape, he sobbed with futile pity for himself.

THE PLANT-THING

BY R. G. MACREADY

"THIS MORNING, DICK, I HAVE SOMETHING SPECIAL FOR you," said Norris, city editor of the *Clarion,* as I approached his desk. "Interview with Professor Carter. You've heard of him, of course?"

"Certainly," I replied. "There are some rather weird stories concerning him."

"Exactly. And the latest of these stories is that Carter is conducting wanton vivisection on a prodigious scale. Holder, of the local Society for the Prevention of Cruelty to Animals, went over yesterday to investigate, but was turned away at the gate. He laid the matter before me and I promised to try for an interview."

"Who started the vivisection story?"

"Several farmers, according to Holder. During the past four months they've sold Carter more than a hundred and fifty pigs, sheep and calves. It is well known that the professor is a scientist and not a stock-raiser; ergo, he dissects the animals . . . Can you start now?"

En route to the Carter home I stopped at a hardware store and bought a thirty-foot length of rope. I foresaw difficulty in securing admittance to the professor's domain.

While driving, I brought to mind everything I knew about him. Four years ago he had bought the old Wells place, ten miles west of town. No sooner had it passed into his hands than he commenced the construction of a high board wall about the five acres, in the center of which the house was situated. The wall completed, he had moved in with a young lady, apparently his daughter, and eight Malay retainers. From that time on he and his household might have been dead for all the town saw of them. Our tradesmen made frequent trips to the place, but all their business was transacted with a Malay at the gate.

I drove rapidly and soon came in sight of my destination, which stood on a hill a half-mile back from the road. Five minutes later I drew up before the gate, and in response to my hail the Malay appeared. He was a nice-looking young chap, dressed irreproachably, and spoke excellent English. I gave him my card and after a perfunctory glance at it, he shook his head.

"I am sorry, sir, but it is the master's order that no one be admitted; and if you will pardon my saying so, least of all, representatives of the Press."

"But my business is urgent. Serious charges have been laid against him, and it is possible that I may be the medium by which these charges are refuted."

The Malay's ivory teeth flashed in a smile.

"Thank you, sir, but I do not doubt that the master is able to take care of himself. Good day." This last was spoken in a tone of polite finality as he turned on his heel and walked away.

I entered my car and drove back to the highway. However, I was determined to get that interview by crook if not by hook; if I may say it, this policy of mine had made me star reporter of the *Clarion's* staff. So I continued on down the road a few hundred yards and parked the car in the grove, where it was hidden well. I then took the coil of rope and made my way through the grove, which swung in a huge, narrowing semicircle up the hillside to the northwest corner of the Carter grounds. Arrived there under the fifteen-foot wall, I looked cautiously about me. So far as I could see, I was unobserved.

Just within the wall grew a great oak, one of whose major branches extended well outside. Quietly I flung one end of my rope over this limb, fashioned a running noose and drew the rope tight. Then slowly I wormed up the barrier.

From the top I gazed down upon a glory of wonderful, luxuriant flora. Stately ferns waved gently in the stirring air, beautiful flowering shrubs were interspersed here and there, while everywhere in the emerald grass, still wet with dew, nodded strange, exotic plants. Ever a lover of flowers, I forgot my mission as I looked. There came to my nostrils odors more fragrant and elusive than any I had heretofore known.

Suddenly I crouched low. On noiseless feet there passed beneath me a Malay, who had emerged without warning from a clump of ferns. He paused for a moment to brush an insect from a shrub, then disappeared from view in a thicket of high, green bushes.

Stealthily I slid to the ground and started toward the house, guiding myself by the observations I had made while on the wall. It was very likely, indeed, that the professor would kick me forth the instant he discovered my presence, but at any odds I should have something to tell the readers of the *Clarion*. Too, my audacity might count in my favor.

I had not gone far before I became conscious of an odor utterly different from the others. It was vague, but none the less disquieting. A feeling of loathing and dread pervaded me, a desire to clamber back over the wall and return to the city. The scent came again, much stronger, and I stood irresolute for several minutes, fighting down a sense of faintness as well as the longing to take flight. Then I advanced. In thirty seconds I came to the edge of a small open space. At what I beheld, I put out my hand to a large fern to steady myself.

In the middle of that tiny clearing grew a thing which, even now I shudder to describe. In form it was a gigantic tree, unspeakably stunted, fully twelve feet in diameter at the base and twenty-five feet high, tapering to a thickness of two feet at the top, from which depended *things*—I cannot call them leaves—for all the world resembling human ears. The whole was of a dead, drab color.

Dreadful as was the appearance of the thing, it was not that which made me reel as I looked. It was writhing and contorting, twisting itself into all manner of grotesque shapes. And *eyes* were boring into me, freezing the current of my blood.

Something rustled in the grass. I looked down and saw an immense creeper snaking toward me. For the first time I observed that it was joined to the trunk of that frightful thing, and so near the ground that I had not seen it for the tall grass. With a cry of horror I turned to run.

The creeper leapt at me and fastened around my middle with horrible force. I felt something in me give way. Frantically, I struck and tore at the ghastly, sinuous girdle that encircled me, undulating like the tentacle of an octopus. Fruitless, fruitless! I was drawn relentlessly forward.

I screamed. In the trunk of the thing there had appeared a mighty red-lipped orifice. The tentacle tightened and I was lifted off my feet toward that orifice. . . .

A beautiful girl was bending over me when I opened my eyes. She spoke in a musical voice: "Please do not move. One of your ribs is broken."

A tall, gray-haired man who had been standing in the background now came to my bedside.

"I am glad that I came in time, my boy. Otherwise . . ."

He was Professor Carter. He presented the girl as his daughter, Isobel.

Here one of the dark-skinned servants entered with some articles, which he deposited upon the center table.

"I am going to set your rib," announced the Professor. And forthwith he took off his coat and rolled up his sleeves. When the job was finished to his satisfaction, I besought him to telephone to town for a taxicab.

"I shall certainly do no such thing," he said. "I insist that you remain our guest until you are recovered."

Isobel Carter proved a wonderful nurse during the three days that followed. Indeed, the moment I had first looked into her deep black eyes, I knew that I loved her. I should have liked to remain in bed indefinitely with her to care for me, but was ashamed to do so. On the third morning I was moving cautiously about the house, she supporting my steps, although there was no need of it. The Professor joined us.

No mention had been made of my weird adventure in the grounds, but at my request he now told me how I had been saved from the hideous creature.

"Your first cry reached my ears as I was walking toward the house, and I immediately dashed in its direction. You were about to be swallowed when I arrived. I gave a sharp command, and my travesty released you."

"It obeyed your command?" I exclaimed incredulously.

"Precisely. It acknowledges me as its master. For six months, its period of life so far, I have superintended its growth and ministered to its needs."

"But *what* is it?"

A dreamy look came into Carter's eyes.

"For many years my brother scientists have sought for the so-called 'missing-link' between man and ape. For my part, I dare to believe that I have discovered the 'link' between the vegetable and animal kingdoms. The creature out there, however, has, to my mind, not as yet passed the initial stage of its development. Whether it will attain the power of locomotion remains to be seen."

He paused, gazing out of the window, then continued.

"Twenty years ago, in Rhodesia, I chanced upon a carnivorous plant that gave me my clew. Since then I have labored unremittingly, crossing and recrossing my specimens, and you have seen the result. It has cost me three-fourths of my fortune, and countless trips to Asia and Africa."

He indicated a vast pile of manuscript on the table.

"The life history, precedents included, of my travesty. It will form the basis of a work which, I do not doubt, will revolutionize science."

Glancing at the clock, he rose to his feet.

"It is feeding time. Do you care to accompany me?"

I assented, and we set out.

The thing remembered me, for the huge tentacle swept out in my direction, curling impotently in the empty air. I shuddered, and kept my distance.

A Malay appeared leading a calf. It was lowing piteously, for it had sensed danger.

The tentacle threshed about, endeavoring to clutch the animal, which lunged back, wild with terror. The man wrapped his arms about it and hurled it forward. It was seized. A loud cracking of bones broke the momentary silence, and was followed by an agonized cry. Six feet from the ground the great orifice gaped wide. The calf disappeared. A fleeting second and the mouth closed. There was no sign of its location; the trunk was smooth and unbroken.

A nausea had gripped me during the scene. The Professor and the Malay were apparently indifferent. They conversed briefly. Then, linking his arm in mine, Carter led the way back to the house. As we walked thither, I broached the subject of departure. He would not hear of it, insisting that I stay till Saturday.

While in his study I had noticed an elephant-gun in a corner. I asked him whether he had done any big-game hunting.

"That gun? Tala had me get it. He asserted that he could foretell tragedy in connection with the creature; that a day would come when I should lose control of it. I scouted the idea, but to humor him, purchased the weapon, which stands there loaded in the event need of it arises. Still, it would assuredly break my heart if anything necessitated the slaying of my travesty."

At the door of his study he excused himself and went in.

Isobel carried me off to the veranda hammock. As we talked it was inevitable that the subject of the plant-thing should come up, and a shadow crossed her face as we discussed it.

"Tala says that Father does not know how dangerous it is. He is right. But Father will not listen."

The next morning I again went with Professor Carter to the little clearing.

It was a sheep this time. The poor beast was paralyzed with fright, and stood passive, waiting for death.

The tentacle shot forth, wavered a second, then encircled, not the sheep, but Professor Carter, who seemed stricken by surprise.

He ripped out an order: "Off!"

The tentacle only tightened. Agony settled upon Carter's face. I sprang forward to drag him back. The tentacle released its hold for one lightning flash, then seized us both. We strove in vain against the vicelike cable. The Malay, with a wild cry, turned and rushed down the path, shouting as he ran.

The thing was playing with us as a cat plays with mice it has caught. It could have crushed us effortlessly, but the tentacle tightened by degrees. In spite of all we could do, we felt that we were being dragged forward to where the frightful red mouth yawned. Our eyes bulged, and I could see that Carter's face was taking on a greenish tinge. I extended my free arm and our hands clasped. Then there was the roar of a gun at close quarters, and the tentacle gave a spasmodic jerk that flung us twenty feet. We rose, staggering.

Tala stood by, the smoking elephant-gun in his hands, staring at the thing. Following his eyes we discerned a large, ragged hole in its trunk, from which a stream of *blood* was flowing and forming a great pool on the ground.

Even as we looked, the travesty went into the death-agonies. And as it writhed it emitted a sound that forever haunts me. Presently its struggles ceased. The professor buried his face in his hands.

I had not noticed Isobel's presence. Now I turned and saw her beside me, gazing with horror-filled eyes at the terrible, drooping form. I took her away from that tragic spot, for I knew that Professor Carter wished to be alone.

DEATH-WATERS

BY FRANK BELKNAP LONG, JR.

WE WERE SEATED IN THE PILOT-HOUSE OF THE "HABAKKUK," a queer little tug which carries daily passengers from New York steamers south along the coast of Honduras, from Trujillo to the Carataska lagoon. We were a chatty, odd group. Shabby promoters elbowed enthusiastic young naturalists (botanists from Olanchito, and entomologists from beyond Jamalteca) and tired, disillusioned surveyors from the plateau. The air was thick with unwholesome bluish smoke from fantastic pipes, which formed curious nimbuses about the heads of the older men. No one had a reputation to lose, and conversation was genial and unaffected.

One of the veterans stood in the center of the cabin and pounded with his fists upon a small wooden table. His face was the color of ripe corn, and from time to time he nodded at his companion. His companion did not return his salutations. The face of his companion was covered; and he lay upon the floor in an oblong box six feet long. No word of complaint issued from the box, and yet, whenever the veteran brought his eyes to bear upon the fastened lid, tears of pity ran rapidly down his cheeks and dampened his reddish beard. But he acknowledged to himself that the tears were blatantly sentimental, and not quite in good taste.

Every one else in the cabin ignored the existence of the man in the box—perhaps intentionally. A man's popularity depends largely upon his attitude. The attitude of the man in the box was not pleasing, since he had been dead for precisely four days. The veteran choked out his words fiercely between ominous coughs.

"My dear friends, you must be sensible of my embarrassment. It is my opinion that I am not an orator, and it is impossible for me to make you understand. I can explain, but you will never appreciate. There were millions of them, and they came after *him*. They attacked me only when I defended him. But it was hard—to see him collapse and turn black. The skin on his face shriveled up before he could speak. He never left me a last word. It is very hard when—one is a devoted friend! And yet his perversity was absurd. He brought it upon himself. 'The man has a warm temper,' I said. 'You must be careful. You must humor him. It is not good to provoke a man without morality, without standards, without taste.' A little thing would have been sufficient, a small compromise—but Byrne lacked a sense of humor. He paid horribly. He died on his feet, with the nasty things stabbing him, and he never emitted a shriek—only a guggling sob."

The veteran looked reproachfully at the six-foot box, and the ceiling.

"I don't blame you for thinking me queer—but how do you explain this?—and this?" he added, rolling up his sleeve and baring a scrawny brown arm.

We pressed forward and surrounded him. We were eager and amused, and a sleepy Indian in the corner ran his fingers through his fragile black beard, and tittered.

The veteran's arm was covered with tiny yellow scars. The skin had evidently been punctured repeatedly by some pinlike instrument. Each scar was surrounded by a miniature halo of inflamed tissue.

"Can any of you explain 'em?" he asked.

He drummed on the taut skin. He was a tried, nervous little man, with faded blue eyes and eyebrows that met above the arch of his nose. He had an amusing habit of screwing up the corners of his mouth whenever he spoke.

One of the young men took him solemnly aside and whispered something into his ear. The man with the punctured arm laughed. "Righto!" he said. The young man closed his eyes, and shuddered. "You—you shouldn't be alive." The youth had great difficulty in getting his lips to shape the words properly. "It isn't a bit of all right, you know! One bite is nearly always fatal, and you—you have dozens of 'em."

"Precisely!" Our man of the scars screwed up his lips and looked piercingly at us all. Some faces fell or blanched before him, but most of the young men returned a questioning gaze. "You know that the culebra de sangre is more certain than the taboba, more deadly than the rattler, more vicious than the corali. Well, I've been bitten ten times by culebras, five times by rattlers and thrice by our innocent little friend, the boba.

"I took great pains to verify these facts by studying the wounds, for each snake inflicts a slightly different one. Then how is it that I am still alive? My dear friends, you must believe me when I say that I do not know. Perhaps the poisons neutralized each other. Perhaps the venom of culebra de sangre is an antidote for that of the rattler, or vice versa. But it is enough that I stand here and talk to you. It is enough that I find within me the strength of youth—but my heart is dead."

His last comment seemed melodramatic and unnecessary, and we suddenly realized that the veteran was not an artist. He lacked a sense of dramatic values. We turned wearily aside, and puffed vigorously on our long pipes. It is difficult to forgive these little defects of technique.

The veteran seemed sufficiently conscious of our reproach. But he kept right on, and his voice was low and muffled, and it was difficult to follow the turnings and twistings of his disconcerting narrative. I remember distinctly that he bored us at first, and spoke at great length about things that did not interest us at all, but suddenly his voice became gritty, like the raucous blundering of an amateur with a viol, and we pressed closer about him.

"I would have you bear this constantly in mind: We were alone in the center of that lake, with no human being except a huge black savage within a radius of ten miles. It was risky business, of course, but Byrne was devilishly set on making a chemical analysis of the water just above the source of our spring.

"He was amazingly enthusiastic. I didn't care to parade my emotions in the presence of the black man, and I longed to subdue the glitter in Byrne's eye. Enthusiasm grates upon a savage, and I could see that the black was decidedly piqued. Byrne stood up in the stern, and raved. I endeavored to make him sit down. From the tone of suppressed excitement his voice rose to a shout. 'It's the finest water in Honduras. There's a fortune in it—it means—'

"I cut him short with a cold, reproachful look that must have hurt him. He winced under it, and sat down. I was level-headed enough to avoid unnecessary enthusiasms.

"Well, there we were, two old men who had come all the way from New York for the privilege of sitting in the sun in the center of a black, miasmal lake, and examining water that would have shocked a professional scavenger. But Byrne was unusually shrewd in a detestable, business-like way and he knew very well that the value of water doesn't reside in its taste. He had carefully pointed out to me that whenever water is taken from the center of a lake directly over a well it can be bottled and sold under attractive labels without the slightest risk. I admired Byrne's sagacity, but I didn't like the way the cannibal in the front was looking at the sky. I don't mean to suggest that he actually was a cannibal or anything monstrous or abnormal, but I distrusted his damnable mannerisms.

"He sat hunched in the bow, with his back toward me, with his hands on his knees and his eyes turned towards the shore. He was naked to the waist, and his dark, oily skin glistened with perspiration. There was something tremendously impressive about the rigidity of his animal-like body, and I didn't like the lethal growth of crisp black hair on his chest and arms. The upper portion of his body was hideously tattooed.

"I wish I could make you perceive the deadly horror of the man. I couldn't look at him without an inevitable shudder, and I felt that I could never really know him, never break through his crust of reserve, never fathom the murky depths of his abominable soul. I knew that he had a soul, but every decent instinct in me revolted at the thought of coming into contact with it. And yet I realized with jubilation that the soul of the monster was buried very deep, and that it would scarcely show itself upon slight provocation. And we had done nothing to call it forth; we had acted reasonably decent.

"But Byrne lacked tact. He wasn't properly schooled to flattery and the polite usages of rational society. He somehow got the queer notion into his head that the water should be tasted then and there. He was naturally averse to tasting it himself, and he knew that I couldn't stomach spring water of any sort. But he had a weird idea that perhaps the water contained a septic poison, and he was determined to settle his doubts on the spot.

"He scooped up a cupful of the detestable stuff and carried it to his nose. Then he gave it to me to smell. I was properly horrified. The water was yellowish and alive with animalculæ—but the horror of it did not reside in its appearance. Hot shame flushed scarlet over Byrne's face. I was brought sharply and agonizingly to a sense of spiritual guilt. 'We can't bottle that. It wouldn't be sportsmanship; it wouldn't be—'

" 'Of course we can bottle it. People like that sort of thing. The smell will be a splendid advertising asset. Who ever heard of medicinal spring water without an excessive smell? It is a great feather in our cap. Didn't you suppose that a smell was absolutely necessary?'

" 'But— ' "

" 'Let us have no "buts." That water has made our fortune. It is only necessary now to discover its taste.'

"He laughed and pointed to the black man in the bow. I shook my head. But what can you do when a man is determined? And, after all, why should I defend a savage? I simply sat and stared while Byrne handed the cup to our black companion. The black sat up very stiff and straight, and a puzzled, hurt expression crept into his dark eyes. He looked fixedly at Byrne and at the cup, and then he looked away toward the sky. The muscles in his face began to contract—horribly. I didn't like it, and I motioned to Byrne to withdraw the cup.

"But Byrne was determined that the black should drink. The stubbornness of a northern man in equatorial latitudes is often shocking. I have always avoided that pose, but Byrne never failed to do the conventional thing under given circumstances.

"He virtually bifurcated the savage with his eyes, and did it without a trace of condescension. 'I'm not going to sit here and hold this! I want you to taste the water and tell me precisely what you think of it. Tell me whether you like the way it tastes, and after you have tasted it, if you feel somewhat out of sorts and a bit dizzy it is only necessary for you to describe your feelings. I don't want to force it upon you, but you can't sit there and refuse to take part in this—er—experiment!'

"The black removed his eyes from the sky and gazed scornfully into Byrne's face. 'Na. I don't want this water. I didn't come out here to drink water.'

"Perhaps you have never seen the clash of two racially different wills, each as set and as primitive and as humorless as the other. A silent contest went on between Byrne and that black imp, and the latter's face kept getting more sinister and hostile; and I watched the muscles contracting and the eyes narrowing, and I began to feel sorry for Byrne.

"But even I hadn't fathomed Byrne's power of will. He dominated that savage through sheer psychic superiority. The black man didn't cower, but you could see that he knew he was fighting against fate.

"He knew that he had to drink the water; the fact had been settled when Byrne had first extended the cup, and his rebellion was pure resentment at the cruelty of Byrne in forcing the water upon him. I shall never forget the way he seized the cup and drained off the water. It was sickening to watch his teeth chatter and his eyes bulge as the water slid between his swollen lips. Great spasms seemed to run up and down his back, and I fancied that I could discern a velvety play of rebellious muscles throughout the whole length of his perspiring torso. Then he handed the cup back without a word, and began to look again at the sky.

"Byrne waited for a moment or two, and then he commenced to question the black in a way which I did not think very tactful. But Byrne imagined that his spiritual supremacy had been firmly established. I could have pointed out to him—but why cry over spilt milk? I can see Byrne now, knee-deep in questions, with his eyes scintillating and his cheeks flushing red. 'I made you drink that water because I wanted to know. It is very important that I should know. Have you ever tasted a bad egg? Did it taste like that? Did it have a salty flavor, and did it burn you when you swallowed it?'

"The black sat immobile and refused to answer. There is no understanding the psychology of a black man in the center of a black lake. I felt that the perversity of Nature had entered into the wretch, and I urged Byrne to ease up. But Byrne kept right on, and then finally—it happened.

"The black stood up in the boat and shrieked—and shrieked again. You cannot imagine the unearthly bestiality of the cries that proceeded out of his revolting throat. They were not human cries at all, and they might have come from a gorilla under torture. I could only sit and stare and listen, and I became as flabby as an arachnid on stilts. I felt at that moment nothing but unutterable fright, mixed with contempt for Byrne and his deliberate tempting of—well, not fate exactly, but the inexcusable phenomena of cannibalistic hysteria. I longed to get up and shriek louder than the savage in order to humiliate and shame him into silence.

"I thought at first, as the screams went echoing across the lake, that the black would upset the canoe. He was standing in the bow, and swaying from side to side, and with every lurch the canoe would ship some water. One cry followed another in maddening succession, and each cry was more sinister and more virulent and unnatural, and I observed that the devil's body was drawn up as taut as an electric wire.

"Then Byrne began to tug at his shoulders in a frantic effort to make him sit down. It was a hideous sight to see them struggling and swaying in the bow, and I even began to pity the black. Byrne hung on viciously, and I suddenly became aware that he was pummeling his antagonist fiercely on the back and under the arms. 'Sit down, or you'll wreck us! Good heavens! To create such a rumpus—and for a triviality!'

"The canoe was filling rapidly, and I expected her to capsize at any moment. I didn't relish the thought of swimming through a noisome cesspool, and I glared incontinently at Byrne. Poor chap! Had I known, I should have been more tolerant. Byrne deserved censure, but he paid—paid horribly.

"The black devil sat down quite suddenly and looked at the sky. All of his rebellion seemed to leave him. There was a genial, almost enthusiastic expression upon his loathsome face. He leered beneficently and patted Byrne on the shoulder. His familiarity shocked me, and I could see that it annoyed Byrne. The black's voice was peculiarly calm.

" 'I didn't mean anything, now. It's just the weather, I guess. I liked the water. I can't see why you shouldn't bottle it, and sell it. It's good water. I have often wondered why no one ever thought of bottling it before. The people who come out here are rather stupid, I guess.'

"Byrne looked at me rather sheepishly. The savage possessed intelligence and taste. His English was reasonably correct, and his manners were those of a gentleman. He had indeed acted outlandishly, and given us good reason to distrust him; but Byrne's tactics had been scurrilous, and deserving of rebuke.

"Byrne had sense enough to acknowledge his error. He grumbled a bit, but in conciliatory mood, and he asked the black to row to shore with a geniality that I thought admirable.

"Byrne put his hand over the side and let it trail in the water. I lit a cigarette and watched the greenish tide swirl and eddy beneath us. It was some time before I glimpsed the first of the little obscenities.

"I tried to warn Byrne, but he suddenly drew his hand up with a shriek and I knew that he would understand. 'Something bit me!' he said. I fancied that the black scowled and bent lower over his oars.

" 'Look at the water,' I replied. Byrne dropped his eyes, rather reluctantly, I thought. Then he blanched. 'Snakes—water snakes. Good Lord! Water snakes!' He repeated it again and again. 'Water snakes. There are thousands! Water snakes!'

" 'These are quite harmless. But I never saw anything like this before!' And I was indeed shocked. Imagine an unexpected upheaving of a million nasty little pink river snakes, from dank depths, and without rhyme or reason. They swam about the boat, and stuck their ugly little heads in the air, and hissed and shot out hideous tongues. I leaned over the boat and looked down into the greenish water. The river was alive with myriads of swaying pink bodies, which writhed in volatile contortions, and made the water foam and bubble. Then I saw that several had coiled themselves over the side of the canoe and were dropping down inside. I felt instinctively that the black devil had something to do with it.

"Such indignities were unthinkable. I stood up in the boat, and stormed. The black lifted his sleepy eyes and grinned broadly. But I saw that he was making directly for the shore. The snakes were crawling all about the boat, and they were attacking Byrne's legs, and their hissing sickened me. But I knew the species—a harmless and pretentious one. Still, the thought of taking them up by the tails and throwing them overboard was repugnant to me. And yet I knew that the noisome things horrified Byrne. He shrieked with the pain of their aggressive little bites and swore immoderately. When I assured him that they were innocuous he eyed me reproachfully and continued to mash them with the heels of his boots. He ground their loathsome heads into a pulp, and blood ran out of their tiny mouths and fairly flooded the bottom of the boat. But more kept on dropping over the sides and Byrne had his hands full. And the black rowed fiercely toward the shore, and said nothing. But he smiled, which made me long to strangle him. But I didn't care to offend him, for his methods of retaliation were apt to be unsavory.

"We finally reached the shore. Byrne jumped out with a shout and waded through several feet of black, sluggish mud. Then he turned about on the shore and looked back over the water. The whole surface was covered with swimming pink bodies, and they crisscrossed, and interlaced on the top of the tides, and when the lurid sunlight fell upon them they resembled unctuous charnel worms seething and boiling in some colossal vat.

"I got out somehow and joined Byrne. We were furious when we saw the black push off and make for the opposite shore. Byrne was upset and nearly delirious, and he assured me that the snakes were poisonous. 'Don't be a fool,' I said. 'None of the water snakes hereabouts are poisonous. If you had any sense—'

" 'But why should they have attacked me? They crawled up and bit me. Why should they have done that? They were scions of Satan. That black ensorceled them! He called them and they came.'

"I knew that Byrne was developing a monomania, and I sought to divert him. 'You have nothing to fear. Had we rattlers or culebras de sangre to deal with, but water snakes —bah!'

"Then I saw that the black was standing up in the canoe and waving his arms and shrieking exultantly. I turned about and looked up toward the crest of the hill in back of us. It was a savage hill, and it rose wild and bleak before us, and over the crest of it there poured an army of slithering things—and it is impossible for me to describe them in detail.

"I didn't wait for Byrne to turn about. I sought to keep him interested in the lake and in the black devil who was standing up in the canoe and shouting. I pointed out to him that the black had made himself ridiculous, and I slapped him soundly on the back and we congratulated each other on our superiority.

"But eventually I had to face them—the things that were crawling upon us from over the somber gray crest of the hill. I turned and looked at the deep blue sky and the great clouds rolling over the summit, and then my eyes went a little lower, and I saw them again, and knew that they were crawling slowly toward us and that there was no avoiding them.

"And I gently took Byrne by the arm, and turned him about and pointed silently. There were tears in my eyes and a curious heaviness in my legs and arms. But Byrne bore it like a gentleman. He didn't even express surprise, although I could clearly perceive that his soul had been mortally wounded and was sick unto death. And I saw shame and a monstrous fear staring at me out of Byrne's bloodshot eyes. And I pitied Byrne, but I knew what we had to do.

"The day was drawing to a close, amidst lovely earth-mists, which hung over the hill; and blue veils made the water gorgeous and hid the canoe and the gesticulating savage. I longed to sit calmly down there by the water, and to dream, but I knew that we had something to do. Near the edge of the water we found a gleaming yellow growth of shrubs and of stout vegetation, and we made stout clubs and strong cutting whips. And the army of reptiles continued to advance, and they filled me with a sense of infinite sadness and regret, and pity for Byrne.

"We stood very still and waited; and the mass of seething corruption rolled down the hill until it reached the level rocky lake shore, and then it oozed obnoxiously toward us. And we cried out when we counted the number of rattlers and culebras and bobas, but when we saw the other snakes we did not cry at all, for the centers of speech froze up in us, and we were very unhappy.

"My dear friends, you cannot imagine, you cannot conceive of our unhappiness. There were charnel reptiles with green, flattened heads and glazed eyes, which I did not attempt to identify, and there were legions of horned lizards, with blistered black tongues, and little venomous toads that hopped nervously about, and made odd, weird noises in their throats; and we knew that they were lethal, and to be avoided.

"But we met them face to face, and Byrne fought with genuine nobility. But the odds were overwhelming, and I saw him go down, panting, suffocated, annihilated. They crawled up his legs, and they bit him in the back and sides, and on the face, and I saw his face blacken before my eyes. I saw his lips writhe back from his teeth, and his eyes glaze, and the skin on his face pucker and shrivel.

"And I fought to keep them from him, and my club was never idle. I flattened innumerable heads that were round, and I rounded heads that were flat, and I made sickening crimson pellets out of quivering gelatinous tissue.

"My dear friends, they went away at last, and left him there. And the blue calm of the hills seemed inexplicable under the circumstances, but I was thankful for the coolness and quiet, and the deepening shadows. I sat down with peace in my soul, and waited. I looked at the tiny punctures on my arms, and I smiled. I was reasonably happy.

"But my dear friends, I did not die. The realization that I was not to die amazed me. It was several hours before I could be certain, and then I did a shocking thing. I took my beard firmly between my two hands and pulled out the hair in great tufts. The pain sobered me.

"I tramped for two days with the body. It was the decent, the proper thing to do. I waited in Trujillo for the fashioning of the coffin, and I personally supervised its construction. I wanted everything done properly, in the grand manner. I have very few regrets—but my soul is dead!"

There was an infinite misery in the veteran's eye. His voice grew raucous, and he stopped talking. We noticed that he shivered a little as he turned up his collar and went out through the cabin door into a night of stars. We pressed our faces against the glass of the one window and saw him standing before the rail, with the rain and moonlight glistening upon his beard, and the salt spray striking against his incredibly chastened face.

MONSTERS OF THE PIT

By PAUL S. POWERS

HOW DID I LOSE MY LEFT ARM? WELL, GENTLEMEN, I HAVE felt that question coming for a long time, and to tell the truth about the matter, I rather dreaded it. For, as well as I have grown to know you during these lonesome nights at the club, I never thought the time would come when I could unburden my mind. I don't expect that you will believe me, either you, Bronson, or Roberts, here. I tried to tell the story once before, to a French doctor at Port Said. He laughed at me at first, and thought me insane afterward. I won't blame you for doing the same. Sometimes I hardly believe the story myself. It seems more like a nightmare than a reality. But here's the proof, gentlemen—this poor stump that was once a fairly serviceable left arm. It looks like a neat surgical operation, doesn't it? But it took my wife three hacks to get it off.

Waiter! Bring the vermouth! There, thank you. You look startled, gentlemen. Perhaps you'd better have a drop of the wine to take the chill of the London fog from your bones. Beastly night, outside. No, I wasn't joking, Bronson, and if you'll be so good as to hand me a cigarette, I'll tell the tale—spin the yarn, as you Americans put it. You won't believe the story, but that makes little difference. I think there is a little saying in your country: "If you believe it, it's true."

It happened four years ago when I was down at Port Said with the engineering company. I was a single man, then, with not a thought in the world other than to take my good money while I could get it, and to get out when there was no more to be had. It was good pay, but rotten work in a rottener country. The town wasn't bad for a headquarters, but it was the trips into the interior that broke us down—from the chief engineer to Tubbs, the youngest apprentice. A year or two and the average man was done, in that country. I saw three white men sent back to the coast on litters, and two more went back in a more gruesome condition. When it wasn't the fever it was the insects, and usually it was both. The snakes and the flies weren't so bad, for a man can kill them, or some of them, but I'll never forget the breath of those awful swamps nor the touch of those ungodly creeping things that were bound to be in your boots in the morning and on your cot at night.

Well, it was halfway across the nigger country that stretches between the company offices and Suakin. There were seven of us white men and a party of blacks. One of the black boys, however, I really grew to like and trust. He knew the country, the desert, and the jungle; and he knew mules. He was in charge of the string we had with us. Kali was this remarkable fellow's name, and I suppose I am the only one who now remembers it.

Can you imagine seeing a beautiful English girl in a filthy native town in the depths of Africa? I couldn't either, until I saw her. Gad! She was white, and young! When I met her in that market place, with a basket on her arm and dressed like a nun, I got the biggest thrill of my life. She was about eighteen, and though I didn't see the beauty of her at the time, I was shocked beyond words. I learned afterward that I was the first Englishman she had ever seen, with the exception of her father—but more of that later. Just that glimpse was all I had that day, but it was enough to set me thinking.

The chief only laughed when I reached the camp with the news, but the chief was a steady old blighter with grandchildren in Southsea, so I didn't wonder. It was the same when I told the other men—they thought I had been drinking. But it was true, and, of course, I asked Kali.

"Why, that is the daughter of the dread father, the mad white man," he winked over the cigarette I had given him. "But no—all white men are mad."

"And who," I asked, "is this white man?"

"A learned man," grinned Kali, "but mad, all the same. He was here when my father was as I am, and even then he was mad. If he was not mad, would he creep in the swamps and in the sand, even as the insects?"

"But how does he live?"

"Ah, he has gold—English gold. Two times, sometimes three times a year, he goes to the coast and brings back all manner of strange things. Wanaki, one of his blacks, once told me that he brought back devils in tiny bottles, from the English ships. To uncork the bottle means death—a terrible swelling death. Wanaki told of his devils and how a black boy died even as cattle die from the cobra. But there was no snake—there was only a white powder."

"Does the girl go with him on his trips to Port Said?"

"If she had, Wanaki would have told me. The girl child is made to stay with the black women. The white man is mad, and if you take the advice of Kali you will forget the white child woman in the long black dress."

Kali looked very wise indeed, and I believe he wanted another cigarette. I cursed him sourly and left him to his mules.

The sight of the woman had set something loose within me. You know well how it is in the wilderness, and it had been long weeks since we had left Port Said. To be sure, there were women there—of a kind. I wanted to know this girl, at least to learn something of her history. Kali's gossip had aroused my curiosity, though I did not believe him. Kali's great sin was his love for talk and his hatred for bare facts. But I vowed to see the girl again.

I'll pass over briefly the days that followed. The very

afternoon following my talk with Kali I saw her again, but only a glimpse and she was gone. Then several days passed, and during them I learned more about the girl and her father. His name was Denham, a doctor, it appeared, with several letters tacked after his name—a scientist. Those were all the facts I could rather, and what he was doing and had been doing the past twenty years was a mystery. Collecting bugs? Possibly. But Kali and the blacks swore that it was more than that—by the burial pits of their fathers it was more than that. He was a devil-devil doctor, and made the milk of the cows turn sour. He was a man-witch who poisoned the swamps, and talked with the spiders at evil hours of the night. He was also a number of other undesirable things, according to the superstitious Kali, who continued to divulge more or less valuable information over my cigarettes.

Then came the day when I met the girl face to face. And that day I learned more than ever before, though what I heard scarcely satisfied me.

The girl was timid, and though she permitted me to walk with her a short distance, I left her more disturbed than before. "Yes," she said, "she was English, though born in Africa." She had never seen England, having been no further than Port Said, and then only once, when a mere baby. Her mother? She did not remember her mother, and she had never heard the English tongue spoken except by her father. This was practically all she told me, but it made me long to hear more.

On that short walk with her I learned several important details, not the least important of which was the fact that she was even prettier than I had at first supposed. And she had been well educated—the professor evidently was an excellent teacher—and she had mentioned books, many books. The next morning I was waiting in the market place.

She came. It was more than I had hoped. Why bore you with details, gentlemen? I met her again and again, and grew to know her better than myself. Yes, I was in love, and beyond that there's no explanation needed, I'm sure.

We talked of many things during that first short week of our acquaintance, and on one subject only was she elusive: her father. Of her father only, she would not speak. When I spoke of him she would turn away with a look on her face much akin to fear. But perhaps I was mistaken. As we grew more intimate it grew upon me that her father, even if he was the dreadful being Kali had made him out to be, was at least a wonderful scholar. I could read it in this child. She was wonderful. In most respects she astounded me with her learning, and then at other times she would show an ignorance that was pathetic. The man she called father had molded her mind to suit his will, but there is that something about a woman's mind, gentlemen, that no earthly cunning can twist from its course. I began to read it in her eyes that she cared for me more than her innocence knew. I haven't told you her name. It was Irene Denham.

"I would like very much to meet your father," I ventured, one evening. "Doesn't he know that you are meeting me here?"

She hesitated.

"I have told him of you, Scott," she admitted. "And—well, he doesn't exactly approve. Of course, it's because he doesn't know you," she added hastily, "but when I suggested that you visit us at our home on the veldt, he was very angry. Father is like that—sometimes I think he hates all white men. I think it's because he's so wrapped up in his work, the work he has been carrying on for twenty years. But to-morrow, Scott, if you will come—"

I shook my head.

"Not if he disapproves of it," I began, and then I had a sudden thought. I would go and, moreover, I would come to an understanding with this man. Surely, I had the right, at least, for I was determined to take Irene back to England with me. There was no other course open—I would see

Professor Denham, and see him the very next day. I told the girl of my plans—and, well, gentlemen, I won't go into details—but she accepted them. I would meet her in the dirty little market place the next morning, we agreed, and would accompany her home.

I found Kali very much worried that night, and when I pressed for further information, and told him that I was planning to visit Professor Denham the next day, he told me bluntly that I would soon die.

"Nonsense, Kali," I laughed. "Why, I expect to find a respectable old naturalist and a fine collection of ants and butterflies. He's harmless. In my country no one is ever frightened at their doings. He's what is called a scientist, Kali."

"One of the black fellah boys from beyond the village told me to watch my mules," answered Kali. "He told me, also, that the white witch-man has been stealing his cattle. What does he do with the cattle? He takes them into dark pits within his great stone house. Tell me, do butterflies eat cattle?"

I was getting very angry, and could have taken the impudent black scoundrel by the throat with pleasure.

"Hold your tongue!" I commanded, but when I left his hut Kali was smoking one of my cigarettes, all the same. This really was getting interesting. On the morrow, I told myself, I would know just how much Kali had lied. At the time I put the whole story down as the product of Kali's vivid if not convincing, creative imagination. I was in love. The next morning, *the* morning, I varnished my boots carefully, and put on my best khaki breeches. I would have given a small fortune for the white linen ones of the chief engineer, but I didn't dare ask him for them. It was hard enough to get away for the day.

Irene was at our rendezvous, and I received the thrill of my life when I saw that she had discarded her nunlike dress for one more fitting to the occasion. It seemed to me to be rather a makeshift affair, but it became her—it brought out beauty that I had not thought her to possess. She was a man's woman, was Irene!

"I don't know why, dear, but I dread the meeting between you and father," she murmured.

We had left the village and were climbing a baking sand dune.

"It won't be so bad," I said, cheerfully. "My education hasn't been along the same lines as your father's, and perhaps he won't be interested in me, yet perhaps we shall have some things in common. A white man, you know, is a white man, and even Africa can't change him. I'll wager you that the first question he asks me is, 'Have you an old London *Times* with you?' "

"White men have been near the village before," insisted the girl. "Never has he admitted them to our home, although one was a scientist like him—an explorer. I believe he hates all men—all mankind. True, he finally gave permission to bring you, but I'm afraid—"

"Does he love—you?" I asked.

"I don't know. There was a time when I was sure he did, just as there were times when he would bring flowers from our garden and put them upon my mother's grave, but for many years he has been changed. He hates the world—he plans to destroy—"

She did not finish the sentence, but stopped as if a cold hand had been laid across her red lips. She paled, and I saw that she was trembling. When I pressed her for an explanation, she changed the subject with a frightened, pathetic smile. From that moment on I felt that a chill had crept down from the dunes like a breath from the swamps. We walked on in silence.

"There!" she said, when we had reached the top of a little hillock. "There is—home."

Home! So this was her home! A melancholy house of stone, crumbling like an ancient ruin. It seemed strangely out of place here in this desolation. It belonged to Carthage, or perhaps to some long dead city. And this child lived here! I shuddered, even though the heat was flickering in waves across the distant veldt.

Her steps became slower, as we approached, and she seemed to be laboring under a clutching fear. I remember that the few cheerful and rather idiotic remarks I made fell flat, and truly I was in no mood for jesting.

As we neared the house I could see half a dozen black slaves working about the *kraal,* but I could see no sign of life within the house. It was fearfully hot, and far, far to the east, I thought I could make out the distant line of the sea, but I knew it was a mirage.

Well, I met Dr. Denham. We had entered the coolness of the hallway, and as I stood wondering what fashion of man it was who had furnished this dreary place so well, I saw a smiling face peering at us from beyond the draperies.

"Mr. Scott, I presume?"

A soft voice, and it fitted the man. In the semidarkness, which was the nearest approach to comfort in sweltering British East Africa, I saw Irene's father. A man of fifty, perhaps, smooth-shaven and neatly dressed in white. The mouth under his rather hooked nose was curved into a smile, and yet, somehow, I felt chilled. No smile of welcome that! Not that there was anything alarming about the doctor's appearance, for he was nearly as I had pictured him, with his scholarly spectacles and abstracted manner. A naturalist and scientist, he looked his part. I bowed.

"I am very glad to know you, Professor Denham," I said, and extended my hand.

That handclasp was like ice! Denham's skin was repulsively cold and moist, like that of a bloated leech. I shuddered, and looked at the man closely.

The eyes! The heavy lenses of his glasses failed to utterly conceal the serpentine power of those greenish eyes. They were at once the eyes of a hypnotist and snake charmer.

Though the professor was smiling with his thin lips, the eyes remained icy and the skin across his lofty brows was wrinkled into a frown. I remember that he made a few commonplace remarks and invited me inside. Dinner, he said, would soon be served. He was happy to have an Englishman for his guest. Yes, it *was* lonely here, but he was fond of loneliness. All the time he was talking I could not keep my eyes from his face. There was some mystery here—some strange secret in this man's life. And Irene knew of it, for I remembered that little slip she had made while we were crossing the sands. She was worried now, and she was watching her father with mingled fear and apprehension, if I read aright.

At dinner, which was served by a good-looking black, the professor talked of many things. Did I like the country? When did I expect to return to Cairo and Port Said? He asked many questions, and for the first time since I met him I felt at ease. Perhaps I had been mistaken after all. First impressions do not always furnish one with a character guide. I warmed up, and we talked until late afternoon, over our wine. I was just about to come to the point, and tell him the real reason for my journey here, when he asked me to look at his specimens.

"Something that you'll find interesting, Mr. Scott, I'm sure," he smiled. "I doubt if you've ever seen anything like them. It has taken years for me to perfect my plans, and it is only recently that I have had any success. Do you know anything of bacteriology?"

"Very little," I confessed. "From what your daughter told me I thought your experiments were confined to insects. I did not know that bacteriology, too, was a hobby of yours, doctor."

He eyed me sharply.

"It's more than a hobby," he said, "as you will soon see. As for insects, well, you will see my insects—later."

I felt much like telling him that he need not go to that

trouble. Creeping things had always horrified me, and I had seen quite enough of them since I had been working in Africa. However, it was my plan to keep him in good humor until we could reach an understanding, so I followed him into a distant portion of the great house.

"As far as bacteria are concerned," I told him, "I haven't even as much as peeped into a microscope."

Professor Denham laughed.

"Microscope!" he leered. "You won't need a magnifying glass to see my collection!"

Was the man mad? I felt a chill creep over me.

We had reached a sort of laboratory, and the professor withdrew a cloth from a glass case. I looked over his shoulder, then, and received one of the shocks of my life. What were these horribly squirming things? Not insects, for never in my dreams had I pictured things like these! They were writhing like maggots in a substance that appeared to be a sticky gelatine. Some of them resembled scorpions, but most of them were rod-shaped things the size of my little finger. They were moving, moving—never still.

"What—what are they?" I stammered in an awed voice.

"Bacilli," chuckled the doctor.

"You mean germs—of disease?" I asked, horrified.

"Exactly! What do you think of my work? I have multiplied them a million times, in size. Some of those organisms literally breathe death. It has taken me twenty years to find the secret, and do you know what it means? I am lord of the world!"

It was devilish, and I longed to get out of the room. This man was mad, surely, yet here was the hideous proof before me.

"There they are," went on the scientist, with a horrible smile. "There they are till I am ready to use them, safe in the glass case and in a culture medium of agar agar."

I wiped the cold sweat from my face, and told him that I had seen quite enough and was ready to leave.

"Not till you have seen the most interesting specimens in my exhibit of insect life," smiled the professor. "I wouldn't have you miss that, for worlds."

I wanted to tell him that I wouldn't see another sight like those writhing things in his laboratory for worlds, either, but I followed him from the room and into a corridor. A huge black was waiting for us there.

"Well, Sahem?" asked the professor, in a harsh metallic voice.

The black giant showed his teeth in a look of anxiety.

"The slaves, master," he muttered. "They threaten to fly. They are afraid, and even the cattle whip cannot make them stay longer. Some of them will talk, unless—"

The doctor whipped a revolver from his blouse and handed it to the great negro.

"Tell them that I will have them thrown into the great pit," he snarled, "if they breathe a word! Kill them, Sahem, if they do not obey; and as for yourself, if you make one slip, the black pit will yawn for your carcass also!"

The slave's face twitched with fear, and it was nearly livid when he bowed to the ground and backed out of the dank passage on his hands and knees. Before I had time to recover from my astonishment a terrible sound echoed at my feet. It was an agonized bellow, ending in a gurgling wail, and it seemed to come from a cavern under the house. The hair tightened on my scalp at that fearful sound—the death sound of some animal in fear and pain. For a moment I heard it and then it died suddenly away into silence.

"My God!" I whispered, "what was that?"

"I fancy," smiled the professor, cheerfully, "that it was an ox."

Kali's weird tale flashed through my head. Perhaps the talkative black man had not lied so much after all. There was a deeper mystery here than I had at first imagined, and for the moment my curiosity was stronger than my dread.

While I followed the bobbing form of the scientist up the passage, I turned over in my mind all I had seen and heard. Again I seemed to see those horrible squirming things in the glass case, and once more I seemed to hear that awful wail. An ox! How long would this distorted nightmare last?

"Now, if you'll be so good," murmured the professor, "we will look over my collection of insects."

He had reached a trap-door and was tugging at the rope that raised it. It suddenly yawned open and I saw the first steps of a staircase leading somewhere down into the dark.

"We'll just leave the door open, so we can see," said the scientist, and he led the way cautiously down the wooden steps. With some misgiving I followed, keeping close to his back. The death cry of the ox still rang in my ears and I determined not to lose sight of my guide. Three steps, then four, then five. At that moment I heard steps on the passage above, and a second later saw Irene's white face framed in the square opening at my head.

"Oh, Scott," she whispered. "Come back—come back!"

Even as the words left her lips I saw a great black hand placed over her mouth, and caught a glimpse of the giant negro, his face distorted by a scowl of rage and fury. I leaped up the steps, and as I did so, down came the trap with a bang and I found myself scuffling in the dark with the professor.

I fought furiously, and was overpowering the wiry little fiend, when I felt myself hanging over the edge of a black void. Something seemed to whirl me closer and then I fell, with the doctor's insane laugh ringing in my ears.

Something strangely yielding broke my fall, something that felt like a suspended mass of silken rope. For a moment I was held there, and as the trap-door was opened above me, I saw the face of the professor looking down at me from above. So this was the pit! I struggled, and tried to wrench myself free from the tangling bands that bound me, for Irene's suppressed cry still echoed in my brain. In vain I tried to tear myself loose, and then, as my eyes grew accustomed to the faint light, I ceased. The silken strands that grasped my arms and legs were as large around as my thumb, and held me like so much steel. The professor was leaning over the edge of the pit. He was speaking, and his voice was quivering with rage.

"Fool! Miserable fool!" he mocked. "So you sought to steal my daughter, did you? And she the future princess of the world! I know your kind, and now I can watch you die. Soon you will see my collection of *insects!*"

And then in the distant corner I could see a huge pair of phosphorescent eyes staring at me through the gloom—then another pair and another! They seemed to appear as if by magic from some dark recess within the pit. Then I saw what covered the floor of the place! Bones! Bones of cattle and of sheep! And in the maze of ropy threads about me hung the carcass of a great ox! I was being held in nothing less than the web of a monstrous spider!

I screamed, and as an echo to the scream I heard the throaty laugh of the demented man in the gallery. *Insects!* God! Great bloated spiders, foul and gigantic, were watching me from their awful lairs! Again I struggled to wrench myself away, but I fell exhausted. Then I saw the hideous monsters begin slowly to advance, and I felt the web tremble as if something of great weight was gliding upon it.

Above me and to the right was one of the ghastly spiders. I saw its multiple eyes watching me as it paused. Fangs, shining like polished ebony, protruded beneath those terrible eyes, and when I saw the thing perched on the great web ready to pounce upon me, I cried out in horror. The web shook again, and I closed my eyes and waited for the dreadful impact. Even now, gentlemen, the sight of a fly buzzing his wings in a spider's web makes me sick and weak. Why I did not faint then, I don't know. Perhaps I was too terror-stricken.

I believe the monster would have leaped at that instant

had it not been for a cry on the other wall of the pit. At the sound I began to hope again. It was Irene.

She was descending by a ladder, under a large trap on the other side, doubtless the one through which the ox had been cast. In her hand was an ax.

"Leave me!" I shouted, sick with fear for her safety. "You cannot save me! Back! Back!"

But she came, and I saw the terrible thing above me turn on its great legs, and watch her. At that second I heard a yell of fury from the professor. He was descending a rope ladder on the other side of the pit, and was foaming with rage.

The great spider had faced me again, and I could feel its legs rasp against the web that held me. I saw that the monster was covered with hair, like a huge bear, though no bear was ever so disgustingly sickening as this dreadful thing. I felt like a helpless fish about to be seized by a bloated octopus. Yet once again it hesitated, as if not knowing whether to turn on Irene or the professor.

Irene reached me first, and her ax whistled through the air at my feet as she cut me loose from the tenacious web. As she did so the hideous monster leaped at her! Like a steel trap and with terrible ferocity, the spider sprang, only to meet Irene's ax.

The keen edge of the tool sank into its horrible flesh. I wrenched the weapon from Irene's hand and finished the awful thing—saw it writhe out its death struggle, entangled by its own web. I struck again and again, and then threw aside the ax with a feeling of nausea and disgust. Irene clung to me and sobbed.

"Quick!" I cried, as I tore my eyes away from the throes of the monster I had killed. "Your father—look!"

The unfortunate professor was pinned under the dreadful body of another spider. It had sprung upon him while I was occupied with my own troubles.

Seizing the ax, I dashed toward him, taking care to avoid

the treacherous web. I struck at the insect of hell with all my strength, and it turned upon me savagely. I saw those awful fangs poised above me as I struck upward again with the ax. My blow landed squarely, but it was too late to avoid the knifelike poison tubes. Something swept into my left hand like a razor, just as the dying and distended body of the spider bore me to the ground. I felt a fetid, cold breath on my neck and something flabby and soft seemed to encircle my chest. For a moment I lost consciousness.

The next thing I remembered was the sense of a great weight being removed from my body. I groaned, and sat upright. Irene helped me to my feet, and she was calm, though the dead body of the professor lay not three feet away. I had been too late, and the spider had accomplished his deadly work. The scientist had been killed by the product of his own insane cunning.

We made good our escape, and it was well, for if another spider—well, I had reached the limit of my sanity.

In the passageway, Irene caught a glimpse of my hand for the first time.

"Scott!" she screamed. "Look!"

My hand was enormously swollen, and even as I watched I could see a blue discoloration working its way toward my elbow. In the excitement I had forgotten the slash from the keen fangs of the spider. I was as good as doomed.

Irene still held the ax, and as I stood there, shaking like a leaf, she raised her eyes in a prayer for courage. I read the answer in her face, and without being told I laid down my swollen arm.

Well, gentlemen, it took her three hacks to get it off. How the blood was stanched I don't know, for the next thing I remember was being jolted along in an ox-cart, bound for the nearest surgeon. A nigger was driving, and I was feeling fine. My head was pillowed in Irene's lap. I looked back, then, and saw a red glow against the evening sky. The slaves had fired the place and fled. From what I have been able to learn, the spiders died in the ruins, for I've never seen a spider any bigger than my hand since that day. To tell the truth, I don't want to.

Irene married me at Cairo, and as soon as I was able, we left for England.

Now there's the story, gentlemen; you may believe it or not. . . . Waiter, will you kindly bring another bottle of vermouth?

FOUR WOODEN STAKES

By VICTOR ROMAN

THERE IT LAY ON THE DESK IN FRONT OF ME, THAT MISSIVE so simple in wording, yet so perplexing, so urgent in tone.

Jack,
Come at once for old-time's sake. Am all alone. Will explain upon arrival.

Remson.

Having spent the past three weeks in bringing to a successful termination a case that had puzzled the police and two of the best detective agencies in the city, I decided I was entitled to a rest, so I ordered two suit cases packed and went in search of a time-table. It was several years since I had seen Remson Holroyd; in fact, I had not seen him since we had matriculated from college together. I was curious to know how he was getting along, to say nothing of the little diversion he promised me in the way of a mystery.

The following afternoon found me standing on the platform of the little town of Charing, a village of about fifteen hundred souls. Remson's place was about ten miles from there, so I stepped forward to the driver of a shay and asked if he would kindly take me to the Holroyd estate. He clasped his hands in what seemed to be a silent prayer, shuddered slightly, then looked at me with an air of wonder, mingled with suspicion.

"I dun't know whut ye wants to go out there fer, stranger, but if ye'll take the advice o' a God-fearin' man ye'll turn back where ye come from. There be some mighty fearful tales concernin' that place floatin' around, and more'n one tramp's been found near there so weak from loss of blood and fear he could hardly crawl. They's somethin' there. Be it man or beast I dun't know, but as fer me, I wouldn't drive ye out there for a hundred dollars—cash."

This was not at all encouraging, but I was not to be influenced by the talk of a superstitious old gossip, so I cast about for a less impressionable rustic who would undertake the trip to earn the ample reward I promised at the end of the ride. To my chagrin, they all acted like the first; some crossed themselves fervently, while others gave me one wild look and ran, as if I were in alliance with the devil.

By now my curiosity was thoroughly aroused, and I was determined to see the thing through to a finish if it cost me my life. So, casting a last, contemptuous look on those poor, misguided souls, I stepped out briskly in the direction pointed out to me. However, I had gone but a scant two miles when the weight of the suit cases began to tell, and I slackened pace considerably.

The sun was just disappearing beneath the tree-tops when I caught my first glimpse of the old homestead, now deserted but for its one occupant. Time and the elements had laid heavy hands upon it, for there was hardly a window that could boast its full quota of panes, while the shutters banged and creaked with a noise dismal enough to daunt even the strong of heart.

About one hundred yards back I discerned a small building built of gray stone, pieces of which seemed to be lying all around it, partly covered by the dense growth of vegetation that overran the entire countryside. On closer observation I realized that the building was a crypt, while what I had taken to be pieces of the material scattered around were really tombstones. Evidently this was the family burying ground. But why had certain members been interred in a mausoleum while the remainder of the family had been buried in the ground in the usual manner?

Having observed thus much, I turned my steps toward the house, for I had no intention of spending the night with naught but the dead for company. Indeed, I began to realize just why those simple country folk had refused to aid me, and a hesitant doubt began to assert itself as to the expediency of my being here, when I might have been at the shore or at the country club enjoying life to the full.

By now the sun had completely slid from view, and in the semidarkness the place presented an even drearier aspect than before. With a great display of bravado I stepped upon the veranda, slammed my suit cases upon a seat very much the worse for wear, and pulled lustily at the knob.

Peal after peal reverberated throughout the house, echoing and reëchoing from room to room, till the whole structure rang. Then all was still once more, save for the sighing of the wind and the creaking of the shutters.

A few minutes passed, and the sound of footsteps approaching the door reached my ears. Another interval, and the door was cautiously opened a few inches, while a head shrouded by the darkness scrutinized me closely. Then the door was flung wide, and Remson (I hardly knew him, so changed was he) rushed forward and, throwing his arms around me, thanked me again and again for heeding his plea, till I thought he would go into hysterics.

I begged him to brace up, and the sound of my voice seemed to help him, for he apologized rather shamefacedly for his discourtesy and led the way along the wide hall. There was a fire blazing merrily away in the sitting room, and after partaking generously of a repast, for I was famished after my long walk, I was seated in front of it, facing Remson and waiting to hear his story.

"Jack," he began, "I'll start at the beginning and try to give you the facts in their proper sequence. Five years ago my family circle consisted of five persons: my grandfather, my father, two brothers, and myself, the baby of the family. My mother died, you know, when I was a baby. Now—"

His voice broke and for a moment he was unable to continue.

"There's only myself left," he went on, "and so help me God, I'm going, too, unless you can solve the damnable mystery that hovers over this house and put an end to that something which took my kin and is gradually taking me.

"Granddad was the first to go. He spent the last few years of his life in South America. Just before leaving there he was attacked while asleep by one of those huge bats. Next morning he was so weak he couldn't walk. That awful thing had sucked his lifeblood away. He arrived here, but was sickly until his death, a few weeks later. The doctors couldn't agree as to the cause of death, so they laid it to old age and let it go at that. But I knew better. It was his experience in the south that had done for him. In his will he asked that a crypt be built immediately and his body interred therein. His wish was carried out, and his remains lie in that little gray vault that you may have noticed if you cut around behind the house. Then my dad began failing and just pined away until he died. What puzzled the doctors was the fact that right up until the end he consumed enough food to sustain three men, yet he was so weak he lacked the strength to drag his legs over the floor. He was buried, or rather interred, with granddad. The same symptoms were in evidence in the cases of George and Fred. They are both lying in the vault. And now, Jack, I'm going, too, for of late my appetite has increased to alarming proportions, yet I am as weak as a kitten."

"Nonsense!" I chided. "We'll just leave this place for a while and take a trip somewhere, and when you return you'll laugh at your fears. It's all a case of overwrought nerves, and there is certainly nothing strange about the deaths you speak of. Probably due to some hereditary disease. More than one family has passed out in a hurry just on that account."

"Jack, I only wish I could think so, but somehow, I

know better. And as for leaving here, I just can't. Understand, I hate the place; I loathe it, but I can't get away. There is a morbid fascination about the place which holds me. If you want to be a real friend, just stay with me for a couple of days, and if you don't find anything I'm sure the sight of you and the sound of your voice will do wonders for me."

I agreed to do my best, although I was hard put to keep from smiling at his fears, so apparently groundless were they. We talked on other subjects for several hours, then I proposed bed, saying that I was very tired after my journey and subsequent walk. Remson showed me to my room, and, after seeing that everything was as comfortable as possible, he bade me good-night.

As he turned to leave the room the flickering light from the lamp fell on his neck and I noticed two small punctures in the skin. I questioned him regarding them, but he replied that he must have beheaded a pimple and that he hadn't noticed them before. He again said good-night and left the room.

I undressed and tumbled into bed. During the night I was conscious of an overpowering feeling of suffocation—as if some great burden was lying on my chest which I could not dislodge; and in the morning when I awoke, I experienced a curious sensation of weakness. I arose, not without an effort, and began divesting myself of my sleeping suit. As I folded the jacket I noticed a thin line of blood on the collar. I felt my neck, a terrible fear overwhelming me. It pained slightly at the touch. I rushed to examine it in the mirror. Two tiny dots rimmed with blood—my blood—and on my neck! No longer did I chuckle at Remson's fears, for *it,* the thing, had attacked me as I slept!

I dressed as quickly as my condition would permit and went downstairs, thinking to find my friend there. He was not about, so I looked about outside, but he was not in evidence. There was but one answer to the question. He had not yet risen. It was nine o'clock, so I resolved to awaken him.

Not knowing which room he occupied, I entered one after another in a fruitless search. They were all in various stages of disorder, and the thick coating of dust on the furniture showed that they had been untenanted for some time. At last, in a bedroom on the north side of the third floor, I found him.

He was lying spread-eagle fashion across the bed, still in his pajamas, and as I leaned forward to shake him, my eyes fell on two drops of blood, splattered on the coverlet. I crushed back a wild desire to scream, and shook Remson rather roughly. His head rolled to one side, and the hellish perforations on his throat showed up vividly. They looked fresh and raw, and had increased to much greater dimensions. I shook him with increased vigor, and at last he opened his eyes stupidly and looked around. Then, seeing me, he said in a voice loaded with anguish, resignation and despair:

"It's been here again, Jack. I can't hold out much longer. May God take my soul when I go!"

So saying he fell back again from sheer weakness. I left him and went about preparing myself some breakfast. I thought it best not to destroy his faith in me by telling him that I, too, had suffered at the hands of his persecutor.

A walk brought me some peace of mind, if not a solution, and when I returned about noon to the big house, Remson was up and around. Together we prepared a really excellent meal. I was hungry and did justice to my share; but after I had finished my friend continued eating until I thought he must either disgorge or burst. Then, after putting things to rights, we strolled about the long hall, looking at the oil paintings, many of which were very valuable.

At one end of the hall I discovered a portrait of an old gentleman, evidently a Beau Brummel in his day. He wore his hair in the long, flowing fashion adopted by the old school, and sported a carefully trimmed mustache and Vandyke beard. Remson noticed my interest in the painting and came forward.

"I don't wonder that picture holds your interest, Jack. It has a great fascination for me, also. At times I sit for hours studying the expression on that face. I sometimes think he has something to tell me, but, of course, that's all tommyrot. But I beg your pardon, I haven't introduced the old gent yet, have I? This is my granddad. He was a great old boy in his day and he might be living yet but for that cursed bloodsucker. Perhaps, it is such a creature that's doing for me; what do you think?"

"I wouldn't like to venture an opinion, Remson, but unless I'm badly mistaken we must dig deeper for an explanation. We'll know to-night, however. You retire as usual and I'll keep a close watch and we'll solve the riddle or die in the attempt."

Remson said not a word, but silently extended his hand. I clasped it in a firm embrace and in each other's eyes we read complete understanding. To change the trend of thought I questioned him on the servant problem.

"I've tried time and again to get servants that would stay," he replied, "but about the third day they would begin acting queer, and the first thing I'd know they'd have skipped, bag and baggage."

That night I accompanied my friend to his room and remained until he had disrobed and was ready to retire. Several of the window panes were cracked and one was entirely missing. I suggested boarding up the aperture, but he declined, saying that he rather enjoyed the night air, so I dropped the matter.

As it was still early, I sat by the fire in the sitting room and read for an hour or two. I confess that there were many times when my mind wandered from the printed page before me and chills raced up and down my spine as some new sound was borne to my ears. The wind had risen, and was whistling through the trees with a peculiar whining sound. The creaking of the shutters tended to further the eery effect, and in the distance could be heard the hooting of numerous owls, mingled with the cries of miscellaneous night fowl and other nocturnal creatures.

As I ascended the two flights of steps, the candle in my hand casting grotesque shadows on the walls and ceiling, I had little liking for my job. Many times in the course of duty I had been called upon to display courage, but it took more than mere courage to keep me going now.

I extinguished the candle and crept forward to Remson's room, the door of which was closed. Being careful to make no noise, I knelt and looked in at the keyhole. It afforded me a clear view of the bed and two of the windows in the opposite wall. Gradually my eye became accustomed to the darkness and I noticed a faint reddish glow outside one of the windows. It apparently emanated from nowhere. Hundreds of little specks danced and whirled in the spot of light, and as I watched them, fascinated, they seemed to take on the form of a human face. The features were masculine, as was also the arrangement of the hair. Then the mysterious glow disappeared.

So great had the strain been on me that I was wet from perspiration, although the night was quite cool. For a moment I was undecided whether to enter the room or to stay where I was and use the keyhole as a means of observation. I concluded to remain where I was would be the better plan, so I once more placed my eye to the hole.

Immediately my attention was drawn to something moving where the light had been. At first, owing to the poor light, I was unable to distinguish the general outline and form of the thing; then I saw. It was a man's head.

I will swear it was the exact reproduction of that picture I had seen in the hall that very morning. But, oh, the difference in expression! The lips were drawn back in a snarl, disclosing two sets of pearly white teeth, the canines over-developed and remarkably sharp. The eyes, an emerald green in color, stared in a look of consuming hate. The hair was sadly disarranged, while on the beard was a large clot of what seemed to be congealed blood.

I noticed thus much, then the head melted from my sight and I transferred my attention to a great bat that circled round and round, his huge wings beating a tattoo on the panes. Finaly he circled round the broken pane and flew straight through the hole made by the missing glass. For a few moments he was shut off from my view, then he reappeared and began circling around my friend, who lay sound asleep, blissfully ignorant of all that was occurring. Nearer and nearer it drew, then swooped down and fastened itself on Remson's throat, just over the jugular vein.

At this I rushed into the room and made a wild dash for the thing that had come night after night to gorge itself on my friend; but to no avail. It flew out of the window and away, and I turned my attention to the sleeper.

"Remson, old man, get up."

He sat up like a shot.

"What's the matter, Jack, has it been here?"

"Never mind just now," I replied. "Just dress as hurriedly as possible. We have a little work before us this evening."

He glanced questioningly toward me, but followed my command without argument. I turned and cast my eye about the room for a suitable weapon. There was a stout stick lying in the corner and I made toward it.

"Jack!"

I wheeled about.

"What is it? Damn it all, haven't you any sense, almost scaring a man to death?"

He pointed a shaking finger toward the window.

"There! I swear I saw him. It was my granddad, but oh, how disfigured!"

He threw himself upon the bed and began sobbing. The shock had completely unnerved him.

"Forgive me, old man," I pleaded; "I was too quick. Pull yourself together and we may get to the bottom of things to-night yet."

I handed him my flask. He took a generous swallow and squared up.

When he had finished dressing we left the house. There was no moon out, and it was pitch dark.

I led the way, and soon we came to within ten yards of the little gray crypt. I stationed Remson behind a tree with instructions to just use his eyes, and I took up my stand on the other side of the vault, after making sure that the door into it was closed and locked. For the greater part of an hour we waited without results, and I was about ready to call it off when I perceived a white figure flitting between the trees about fifty feet away.

Slowly it advanced, straight toward us, and as it drew closer I looked, not *at* it, but *through* it. The wind was blowing strongly, yet not a fold in the long shroud quivered. Just outside the vault it paused and looked around. Even knowing as I did about what to expect, it was a decided shock when I looked into the eyes of the old Holroyd, deceased these past five years. I heard a gasp and knew that Remson had seen, too, and recognized. Then the spirit, ghost, or whatever it was, passed into the crypt through the crack between the door and the jamb, a space not one-sixteenth of an inch wide.

As it disappeared, Remson came running forward, his face wholly drawn of color.

"What was it, Jack, what was it? I know it resembled granddad, but it couldn't have been he. He's been dead five years!"

"Let us go back to the house," I answered, "and I'll do my best to explain things to the best of my ability, I may be wrong, of course, but it won't hurt to try my remedy. Remson, what we are up against is a vampire. Not the female species usually spoken of to-day, but the real thing. I noticed you had an old edition of the *Encyclopædia Britannica.* If you'll bring me volume XXIV I'll be able to explain more fully the meaning of the word."

He left the room and returned, carrying the desired book. Turning to page 52, I read:

> *Vampire.*—A term apparently of Servian origin originally applied in Eastern Europe to blood-sucking ghosts, but in modern usage transferred to one or more species of blood-sucking bats inhabiting South America. . . . In the first mentioned meaning a vampire is usually supposed to be the soul of a dead man which quits the buried body by night to suck the blood of living persons. Hence, when the vampire's grave is opened his corpse is found to be fresh and rosy from the blood thus absorbed. . . . They are accredited with the power of assuming any form they may so desire, and often fly about as specks of dust, pieces of down or straw, etc. . . . To put an end to his ravages a stake is driven through him, or his head cut off, or his heart torn out, or boiling water and vinegar poured over the grave. . . . The persons who turn vampires are wizards, witches, suicides, and those who have come to a violent end. Also, the death of any one resulting from these vampires will cause that person to join their hellish throng. . . . See Calumet's "Dissertation on the Vampires of Hungary."

I looked at Remson. He was staring straight into the fire. I knew that he realized the task before us and was steeling himself to it. Then he turned to me.

"Jack, we'll wait until morning."

That was all. I understood, and he knew. There we sat, each struggling with his own thoughts, until the first faint glimmers of light came struggling through the trees and warned us of approaching dawn.

Remson left to fetch a sledge hammer and a large knife with its edge honed to a razorlike keenness. I busied myself making four wooden stakes, shaped like wedges. He returned bearing the horrible tools, and we struck out toward the crypt. We walked rapidly, for had either hesitated an instant I verily believe both would have fled incontinently. However, our duty lay clearly before us. Remson unlocked the door and swung it outward. With a prayer on our lips we entered.

As if by mutual understanding, we both turned toward the coffin on our left. It belonged to the grandfather. We unplaced the lid, and there lay the old Holroyd. He appeared to be sleeping; his face was full of color, and he had none of the stiffness of death. The hair was matted, the mustache untrimmed, and on the beard were matted stains of a dull brownish hue.

But it was his eyes that attracted me. They were greenish, and they glowed with an expression of fiendish malevolence such as I had never seen before. The look of baffled rage on the face might well have adorned the features of the devil in his hell.

Remson swayed and would have fallen, but I forced some whisky down his throat and he took a grip on himself. He placed one of the stakes directly over its heart, then shut his eyes and prayed that the good God above take this soul that was to be delivered unto Him.

I took a step backward, aimed carefully, and swung the sledge with all my strength. It hit the wedge squarely, and a terrible scream filled the place, while the blood gushed out of the open wound, up, and over us, staining the walls and our clothes. Without hesitating, I swung again, and again, and again, while it struggled vainly to rid itself of that awful instrument of death. Another swing and the stake was driven through.

The thing squirmed about in the narrow confines of the coffin, much after the manner of a dismembered worm, and

Remson proceeded to sever the head from the body, making a rather crude but effectual job of it. As the final stroke of the knife cut the connection a scream issued from the mouth; and the whole corpse fell away into dust, leaving nothing but a wooden stake lying in a bed of bones.

This finished, we dispatched the remaining three. Simultaneously, as if struck by the same thought, we felt our throats. The slight pain was gone from mine, and the wounds had entirely disappeared from my friend's, leaving not even a scar.

I wished to place before the world the whole facts contingent upon the mystery and the solution, but Remson prevailed upon me to hold my peace.

Some years later Remson died a Christian death, and with him went the only confirmation of my tale. However, ten miles from the little town of Charing there sits an old house, forgotten these many years, and near it is a little gray crypt. Within are four coffins; and in each lies a wooden stake stained a brownish hue, and bearing the finger prints of the deceased Remson Holroyd,

THE DEVIL BED

By GERALD DEAN

I MAY AS WELL STATE AT THE BEGINNING THAT I AM NOT, either by gift or inclination, a writing man; this story must, therefore, be pardoned in advance for its rough manner of narration, its absolute lack of all literary polish. Fortunately, the fantastic and well-nigh incredible happenings which make up my narrative stand by themselves. They need no furbishing of brilliant phrases, but rather a stark and truthful simplicity for their telling. Let me commence, then, without further apology or explanation.

My name matters little to the story. I am a man of middle age, a bachelor, and fairly successful in the practice of the law. The one hobby which I possess is the collecting of Colonial furniture of the earlier periods, and it was through this interest that I first made the acquaintance of Harry Ware.

Harry, unlike me, is rather an unusual fellow. He is, first and foremost, a scholar; widely traveled, tremendously learned and well read. As a friend old Harry is the salt of the earth. I know of no other man whom I would choose in preference to him as a companion and intimate. He is, incidentally, the last male descendant of a fine old American family of English stock, and one of the most discreet and intelligent of collectors of early Americana. What with me is merely a diverting hobby and pastime is to Harry an overpowering obsession—a life-work, almost.

We met for the first time at an auction in White River Junction, Vermont, some eight or nine years ago, on which occasion we fought each other amicably enough, for the possession of an unusual block-front highboy. We returned to New York together, and from then on our acquaintance gradually progressed and developed into the closest and happiest friendship I have ever known. For several years it was our habit, every summer, to make collecting trips together through the South and New England. Once each week during the rest of the year we dined together, alternately at Harry's huge barracks of a place, and my rooms in town.

I remember that it was on a cheerless and murky morning in early February, about three years ago, that Harry called me up at my office.

"I've got something very interesting to tell you," he said. "If you're not going to be busy to-night, come up to the house." And then, before I could reply: "Why not come straight out from the office, and have dinner with me?"

I replied that I had nothing else on hand, and promised to be at his home, which is in Fieldston, on the northern outskirts of the city, at about eight o'clock. I presented myself there, accordingly, at the stated time, and after an excellent dinner we repaired to the library for cigarettes and coffee. I could see that something had happened to disturb Harry's usual calm, sleepy manner; for the first time in my experience he seemed bubbling over with suppressed excitement. As soon as the manservant had withdrawn, closing the great doors silently after him, Harry extinguished his cigarette and drew his chair up closer to mine.

"Charles," he announced dramatically, "I've had the most unusual thing happen to me—it's like something you'd read about. If it weren't that I have tangible proof, I'd think I'd dreamed it. You can't possibly imagine what is it."

"Well, for Pete's sake, man, let's have it!" I demanded, somewhat testily. "You sound as though you'd seen spooks. What's it all about?"

Harry leaned forward.

"You know the Collingwood escritoire, of course," he began.

And of course I did. A wonderful and priceless piece of furniture; one of the prizes of Harry's collection, which he has had in his possession for all of twenty years. It stands in his bedroom, and he uses it for a writing desk, but it is willed to the Metropolitan Museum, to be added to that institution's collection after Harry's death. . . . I nodded, therefore, without answering.

"What would you say," Harry went on, "if I were to tell you that I have just discovered a secret drawer in it?"

It was my turn to lean forward. "Not really!" I exclaimed. "When? Where? How?"

"It was quite accidental. You know the desk has been sounded, time and again, for any possible secret cubbyholes or recesses—always unsuccessfully. Last night I'd been very prosaically making out checks to pay my various bills, and I reached for one of my old books of stubs in another receptacle. Something happened. . . . I was awkward, perhaps, and lost my balance. Anyway, my elbow struck sharply against a corner, and at the same instant a panel of wood moved smoothly across, and a tiny drawer came sliding out. I think I sat there staring at it for fully five minutes, before I appreciated the evidence of my eyes. Think of it, man, after owning it for twenty years. A secret drawer!"

"It was—empty, of course?"

Harry shook his head. I could see that he was enjoying the whole thing vastly. "No. Interesting and exciting though it was even to discover such a drawer, there was a further thrill to come. The drawer held a miniature and a letter. Wait—I'll get them and let you see them."

For a minute I suspected Harry of tricking me, and believed the whole affair an elaborate joke at my expense. When he returned, therefore, and placed a small miniature in my hand, I accepted it silently and took it over to the table, where I examined it with critical attention under the shaded lamp.

The miniature was undoubtedly authentic—a lovely bit of early eighteenth century work, in perfect condition. The portrait was of a boy, a charming, aristocratic, rather haughty youth of not more than eighteen or twenty years. I turned the miniature over. Pasted to the back was a slip of paper, and on it written in characters so faded as to be almost indecipherable, the following words:

Lennox. Born July 18th, 1694.

Died, by his owne hande, Aprille 10th, 1713.

As I stood there, staring wordlessly at the inscription, a vague pity swept over me; an intolerable sadness for some unknown and long-forgotten tragedy which I could never hope to comprehend. Who was this handsome lad who had, at the age of nineteen, ended his own life? Why, how, and where? . . . I looked over at Harry, who was watching me from across the room.

"Rather pathetic, eh?" I said brusquely.

He merely nodded. "Yes. Handsome boy, too. I'd like to find out who he was. But here's the prize find—this letter. Read it, and tell me what you make of it."

I took the letter, a folded slip of paper, written apparently by the same feminine hand that had inscribed the tragedy on the back of the miniature. As well as I can remember, it ran as follows:

KIRKWOOD,

All is well. A merciful God hath seen fit to spare us frightfulle shame and ignominie. No slightest shade of suspicion hath fallen upon Lennox, and he may proceede safely to Philadelphia. He is doubly safe in that the suspicion of the people hath fallen upon a poore half-wit, whom yesternight they did take and burn alive. So once againe the family fate is averted.

Our bond-man, Foulke Barton, goes to Fort La Tour

within the week. I give him £50, and household belongings. Also in obedience to your wish, the Deville Bed.

A thousands fonde kisses to you and our poor boy,

ANTOINETTE.

I read this strange letter once, standing up beside the table. Then I seated myself, lit another cigarette, and read it over. Harry still watched me, enjoying my complete mystification. "Well? What do you make of it? Tell me just your impressions," he demanded, finally.

"I can't make anything of it," I said in exasperation. "Unless—well, let's see." As Harry waited impatiently, I groped for words to convey my bewildered impressions. "This young man of the miniature—Lennox—has apparently committed a crime, and fled from the scene. A terrible crime, I imagine, since the people burned alive a half-wit whom they suspected of it. . . . But the second paragraph is meaningless, to me. What has this bondman to do with the affair? There's no way of telling whether he was an accomplice, or a witness. Yet it seems irrelevant, doesn't it, that the mother should mention his leaving for some fort, and that she gave him household furnishings? And what in the name of all that's holy, is a Devil Bed?"

Harry laughed. "Your deductions are admirable, Dr. Watson," he said. "But I must say that the crime and the burning alive do not interest me. It's the reference to the bed—the Devil Bed—that has me fascinated. Don't you realize that the writer of this letter is probably referring to something that I've been trying to find for years—one of those marvelous old carved oak bedsteads with gargoyle heads that we know were brought over from England by a few wealthy families, and have never been able to trace? Great Kingdom, Charles! Just think! This hidden drawer and this letter may be the means of our discovering one of those beds. I tell you, I'd give ten years of my life, and all I own, if I could be lucky enough to find one, or even part of one. It would be the most wonderful thing in my life. It would make my collection the most famous in America!"

I sat wordless before Harry's unexpected enthusiasm and excitement. To tell the truth, the personal side of the story unveiled by this mysterious letter interested me far more than the reference to the bed. The sinister hints of a nameless crime, its innocent victim, and the unhappy, guilt-burdened Lennox reached out to me across the span of two silent centuries, and held me enthralled. But I realized that Harry had valid cause to place more stress upon the reference to the bed, that collectors' will-o'-the-wisp. What, after all, did it matter who had committed a crime two hundred years ago? The guilty man had paid the price of his sin long years past, having died by his own hand. But the bed, if it could be traced, was a matter of living importance. . . . Still, how could the fact that one Foulke Barton, a bondman, had taken such a piece of furniture to Fort La Tour, two hundred years ago, lead one to believe that it might be traced now, after such a lapse of time? I said as much to Harry.

"There's just a chance," he replied quickly. "Just one chance in ten thousand. God alone knows why the bedstead was given to him, but the man must have realized its value, and been overcome by such a gift. Even then a carved bedstead of that type would be worth an enormous amount of money. He, and possibly his descendants, could not help but recognize its beauty and worth. Just think! It may be standing even yet, in the bedroom of some little New Brunswick farmhouse!"

"New Brunswick?" I repeated stupidly. "You mean New Brunswick, in Jersey?"

Harry shook his head impatiently. "No! Fort La Tour is the old French settlement in Canada where the city of Saint John, New Brunswick, now stands. I tell you, Charles, if it's the last thing I do, I'm going up to the province and hunt for that bed!"

I remember laughing a little at Harry's impetuous manner. "Starting to-night?" I asked lightly.

And then Harry Ware gave me the surprise of my life.

"I've already packed," he said, "ready to leave in the morning. Why don't you skip business for a week or so, and come along with me?"

As it happened, I was not in a position at that time to leave the city, my firm was working under heavy pressure, and I could not possibly hope to take a vacation. It was rather regretfully, therefore, that I declined Harry's invitation, for the Devil Bed had me interested, and even a wild goose chase can be exciting under certain conditions and with certain companions.

However, I accompanied Harry to the Grand Central Station next day, and wished him the best of luck in his search. Even at the last minute, standing in the noisy train shed, he tried again to coerce me into the hunt. "I'm going to scour every inch of New Brunswick," he said. "Lord knows what other finds I may run across in the meanwhile. Come along!"

I hated to refuse, but business is business, and unlike Harry I was dependent for bread and butter upon my profession. So I let him go alone, and in the heavy stress of work during the next few weeks I put the whole affair out of my mind completely, so that the secret drawer and the miniature and the Devil Bed faded slightly in my memory, and lost something of the entrancing glamor they had held that evening in Harry's library.

It was some time during March that I next heard anything of interest from my adventurous friend. He had written me one or two brief letters during that time, describing his various attempts to trace the descendants of Foulke Barton, which attempts had been, so far, a complete failure. Now there came a note that was almost jubilant in tone—the baying of the bloodhound in full scent:

I think I've found them, and strangely enough, through another crime or rather a series of crimes. This time, it's something rather ghastly. A man named Amos Barton, whom I have found to be a direct descendant of Foulke Barton, was hanged in the prison here in 1848, having been condemned for the wanton murder of (just imagine!) a family of nine people. I've found all sorts of details concerning him and his forbears from the old files of newspapers. They were a bad lot, and Amos wasn't the first to end his days inside prison-walls. The whole family, from away back, seemed tainted with homicidal mania, which cropped out every few generations in some atrocious crime. Amos Barton was a farmer, settled in a small place called Rothsay. He was apparently a mild and peaceable man. One night, so the old records say, he ran amuck and slaughtered a household of neighbors, against whom he had no discoverable grudge or grievance. When found, he made no attempt to disprove his guilt, and was summarily hanged by the neck until dead, a week later. Justice moved more quickly in those days, apparently. Well, the interesting and hopeful fact remains that he left a family of generous size, which is doubtless scattered through the province. The deuce of it is, they are supposed to have changed their name, because of the disgrace. However, I'm out to find them, and I feel in my very bones that some one of them will be found, and I'll still trace my Devil Bed. Why don't you come on now, and help me in the search?

That letter made a deep and strange impression upon me. I'm no believer in ghosts, the Lord knows; no one could be more skeptical or coldblooded in that sort of thing than I am. And yet—

Well, I didn't like this constant shadow of murder connected with the Devil Bed. The laughing, charming face of the boy in the miniature rose up before my mind's eye. What evil impulse could have caused such an innocent-looking chap to commit a horrible crime? What could have made this unknown farmer, Amos Barton, wantonly slay an entire family? What legacy of evil had descended through the Barton family? Was there a pursuing demon—?

So far my reverie went, and then, with a conscious effort, I turned my thoughts deliberately from the whole affair. Yet the lurking horror remained in the background. I found myself wishing that my friend Harry had never discovered the secret drawer in his escritoire; had never started out on his mad hunt for the Devil Bed. And I wrote Harry, what was quite true, that an important case forced me to remain indefinitely in New York.

And then, perhaps two months later, came a triumphant telegram. The search was over; the Devil Bed had, unbelievably, been found at last. The message was sent from the village of X——. I cannot for obvious reasons give the correct name of the little New Brunswick hamlet in which the bed was discovered.

> Come at once. Search successful. Want you to verify and help in packing and crating. Have notified Blank at the museum. Reply immediately when you will arrive.
>
> (Signed) WARE.

Of course, there was nothing else to do, in the light of my friendship and various obligations to Harry, but to comply. I dropped everything, put my affairs in hurried order, and having sent a wire in response, I took the train the next day for Boston.

Harry met me at the station, in Saint John. He was glowing with triumph, almost ecstatic in his delight. "Wait till you see it," were his first words. "Man, I can't believe my own luck! It's too marvelous—the bed, you understand. Almost perfect condition; the most exquisite carving in oak I've ever seen. But I mustn't rave. I mustn't spoil it for you. Just think, though. Out in the hay-loft of an old barn; hidden behind the filth and débris of years. I tell you, when I first saw it I couldn't speak, or think. I just stood there, and gibbered like a madman!"

Harry's enthusiasm was contagious. "They're tremendously excited at the museum," I told him. "Are you sure the present owners will be willing to sell?"

He nodded briefly. "Oh, yes. They have no idea how important, how priceless, it is. In fact, they dislike it." Talking constantly, he led the way from the station to his hotel. It was then early evening—we were to stay at the hotel overnight, and proceed to X—— by train in the morning.

Over our dinner, and later, in my somewhat rococo sitting room, Harry described his search and all its heartbreaking disappointments and failures. "I had the devil's own time, tracing the children of Amos Barton," he said. "There were six of them, five sons and one daughter, and they'd changed their name to Shilling, after their father was hanged. I thought from the first that if any of the children had got the bed, it would be the daughter. As events proved, I was right. . . . But, in the beginning, I couldn't find any of them. Lord, what a job! Searching birth records, death notices, newspaper files. Yet the thing had me fascinated, and I couldn't give up. Finally I found them, first one, then another, and so on. You see, there was one thing that made the whole affair comparatively simple; they hadn't any of them left New Brunswick. They're quiet, unprogressive, narrow people. The whole stock seems sort of stunned by the family disgrace and trouble that's followed them so long. Even—"

"But tell me," I interrupted, as Harry fell silent, "how did you finally locate the people that had the bed?"

Harry stretched his long, lanky frame in a spindling gilt chair, and stared up at the ceiling. "Well, there was that daughter of old Amos," he said. "She was the oldest, and the only girl. After infinite trouble I found she'd married a man named Lyons. They'd been married before this wholesale murder affair, and her husband didn't like the disgrace, or else he objected to the sort of family he married into—anyway, he ran off, leaving his wife with a boy about two years old. She left Rothsay, sold the house there, and went into service as housekeeper for an old farmer in X——, named Nagle. The important thing for us is, that she took with her all her household belongings, including the Devil Bed. She must have been canny enough to realize its value. This old fellow whom she went to work for must have taken a liking to her, for they got married, later on, and he left the farm to her when he died. And the boy (Fanny Barton Lyons' son, you understand) took the name of Nagle and got possession of the place when his mother died. So there you are. To-morrow, at X——, you'll meet him; he's still alive and as spry as a cricket. He's the owner of the bed, and his granddaughter, who lives wih him, is the one who helped me to find it in the hayloft. Pretty piece of work, eh?"

I stared at Harry with infinite admiration. "You should have been a detective," I declared. "You're wasting excellent talents in the mere tracing of old furniture." Then a new thought struck me, or rather a thought I had so far deliberately submerged. "Harry," I said, "what do you make of the fact of these—murders? Here are several nasty crimes in connection with this bed, or in connection with the owners of it. Is there—can there be—any *real* connection?"

Harry stared at me, very oddly, I thought. He started impulsively to say something, then checked himself.

"Pure coincidence," he said, lightly. "What else can it be? . . . *What are you trying to say?*"

Something angry, something almost furious in his eyes and voice, a strange, half-suppressed rage, made me draw back from him.

"Why, Harry, my dear old chap!" I stuttered. "I don't mean a thing. Just a fancy of mine!"

The subject was changed immediately, but I went to bed that night with somber, undefined horror lurking in the shadowy depths of my consciousness.

We started out early the next morning, complete harmony restored between us, and arrived about noon at the little village of X——. From there we took a carriage, hired at a local livery-stable, and drove out through pleasantly hilly and wooded country to the Nagle farm. It was an unkempt and run-down place, hidden snugly between low, rolling hills; the farmhouse itself a dull, indefinite-looking yellow building, with barns and outhouses in an almost inconceivable state of dilapidation.

As our carriage drove up, a huge mongrel dog darted out, barking vociferously, and ran along at our horse's heels. A moment later a sturdy young woman came out to the side door, and called the dog away. Behind her I could see an old wizened man, who later came hobbling down the pathway to our carriage. His faded eyes stared at me in blinking amazement, and at our introduction he bowed and scraped most obsequiously. I, in turn, stared back at him. So this was the descendant of that almost mythical bondman, Foulke Barton, and of the strange murderer, Amos Barton! Well, there was nothing of murderer about this poor, doddering old nondescript, surely. The girl, his granddaughter, Sophie, rather pleased me. She was a rosy-cheeked, strong young thing, and whatever the outside condition of the place, the interior, due to her efforts, was spotlessly clean and tidy.

I was shown to a pleasant though sparsely furnished bedroom, but almost before I could set my luggage down, Harry was insisting that I come out to see the Devil Bed. He had, himself, gone straight to the barn as soon as we arrived, to assure himself that his discovery was quite safe. Now, his suit powdered with cobwebs and dust, he stood in the doorway, commanding that I hurry

Nothing loath, I followed him down the narrow staircase and out through the back yard to the barn. The place seemed unusually dark and gloomy after the cheerful radiance of out-of-doors, and my eyes, blinded by sunshine, were at first unable to make out my surroundings. Gradually becoming accustomed to the dimness, I looked about me. Rusty rakes and hay-forks leaned disconsolately against the sweating walls, and the empty stalls were piled high with discarded farm machinery of all sorts. Though the place had obviously been long unused, a faintly ammoniac odor filled the air, struggling through a dank, mildewed atmosphere, and creating a ghastly combination of filth and decay. At the rear of the barn stood a ladder that reached up to the hayloft above. Harry ascended this, deftly as a monkey, and I followed, protesting faintly; my hands were reluctant to take hold of the dirt-encrusted sides. At every step, huge spiders drew back cautiously into quivering webs, and as I halted for a moment at the top, I experienced again that strange, indescribable fear which had tormented me the night before. Then I threw the unreasonable horror from me, and stepped up into the hayloft.

There, in a pale, hazy light, stood the four carven pieces of oak that made the Devil Bed. Harry had pulled them out from their ignominious hiding-place to the center of the loft floor. For an instant, as he had done, I merely stood there looking at it, and "gibbering like a madman." The bedstead was truly a gorgeous thing, the most marvelous piece of furniture I have ever laid eyes upon. Only those who love the rare and exquisite work of old-time craftsmen who gave their whole lives to the fashioning of beautiful objects, can understand the thrill that tingled through me. Never, anywhere, have I seen human handicraft of greater loveliness.

And then, even as I stood there, that perfect feeling of delight passed, and a chill came over me. For there was something nameless, something horrible and full of evil coming to me, like a sluggish wave, from the direction of the Devil Bed. I came closer to it, staring intently. The carvings that at first glance were so admirable in their perfection, I now saw to be of a most perverse and suggestive obscenity. Here were strange, writhing forms struggling in bestial embraces; snakes, knotted and upreared; a thousand morbid visions emanating from an unclean mind. . . . And all the while, the power of that evil, hypnotic spell drawing me! . . . I looked up suddenly, as one does who feels the steady gaze of human eyes. And then I saw what had, undeniably, given the Devil Bed its name. All along the sides of the tester ran a carved series of faces, the evil, the vileness of which, I can never hope to express. Contorted, leering faces; faces of imbeciles in lustful paroxysms; faces only half human, yet doubly disgusting in their perverted humanity. The most hideous gargoyles of Gothic architecture were angels of serenity beside these frightful visions. No nightmare could evoke a more terrible crew.

And then, abruptly, came Harry's triumphant voice. "Well, what do you think of it?"

It was with a definitely physical effort that I drew my eyes away.

"Marvelous, but how evil!" I cried. "No wonder they called it the Devil Bed. . . . It's—Harry, can't you see?—it's wicked! It's the most wicked thing I've seen."

He brushed me aside. "Yes, perhaps so. Perhaps you're right. It's hardly the thing to grace a Victorian bedroom, eh?"

A thin, mocking laughter filled the hayloft, and tinkled into silence. I looked up. The leering lips of the grimacing devil nearest me seemed still curved in malicious scorn. Yet it must have been Harry who laughed.

Something within me protested. "It's a gorgeous piece," I said slowly, almost grudgingly. "You're lucky, Harry, to have discovered it. And yet it seems to me that it were better if it had not been found. It's decadent. It hasn't the splendid sturdy quality I had expected to find in it. I'm disappointed."

No sooner were the words said than I regretted them. For Harry glared at me with a rage and contempt beyond words. His face, usually so pale and calm, was mottled with angry red, and his eyes fairly bulged from their sockets. I think he suspected me then of the rankest jealousy.

"Doubtless I should leave it here," he suggested furiously. "Or better still, burn it up, because it offends your prudish taste! Or, perhaps, you're afraid of it?"

And then, instantly, I knew that Harry had hit upon the truth. I *was* afraid of it. As God is my judge, I hated and feared that inanimate thing—that mere bulk of carved wood! And I felt, somehow, that Harry was afraid of it also, and was masking his own inexplicable horror behind this false indignation and bravado. For neither of us would, or could as sane men, admit the truth.

"We're talking nonsense," I said. "It's undeniable that you've made the discovery of a century. The bed is far too valuable to be destroyed, and it will make a tremendously interesting museum piece. I only know that I dislike the ornamentation, and that I wouldn't sleep under those faces for a fortune!"

Harry eyed me curiously. "It's odd that you should have said that," he remarked. "Because I intend to rope up the bed, and sleep in it to-night, myself."

There was no deterring him. He had made up his mind, and like many men of his type he was as immovable in his intentions as a block of granite. I don't know what subconscious premonition made me attempt to dissuade him, but at all events my vague objections were quite ignored. Harry had determined to set the Devil Bed up in one of the farmhouse bedrooms, and he carried out that purpose without further discussion.

Between us, with infinite pains and precautions, we carried the tremendously heavy pieces down that tottering old ladder, out into the yard, and into the farmhouse. I remember that the old man and his granddaughter watched us closely at our task, but made no offer of assistance. When the bed was finally set in place in the spare room, its bulk filled almost every inch of available space, and it towered aloft, barely missing the ceiling. Harry and I stood together in the doorway, breathing gustily from our efforts. I must admit that here, between practical, sunny walls, something of horror and mystery seemed to have departed from the great bedstead. The carven heads were just as appallingly hideous, but less terrifying. I remember thinking that I had been rather a fool to have felt any horror of the thing. After all, a bed was nothing but a bed, no matter how peculiarly ornamented, and if Harry wished to sleep in it, what possible harm could ensue therefrom?

A minute later we went downstairs to supper in the best of spirits. The table was laid in the kitchen and Sophie bustled cheerfully to and fro, serving us. As I ate, I marveled at the equable manner in which Harry and I had been accepted in this quaint home. Even the mongrel dog had become friendly, and now sat at Harry's feet, begging for an occasional scrap with pleading eyes. Through the window at my right, I could see the old man pottering about the yard, puffing peacefully at a villainous-looking pipe. In this simple, homely atmosphere, how shadowy and far away seemed the annals of horror and bloodshed connected with the Barton clan! And how ridiculous seemed my own vague fears of the Devil Bed!

When we had finished our meal, Harry called to Sophie, with whom he was plainly on the best of terms.

"I wonder whether you have a spare mattress for the old bed," he said. "I intend to sleep in it to-night."

Sophie had been standing in the doorway, looking out into the yard. At Harry's words she swung around, and her face turned slowly paler and paler, until it was almost gray in the half-light.

"Oh, Mr. Ware," she said. "You're not going to—to sleep in it?"

Harry laughed irritably. "Yes. Why not? Are you afraid of it, too?"

I waited what seemed an interminable time for the girl's reply. Sophie stood immovable for a moment, then she came quickly over toward us, and stood gripping the edge of the table.

"Yes, I *am* afraid of it," she said, simply. "I've always been, and so has all our family. We've even been afraid to destroy it. There was an old French Priest who saw it once, and he said it was unholy. There's a curse'll fall on anybody who sleeps in it. Oh, Mr. Ware! Buy it if you want, and put it into a museum for people to look at, but don't sleep in it. Something terrible will happen to you. I *know!*"

There was a certain quiet earnestness in the girl's voice that brought back to me, with sickening force, all my own indefinable dread. I hoped against hope that Harry would accept her warning. But his first words showed that hope to be vain.

"There's nothing you could have said," he returned lightly, "that would have made me more determined to sleep in the bed. I tell you, Sophie, that you and other people have allowed yourselves to be frightened by the cowardly superstitions of priests and old women. Don't think me discourteous in saying this. I know how ghost stories can persist, unreasonably, from one generation to another. A horrible tragedy is often connected with an inanimate object, but I for one have no faith in such nonsense as haunted houses, and accurst beds. How much will you wager that I sleep better to-night and have better dreams, than you or my friend, here—either of you?"

Sophie seemed to realize that there was nothing more to say. Without answering she turned away and went upstairs. Half an hour later she came out to us, where we were smoking and chatting on the porch in the fragrant dusk, and announced that the big bed was ready to be slept in.

And now I come to that part of my story which must tax the credulity of the ordinary reader. I can only say that these eyes have seen the sights I tell of; these ears have heard the sounds.

At nine-thirty, Sophie and her grandfather having gone up to bed, Harry and I extinguished our last cigarettes and walked upstairs together. At the door of the spare room where the Devil Bed had been placed, we paused and stood for an instant. Then Harry pushed open the door and went in, and I followed him.

The bed filled the room so completely that no other piece of furniture save a plain wooden chair could be squeezed in. On this one chair Sophie had placed a small kerosene lamp with a plain glass shade. A thin, flickering light drifted across the carved surface of the bed, so that the gargoyle faces seemed ever leering out into the light, and then withdrawing into obscene darkness again. The bed, in that first hurried glimpse, struck me as even more ghastly than before. I can only say that it seemed—living.

I commenced speaking hurriedly, stammering in my excitement.

"Harry! Call me an old woman—an old fool—anything you want!" I said. "But don't sleep in that infernal bed. I don't believe in ghosts or spooks any more than you do, but I tell you this thing has *got* me!"

Harry shook his head obstinately, without answering.

Yet I couldn't give up.

"Humor me this once, for old friendship's sake," I pleaded. "Sleep in the bed some other time. Not to-night."

"This is my only chance," Harry replied. "To-morrow it is to be crated, remember. And once in the museum—well, I couldn't very well sleep in it there! No, Charles, my mind is made up." We looked at each other for a moment, in complete silence. Then Harry stepped closer to me, and gripped my shoulder. "Don't think me just an obstinate fool!" he said. "I have reasons—for wanting to sleep in the Devil Bed! If you could guess the things I've heard whispered—and it's all nonsense, Charles! Nonsense!"

"You're quite sure?" I said, grimly.

"Positive! But the only way to prove it, is by sleeping in the thing myself. So—good-night, Charles, old fellow! We'll be laughing over this scene to-morrow morning at breakfast!"

There was no use in wasting any further words; I bade Harry good-night and went to my own room. Here I undressed, and lay down. For a long time I remained awake, listening for—what? Eventually I fell into a restless sleep.

Some hours later I was awakened suddenly by a most strange and dreadful sound. It can be described only as something between a scream and a howl, and it was not human. . . . I sat up in bed, trembling all over. And at the same time a queer relief came over me. Here, at all events, was actuality at last, and no matter what the horror might prove to be, it was better than blind dread and waiting. I got out of bed, stumbled across the room in the dark, and lit my lamp with shaking fingers. Then, barefooted, holding the lamp high, I hurried out into the hallway.

The house was now absolutely still. I went first to Harry's room. The bed was empty, and I knew that Harry must be connected in some way with that fearful, agonized, inhuman cry. . . .

At the head of the staircase I halted for a moment, then slowly descended. Since I was quite unfamiliar with the house, I was unaware that these were the back stairs which would lead me to the kitchen. There was not the slightest sound to be heard anywhere—yet I felt, I *knew*, that some one was crawling about, somewhere, in the turgid darkness below.

At the foot of the stairs I met with a closed door. I threw it open, and then stopped short on the threshold. The feeble rays of the lamp showed me that I had found what I sought. On the floor of the kitchen, in a spreading pool of blood, lay the unfortunate mongrel dog whose death scream I had heard. And facing me, his back to the wall, stood Harry, the lamplight flickering on the wet blade of a carving-knife he brandished in his hand!

May I never again see, in dreams or in reality, such a face as Harry presented then to my horrified gaze! His eyes were wide and staring—his lips curled back in a snarling grimace. If I had never before seen blood-lust and fury in a human face, I saw it now. . . . Just an instant we looked at each other, then he came hurtling toward me. I knew him for a maniac, and I set down the lamp, and grappled with him for the possession of the knife.

He was too strong for me. Ordinarily, I could have conquered and disarmed him, for Harry is a lighter man, and possessed of less physical strength. But now he was not a man; he was a killer, and he had gained the terrific force of a maniac. In the implacable grip of his hand about my throat I felt that my last moment had come; I could see the knife in his right hand poised for the thrust that would mean my death! Then suddenly, I heard running feet on the stairs behind me, a woman's sharp cry, and the deafening explosion of a revolver shot. At the same instant, Harry's grip on my throat relaxed, and he slid grotesquely to the floor. I turned weak and shaking, toward the direction from which the shot had come. Sophie stood there, at the foot of the stairs, with a smoking revolver in her hand.

"I had to kill him," she cried, hysterically. "I had to kill him, or he would have murdered us all."

Harry did not die. The wound which Sophie had given him, and which had saved my life, was merely a deep and extremely painful flesh wound in the shoulder, from which he soon recovered.

But the shock to his nervous system—to his very mind

and soul—went deeper. It was only after many days of rest that he could bear to speak of the terrible experience through which he had gone.

And then, strangely enough, he had nothing to tell us which we did not already know. He remembered nothing, from the time he fell asleep in the Devil Bed, till the moment when he dropped to the floor wounded by Sophie's shot. What malignant and mysterious impulse had entered his body, guiding him to the kitchen, putting the knife in his hand, filling him with a fierce lust to kill—he could no more guess than we could. His amazement and horror when we told him what he had done were unspeakably piteous to see, as was his utter remorse over the stabbing of the hapless dog.

"I didn't know what I was doing," he kept repeating dully, over and over. And my mind flashed to the boy Lennox, who also had killed, and all those notorious members of the Barton clan, who had swung for dreadful murders of which they were, in a deeper sense, completely innocent.

On Harry's recovery, there remained but one thing to do before our return to New York. The Devil Bed was taken apart, and hauled unceremoniously to the yard, where we burned it. Not again should this accurst thing bring death and tragedy to innocent victims! Sophie and Harry and I watched it burn, in silence. The flames licked hungrily about those leering gargoyle faces, and we shivered a little, for the eyes seemed almost human. So heavy was the wood that it took hours before the last vestige of it was destroyed.

There is still one thing to tell. As I was hacking the bed apart for easier burning, I found a crude scrawl carved in the under-bracing of the tester:

BLOODE WARM AND RED
ON HIS HANDS THATTE CARVED THIS BED
BLOODE SHALL BE SHED
BY HIM WHO HEREON RESTS HIS HEAD.

Doggerel? Curse? Joke? Who knows. . . . For an instant the old chill and horror went through me as I read it, then I tossed the piece vindictively into the flames, and it too was consumed.

www.ingramcontent.com/pod-product-compliance
Lightning Source LLC
Chambersburg PA
CBHW020943310726
48980CB00001B/33

* 9 7 8 1 4 3 4 4 7 1 2 9 1 *